DECISION AT TRAFALGAR

by the same author:

Flag 4: The Battle of Coastal Forces in the Mediterranean

Graf Spee: The Life and Death of a Raider

73 North: The Defeat of Hitler's Navy

DECISION
AT
TRAFALGAR

**From the Library of
Frank Madsen**

BY DUDLEY POPE

1960

J. B. LIPPINCOTT COMPANY

PHILADELPHIA & NEW YORK

To

Lt.-Col. and Mrs. Harold Wyllie,

whose knowledge and artistry have contributed so much to our understanding of the great days of sail.

Contents

Illustrations

ACKNOWLEDGMENTS

THE AUTHOR would like to thank the following for kind permission to reproduce the illustrations in this book: The Admiralty for Numbers 5, 8 and 19; Lt.-Col. Harold Wyllie, O.B.E., for 9, 10, 16 and 17; Viscount Digby, for 15 and 21; the Misses Duff, for 14; the Gresham Committee, for 1, Mr. Christopher Marsden, for 20; Mr. Colin Mudie, AMINA, for the drawing of the *Victory* facing page 360; the Musée de la Marine, for 6 and 7; the Museo Naval, Madrid, for 12; the National Maritime Museum, Greenwich, for 3; the National Maritime Museum, Greenwich Hospital Collection, for 4 and 18; and the National Portrait Gallery, for 2.

AUTHOR'S PREFACE

MY REASON for writing this account of the year of Trafalgar is that it seemed a curious omission that no book has hitherto set out to describe the most famous naval campaign and battle in history from all practicable points of view. One of the aims of my account, therefore, is to tell the story of the actual battle as it was seen through the eyes of the contending British, French and Spanish admirals, captains, lieutenants and ratings, frequently using their own words.

Since it is difficult to understand the significance of a battle unless all the many and varied circumstances surrounding it are known, I have also tried to present a picture of life and events in Britain and France during 1805: of Napoleon and Pitt, and the ordinary British folk who faced the threat of invasion and drilled with pike and pitchfork on the village greens when the French Emperor's "Army of England" was poised on the cliffs above Boulogne and his harbours were full of landing craft.

Yet the men who actually fought the battle and helped to preserve freedom for Britain served on board the ships of the Royal Navy in conditions little removed from slavery. They lived on salt meat said to be often so hard that it could be carved and would take a polish like a fine-grained wood; they were flogged for the slightest misdemeanour; and they were frequently cheated out of what miserable wage they were paid. Yet it was these men, many of them press-ganged jailbirds, who fought the enemy like demons —and who broke down and wept when Nelson died. Nelson made these men believe they were each worth three Frenchmen or four Spaniards; such was the magnetism of his leadership that in battle these odds were often achieved. So this account also tries to give the reader a glimpse into the Admiralty and the massive wooden ships that carried out its bidding, and to portray life afloat in the year 1805.

The victory off Cape Trafalgar was unique in many ways. Nelson, its victor and victim, was the first and last man to use gun and sail in a perfect combination on such a scale. But more important, it gave the world a standard by which daring and bravery would henceforth be measured, and established a tradition for Britain and the Royal Navy which was to prove powerful and enduring. Many of the facts surrounding this great sea battle have been or are still in dispute. Rather than go into arid detail and relate how learned men have argued through succeeding generations, I have usually given my own interpretation, but I have noted where this varies from certain hitherto accepted accounts.

In dispute at some time or another have been Nelson's actual method of attack; his intentions during the battle—whether or not he began the attack according to the pre-arranged plan; the circumstances surrounding his memorable "England expects . . ." signal; the design of the signal flags; and what several ships did—in particular the rear ships.

There were many reasons for the spectacular victory, when twenty-seven British ships attacked the thirty-three of the Combined Fleet of France and Spain, capturing seventeen and blowing up the eighteenth, and capturing several more a few days later; yet, as related in these pages, Napoleon himself played a significant part in the defeat of his own fleet.

While Britain waited for the Combined Fleet to sail from Cadiz, Napoleon was calling his Commander-in-Chief a traitor, and an hour or so before the battle began one of the ablest Spanish captains commented: "The fleet is doomed. The French admiral does not understand his business." Muttering *"Perdidos,"* he turned up his men to prayers. Against this picture we have Nelson, dramatic, warm-hearted, cool-brained, and his sailors—men longing to see their wives, yet excited at serving once again under Nelson, painting their ships in the same yellow-and-black style of the *Victory*, and honoured to pay for the paint out of their own pockets. On the eve of the battle, a British captain complained of his indigestion, while French and Spanish captains complained that their ships were rotten. Most of the British captains were fulfilling their greatest ambition in fighting under Nelson, while the French and Spanish captains held a council of war where many argued that their Fleet should not sail.

Yet the Britain Nelson's men made safe presented in 1805 a curious and often contradictory pattern: a man could be hanged for stealing a handkerchief, and M.P.s represented villages which had been washed away by the sea, while great new towns had no Member. France was equally contradictory. Despite the Revolution, which sent the King to the guillotine, Napoleon's Court was, in the year 1805, more splendid than ever before.

These are some of the reasons why the battle of Trafalgar gave a crushing victory to the British, and why it was the final and calculated act in a campaign, and not an isolated action fought by chance off a Spanish cape.

I have had a great deal of help and encouragement in carrying out the research for this book, particularly from two acknowledged experts of this period. The first is Rear-Admiral A. H. Taylor, C.B., O.B.E., D.L., J.P., an authority on Trafalgar, who placed much valuable material, particularly a time-table of the battle, at my disposal and has given me many hours of his valuable time, and who read the Ms.

The second is Lt.-Col. Harold Wyllie, O.B.E., perhaps best known as the brilliant marine artist, but who is also one of our greatest authorities on the construction and rigging of the "wooden walls." He has given me much advice on many aspects of life afloat in 1805, and read the Ms. I am also greatly indebted to him for allowing me to reproduce some of his paintings and also one by his father, the late W. L. Wyllie.

I am very grateful to Professor Michael Lewis, C.B.E., M.A., F.S.A., F.R.Hist.S., who read the Ms. and made some valuable suggestions which have been incorporated.

The role of the Earl of Northesk, the third-in-command at Trafalgar, has tended to be overshadowed by Nelson and Collingwood; but I have been fortunate in being allowed by the present Earl to make use of interesting material, including letters, which came to light only recently and has never previously been published. The papers are at present in the custody of his cousin, Mr. John Carnegie, for whose help I am also grateful.

The Misses Duff, of Bolton Gardens, South Kensington, descendants of Captain George Duff of the *Mars,* one of the two British captains killed in the battle, have allowed me to use hitherto unpublished documents concerning the four members of the Duff family at Trafalgar, and I am also grateful to Lt.-Col. T. Gordon-Duff of Drummuir Castle, Banffshire.

I am indebted to Lord Digby, concerning the captain of the *Africa;* to the Earl of Radnor for permission to use certain correspondence; to Lord Cottesloe, for material concerning Captain Thomas Fremantle, and also the Hon. Mrs. Christopher Fremantle for permission to quote from *The Wynne Diaries,* which she edited; to Mr. Christopher Marsden, for letters written to and by his forebear, William Marsden, Secretary to the Board of Admiralty at the time of the battle; and Sir William Codrington, Bt., for permission to use material concerning Captain Codrington of the *Orion.* I have also to thank the descendants of Captains Tyler and Blackwood for their efforts on my behalf.

My thanks are due to Lt.-Cdr. P. K. Kemp, R.N. (Retd.), F.R.Hist.S., Head of Historical Section, Admiralty; to the staff of the Admiralty Library, and in particular Mr. G. Young; to Miss Lindsay-MacDougall, National Maritime Museum; to the staffs of the Public Records Office and British Museum, for their ready and expert help; and to Mr. E. Smith, Head of AMS, Admiralty.

Many of my friends have given me encouragement and advice, but I must particularly thank Mervyn Ellis, of the Department of the Chief of Naval Information, Admiralty; Cdr. T. Marchant, D.S.C., R.N. (Retd.); and David Wainwright, all of whom have also read the Ms.; Count Henry Bentinck and Basil Bowman. Patrick Satow, D.S.C., and H. W. Bailey read the galley proofs and made many valuable suggestions.

Once again it is an understatement to say that without help, encouragement and constructive criticism from my wife—who has typed more than a quarter of a million words in connection with the narrative—this book would not have been attempted or completed.

To avoid having too many footnotes, various comments and additional facts are given in the Notes and Bibliography, beginning on p. 366.

DECISION AT TRAFALGAR

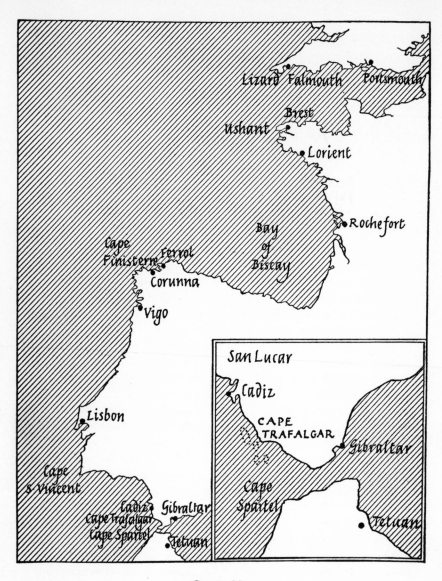

Lizard Falmouth Portsmouth

Brest

Ushant

Lorient

Rochefort

Bay of Biscay

Cape Finisterre

Ferrol

Corunna

Vigo

Lisbon

Cape S. Vincent

Cadiz

Cape Trafalgar

Cape Spartel

Gibraltar

Tetuan

San Lucar

Cadiz

CAPE TRAFALGAR

Gibraltar

Cape Spartel

Tetuan

CHART No. 1
South-western Europe.

16

ONE

PICKLE COMES HOME

*Yet when we achieved and the new world dawned, the
old men came out again and took our victory to remake
in the likeness of the former world they knew . . .*
—T. E. Lawrence

TWO HOISTS of flags quivered in the moaning wind as they
streamed out from the signal halyards at the yardarm and mizen-
mast-head of the 38-gun frigate *Euryalus* which was, on this stormy
October day in 1805, serving as the flagship of Cuthbert Collingwood, Vice-Admiral of the Blue.

For the past five days—since Lord Nelson died at the close of the
battle—Collingwood had been in command of the victorious but
battered British Fleet now fighting for its very life in heavy seas
only a few miles to windward of Cape Trafalgar. He had seen
many of his prizes, vast French and Spanish three-deckers which
had been the pride of the Emperor and of His Catholic Majesty,
smashed by the great waves; he had even been forced to give
orders for prize-crews and prisoners to be taken off and ships
scuttled or set on fire.

Nature, in the shape of winds raging at more than sixty knots
across the wide Atlantic, with nothing to break their fury or
quieten the great singing waves they drove before them, was blunt-
ing the sharp edge of victory; yet despite the gales Collingwood
could no longer delay the task of informing the Admiralty in London of the best news—that the Combined Fleet of France and
Spain had been defeated, with eighteen of its ships captured or
destroyed—and the worst, that Nelson had perished, though not
before learning that the toll of the enemy had been only two short
of the twenty for which he had bargained.

Downwind from the *Euryalus,* and often almost completely

hidden as sheets of spray sluiced over her flush deck, was the tiny topsail schooner *Pickle*. Her mainsail was furled on its long boom and the foresail brailed up, while the three headsails were lashed in untidy bundles at the foot of their respective stays. For the previous five days she had been under way, sails well reefed, hatches battened down, tidying up after the battle. More than 120 French and Spanish prisoners had been saved from the sea or brought aboard from prizes about to be scuttled, and herded down below where, under four feet three inches of headroom, the stench of bilge-water, rotting food, wet clothes and vomit did little to comfort them.

Now, after a few hours lying hove-to while some of her thirty-three crew tried to snatch some rest in between standing a watch and keeping a guard on the prisoners, the flagship was signalling. Bloodshot and salt-rimmed eyes stared up to windward, trying to focus through unsteady and spray-soaked telescopes to identify the flags. The *Pickle*'s pennants flew from one yardarm of the *Euryalus*, indicating the signal was to her. The other hoist consisted of two flags, the upper one white and the lower one quartered in red and white—eight and four. And in the signal book, Number 84 meant "Pass within hail."

Wearily Lt. John Richards Lapenotiere, the thirty-five-year-old Devonian who was commanding the schooner, gave the order to get under way. Each man in the crew moved cautiously, using one hand for his task and the other to hold on, for the ship was rolling and pitching like a log launched into a mountain torrent. Some of the seamen went to the brails to loose the foresail, others to the halyards ready to haul up the big mainsail as soon as the gaskets lashing the stiff, sodden canvas and gaff to the boom were let go. More men stood by at the sheets, ready to trim the sails the minute they were hoisted.

Above the noise of the wind in the masts and rigging—which tore at already frayed nerves like the shrill voice of a shrewish woman—came orders shouted by George Almy, the Second Master, whose accent betrayed his American origins.

The constant soaking and the cold made the skin of the men's hands white and dead-looking, and the ropes they seized were stiff and swollen, intractable and unwilling to run through the blocks. And as is the way with ropes in bad weather, they looped themselves in tiresome bights round any and every projection on deck and masts, exasperating the tired seamen and slowing up their tasks.

"Ease away vangs, downhauls and tack tricing lines . . . ease away boom sheets!" With the help of a speaking-trumpet Almy's voice won its fight against the wind. "Man the main halyards . . . haul taut!" The men, having taken the strain on the halyards, prepared to haul up the big mainsail now that everything was clear.

"Hoist away!"

With maddening slowness the sail crawled up the mast, the canvas beginning to flog as the wind got into it. Eventually it was hoisted and sheeted in. The middle jib followed, and a few minutes later the foresail was sheeted in and drawing. Slowly the *Pickle* began to move through the water, her bluff bows shouldering through the waves and bursting the crests into showers of spray. Right aft, unprotected from wind and sea, the quartermaster watched the leech of the jib as he moved the tiller inch by inch to bring the schooner hard on the wind to start the wearisome beat up to the *Euryalus*.

As soon as the leech began to quiver—showing the ship was sailing as close to the wind as she could without losing speed—he eased the tiller a fraction. With his legs straddled to keep his balance on the heaving deck, his eyes were busy watching the leech of the *Pickle*'s jib and the relative position of the *Euryalus,* while his ears listened for any orders which might be shouted at him. He became part of the quivering, plunging ship, sensitive to her every yaw and anticipating the way an extra heavy sea would try to barge her bows off course. He knew, by a mixture of instinct and experience, just how a sudden stronger squall could run her head up into the wind, with every resulting vicious flap and slat of the sail liable to slit the canvas from top to bottom. Slowly the *Pickle* worked her way across the desolate and heavily furrowed grey waste separating her from the *Euryalus,* and when Lapenotiere sailed her close down the frigate's lee side, someone bellowed from the quarter-deck through a speaking-trumpet, and ordered him on board. The *Pickle* was hove-to, the set of her sails so balanced that the pressure of the wind on one neutralized the other. The jolly-boat was lowered, and as it rose and fell several feet on the restless water, Lapenotiere scrambled in.

On board the *Euryalus* Vice-Admiral Collingwood was waiting.

His despatch, addressed to William Marsden, the Secretary to the Board of Admiralty and dated "*Euryalus,* off Cape Trafalgar, October 22nd, 1805," was ready in his cabin, together with copies of a general order to the Fleet issued on the day after the battle, paying his tribute to the fallen Nelson and thanking every man in the Fleet for his "highly meritorious conduct." He had also written, with a heavy and anxious heart, a second letter to Mr. Marsden describing the damage the gale had since wrought to the prizes. He had been forced to order the scuttling of the huge 130-gun *Santissima Trinidad,* the greatest warship ever built and flagship of Rear-Admiral don Baltazar Hidalgo Cisneros; the 112-gun *Santa Ana,* flagship of Vice-Admiral don Ignatio Maria de Alava, had no doubt also sunk. Of the remaining prizes, he had written, "Unless the weather moderates, I doubt whether I shall be able to carry a ship of them into port."

Captain Henry Blackwood, commanding the *Euryalus,* had been writing regularly to his wife and was waiting to send the letters home by the first ship—which he hoped would be his own frigate, so that he should have the honour of carrying back the first news of the battle, and also Captain Hardy with Nelson's body. To his wife at 1 a.m. on the night after the battle he had begun his letter with: "The first hour since yesterday morning that I could call my own is now before me, to be devoted to my dearest wife, who, thank God, is not a husband out of pocket. My heart is, however, sad, my Harriet, and penetrated with the deepest sorrow. A victory, and such a one was never before achieved, took place yesterday in the course of five hours; but at such an expense, in the loss of the most gallant of men—the best and kindest of friends, as renders it to be a victory I could hardly have ever wished to witness on such terms. . . ."

But Blackwood was disappointed: by the 26th, five days after the battle, Collingwood had decided to send his despatches home in the second smallest ship in the Fleet, the *Pickle.* According to descendants of her commanding officer, the reason why Collingwood chose Lapenotiere and his little schooner was that several years earlier the Admiral had been travelling in a ship with the young lieutenant. An order had been given to the man at the wheel and Lapenotiere, although only a passenger, had realized that if it were obeyed the ship would go on the rocks. He promptly gave another order and saved the ship. A grateful Collingwood

had said: "If ever I have the opportunity, I will do you a service."
Now that opportunity had come and Lapenotiere—whose family
came to England in the revolution of 1688 with "Dutch William,"
and whose father and grandfather had served in the Navy—had
been chosen to take the despatches home.

When Lapenotiere finally scrambled on board the *Euryalus* from
his jolly-boat he was taken to the Admiral's cabin. According to the
same source Collingwood reminded the young lieutenant of his
promise and said: "Now take these despatches to England; you will
receive £500 and your Commander's commission. Now I have kept
my word." After collecting various other letters—including Blackwood's—to deliver in England, and receiving orders to transfer
the rest of the prisoners he still had on board to the *Revenge,*
Lapenotiere went back on board the *Pickle.* By noon the jolly-
boat had returned from its task of moving the prisoners, and once
again Lapenotiere had a full crew to work the ship, instead of having to use some of them as guards. "In boat and made sail for England," Almy's spidery handwriting noted in his log.

With more than a thousand miles to go from Trafalgar—which
is only a few score miles along the Spanish coast from Gibraltar—
the *Pickle* had a long, tedious and dangerous voyage ahead of her.
The four enemy battleships[1] under the French Rear-Admiral
Dumanoir, which had fled from the battle, might fall upon her;
French or Spanish ships could swoop out from Vigo, Corunna,
Ferrol or Brest. In addition, another French admiral, Allemand,
was at sea with at least five more battleships. But, despite the threat
of enemy ships lying across his track, Lapenotiere knew that the
weather would probably turn out to be his worst enemy. The
Pickle had already endured a heavy pounding in gigantic seas—
Blackwood had written on the 23rd, "It has blown a hurricane"—
and the wrenching strain on her frames and timbers was probably
squeezing the caulking oakum out from between the planks of
her hull.

Now, on Saturday, October 26, from off Cadiz (where three
years later she was to be wrecked while entering the harbour) the
quartermaster steered the *Pickle* west-north-west to round Cape
St. Vincent. The gale slowly eased down until there was only a

1 The more conventional phrase "line-of-battle ship" will be rendered as
"battleship" in this narrative.

fresh breeze blowing under a cloudy sky, but the strong winds on the previous days had left a heavy swell which made the ship's timbers creak and groan, as if she resented every wave which alternately lifted her on its crest and then tumbled her into the trough. Soon she could carry more sail. The main-topmast, which had been sent down and lashed on deck at the beginning of the gale, was sent up again; reefs were shaken out of the mainsail and the topsail was set. But the topsail stood for less than an hour, because the wind quickly piped up again and backed just before midnight, forcing Lapenotiere to sail the *Pickle* in almost exactly the opposite direction to the course for England. His great danger now was that the *Pickle* would be trapped in the great bay formed by the rocky outcrop of Cape St. Vincent. Wise seamen feared a lee shore in a gale more than the most heavily armed enemy.

By dawn on Sunday the wind had veered, and at noon the *Pickle* was back on course some twelve to fifteen miles off Cape St. Mary, with Cape St. Vincent yet to be weathered. On Monday, with the wind lighter and more canvas set, Lapenotiere decided to muster the crew. The *Regulations and Instructions Relating to His Majesty's Service at Sea* laid down that a commanding officer "is himself to muster the Ship's Company at least once a week at sea," and in addition to checking them against the ship's books, Form Number 15 had to be filled in.

This had several columns with different headings—the date the man joined the ship, whether "prest" (press-ganged) or a volunteer, name, rating, age, stature, complexion, leave allowed, etc. There was one column headed ominously "D., D.D., or R."—discharged, discharged dead, or "run" (deserted). Of the ship's complement of forty there were now only thirty-two men on board; the rest had "run" or been discharged. And even though the *Pickle* had been at sea continuously for several weeks, there were no sick men wanting the attentions of Mr. Britton, the surgeon from Bristol.

The muster list gave a good indication of the cosmopolitan crowd of men who, volunteers or prest, manned His Majesty's ships at this time. Of the thirty-two men whose names appeared on Form 15, seventeen were English, nine Irish, two American, one Norwegian, one Scots, one Welsh and one a Channel Islander. But compared with battleships this was nothing—the *Victory*, as we shall see later, numbered Americans, Swiss, Germans, Maltese, Russians, Swedes, Italians, Norwegians and even Frenchmen among her crew as well as men from Salvador and Guadeloupe.

With the *Pickle*'s crew mustered on deck, the first man's name was called and his details noted down—James Rowden, bosun's mate, joined the ship on December 1, 1804, volunteer, born at Saltash, Cornwall, and aged thirty. One after another the men were checked. The ninth and tenth names on the ship's books were of Irishmen, one from Cork and the other from Dublin, who were marked "run." The eighteenth and nineteenth names were of Norwegians—John Ellingson, who was rated a carpenter's mate, and Wildred Andrus, able seaman. Both were volunteers, joining the ship on December 1, 1804, and both were marked down as having "run" at Plymouth. One prest American, Thomas Bascombe of New York, rated able seaman and twenty-six years old when he suddenly found himself in His Majesty's Service, was noted down as having been discharged at Bermuda in time to have missed Trafalgar. Farther down the list was another Norwegian, I. Ellingson, the brother of John. He had joined as a carpenter's mate five weeks before his brother—and deserted in September, just before the *Pickle* sailed from Plymouth for Cadiz. Immediately below, Wildred Andrus's name appeared once again—he had rejoined the ship after having "run" on the same day that his countryman deserted, and he was marked down "returned after run." The name of Almy, the Second Master,[2] with a note that he came from Newport, Rhode Island, was next to that of John Oxford, a twenty-four-year-old able seaman from the same town.

The *Pickle*'s crew had just been dismissed after the muster when a look-out hailed the quarter-deck: "Sail in sight to the west-north-west standing towards us."

A few minutes later, as the *Pickle*'s bluff-bowed hull was lifted up on the crest of an extra high wave, thus helping the eyes of the anxious men on the quarter-deck to see a little farther over the curvature of the earth, they identified the approaching sail as a ship-rigged sloop. From her course she was obviously steering to intercept the *Pickle*, so Lapenotiere decided to keep sailing as fast as possible, to be on the safe side until he was sure of her identity. He

2 The *Pickle* did not at this time have a Master. See Notes, p. 366.

ordered the fore-topsail to be set. However, the sloop slowly closed on the *Pickle* and Lapenotiere had the private signal hoisted. As soon as the flags were streaming from their halyards the sloop answered and ran up the numbers which identified her—451.

She was the 26-gun *Nautilus*—a new ship built eighteen months earlier at Milford Haven and now commanded by Captain Sykes. Soon the two ships were hove-to near each other, and the *Nautilus* lowered a boat for Captain Sykes to go aboard the *Pickle*. As soon as a weary Lapenotiere had told him the news of the victory and of the tragedy Sykes, realizing its importance, decided to go at once to Lisbon to warn the British Ambassador. The *Nautilus* headed for the Tagus, but darkness brought a fresh gale and both ships had to reef down hurriedly. The *Nautilus* finally reached the mouth of the Tagus early on Tuesday, firing several guns to bring out a pilot boat. None came, and after waiting two hours the sloop hove-to while a Portuguese fishing boat was boarded and her master paid to take a despatch into Lisbon and have it delivered to Mr. Gambier, the British Consul. By 9.30 a.m. the *Nautilus* was under way again—this time heading for England, because Captain Sykes had decided that the task of carrying the news of the victory off Cape Trafalgar was too important, in case she was captured, to leave entirely to the *Pickle*.

By Wednesday, October 30, the *Pickle*'s log noted that they were off the Burlings, the rocks to the north-west of Lisbon, and they "saw the *Notlas*" (Almy's spelling of the *Nautilus*). Despite her long detour to the Tagus she had caught up. She was, of course, a larger ship and she was still in sight next day when yet another gale blew up from the south-west.

Once again the crew of the *Pickle* went through the back-breaking task of shortening sail, starting by sending the topgallant yard, with its heavy weight and windage, down to the deck and lashing it. Mainsail and middle jib were reefed, but still the *Pickle* plunged and pounded, as if she were trying to run amok in the screaming wind. Finally, with topsail furled and the yard sent down, and the foresail brailed up, she seemed to ride a little easier. But it gave the crew only a short respite—at 9 a.m. on Thursday, as they were rounding Finisterre before entering the Bay of Biscay, a heavy sea swept the ship, wrenching away the jib-boom and spritsail yard. Within a few minutes Copeland, the carpenter's mate, was reporting that the limber holes in the frames which drained the forepeak were blocked up, preventing the water running aft to the pump. As a result the forepeak was flooding. Lapenotiere sent men down to start baling with buckets.

By 11 p.m. the little *Pickle*'s position was rapidly becoming critical. Somewhere forward below the waterline there was a leak, and the more the ship laboured the worse it would get. The wind increased in the darkness, whipping up vicious seas which were superimposed in complicated patterns on the heavy swell already rolling in without interruption from another great storm centre in the heart of the Atlantic. As each crest passed under the bows, the ship reared up and then plunged into the next trough, sending a great shudder through her timbers. In the forepeak, barely able to keep a foothold on a deck which seemed more like a seesaw, men scrambled and cursed, filling buckets and passing them up to be emptied. But however fast they baled, the level of the water swilling and sucking round their legs seemed to remain the same. Further aft men manned the pump which gushed and gurgled but, however hard they worked, never sucked dry. Midnight came unnoticed, bringing in its train Friday, November 1.

In the small hours, in the darkness of a night which brought a chill to men's spirits, the wind increased its frenetic screaming in the rigging and masts. Extra men at the tiller struggled to keep the *Pickle* on something approaching a safe course. By 5 a.m. the gale was worse. The wind, exerting a pressure of many pounds on each square foot of the weather side of the hull and the masts and rigging, was now so strong that as the ship rolled to leeward she hung there sluggishly for minutes on end, seemingly reluctant to steady herself and roll back to windward. She began to feel dead in the water and Lapenotiere, weary and worried, anxious both for his ship and the despatches entrusted to him, decided he would have to clear some of the top-weight off the ship. The easiest way of doing that was to get rid of some of the 12-pounder carronades on deck. Each weighed six hundredweight on its wooden slide, and since they were fitted high up and well out against the ship's side, where they exerted a great leverage, they were from the point of view of stability in almost the worst possible position. Lapenotiere therefore ordered four of them, with their slides, to be heaved over the side. Lightened by more than a ton, the *Pickle* then seemed to ride a little easier, but still she plunged and pounded, her apple-cheeked bow lifting and then smashing down in a welter of solid water and spray, straining the whole ship.

Dawn came cold, grey and disheartening, and it brought no improvement in the weather. By 10 a.m. this miserable Friday, the time had come to reduce sail even more. Men scrambled to halyards, sheets and vangs, while others had to cling precariously to the boom to stifle the flogging canvas as the halyards were slackened away and the sail brought down. The wind whipped and tore it like a petulant giant until gaskets could be passed and secured. But the crew still had work to do: the fore-topmast had to be sent down in an attempt to reduce the windage, and lashed securely to the deck. At noon Almy recorded in the log that a strong gale was still blowing, but under the low scudding clouds it seemed to be getting a little lighter, and the more hopeful among the crew hazarded a tentative guess that the wind was easing slightly. And indeed it was, though to men who had not had a decent sleep for eleven days and whose clothes had been wringing wet for most of that time it seemed to do so with tantalizing tardiness. More sail was set as gradually the wind veered and dropped to a fresh breeze. The fore-topmast was sent up once again, and at 5 p.m. the fore-topsail yard was swayed up. By the time it was dark the *Pickle* had all her working canvas set and drawing. The leak had stopped and although the swell kept the *Pickle* pitching and rolling violently, the watch below thankfully wriggled into their sodden hammocks and slept.

The next day was Saturday, November 2, and the *Pickle* reached the entrance of the Channel, west of Ushant. The Lizard was 151 miles away to the north-north-east according to Almy's calculations, though much of them had to be guesswork and dead reckoning because of the gales. The quartermaster at the helm was steering the ship on a north-easterly course, and a following wind kept her sailing fast. On deck and down below the crew were hard at work tidying up, sorting out the sodden tangle of gear and clothing. By now the *Pickle* was no longer alone: on the horizon all round were sails, sails of merchant ships converging on or leaving English ports, bringing in much-needed cargoes and outward bound with others, and sails of warships—battleships going out on patrol or returning frigates bearing despatches to far-flung commanders-in-chief or bringing some back—and tiny sloops and cutters of all descriptions on a variety of missions.

Yet even now, within a day's sailing of the Lizard, given a decent wind, Nature had not finished with the *Pickle:* the wind dropped right away so that the once arched and overstrained sails flattened like limp curtains, and as the way came off the schooner they slatted and flapped while she rolled in the slight swell, the trucks of her masts scribing invisible circles in the sky. And slowly the ships on the horizon faded from sight, blurred and then hidden by banks of sea mist forming as the warm air rolled in across the cold sea, to be chilled and its invisible water vapour condensed into myriads of dank and visible droplets. Lapenotiere, knowing how urgent was his task of delivering Collingwood's despatches, set the crew to work with sweeps. These large oars, with three or four men thrusting at each of them, soon had the *Pickle* heading the right direction with a knot or two of way on her.

The oars had been groaning rhythmically for more than four hours when the perspiring men—and Lapenotiere on the quarter-deck—saw a ruffle on the water ahead: a breeze was coming up from the eastward. A light head wind was certainly better than rowing; but would they never get a reasonable beam wind to give them a fast reach, which was the schooner's fastest point of sailing? Thankfully the men hauled the sweeps inboard and stowed them while others hurried to sheet in jibs, foresail and mainsail, to catch every miserable cat's-paw of wind and enable them to creep nearer to the Lizard. The breeze pewtering the sea soon became steady and then it increased to fresh and later strong, so that the *Pickle,* from heeling gently and steering through calm seas with almost feline grace, was soon lumbering along like an overloaded farm cart, with more wind and sea than she wanted. At 5 p.m. Lapenotiere ordered the fore-topsail to be taken in, and a few minutes later he ordered the yard to be struck down on deck.

Late this Sunday afternoon a powerful 74-gun ship, the black-and-yellow hull identifying her as one of Nelson's fleet, came down on them fast, ploughing her way south-westward out of the Channel. After the private signal was run up on each ship they exchanged numbers. Three flags from the 74 identified her as the *Superb,* commanded by Captain Richard Gardiner Keats. The signal flags 351—"I have some intelligence to communicate"—hoisted from the *Pickle*'s yardarm soon brought a scurry of activity aboard *Superb:* her jibs and staysails came tumbling down, the courses—the lowest of the big sails on the fore- and mainmasts—were clewed up, and her topgallants lowered. Her helm was put a'lee to bring her up to the wind and then her main-topsail backed, so that the wind filling the fore-topsail tried to move the ship ahead but was counterbalanced by that on the backed sail trying to push her astern. She was now hove-to and in the meantime the *Pickle* had lowered a jolly-boat which was bringing Lapenotiere across.

For Keats, the news that Lapenotiere took only a few moments to relate was one of the greatest shocks of his life. His reactions can easily be imagined, for he was Nelson's special favourite, and up to this moment he had been hurrying to Cadiz, hoping desperately that he would be in time for the battle. Now, on this drab November Sunday, with the battle fought and his friend and patron dead, perhaps Keats's mind went back to a morning some seven weeks earlier in the grounds of Nelson's home, Merton Place, in Surrey. There he had walked with the Admiral, who in an excited voice had described his plans for fighting the Combined Fleet of France and Spain. When Lapenotiere left to return to the *Pickle* he left behind men who were openly shedding tears. As the *Superb* got under way again for Cadiz, every man aboard was conscious that he had missed a rendezvous with history and, in Nelson's death, suffered a personal loss.

The *Pickle* was less than sixty miles from the Lizard and with night falling the wind eased and veered, and Almy noted in the log that the ship had "all sail set to advantage" as she made her way up to the north-east. Here, as the broad Atlantic funnelled into the narrow Channel between England and France, the tidal stream was getting stronger every mile made to the eastward, adding to the problem of dead-reckoning navigation. At midnight the deep-sea lead was got out and a cast gave fifty-two fathoms under the *Pickle*'s keel. Two hours later a sharp-eyed look-out spotted the Lizard Light perched some two hundred feet up atop Lizard Head and bearing east by north, an estimated nine miles away.

Sailing ships had made this very landfall for centuries, returning from the four corners of the earth laden with rare cargoes which had made England rich, or bearing the scars of sea battles which had created—and maintained—her greatness. And the Lizard was often the last sight of land for ships making their departure, bound for remote ports and unexplored coasts to trade or blockade, survey, barter or battle. Even as the Lizard was the first sight of England for the Duke of Medina Sidonia and the Spanish Armada, so it was the last for the Pilgrim Fathers sailing for America. Drake's last glimpse of England before he died on board his own ship off Porto-bello in 1596 had been this very headland, and Nelson, too, had seen it for the last time a bare few weeks before the *Pickle* nosed her way past.

In the darkness she sailed past the sleeping villages along the Cornish coast: past Landewednack, hidden under the lee of the Lizard, whose parish church was the most southerly in England, past Cadgwith Cove, and the hump of Black Head. Beyond was Coverack, a small fishing village with its own stone quay, a favourite landing place for smugglers. These men still managed to bring in brandy from across the Channel after successful deals with equally unscrupulous enemy traders who, like themselves, placed cash above conscience to satisfy customers who put palate above patriotism.

By the time dawn diluted the black night to a chilly grey, the *Pickle* was abeam of the Manacles, that most dreaded group of rocks lying near the track of ships off this coast. Many seamen, washed ashore lifeless from ships which came in too close under the cliffs through faulty navigation or were driven ashore by gales, were buried in St. Keverne's churchyard a mile or so inland. Lapenotiere could see Falmouth Bay and the whole of the Cornish coast up to Rame Head opening out as he brought the schooner round to the north, following the shore line and broad-reaching —at long last—the last few miles to Falmouth, whose entrance was guarded by the twin castles of Pendennis and St. Mawes, constructed by a thoughtful Henry VIII. As the *Pickle* reached Falmouth Bay with the wind light and the tide foul, Lapenotiere gave his orders to Kingdom, his second-in-command, who was taking the ship on to Plymouth. Lapenotiere went below to his tiny cabin and struggled into his best uniform, mildewed and creased as it was. He then took a pouch containing Admiral Collingwood's despatches, Blackwood's letters and various other papers from the desk in which he had kept it under lock and key, buckled on his sword and went back on deck.

It was at 9.45 a.m. on Monday, November 4, that he gave the order first to shorten sail, and then heave-to. The jolly-boat was swung over the side once again and he stepped into it.[3] The menacing bulk of Pendennis Castle was more than half a mile away, and it was some time before the tall, quiet-spoken lieutenant stepped ashore from the boat and began to arrange for a postchaise to take him and his precious despatches the 266 miles to the Admiralty in London.[4]

Lieutenant Lapenotiere and his coachman were not, however, the only carriers of the news. Captain Sykes and the *Nautilus* had been following close astern of the *Pickle*, but on the previous Saturday had narrowly escaped being captured a hundred miles south-west of Ushant. Steering north-eastward in a light breeze, the horizon fading in the haze so that it was impossible to see where sea ended and sky began, the *Nautilus*'s look-outs had sighted the sails of four ships to the eastward. Through telescopes her officers saw they were steering towards her and would pass across the sloop's bows from starboard to larboard. The private signal was hoisted at one of the *Nautilus*'s yardarms and two guns were fired to draw attention to it. But the four ships made no reply.

Sykes, uncertain what was going on, kept a respectable distance and his wariness was rewarded. After identifying the vessels as a battleship, two frigates and a brig, he saw another brig come into sight and pass near the battleship, which hoisted French colours to it. He was just digesting this fact when the battleship hoisted a French pennant over two strange flags at the mizen peak. That was more than enough for Sykes. He gave the order to beat to quarters, and the staccato rattle of the drum beating to the tune of "Hearts of Oak" sent the *Nautilus*'s crew of 121 to their stations. Bulkheads were hinged up or taken down; decks were wetted and sanded against fire and slipping feet; the galley fire was doused.

3 For a painting of the *Pickle*'s arrival, see illustration Number 19.
4 The semaphore telegraph stations between London and Plymouth were being built at this time but were not yet completed; the nearest was at Portsmouth.

Fighting lanterns, with candle-ends in them, were put ready; the gunner went to the magazine, and the carpenters stood by with their sounding irons and shot plugs. The gun captains had their powder horns and priming irons ready; slow matches—long twists of cotton or worsted impregnated with a composition which made them burn slowly—were lit and hung over tubs half-filled with water; powder boys brought up cartridges; fire screens—mostly wet blankets—were rigged.

The little sloop had eighteen 9-pounders on the upper deck, with six 12-pounders on the quarter-deck and two more 12-pounders in the fo'c'sle. At the first roll of the drum the crews had swarmed to their guns, cast off the lashings and tackles securing them, and run them in ready to load. While this was going on the ship's fore-topsail and fore-topgallant were being set. All sails were sheeted in hard as Sykes turned the *Nautilus* away to make her escape to the south-east. But the French ships did not follow him and by 5 p.m. had gone out of sight over the horizon to the north-west.

At 10 a.m. on Sunday, after an uneventful night, Sykes came on deck and ordered the lieutenant to send the hands aft to witness punishment: two seamen were to be flogged for "insolence and neglect of duty." A midshipman passed the order on to the bosun's mates, and to the accompaniment of their shrill pipes it was shouted throughout the ship. Marines in white breeches and red tail coats, their white crossbelts newly pipe-clayed, hats high and round, the brims looped up at the side like a bishop's, fell in on the poop with muskets and side-arms; the captain and lieutenants waited on the weather side of the quarter-deck, with the junior officers gathered respectfully to leeward. The rest of the crew fell in anywhere—on the boats, on the booms—wherever they could get a view.

Sykes ordered: "Rig the gratings." Two of the gratings covering a hatch were brought aft, and while one was put flat on the deck, the other was lashed vertically above it, against a bulkhead. Then Sykes called for Alexander Petrie, sentenced to thirty-six lashes. Had he anything to say in extenuation? That formality over, the next order was "Strip," and Petrie took off his jacket and shirt. At "Seize him up" he leaned against the vertical grating and the quartermaster lashed him to it. Sykes then read out the particular

Article of War which Petrie had infringed, and while he was doing so one of the burliest of the bosun's mates took the red-handled cat-o'-nine-tails from a red baize bag. The cat was a brutal weapon, symptomatic of a brutal age. It consisted of nine long and thin lines (knotted if the punishment was for theft) which hung like poisonous tentacles from a short, rigid handle. One lash stripped the skin from the man's back wherever the tails fell, the knots biting deeper and drawing blood. Six lashes—for each was skilfully placed by the bosun's mate in a different place—made all the skin completely raw, while twelve mangled the flesh so that it looked like butcher's meat. A man who frequently witnessed flogging said that after two dozen lashes—which left the bosun's mate exhausted, so that another man took over—"The lacerated back looks inhuman; it resembles roasted meat burnt nearly black before a scorching fire." Yet seventy-two lashes were regarded as common, and even five hundred were sometimes given.

The punishment for striking an officer was invariably flogging through the fleet. For this a man was lashed to a grating in a boat and, to the accompaniment of half-minute bells and a drummer beating the "Rogues' March," he was rowed to each ship in turn and flogged. If he became unconscious half-way through he was often brought back, nursed to health, and weeks later the flogging resumed. Even if he died on the grating—and many men did, from shock—the punishment often was completed. It was rare but not unknown for a corpse to be brought alongside a ship, and the remaining lashes administered before it was rowed ashore and buried, without religious rites, below the tide line.

Yet some captains used the cat rarely, if at all. Collingwood, a stern disciplinarian, had his men working cheerfully and efficiently and yet he used the cat less than once a month. When bad sailors were brought before Nelson he had often said: "Send them to Collingwood: he will tame them if no one else can." The Vice-Admiral could deal with the worst of them, making good seamen of those whom others might have flogged to death or hanged from the yardarm.

A few captains in Nelson's time were complete tyrants; bolstered up by the Articles of War, they were able to use the cat indiscriminately to work off deep-rooted grudges against life in general. At least one captain flogged the last man down on deck

after setting sail aloft—which often meant the best man got the
cat, since it depended how far out on the yard he was working.
One man who served in nine battleships said only two had humane
commanders. It is a sad fact that a tyrant—in defiance of Admiralty
regulations—could so harry and haze a seaman he disliked (and
men served for upwards of two years in the same ship without
setting foot on shore) that the wretched fellow was goaded into
an offence for which the only punishment was death; a comparatively quick end if hoisted in a hangman's noose from a yardarm, or
the slow, agonizing death resulting from being flogged round the
fleet.

So Alexander Petrie paid the price for "Insolence and neglect
of duty," and at the end of his thirty-six lashes he was cut down
from the grating and taken away to the sick bay, where the surgeon
tried to patch him up. The second offender, William Donaldson,
was then tied up to receive two dozen lashes. And in the *Nautilus*'s
log it was noted down briefly: "At 10 punished Alexr Petrie and
Wm Donaldson seamen with 36 lashes and 24 lashes for insolence
and neglect of duty. . . ."

Late on Monday night, nearly twelve hours after Lapenotiere
left Falmouth in his postchaise, the *Nautilus* hove-to off Plymouth
and Captain Sykes went ashore by boat, reported and took a postchaise for London.

Lying-to in heavy weather with a mizen (*left*), a close-reefed main-topsail (*centre*) and main-staysail (*right*).

TWO

PRICE OF VICTORY

*The death of Nelson was felt in England as something
more than a public calamity; men started at the intelligence,
and turned pale, as if they had heard of the loss of a dear
friend.* —Southey

LIEUTENANT LAPENOTIERE was already well on his way. By
noon on Monday his postchaise was clattering out of Falmouth
up the road to Penryn, where it took the right-hand fork for Truro.
Lapenotiere was glad the roads were dry—it had not rained for
five days—and his coachmen kept up a good speed, unaware that
he was bearing momentous news.

The coach clattered into Truro, Cornwall's only city and placid
with good breeding, where the county gentry had their town
houses and paced over cobblestones along walks lined with palm
horses, and as soon as they were changed the coach drove on to
trees. At the Royal Hotel the ostlers were ready with four fresh
Liskeard, the old market town which had been the Royalist headquarters when England was torn between Cavalier and Roundhead.

Changing horses once again—they, and sometimes the postchaise
as well, were to be changed nineteen times before he reached London—Lapenotiere approached the Devon border. He left behind
him a Cornwall full of colour and contradictions. Wesley's influence
was strong and there were books of his hymns in nearly every house,
while each village had its thatched chapel. Men played kayle, or
skittle-alley, while they drank ale or cider; they held competitions
among the tin mines to catch greased pigs, and watched cock-fight-
ing and bull-baiting, or a lunatic in a cage. From Cornwall a lumbering stage wagon took three weeks to get to London, and many a
man made his will before embarking on such a journey.

The young lieutenant was soon at Tavistock, passing within a

mile of where Sir Francis Drake was born. Then on the postchaise
thundered, to Dartmoor bleak and foreboding, passing close to
Princetown, soon to have a huge prison built there to house
French prisoners-of-war, but now just a village with quarries and a
few farms.

The road swept slowly down among gaunt tors on its way to
Postbridge, with its ancient clapper bridge across the West Dart.
On and on the horses galloped, with Lapenotiere sitting in uncomfortable silence grasping his despatches. From Exeter the 'chaise
turned on to the post road for the lace-making town of Honiton,
with its fourteenth-century leper hospital. Once clear of its wide
streets he was soon heading on to Axminster, past rich meadows
whose sturdy-framed and red-coated South Devon cattle yielded
milk of just the right type for the country's famous scald cream, past
orchards whose apples, under the farmers' presses, gave up a fine
and potent cider.

This was the land that Nelson's victory had made safe for another
century, although few men working in the fields bothered to glance
up to see the messenger who was bringing the news. It was a land
where poverty rubbed shoulders with richness, but which bred a
sturdy race of people. Veal and pork cost about threepence a pound
and rhubarb was the main medicine.

A woman was paid sixpence a day for weeding a field, plus a
penny-ha'penny for beer. A maid received £5 a year and a farm-
hand £10 if he lived in. They ate their food from wooden plates,
and their homes were lit by candles and cruses fed with fish or animal oil. Schoolteachers were paid a pound a month, and burying
a pauper cost the parish twenty-seven shillings for a coffin and half
a crown for the minister. If the local people went far afield they
would travel by wagon. Those with first-class tickets stayed in when
they reached a hill while the second-class got out and walked, and
those with third-class tickets had to push.

It was a jaded and weary Lapenotiere who sat back as the fresh
horses galloped through finely wooded country alongside the Test
at Laverstoke and Overton, and then on to Basingstoke, where
seven roads met at what was once one of the manors held by King
Harold before the Conquest. There remained some fifty miles to
London. Many miles farther back along the road—which, coming
from Plymouth, he had joined at Two Bridges—was Captain Sykes,

of the *Nautilus,* also bound for the Admiralty as fast as postchaise would bear him.

Lapenotiere left Basingstoke in the late afternoon of November 5 and the weather gave a warning of fog to come. Smoke from the chimneys of the cottages along the side of the road rose in vertical threads or mingled with hints of mist, and the smell of burning logs introduced a new and welcome odour into the musty 'chaise. Sure enough, as he approached the outskirts of the great capital, the stratified sheets of mist lying in the hollows gradually thickened into banks of fog, white in the glow from the lamps at first, but yellowing with the throat-catching tang of sulphur as bunches of cottages merged into terraces of houses. The cursing coachman slowed from a gallop to a trot, from a trot to a walk, and from a walk to a crawl. Gales and calms, head winds and leaks had conspired to slow the *Pickle,* and now one of London's famous November fogs was marking down the bearer of Collingwood's despatches for its special attention.

The fog which hampered Lapenotiere also caught, among hundreds of others, the vivacious Lady Bessborough, who wrote: "I drove to town intending to go . . . to Queen Street and Duncannon's house, where I had appointed people to meet me. The fog, which was bad when I set out, grew thicker and thicker, but when I got into the Park was so complete it was impossible to find the way out." But the woman who was four years later, when a grandmother, to suffer the attentions of the corpulent and dissipated Prince Regent, was not put out. "My footman got down to feel for the road, and the hollowing of the drivers and the screams of people on foot were dreadful. I was one hour driving through the Park; Queen Street was impossible to find . . . I set out with two men walking before the horses with flambeaux, of which we could with difficulty perceive the flame—the men not at all. Every ten or twenty yards they felt for the door of a house to ask where we were—it was frightful beyond measure. . . . I find Lady Villiers, who rode to see me, was overtaken by it on her return, and nearly drown'd by riding into the Thames. How many accidents she has!"

Her Ladyship had safely negotiated the worst fog the capital had seen for many years by the time the fretting Lapenotiere approached Westminster Bridge and Whitehall, stiff and weary from nearly thirty-seven hours' hard driving from Falmouth. Midnight had struck and November 6 had been ushered in.

A fog-bound Whitehall was deserted and in the Admiralty the silver-haired and sharp-eyed Lord Barham, now seventy-nine and First Lord, had retired to bed. England owed much to Lord Barham, a tough man and a brilliant administrator, whose life was devoted to the good of the Service he loved. He had been Comptroller of the Navy from 1778 to 1790 and thus was responsible for its material. As we shall see later, he had set the stage for Nelson to fight the Combined Fleet in the same competent, clear and concise way that he had, within a few days of taking over as First Lord, set out the duties of the Board of Admiralty. His own role occupied a sentence—"The First Lord will take upon himself the general superintendence of the whole." The duties of the "Senior or First Professional Lord,"[1] the Second and Third Lords, and Civil Lords took only a few lines. Then he outlined the tasks of the Secretary, Second Secretary, clerks ("To be in their desks by 10 o'clock"), confidential clerks, nine principal clerks "and an extra clerk to be under the First Lord's Secretary."

The Secretary to the Board probably had the hardest task of all. With the help of the Second Secretary he had to open all incoming correspondence, examine and sign outgoing letters, countersign orders, commissions and warrants signed by the Board, and run the whole office through the First Clerk.

It was the weight of all this work that kept the Secretary working late in the Board Room on this foggy November night. He was an Irishman, William Marsden, son of an Irish banker with shipping interests. Originally intended for the Church, he had, via the East India Company, become Secretary to the Board of Admiralty, thanks to the influence of Earl Spencer (such appointments were held almost entirely by influence in those days). The Board Room where Marsden worked had been the centre of Britain's dominion of the seas since Ripley constructed the building in 1725. From here orders had gone out which sent Anson on his great voyage of exploration in 1740; Byng to Minorca—and his death before a firing squad after a court-martial in England; Cook

[1] Now termed the First Sea Lord.

on three voyages which opened up the entire Pacific; Howe to his great battle in 1794 on the "glorious first of June"; Admiral Sir John Jervis to the St. Valentine's Day victory off Cape St. Vincent in 1797, and Nelson himself to the great victories of the Nile, Copenhagen and now against the Combined Fleet of France and Spain.

The ebb and flow of British naval history—and land history, for the two were interdependent—had been planned in this room, and somehow it had absorbed this atmosphere. It was rectangular, with three windows on one long side overlooking some stables. The high white ceiling was decorated with gilt emblematic roses and heavy seventeenth-century oak panelling covered the walls. A log fire burnt in the grate which still bore the arms of Charles II, and on the wall over the fireplace were several charts, wound round rollers so that they looked like white sun-blinds. A long, heavy mahogany table occupying the middle of the room had its legs inset so that people sitting round it were not inconvenienced as they discussed, argued and decided policies which could send fleets to victory or to their doom, break an admiral or promote the humblest lieutenant. On the north wall, flanked by bookcases, was what at first glance appeared to be a huge clock face, but closer inspection showed that it was a circular map depicting Europe from the Baltic to the north of Spain. In its centre was fixed a gilded pointer, and round the edge were marked the points of the compass. The pointer was geared to a wind-vane on top of the Admiralty building. Sitting round the Board Room table, the members could see which way the wind was blowing and thus have an idea whether or not the Fleet could sail. The dial had worked continuously since 1695, having previously been in Wallingford House, on the site of which Ripley built the present building. The North Sea bore the name "The British Ocean"; the Scillies were labelled "Silly I."; Calais was "Calice," and Dieppe was spelled "Diep." The arms of the royal houses of Europe were painted in their once-appropriate geographical locations.

The most striking features of the whole room were the magnificent Grinling Gibbons carvings in pear wood. Among them were intricate working models of dividers and cross-jacks, a pelorus, astrolabes and a shot-gauge. Almost hidden was a tiny open pod of peas, Grinling Gibbons's own trade-mark. And tucked away, where it was to remain undiscovered for 263 years, was carved a date, 1695. In a corner of the room a tall and stately grandfather clock told both time and date, as it had been doing for the past 105 years, ever since it was made by Langley Bradley, the man who constructed the great clock of St. Paul's Cathedral. The mirror on the door of the clock had reflected the Board's deliberations since 1700.[2] The fire glowed and Bradley's clock ticked away the passing minutes as Marsden sat working in the light of a few candles set in silver candlesticks on the huge table.

Out in Whitehall Lapenotiere's postchaise carried him the last few yards of his long journey, turning through the narrow arch of the Admiralty and into the cobbled courtyard. It rumbled to a stop in front of the four columns guarding the main door, and in the fog two lanterns guttered fitfully as the young lieutenant climbed stiffly from the carriage and walked up the shallow steps. The clatter of the horses' hooves had roused the night porter from the comfort of his hooded chair and he opened the door. Lapenotiere quickly told him that he bore urgent despatches for Mr. Marsden. His mission was too urgent for him to be left in the little waiting-room on the left of the glowing fire, so he followed the porter out of the hall and past another room where Nelson's body was soon to lie in state. Climbing up two flights of narrow stairs, he came to the door of the Board Room.

Inside the room a tired Marsden had just finished his work. "It was," he wrote, "about one o'clock a.m. of the 6th November, when I was in the act of withdrawing from the Board Room to my private apartments, after having opened the common letters received in the course of the evening." The night porter knocked and went in, announcing an officer bearing despatches. Lapenotiere, unshaven, uniform crumpled, his face lined with tiredness, but still alert in his unaccustomed surroundings, strode into the candlelit room and stopped before Marsden. Without any preamble he said: "Sir, we have gained a great victory; but we have lost Lord Nelson."

2 The Board Room has been changed only slightly since Nelson's day. The wind dial is over the fireplace, but the table, clock, carvings, panelling, fireplace and most of the chairs still remain. The date on Gibbons's carving was discovered by Mr. E. Smith, of the Admiralty, in September, 1958.

Lapenotiere then handed over the despatches, addressed simply to "W. Marsden Esq." The Secretary broke the seal and started reading. The despatches said:

> *Euryalus,* off Cape Trafalgar, Oct. 22, 1805
>
> The ever-to-be lamented death of Vice-Admiral Lord Nelson, who, in the late conflict with the enemy, fell in the hour of Victory, leaves me the duty of informing my Lords Commissioners of the Admiralty, that on the 19th instant it was communicated to the Commander-in-Chief, from the ships watching the motions of the enemy in Cadiz, that the Combined Fleet had put to sea. . . . On Monday, the 21st instant, at daylight, when Cape Trafalgar bore E. by S. about seven leagues, the enemy was discovered six or seven miles to the eastward, the wind about west, and very light.
>
> The Commander-in-Chief immediately made the signal for the Fleet to bear up in two columns, as they are formed in order of sailing; a mode of attack his Lordship had previously directed, to avoid the inconvenience and delay in forming a line of battle in the usual manner. . . . The Commander-in-Chief, in the *Victory,* led the weather column, and the *Royal Sovereign,* which bore my flag, the lee. The action began at Twelve o'clock by the leading ships of the columns breaking through the enemy's line. . . . The enemy's ships were fought with a gallantry highly honourable to their officers; but the attack on them was irresistible, and it pleased the Almighty Disposer of all events to grant His Majesty's arms a complete and glorious victory. . . .
>
> His Lordship received a musket ball in his left breast, about the middle of the action. . . . I have also to lament the loss of those excellent officers, Captains Duff, of the *Mars,* and Cooke of the *Bellerophon.* . . .

Shocked as he was by this double-edged news, Marsden remembered he was the Secretary to the Board. "The effect this [news] produced, it is not my purpose to describe," he wrote later, "nor had I the time to indulge in reflections, who was at that moment the only person informed of one of the greatest events recorded in our history, and which it was my duty to make known with the utmost promptitude.

"The First Lord [Barham] had retired to rest, as had his domestics, and it was not till after some research that I could discover the room in which he slept. Drawing aside his curtains, with a candle in my hand, I awoke the old peer from a sound slumber; and to

the credit of his nerves be it mentioned that he showed no symptoms of alarm or surprise, but calmly asked: 'What news, Mr M.?' "

There were many people to inform—among them the King at
Windsor, the Prince of Wales, the Duke of York, Mr. Pitt in Downing Street, other Ministers and the Lord Mayor, "who communicated the intelligence to the shipping interest at Lloyd's Coffee
House." A notice for the royal salutes was also necessary and preparations had to be made for a *Gazette Extraordinary* that would,
as Marsden noted, "be eagerly read with mixed feelings of exulta-
tion and grief."[3] The night porter was sent round the Admiralty
building to rouse anyone who could help—even if he were only useful for sending out into the fog to fetch in regular clerks.

The first task was to make several copies of Collingwood's
despatch. One of the first completed was sent round by a messenger
at 3 a.m. to the Prime Minister, who had just gone to sleep after
writing a long letter to Nelson. "I shall never forget," wrote Lord
Malmesbury, "the eloquent manner in which he described his
conflicting feelings when roused in the night to read Collingwood's
despatches. Pitt observed that he had been called up at various
hours in his eventful life by the arrival of news of various hues;
but that whether good or bad he could always lay his head on his
pillow and sink into a sound sleep again. On *this occasion,* however,
the great event announced brought with it so much to weep over,
as well as to rejoice at, that he could not calm his thoughts, but
at length got up, though it was three in the morning."

An Admiralty messenger arrived at Windsor Castle at 6.30 a.m.
with the news for the King, who on hearing of Nelson's death
"was so deeply affected that a profound silence of nearly five minutes ensued before he could give utterance to his feelings." The
Queen called the weeping princesses round her and read Collingwood's despatch to them. "The whole Royal group shed tears to the
memory of Lord Nelson."

The Duke of York arrived at the castle "to congratulate Their
Majesties on the victory and to condole with them on the heavy
and great loss by which it had been purchased." The Royal Family
then went to St. George's Chapel, "to return thanks to Almighty

3 The people of Britain were not, however, the first to hear the news: the
Gibraltar Chronicle printed on October 24 a letter from Collingwood to
Lt.-General Fox, the Commander-in-Chief of the fortress.

God to the success of His Majesty's arms," and at one o'clock the Staffordshire Militia marched to the Little Park, where "they fired three volleys in honour of the great event."

Back in London a great deal of work had already been done by the time the Second Secretary to the Board, Sir John Barrow, arrived at the Admiralty. "Never can I forget the shock I received, on opening the Board Room door . . . when Marsden called out— 'Glorious news! The most glorious victory our brave Navy ever achieved—but Nelson is dead!' " Barrow wrote.

Despite the fog—which had also delayed Captain Sykes, of the *Nautilus,* who arrived later in the day—rumours of Nelson's great victory and of his death spread across London like wildfire. The Park and Tower guns boomed out at ten o'clock, while the *London Gazette*'s compositors worked hurriedly to set up Collingwood's despatch in type and rush out the *Gazette Extraordinary.* As soon as it was printed, three thousand copies were sped to Yarmouth by coach and loaded aboard a fast cutter, which immediately set sail with a fair wind to take the news to the Continent. The Government was well aware of the propaganda value of the victory.

"Good heavens! What news!" wrote Lady Bessborough to Lord Granville Leveson-Gower. "How glorious if it was not so cruelly damp'd by Nelson's death. How truly he has accomplish'd his prediction that when they meet it must be to extermination. To a man like him he could not have pick'd a finer close to such a life. But what an irreparable loss to England! . . . Do you know, G., it makes me feel almost as much envy as compassion; I think I should like to die so. Think of being mourned by a whole nation, and having my name carried down with gratitude and praise to the latest generations."

Crowds besieged the newspaper offices, clamouring for news: not news of the victory, but to discover whether it was true that Nelson, the man they had huzza'd so recently, was dead. "The scene at the Admiralty," reported Lady Bessborough, "was quite affecting—crowds of people, chiefly women, enquiring for husbands, brothers, children. . . ."

The *Gazette Extraordinary* was not on sale until late afternoon, but by then shop windows had been draped with hurriedly purchased purple cloth. Within a few hours, "almost everybody wears a black crape [sic] scarf or cockade with 'Nelson' written on it—this is almost general high and low."

That evening "the Metropolis was very generally and brilliantly illuminated on the occasion; yet there was a damp upon the public spirit, which it was impossible to overcome. Even many of the devices and transparencies indicated that the loss of Lord Nelson was more lamented than the victory was rejoiced at," reported the *Naval Chronicle*. And Lady Elizabeth Harvey, writing to her son in America, said that illuminations were begun but discontinued, "the people being unable to rejoice." Later she wrote: "As we came away [from the Admiralty] there was a vast rush of people, but all silent, or a murmur of respect and sorrow; some of the common people saying, 'It is bad news if Nelson is killed,' yet they knew twenty ships had been taken."

The theatres quickly added their tribute. That same evening at Drury Lane, after the performance of *The Siege of Belgrade*, the actors sang "Rule Britannia," and were followed by Mr. Wroughton, the acting manager, who recited:

> Is there a man who this great triumph hears
> And with his transports does not mingle tears?
> For, whilst Britannia's Flag victorious flies,
> Who can repress his grief when *Nelson* dies?

Those lines, and several more, had been written that afternoon by Mr. Cumberland, "a veteran favourite of the Muses," and, said the *Naval Chronicle*, "this simple yet elegant address, which spoke the genuine language of the heart, was delivered by Mr. Wroughton with that propriety, pathos and energy, which can never fail of making a powerful impression."

At Covent Garden the stage manager had worked even harder. After the nightly performance of the comedy *She Wou'd and She Wou'd Not* the curtain went up to show the British Fleet riding triumphantly, with a group of naval officers and seamen at the front of the stage in attitudes of admiration. "Suddenly a medallion descended, representing a half-length of the Hero of the Nile, surrounded by rays of glory, and with these words at the bottom— 'Horatio Nelson.' The effect was electrical and the house resounded with the loudest plaudits and acclamations." The audience was soon on its feet singing "Rule Britannia," and the orchestra then played the "Dead March."

At Chester, when the city heard the news, the cathedral's bells rang out first with joyful peals for the victory, and then alternated with solemn tolling for Nelson; at Christ's Hospital the schoolboys "lit the fireworks for the victory and then drank a little glass of sherry for Lord Nelson in solemn silence." Countess Brownlow, then a child at school, fainted in horror, although she had never seen Nelson. Army officers went on parade in full mourning and with their colours and brightly polished band instruments "draped in crape ribbon."

Off Elsinore, north of Copenhagen, all the ships anchored under Kronborg Castle, Hamlet's legendary home, "fired three discharges in celebration of the victory off Cadiz. Immediately afterwards their flags were lowered and three-minute guns fired, on account of the death of Lord Nelson." At Kingston, in Jamaica, a funeral pyre forty-seven feet high and forty-seven feet in breadth—representing Nelson's age—was lit in forty-seven places at once by the militia, and as it blazed a funeral oration was delivered by the governor, followed by the firing of forty-seven minute-guns and forty-seven rockets. In many ships of the Royal Navy hardened seamen broke down and wept openly when they heard the news.

At the Admiralty a messenger soon arrived from Windsor Castle with a letter for Marsden from the old King's private secretary, Colonel Taylor. "However His Majesty rejoices at the signal success of his gallant fleet, he has not heard without expressions of deep regret the death of its valuable and distinguished commander; although he added that a life so replete with glory and marked by a rapid succession of such meritorious services and exertions, could not have ended more gloriously." And Colonel Taylor added: "I have not upon any occasion seen His Majesty more affected." Four days later Taylor wrote again to Marsden, and a postscript said: "The King is of opinion that the battle should be styled that of Trafalgar." (See illustration Number 20.)

The women who did not know whether the great victory had also taken their loved ones behaved bravely. Lady Arden was worried about her son serving in the *Orion* in the battle, but her husband wrote she was "full of hope that the *Orion* had not had less than her share in this glorious conflict! This was worthy of a Roman matron in Rome's best days."

The wife of Captain Edward Codrington, who commanded the *Orion*, was startled by her maid coming into her room at Brighton and saying suddenly "There has been a great action and Lord Nelson is dead." A friend with her tried to get more news from Colonel Savery, then in waiting on the Prince Regent at Brighton. "After *to me* ages of misery," she later wrote to her husband, "he returned with a very kind note with all the particulars the Prince had had: and all the officers names who had been wounded. Never did Heaven pour such balm into a distracted mind as this communication. For your glorious leader I grieve most sincerely; but for the safety and honour of my husband how can I picture to you my ecstasy and gratitude!!"

As an English refugee Betsey Fremantle had been evacuated from Italy by a British warship, the *Inconstant*, a few hours before Napoleon's troops arrived. She had fallen in love with the warship's captain, Thomas Fremantle, and married him. Now she wrote in her diary on November 7: "I was much alarmed at *Nelly's ghastly* appearance immediately after breakfast, who came in to say Dudley had brought from Winslow the account that a most dreadful action had been fought off Cadiz, Nelson and several captains killed, and twenty ships were taken, I really felt undescribable misery until the arrival of the post, but was relieved from such a wretched state of anxious suspense by a letter from Lord Garlies, who congratulated me on Fremantle's safety and the conspicuous share he had in the victory. . . . In the midst of my delight to hear Fremantle had been preserved in this severe action, I could not help feeling greatly distressed for the fate of poor Nelson. . . . Regret at his death is more severely felt than joy at the destruction of the Combined Fleets."

Betsey's sorrow at the Admiral's death was deep and genuine, for when she and the *Inconstant*'s captain had fallen in love on the way from Leghorn, Nelson and Lady Hamilton had been two of the witnesses at the wedding which soon followed in Naples.

Fanny, the wife from whom Nelson finally parted in 1801, had the news of her husband's death direct from Lord Barham. Although the First Lord was more than busy the day Collingwood's despatches arrived he found a few minutes to write to Lady Nelson.

"Madam," his letter began: "It is with the utmost concern that in the midst of victory I have to inform Your Ladyship of the death of your illustrious partner, Lord Viscount Nelson . . . it is the death he wished for and less to be regretted on his own account. . . ."

At Merton, the home Nelson had left for the battle, his beloved Emma was grief-stricken, sending messages to her friends that she was very ill. Her lover and protector was dead. England would now turn its back on her.

Honours were soon awarded: three days after his despatches arrived, Collingwood was made a baron and promoted, while Nelson's brother, the Reverend William Nelson, within three days of hearing that he had inherited Nelson's barony, received an earldom.

(Later there was a Parliamentary grant of £120,000 to the Nelson family. Of this the new Earl received £90,000 to buy an estate to go with the title [another £9,000 was added later by Parliament] and Nelson's two sisters received £15,000 each. An income of £5,000 a year was granted to those who succeeded the title, and Nelson's widow received £2,000 a year.)

But Nelson's last wishes were ignored. In a codicil to his will he had detailed Emma's "eminent services" to her King and country, and said "Could I have rewarded these services, I would not now call upon my Country, but as that has not been in my power, I leave Emma Hamilton therefore a legacy to my King and Country, that they will give her an ample provision to maintain her rank in life."

There remained one other dearly loved person to be cared for —his daughter Horatia. "I also leave to the beneficence of my Country my adopted daughter Horatia Nelson Thompson, and I desire she will use in future the name of Nelson only. These are the favours I ask of my King and Country at this moment when I am going to fight their Battle. . . ." But to the majority of the ruling class in England, Nelson and Lady Hamilton had committed almost the greatest sin of all—they had sinned openly; and Emma and Horatia were left to their own devices.[4]

---

[4] Lady Hamilton received private assistance, but was so badly in debt in 1807 that she had to sell Merton. Harried by creditors and twice arrested for debt, she fled to France where she drank excessively and died in misery, poverty and squalor in 1815. In 1822 Horatia married a parson, the Reverend Philip Ward, and had eight children.

THREE

JUMPING "THE DITCH"

Now tell us all about the war,
And what they fought each other for.

—Southey

VERY FEW sea battles are merely haphazard clashes of opposing
ships and seamen: the actual fighting is usually the final climax,
the ultimate test of plans made and matured amid rapidly changing
circumstances, with luck and weather intervening capriciously, fa-
vouring one side and then the other. For this reason the battle
of Trafalgar was not only the greatest sea victory ever won by
British arms but the climax of the greatest campaign fought up to
then in the whole of British history.

After a long and bitter struggle against France which had started
in 1793, the Treaty of Amiens in 1802 brought a brief fourteen
months of peace. During that time Napoleon swiftly tidied up
after the war and the Revolution and started to get France's
economic life running smoothly once again. He had every reason
to be pleased with himself: victorious in his land battles against
the best troops that Europe had up to then put in the field, he had
also won in the diplomatic field, for under the terms of the treaty
his African, Indian and West Indian colonies were returned to
him. But he made one big mistake, and this was to think that
Britain's urgent and honest desire for peace was the subservient
cringing of a defeated people. While Napoleon put all his efforts
into filling his arsenals, forging more guns, building new and more
powerful warships and restocking a France whose storehouses had
been emptied by the British blockade, most of Britain sighed with
relief and sat back to enjoy the peace.

True to form, the British Premier, Addington, halved the size of the Army, demobilized the Volunteers, and paid off more than sixty of the Royal Navy's hundred battleships. Worse than that, more than forty thousand trained seamen were discharged—veterans of Camperdown and Cape St. Vincent, the "glorious first of June," the Nile, Copenhagen and the never-ceasing blockade through high summer and winter storms alike. Surplus war stores were sold to the highest bidders—and they were often French agents, who gleefully shipped them across the Channel, where Napoleon watched, waited and planned.

While the wealthier Britons flocked to France to sample once again its geographical, artistic and culinary delights, their coaches rattled and clattered through a land which was, without question, then the most powerful nation the world had ever seen—whose Navy and Army were still mobilized, biding their time and gathering their strength.

However, not every Briton was taken in by Napoleon's outwardly peaceful intentions. There was Richard Brinsley Sheridan, for instance, the Irish playwright who had exchanged pen for politics and brought his brilliant eloquence to bear as Member of Parliament for Stafford: he told the House that Napoleon's great ambition was to rule England. "This is the first vision that breaks on the First Consul through the gleam of the morning," he declared; "this is his last prayer at night, to whatever deity he might address, whether to Jupiter or Mahomet, to the Goddess of Battles or to the Goddess of Reason."

But Britain wanted peace so blindly and passionately that few heeded the warnings; even the great Earl St. Vincent, at that time one of Britain's finest sailors, plunged headlong into the task of pruning the Royal Navy—although at the same time he succeeded in stopping many nefarious practices, particularly in the dockyards.

So peace there was throughout the length and the breadth of the British Isles. Betsey Fremantle stoically bore more children and wrote in her diary, "Fremantle went with my three sisters to the Buckingham Ball, I stayed at home with my four brats. . . . He has ordered a new carriage and a new gig prices £160 and £80. . . . Fremantle offered himself for election. . . . Fremantle dined at Lord Nelson's, and met us in the evening at Sir Lionel Darrell's at Richmond where there is a very pleasant ball every Friday. . . . Poor little Harry's humour is breaking out again violently. Mr.

Nagle calls it an inveterate species of the tetters, and will try something to cure them, he don't approve of bathing him in salt and water, which would throw the child in agonies. He really suffers very much and is a miserable little creature. . . ."

Across the Channel, Napoleon reviewed his veteran troops in the Place du Carrousel while newly arrived British tourists watched open-eyed before going to gaze in awe and admiration at the priceless paintings and statues in the Louvre; much of it, however, was plunder transported from pillaged palaces and castles, stately châteaux and galleries all over Europe. But as the First Consul, plainly dressed in a simple blue uniform, strode through his magnificent apartments in the Palais des Tuileries, past bowing footmen decked out in green and gold, he thought and planned and plotted new conquests; he was living, waking and praying even as Sheridan had said. He had conquered Europe, and it had seemed easy.

From being an insignificant but rebellious Corsican boy knowing scarcely a word of the French language, taciturn, shy and small in stature, born in an island where an insult could be answered only with a dagger and where overnight neighbours' quarrels became vendettas, he had gone to the Paris Cadets' School. After graduating and becoming an artillery subaltern he had then but a single dream—of freeing Corsica from the bondage of France. Now, amid the splendour of his home in the Tuileries, he had another dream—of conquering a world whose sun would rise and set over Paris.

Only one country apparently stood in his way—that damnable nation of shopkeepers across the Channel and their thrice-damned Navy. However much he might overrun Europe, defeating or double-crossing kings and princes, making promises and treaties he never intended to honour, wheedling where necessary or threatening with cold fury when wheedling failed—his great enemy was Britain. Placed by a geographical quirk so that she was the main gateway on the sea highway to Europe, Britain had stood firm behind her moat, safe up to now from his Grand Army. Her Navy was a net cast round his great continental conquests, preventing him from breaking out to sail down the trade routes of the world and conquer the lands at the end of them.

He cast greedy eyes towards the riches of the East: to India whose very name conjured up visions of wealth and splendour and to the great continents of America and Australia. Despite the beating which the French Fleet had taken from Nelson at the Nile, Napoleon's spies were once again hard at work in Egypt. The world, Napoleon thought, was a ripe fruit waiting for him to pluck. Indeed, this was true; but between him and the trees that bore it was a fence—the ships of the Royal Navy. They had to be destroyed before Napoleon could regain and extend France's colonial greatness to make Paris the centre of the world, a city to which kings and princes, queens and envoys, premiers and pashas would come to pay him court, beg his favour and plead their cause.

Being a land animal, unable to understand sea power and its uses, he could visualize only one sure way in which France, the greatest of land powers, could challenge, fight and defeat the greatest of the maritime powers—by invasion. If the Royal Navy was a thousand-headed hydra (and he began to think it was) then its heart was London. Destroy that heart, he decided, and the heads would wither and die of their own accord.

However, because of the unpredictable British, war broke out again before Napoleon was ready, but he was quick to recover his stride. "They want us to jump the ditch," he declared, "and we *will* jump it." Napoleon, with all the zest, dynamism and fire in his belly that lifted him from an artillery subaltern to be the First Consul and the only contender for the title of Emperor of the World, set his nation to work: she was to produce the craft which would bridge the Channel and set the Grand Army ashore on the Kent coast for its triumphal march through the Garden of England to London.

Surrounded by sycophants who hardly dared to disagree on even the slightest tactical question, let alone the broad strategic concept, Napoleon received the reports of his naval officers. With few exceptions they thought the best type of craft to carry the Grand Army would be flat-bottomed and propelled by simple sails and oars (we can call them by the more modern term of landing craft). There would be four types—barges, sloops, pinnaces and gunboats.

Napoleon reckoned that his Grand Army—by now camped 150,000 strong on the cliffs above Boulogne and rechristened the "Army of England"—need take only 6,000 horses with it. The rest of the cavalrymen would go over carrying their saddles and capture or commandeer horses in England. Within a few days of the war's beginning once again, Napoleon had ordered several hundred landing craft to be built at Dunkirk and Cherbourg, while Boulogne was chosen as the point where they would be assembled. His plans changed frequently, but to begin with he calculated that he would need about 2,500 craft. As the invasion planning got under way, more craft were ordered to be built in twenty other Channel ports. The Minister of Marine, Admiral Denis Decrès, who at the age of forty-two had a great reputation for hard work, bore the brunt of Napoleon's broadside of orders and determined prodding: instructions arrived almost daily from the First Consul concerning the invasion flotillas.

France's pulse quickened under the influence of Napoleon's tremendous drive. In all the Channel ports, both large and small, the shipyards echoed to the rhythmic thud of shipwrights' adzes, the clatter of hammers and the hoarse cough of long rip-saws as they shaped great baulks of oak, spruce and pine into planks and frames, beams and masts, keels and yards. In the forests tall trees tumbled under the violent assaults of foresters' axes, and in the clearings large ovens glowed and turned wood into charcoal. In the arsenals skilled men mixed the charcoal with the appropriate portions of saltpetre and sulphur to make gunpowder, and in the foundries perspiring men worked day and night, fired with Napoleon's enthusiasm, casting cannon and round-shot, musket balls and grape-shot.

This massive plan for the invasion needed a great deal of money to put it into execution. The bankers of France, realizing that the defeat of England was a good proposition in which to invest, readily lent the First Consul twenty million francs. But this was by no means enough, and the wily Napoleon ordered his ministers to tackle all the wealthy people whose vanity and patriotism could be played on to produce the money to build warships which would be named after them. To Napoleon's surprise and disgust, the majority of the wealthy citizens of the Republic apparently saw little to appeal to their vanity or patriotism, and only a few paid up for the pleasure of having their names carved across the transoms of invasion craft.

Since the people appeared to be keen enough to defeat England as long as it did not affect their personal pockets, the Minister of the Interior was instructed to attempt to broach the coffers of cities and departments. He wrote to the chief magistrates the length and breadth of France, enclosing a price list, and adding that the craft would be distinguished by the names of the authorities paying for them. "If each department by a rapid movement puts the vessels on the stocks," he wrote, "the French Army will soon go and dictate laws to the British Government."

This time Napoleon was to be pleasantly surprised by the response: offers came flooding in—and they were handsome offers, too, as if the towns and departments had at last caught his hitherto uninfectious enthusiasm. Lyons offered a 100-gun battleship, and Bordeaux an 84. The department of Loiret paid for a 30-gun frigate and Seine-Inférieure put up a 74, while Seine-et-Marne, not to be outdone, came along with a similar offer. Various battalions of the Army of England gave a day's pay; Paris, the city from which Napoleon proposed to rule the world, dipped deep into its coffers to buy a 120-gun battleship, while the Senate followed suit. Small towns bought barges or pinnaces to carry their names to victory.[1]

Napoleon and his wife Josephine went on a grand tour of the invasion ports in the summer of 1803. The *Times* reported that at Calais the First Consul arrived "on a small, iron-grey horse of great beauty. He was preceded by about 300 infantry, and about 30 mamelukes formed a kind of semi-circle round him."

He was not at all pleased with what he saw at Boulogne; and as if to display how the Royal Navy ruled the Channel, one of its frigates came close in to attack seven landing craft which were sailing into the port. The guns of Boulogne opened fire but their shot fell short, infuriating the First Consul, who had all the pride of an old artilleryman. According to a Briton living at Boulogne at the time, he "became fidgety, uttered a few *sacrés*"—and then discovered the guns were accidentally being loaded with saluting charges. He promptly flew into a fury, tearing the epaulettes from the shoulder of the officer responsible and telling him he was no longer in the French Army.

[1] The three main types of landing craft were:

Type	Length	No. of crew	Armament	Troops
Barge	100 ft.	38	24-pounders (12)	120
Sloop	70–80 ft.	30	24-pounders (3)	120
Pinnace	60 ft.	5	- -	55

By July, 1803, Napoleon's plans allowed for this: the Dutch division, with its headquarters at Flushing, would consist of three hundred landing craft; the right division, based on Ostend and Nieuport, would also have three hundred. The centre division, at Dunkirk, Gravelines and Calais, would handle three hundred while the left division, based on Wissant, Ambleteuse, Boulogne and Etaples, would have about 1,650 landing craft of various types and a thousand transports. That, at least, was Napoleon's great plan on paper, but when one came to examine the actual craft on moorings

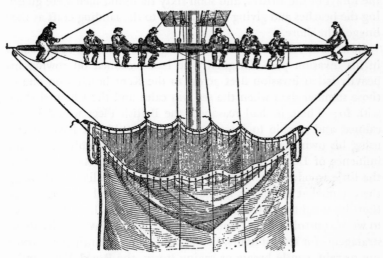

Hoisting up the foresail to bend it to the yard. The men in the centre are standing on the foot-ropes, or horses, with their arms over the yard.

in the Channel ports the position was vastly different. The man who had to discover the sobering difference between the fleet of fantasy represented by the piles of orders and the fleet of reality represented by craft on the stocks, afloat or hauled out, was Forfait, the Inspector-General of Flotillas. With the date that Napoleon decreed the whole invasion force must be ready to sail only six weeks away, Forfait had to report a deficit of a thousand craft.

Apparently ignoring these unpalatable figures, Napoleon's blood stayed hot with fever heat engendered by his desire to become

Emperor of the World, but the summer of 1803 gave way to autumn. Although the adze hacked and sliced trunk and bough into frames and timbers, the furnaces ran hot metal into the moulds of great guns, and patriots gave francs and sous for the war chest according to their means, September brought the vicious equinoctial gales in the Channel, and still Napoleon waited.

The Royal Navy continued to harry the landing craft as they sailed from the shipyards to the assembly ports, and in desperation Napoleon ordered batteries to be set up along the coast. Two stone forts and a wooden one were built to cover Boulogne harbour from the forays of the British, and soon sixty thousand men were guarding the beaches and giving covering fire to the landing craft as they hugged the shore.

Slowly but reluctantly Napoleon began to see some of the snags in his invasion plan. Originally he had reckoned on rowing his heavily laden invasion fleet across to the Kent beaches on one of those summer days when the sea was calm and the Channel thick with fog. Then, he had reasoned, the British Fleet would be becalmed and unable to interfere, and he would not have to risk using his own Fleet as a covering force. But, probably under the influence of Decrès, he slowly changed his mind. As he stood in the little wooden hut which he had built on the cliffs overlooking the Channel at Boulogne, he realized that the ideal weather conditions he sought rarely occurred. His Fleet would have to be used to wrest control of the Channel from the Royal Navy—by battle or stratagem—for several hours. Yet off the French Atlantic ports, come sun or rain, gentle breeze or raging storm, the Royal Navy under Cornwallis was waiting. At the Texel, Admiral Keith kept guard, and off Toulon, in the Mediterranean, Nelson waited fretfully.

As Admiral Mahan wrote, "Those far-distant, storm-beaten ships upon which the Grand Army never looked stood between it and the dominion of the world."

FOUR

MARTIAL MUDDLE

Their force is wonderful, great and strong, yet we
pluck their feathers by little and little . . .
—Lord Howard of Effingham, on the Armada, 1588

WHILE NAPOLEON drove the French nation even harder, England, whose Government had cut the Navy and Army so drastically that its very freedom stood in mortal danger, viewed his invasion plans with mixed feelings. Some people became alarmed and excited; some refused to believe he would be so foolhardy. Others affected not to worry whatever the Corsican proposed doing. At his home at Dropmore Lord Granville wrote: "You will find me here, very peaceable, rolling my walks and watering my rhododendrons, without any thought of the new possessor to whom Napoleon might dispose them."

Captain Fremantle managed to get a ship, and poor Betsey wrote: "He really goes to sea quite *à contre coeur* as he was now so comfortably settled here, and I feel not a little anxiety at being left alone with five such young children." Later she added, "I begin to be half alarmed at the attempt to invade which is now daily expected to take place, and these horrid French are such desperate wretches that I quite dread their attack, tho' I trust it will prove unsuccessful." Already that autumn she had been badly scared when she went to visit her husband at Portsmouth. They had gone for a walk on the walls of the town "where we were not a little surprised at seeing a great concourse of people on the beach, the yeomanry out, guns frequently fired, signals made, the telegraphes at work and many sails in sight. On enquiring I was told it was supposed the French were affecting a landing as numbers of the flat-bottom boats were seen making towards the shore." "This created a very great alarm," wrote Betsey, but next day she was happy to hear "that a fleet of coasters who had been becalmed at the back of the Isle of Wight had occasioned our alarm."

In the face of Napoleon's massive threat, Britain quickly roused —and frightened—itself. To the uneducated but sturdy masses of the people, rapidly arming themselves with whatever weapons they could lay their hands on, from musket to pike and pitchfork, Napoleon appeared an ogre whose size, villainy and cruelty grew in the telling: he poisoned the sick to save food, he gloated over corpses scattered on the battlefields. Now he was variously building a massive bridge from Calais to Dover, across which his Army of England would march to the sound of fifes and drums and directed by the equivalent of military policemen stationed in balloons overhead; serving as a seaman in an English fishing smack off the south coast, tending his lines at night and searching the shore with his spy-glass by day; and digging a tunnel under the Channel, out of which he was to pop to stride across the Kentish meadows at the head of his huge army.

The Government under Addington tried to arm Britain overnight. Producing arms was the most difficult task, while there were three ways of finding the men to handle them—offering bounties to lure them into the regular Army, appealing to their patriotism to join the Volunteers, and balloting to raise a Militia. But one method tended to cancel the other out. For instance, any man picked by the ballot for the Militia—which was a home defence force—could pay someone else to take his place, and the price for substitutes soon went up to £30 a head. But the harassed and brass-lunged recruiting sergeant trying to drum up recruits for the regular Army could offer a bounty of only £7 12s. 6d. Most men preferred to take the £30 and serve only in Britain with the Militia rather than accept the recruiting sergeant's meagre bounty and risk being sent overseas in the regular Army. As a result, the Government soon discovered that, instead of raising a large regular Army which could defend Britain and then strike back at Napoleon on his own soil, they had landed themselves with a completely untrained "Home Guard."[1]

[1] The regulations for Volunteers laid down that "two shirts, a pair of shoes and stockings, combs, brushes (and a horseman what is necessary for the care of his horse) is all a soldier ought to carry." He would have bread for four days and sixty rounds for his musket.

After a series of confused, overlapping and frequently contradictory orders, the Government finally decreed that 40,000 men were to be raised by ballot in Britain and 10,000 in Ireland. This was followed by a levy *en masse* which gave the old King powers to make each parish in the country provide (at its own expense) "the necessary implements of warfare for the male inhabitants." These unspecified implements would be kept locked up in the parish church under the watchful eye of the churchwarden. The men were to be trained for at least two hours every Sunday "either before or after Divine Service." The local constable was to attend—and be paid £5 a year out of the poor rate for doing so. The Volunteer who dodged a drill would be fined five shillings, and dodging it three times would land him in jail. If Army pensioners put the Volunteers through their paces on the village green they would get a wage "not exceeding 2s. 6d. a day"—also out of the poor rate.

The Volunteers went to work with a will: armed with ancient fowling-pieces, home-made pikes, pitchforks, and muskets if they could be obtained, they drilled on the greens, marched along country lanes, drew up plans for the defence of their villages over pints of home-brewed ale, and waited hopefully for Boney's Army of England to appear so that they could give it a drubbing. Meadows were used as firing ranges and resounded to the rattle of musket and fowling-pieces; local pensioners assumed a new importance in their villages and strutted and yelled at squire and yokel alike, marching and wheeling them in some semblance of martial formation.

Local tailors worked to make uniforms to the specifications of individual commanding officers, for each company could design its own. Men vied with one another to become the most efficient on parade. In the secrecy of their kitchens they practised musket drill with broomsticks and gave their wives the benefit of their new-found military knowledge by describing where Napoleon would land and how he would be beaten—by the Volunteers, of course. Naturally all this martial fervour affected women's fashions: one of the dresses which soon became the vogue was "a short round dress of white muslin, with a rifle dress of dark-green velvet and a rifle hat to correspond."

From the time the war began again in May, 1803, until the battle of Trafalgar was fought in October, 1805, the "Corsican ogre" dominated the lives of the people of Britain. When invasion failed to materialize in the summer or autumn of 1803 it was assumed that Napoleon would arrive in the summer of 1804. Having been made Lord Warden of the Cinque Ports in 1791, William Pitt— now out of office—was living at Walmer Castle on the Kentish shore opposite Calais. He stayed away from Parliament and, as Colonel of the Cinque Ports Volunteers, drilled his troops on the foreshore and kept an eye open for a sight of the enemy's invasion barges. Even Charles James Fox, previously so violently against the war and forever finding excuses for the French, joined the Chertsey Volunteers as a private soldier.

The Church became militant. Dr. Watson, the Bishop of Llan- daff, told the clergy of his diocese: "You will not, I think, be guilty of a breach of Christian charity in the use of even harsh language when you explain to your congregations the cruelties which the French have used in every country they have invaded . . . they everywhere strip the poorest of everything they possess; they plun- der their cottages, and they set them on fire when the plunder is exhausted; they torture the owners to discover their wealth, and they put them to death when they have none to discover; they violate females of all ages. . . . Can there be men in Great Britain of so base a temper, so maddened by malignity, so cankered by envy, so besotted by folly, so stupefied as to their own safety, as to abet the designs of such an enemy?"

And so from the pulpits the length and breadth of the country hitherto timorous parsons girded their loins, took deep breaths, and called the nation to arms. The Reverend Cornelius Miles took the thirty-sixth verse of the twenty-second chapter of St. Luke—"And he that hath no sword, let him sell his garment, and buy one"—for his stirring sermon, while at Colchester a prayer offered up for preservation from the invasion of Napoleon ended with: "O Lord God, be pleased to change his wicked heart or stop his wicked breath."

George Cruikshank, the famous cartoonist of the period, wrote: "Every town was, in fact, a sort of garrison—in one place you might hear the tattoo of some youths learning to beat the drum, at an- other some march or national air being practised upon the fife, and every morning at five o'clock the bugle horn was sounded through the streets, to call the Volunteers to a two-hour drill, and the same again in the evening."

But martial glory was not only the aim of every man in the country: the boys wanted it too. They banded themselves into juvenile regiments. Cruikshank's brother formed one and appointed himself its colonel. "We had our fife and drum," he wrote, "our 'colours' presented by our mammas and sisters who also assisted in making our accoutrements. We procured gun-stocks into which we fitted mop-sticks for barrels." These sticks were polished with bootblack by the maids of the house to make them look like real metal. The boys held their parades and manoeuvres in the no-man's-land between Bloomsbury Church and where Russell Square and Tavistock Square now stand.

In south-east England the invasion scares were frequent. Eastbourne, for instance, nestling under the lee of Beechy Head, was almost deserted in the autumn of 1803 after rumour selected it for Napoleon's landing place. A barracks for ten thousand men was hurriedly built on the beach, and another was built at Pevensey Bay nearby. Farmers had orders that if the French came they were to burn the crops and houses. In Wales, Mr. James Nield was innocently enjoying a tour of the countryside round Radnor when some people thought they recognized him as Napoleon, and without waiting to see if his Army of England was at his heels they wanted to throw him into prison.

The Press loved the situation and spread itself in a rash of adjectives and adverbs. The *Bath Herald* declared: "If you have qualities for a soldier you are imperiously called upon, by everything valuable to man, to be a soldier." Later it was able to report: "Sixteen honest sons of St Crispin have been taken down by their employer, Mr James Phipps [a bootmaker] of St Margaret's Buildings and entered as Volunteers—each man determined to sacrifice his all."

As the months slipped by, so the nation's plans to beat an invasion became more effective. The Government stored enough flour in London to last the capital a fortnight, while the millers had enough for another three weeks. Beacons made of at least eight wagon-loads of faggots, brush and cordwood and several barrels of tar were set up all round the coasts, ready to be lit at night as a warning visible for at least three miles. By day wet hay was to be burned to make smoke signals. Inevitably some of the beacons were lit by accident or because of a false alarm. The poet Crabbe was staying at Aldeburgh, in Suffolk, when his son ran into the room and woke him with, "Do not be alarmed, but the French are landing and the drum on the quay is beating to arms." His father replied, "Well, you and I can do no good, or we would be among them; we must wait upon the event." With that he went back to sleep.

The way in which the Mortella Tower in Corsica held out in 1794 against British troops had created a great impression. The tower had but three guns and only thirty-three soldiers manned it. Its effectiveness led the British Government to build seventy-four such towers round the south-eastern coast of England. Looking like inverted flower-pots, they were eighty feet high and cost more than £7,000 each to build. The forts, which were called martello towers (the English rendering of the original name), had two storeys, the lower acting as a magazine and the upper as accommodation. On the seaward side the brickwork was nine feet thick. Each mounted a swivel gun or howitzer.[2]

The great flat area of Romney Marsh, stretching inland from Hythe, in Kent, to Rye, in Sussex, with its long and flat beaches, was reckoned to be an ideal place for Napoleon to land. A plan for flooding it by damming up the sluices was abandoned, so it was cut off by digging a deep canal along its inland edge. It would probably have been of no practical use had the French landed, but more than a century and a half later it still served as an excellent fishing ground for small boys.

Under Addington's vacillating leadership Britain stayed on the defensive, and through his Government's muddle and indecision the people lost what little trust they had in him. They wanted to fight back, and they felt that William Pitt was the only man who could give them the leadership they wanted. So, by circumstances we need not go into here, Pitt became Prime Minister on May 18, 1804—on the same day that Napoleon was declared the Emperor of France. Britain's leaders—or was it the Channel?—had so far

[2] Many of the martello towers still exist along the coasts of Kent and Sussex.

saved the island from capture, yet to establish a lasting peace they had to rid themselves, and Europe, of Napoleon. Drained by a long and expensive war in which many mistakes had cost them dearly, they could only wait until the few remaining free states in Europe could be rallied into a Third Coalition; they could then be led united against Napoleon. Pitt was a sick man when he went to Downing Street—indeed death had already given him a warning tap on the shoulder—but he knew only too well that the sole hope for Britain lay in gaining allies on the Continent. He therefore began negotiations with young Alexander, the Czar of All the Russias, to begin the Third Coalition.

Meanwhile Napoleon had frequent and tantalizing glimpses of his objective. He liked to ride along the beaches round Calais and Boulogne, when the waters of the Channel lapped or raged as if mocking him. "I have passed these three days amidst the camp and the port," he wrote; "from the heights of Ambleteuse I have seen the coast of England as one sees the Calvary from the Tuileries. One could distinguish the houses and the bustle. It is a ditch that shall be leaped when one is daring enough to try."

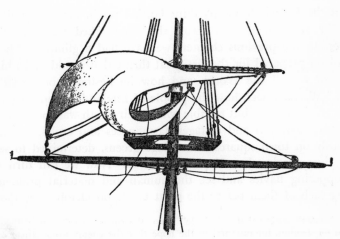

Clewing up a topsail to take in a third reef.

FIVE

THE NAVIES

*If they are kept off the sea by our superior strength, their
want of practice will make them unskilful and their want of
skill, timid.*
                                                          —Pericles

IN SPITE of Atlantic storm, the Royal Navy had blockaded Brest
and Rochefort, and despite Mediterranean mistral it had blockaded
Toulon.[1] While its ships tacked and wore in every sort of weather,
beating up close to the entrance of the harbours when the wind
was off shore and the enemy could sail, and clawing off shore
when the wind came from seaward, the sweepings of the jails were
transformed into hardened seamen.

But the French Navy, its ships bottled up in harbours, sailed
only in men's memories, across the wine-soaked tables in the
bistros. In the previous chapters we have had a glimpse of how
Napoleon prepared for the last great thrust that would make him
Emperor of All the World, and how he hesitated before "the
ditch." We have seen how the people of England, blundering yet
brave, slow to anger but terrible when their wrath was roused, had
left their mansions and cottages, farmhouses and crofts, to drill
furiously on town squares and village greens, determined to sell
their lives dearly when Napoleon arrived.[2] Now we can turn to
the opposing navies and see the human and material problems
facing each of them before the great battle on October 21, 1805.

[1] It is worth noting that "blockade" is not the correct word to use: Nelson
waited off Toulon, for instance, in the hope that the enemy would come out
and fight, giving him an opportunity of destroying it.

[2] More than a century and a quarter later Winston Churchill, the Premier
of the day, had an appropriate slogan ready should Hitler's invasion have
taken place—"You can always take one with you."

The greatest defeat suffered by the French Navy up to the eve of Trafalgar had been at the hands of its own people. While a King sat on the throne of France, service as an officer in the French Navy had been one of the most aristocratic of professions, but during the Revolution which dragged Louis XVI from the throne to the guillotine, Paris had rung to Danton's impassioned cries in the Champs de Mars. It had also rung to the screams of hundreds of aristocrats—or any person that looked like one—being marched off to jail or to meet the hooded executioner. And while a young Corsican artillery captain named Bonaparte watched the mob in Paris worship the red cap of liberty as the symbol of its new-found freedom, the revolutionaries had started to democratize the French Navy, after their own crude and short-sighted fashion. Almost every officer, from admiral to the most junior *ensign de vaisseau,* who had the taint of blue blood in his veins was arrested and flung into jail or forced to flee. Despite the invaluable experience and skill they had, many of them were later dragged from their dark cells into the blinding sunlight and carried to town squares, where hastily erected guillotines rewarded their services with a mercifully quick death.

On board the ships the revolutionary cry of *"Liberté, fraternité et égalité"* had put the heaviest emphasis on *égalité,* and the revolutionary with the shrill voice and glib tongue held sway. When the *Patriote* and *Entreprenante* (the latter shortly to be captured by the British and later used at Trafalgar) sailed into Brest from Toulon, all their officers had been arrested in the name of the Committee for Public Safety and flung into jail. The officers of the *Apollon* were less fortunate when they brought their ship into Rochefort: Citizen Hugues, "an excellent Jacobin, whose *civisme* and activity were of the desirable degree," denounced them and they were led from the quarter-deck to the town square, and once again the guillotine's sharp blade flashed in its sudden downward drop as it did its swift work of purifying the post-Revolution Navy.

In the place of the "aristos" had come men whose single-minded devotion to the Revolution far outweighed their professional abilities as seamen: surviving junior lieutenants with the correct political outlook had become captains almost overnight; captains of small merchantmen were given great ships of the line to command; ratings were made into officers on the strength of their Jacobinism. And quite inevitably discipline had vanished: any attempts by newly appointed officers to enforce it put them in peril of being denounced by Citizen Hugues and his numerous colleagues. The seamen and the revolutionary committees ashore found their new freedom more heady than the strongest draught of cognac, but it certainly gave them no stomach for going to sea.

When Napoleon had lifted himself by his boot-straps to power he saw the reason for the Navy's weakness and restored some of the surviving "aristos" to high commands, but those he chose were, for the most part, of an inferior breed when compared to their equivalents in the Royal Navy, which sent its would-be officers to sea at the age of twelve or thirteen and kept them there. Much of the fighting spirit was thus driven out of the French Navy by its own people. The names of ships—names proudly borne for centuries—were changed; old emblems of the Fleet were destroyed, and in place of discipline, tradition and experience, the red cap of liberty was unceremoniously placed on the quarter-deck.

The French Navy's position had only slightly improved when nineteen of its ships, manned by more than 11,000 men, were attacked while at anchor in Aboukir Bay in 1798 by a British Fleet of fourteen ships, manned by just over 8,000 men. By midnight, when the battle of the Nile had ended, nine of the French ships had been captured, two more destroyed, and 9,830 men killed, wounded or taken prisoner. Napoleon's Army in Egypt was thus isolated and doomed to failure, and the French Navy suffered a blow to its self-confidence from which, under Napoleon, it was not to recover.

Many years later when sadder, defeated, and perhaps wiser, Napoleon, while he was in exile at St. Helena, said that he had been unable to find a man sufficiently strong to raise the character of the French Navy. "There is in the Navy a peculiarity," he declared, "a technicality that impeded all my conceptions. If I proposed a new idea, immediately Ganteaume [who commanded the blockaded squadron at Brest] and the whole Marine Department, were against me. 'Sire, that cannot be.' 'Why not?' 'Sire, the winds do not admit of it.' Then objections were started respecting calms and currents, and I was obliged to stop short." Hitler, just a century and a quarter later, also blamed the Navy for not performing the miracles that his own orders precluded.[3]

Yet it was not only the leadership problem at all levels which bedevilled Napoleon's efforts. The dockyards were centres of inefficiency, short of everything needed to make them function. There were not enough shipwrights, carpenters, seamen and soldiers for the ships or the forts and dockyards. The mountings of the guns in the forts protecting the dockyards and harbours were rotten and the guns themselves were unfit to be used. Soldiers had to be drafted in to man the ships, and the seamen were deserting. As will be seen later, Nelson was well aware of the quality of the enemy ships and seamen he had to fight, for the Spanish Fleet was in no better shape than the French.

Nevertheless it would be very wrong to assume that the Royal Navy at the time of Trafalgar was faultless, although it is a common assumption that because the victory was so overwhelming the Navy must have been in almost perfect shape. There was considerable corruption in the dockyards (a former First Lord of the Admiralty was charged the year after Trafalgar with malversation) and British warships were, for the most part, not nearly as well designed as all their French and Spanish counterparts. They were generally slower, could not sail as close to the wind, and were not so weatherly. The seamen manning the ships were seldom paid the wages due to them and the press-gangs which combed the countryside were little better than kidnappers covered by laxly interpreted laws.

The Navy Estimates[4] for 1805 proposed "that 120,000 men be employed for the sea service, including 30,000 Royal Marines." Of actual battleships, the Royal Navy had a total on paper of 181 —this being made up from 26 building or ordered, 39 on harbour service, 33 "in ordinary" (i.e., officially ready for fitting out, but usually in need of repairs costing nearly as much as rebuilding

---

[3] After an abortive action on New Year's Eve, 1942, Hitler flew into a fury and paid off every ship larger than a destroyer. Yet the defeat had been due to his own cautionary orders and a complete lack of understanding of naval strategy. See the author's *73 North* (J. B. Lippincott Company, 1958).

[4] The Estimate was for just over £15 million and included £2,886,000 for wages, £2,964,000 for victualling, and £582,000 for the upkeep of prisoners-of-war confined in hulks.

them) and 83 in commission. Among the 83 were included ships such as Nelson described in a letter to the Prime Minister only three months after the war had started again. Of his fleet, only four could keep the sea in winter, he said. Of seven others "it is not a storeship a week which could keep them in repair."

That autumn of 1803 he wrote, "I bear up for every gale. I must not, in our present state, quarrel with the north-westers— with crazy masts and no port or spars near us. Indeed, on the whole Mediterranean station there is not a topmast for a seventy-four."

At the beginning of December he was writing to Sir Evan Nepean, then Secretary to the Board, about the *Excellent,* enclosing a survey report on the main and mizenmast rigging. "It is to be lamented that a ship so recently from England, and coming direct abroad from a King's Yard, should have sailed in such a state; the Master-Attendant at Portsmouth must either have been blind to the situation of the rigging, or not have given himself trouble to discover its miserable state."

Since the ships of the Royal Navy had to stay at sea almost continuously to contain Napoleon's fleet, much of the damage to the ships was "fair wear and tear," but much of it was not. There was corruption everywhere in every service. When a firm of London copper merchants was condemned for having naval stores—copper nails marked with broad arrows—the Attorney-General said the jury "would hear with astonishment, but it was a fact capable of the strictest proof, that the depredations upon the King's naval stores did not annually amount to less than £500,000."[5] The *Naval Chronicle* estimated that the losses in the war up to 1802 "in consequence of the peculation or negligence of its servants in the naval departments" amounted to £20 million.

At Portsmouth it was discovered that John Freeborne, the foreman of the labourers, and two other men, kept hogs in the warehouses and fed them with "the King's serviceable biscuits." The same trio also stole planks, spars, staves and barrels, which were sold at a shop which Freeborne kept in Portsmouth. When a commission checked the accounts some time before Freeborne was discovered, it was found that the dockyard was short of 278,042 pounds of bread, 11,162 pieces of beef, 4,649 pieces of pork, 3,746

5 Equal to more than a sixth of the Navy's wage bill in 1805.

pounds of flour and 2,798 pounds of suet, "besides considerable deficiencies in other species of victualling stores." A report by the same commission twenty years later showed no improvement.

This type of corruption was partly due to the natural dishonesty which spread through every branch of what would now be called the Civil Service; but perhaps most of the blame must be put on the men in authority—up to and including Ministers of the Crown —who, as rewards for votes in Parliament or the exercise of some favours or "interest," gave unqualified and unscrupulous men jobs in various departments. The pay was poor, but there were plenty of opportunities for fraud which were exploited to the full.[6] The net effect of this was that many of the ships which went out to fight the enemy and keep England free from invasion sailed from the dockyards incompletely repaired or equipped so that the dishonest could flourish. Twelve days after Nelson wrote home from the Mediterranean about the dreadful condition of the *Excellent,* Collingwood wrote from the Channel saying that the *Venerable*'s condition was so bad that "we have been sailing for the last six months with only a sheet of copper between us and eternity." However, much of the rot so frequently discovered in the ships was due to the methods of building and the types and condition of wood used.

Most of the King's ships were built at Deptford and Woolwich on the Thames, at Chatham on the Medway, and at Plymouth. But there were other yards, often privately owned. One was at Buckler's Hard, a small and picturesque village three miles from Beaulieu on the west branch of the Beaulieu River, which flows into the Solent. Three of the British ships that fought at Trafalgar were built there. As the second Lord Montagu of Beaulieu wrote, the yard "helped in no small degree to lay the foundations of our Empire."

In the 1740's John, the second Duke of Montagu (not to be confused with the second Lord Montagu), was looking for a suitable place to create and encourage local industries, and Buckler's Hard (originally called Buckle's Hard, probably after the local family of Buckle, who lived there for generations) was, with its

6 Lord Melville was impeached for alleged misappropriation of public money during his term as Treasurer of the Navy.

hard gravel foreshore (The Hard), an ideal place. The Duke's manor at Beaulieu had a great number of oak trees growing on it, and there was an ironworks—where the great forge hammer was worked by a water-wheel—at Sowley Pond only four miles away. And thanks to a legacy from the Abbots of Beaulieu, the manor enjoyed all the privileges of the Cinque Ports as a free harbour.

The small shipbuilding firm of Wyatt & Company, then at Bursledon, accepted the Duke's offer and moved their business to Buckler's Hard in 1743, bringing with them their overseer, Henry Adams. While houses were built for employees, "ways"—strongly built ramps leading down into the water—were constructed, and a kiln for boiling wood erected. Very soon great oaks on the Beaulieu estate toppled under the woodmen's axes, startling the herons and swans abounding along the muddy edge of the river. The branches were lopped and teams of horses dragged the trunks to the Hard. Here they were cut into planks and left to season in great stacks between the two rows of houses which were then being built.[7] Wyatt's soon had their first order, and over the years the orders were for larger vessels, until they were commissioned to build a 64-gun ship. A cradle on which the hull would rest was constructed; then long sections of elm were put down to form the keel, or backbone, of the new vessel. On this backbone were built the ribs—each made up of several pieces of wood called futtocks. Because these were curved, like ribs of a skeleton, trees of the right shape had to be found. For the smaller and thinner pieces, the wood could be put into the kiln and boiled until it became pliable enough to be bent to shape.

So the fast-growing little village nestling among the trees, beside the quietly ebbing and flowing water of the river, rang to the sound of the saw and the adze—a tool used for shaping wood and looking like a heavy, short-handled hoe with a very sharp edge. Quickly the ship took shape on the slipway. The hull planks were clenched to the frames and timbers by copper nails and bolts or wooden tree-nails, and then the caulkers got to work hammering twists of oakum into the gaps between the planks. Finally, on April 10, 1781, the *Salisbury and Winchester Journal* reported, "There was

---

[7] This is the reason why the street is so wide today. The houses are still in-habited.

launched at Buckler's Hard the *Agamemnon,* a fine 64-gun ship, built by Mr Adams of that place." After the launching she was towed round to Portsmouth and entered a dry-dock to have her hull copper-sheathed. A ship's great enemy—particularly in a warm climate—were the tiny little teredo worms which bored into the hull and then, making thousands of tunnels up and down the lengths of the planks, reduced them to mere honeycombs. But the teredos were powerless against the thin sheets of copper.

Twelve years after the *Agamemnon* was commissioned a young Captain Nelson, after spending five years unemployed "on the beach," was appointed to her. There was no prouder man in the Navy. He wrote to his parson brother, "My ship is, without exception, the finest sixty-four in the Service, and has the character of sailing most remarkably well."

The years slipped by, and although the map of Europe changed at the hands of Napoleon, Buckler's Hard remained much the same: Henry Adams lived in the master-builder's house; timber was stacked high in the street and the village kept busy. Nineteen years after the *Agamemnon* was built Adams supervised the laying down of the keel of a frigate for the Royal Navy. She was the *Euryalus,* due to become, as a result of Trafalgar, perhaps the most famous frigate of all time. It took fifteen months to build her. Most of the oak came from the Forest of Dean, in Gloucestershire, and the New Forest, and she cost £15,568. But before she was completed Henry Adams had another order—the biggest yet. It was for a 74-gun ship, to be called the *Swiftsure,* third of the Buckler's Hard ships which was to be at Trafalgar. By the time she was completed two thousand great oaks had been used in her construction, along with a hundred tons of wrought ironwork from Sowley Pond, and thirty tons of copper nails and bolts. When he finished his task of building the *Swiftsure,* which took thirty months, Henry Adams was ninety-one; he had only one year more to live.

Yet for all the romance in the building of the ships which made the Royal Navy the greatest maritime force the world had known, there were many bad constructional practices which meant that the wood started to rot even before the ships had been launched. At least one great three-decker was condemned within a year of being launched. The timber used to build the ships in the yards of England should have been seasoned for a year or more, but all too often it was used green, making it more prone to rot quickly. To make matters worse, the ships were built in the open air and it was the custom to let the vessel stand exposed "for a twelvemonth or a little more" before the deck and hull planking was put in place. It was not unusual to have the whole frame green with the growing spores of rot before planking-up started.

Some of the fastest ships in service with the Royal Navy were, ironically enough, those captured from the enemy. The *Tonnant,* which kept her name although she had her Tricolour changed for the British ensign, was "the finest two-decker ever seen in the Royal Navy," and the *Egyptienne,* captured in 1800, "the finest ship on one deck we ever had." The reason for this state of affairs is not hard to find: the French were imaginative in their approach to ship designing. Some of the country's finest brains drew up the lines for them, or shaped them in model form, striving for three main and often (from the naval architect's point of view) opposing characteristics. They aimed at producing a fast ship which must have fine lines and a long and narrow-beamed hull. It must carry a large number of guns, requiring a hull with plenty of beam and rising high out of the water. Finally the ship must point high (i.e., sail close to the wind); this called for a long, low hull but with a broad enough beam and sufficient stability to carry a lot of sail.

In Spain an Irishman named Mullins, who as a master-shipwright was a genius, improved the Spanish Navy's warships considerably. Only in Britain did conservative methods mean that the shipyards continued to build badly designed ships which were frequently slow, difficult to manoeuvre and not particularly good in heavy weather. It was a common saying that our ships were built by the mile and cut off as required. Naval officers were usually very free in their praise of the French ships, but the constructors failed to learn anything from the prizes.

In view of this, it should seem strange that the Royal Navy was so successful in battle. The answer is that—apart from the quality and experience of the officers and men compared with the French and Spanish—the British gunnery was superb, and in addition they had plenty of carronades—short-barrelled guns, rather like mortars, which had a very big bore. They received their name from the Carron Company, who made them. They were easily handled and very destructive at short range. "In this war," wrote Napoleon, "the English have been the first to use carronades, and everywhere they have done us great harm." Later he wrote to Decrès: "For God's sake ship me some more carronades."

Battles were fought at close quarters: ranges varied from a few hundred yards to a few feet, ships sometimes being lashed together or locked by their rigging. This reduced warfare, once the opposing fleets had closed with each other, to a battle of broadsides, and the ships which could fire the fastest generally won. Because of their training this was usually achieved by the British.

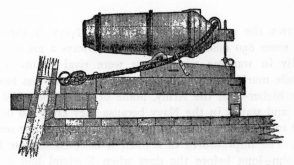

A carronade, showing the slide and a section of the deck and bulwark.

SIX

SALT-PORK DAYS

*The man who wants to be fully employed should procure a
ship, or a woman, for no two things produce more trouble.*
                                                —Plautus

MANNING the great ships of the Royal Navy (a three-decker
needed some 850 officers and men) was always a great problem,
especially in wartime when there were rival claims from the
mercantile marine—in which discipline was much less harsh and
the pay higher—and the Army. Some of the seamen had joined
as boys and stayed in the Navy because they knew no other life
or were too closely watched to escape, but many of the men were
pressed. The impressment of seamen is believed to date back to
King John—long before the days when England had a regular
royal fleet.

By law the whole of the seafaring population of Britain was
liable to serve the King at sea, and if a man was given an "imprest"
or advance payment by a King's agent—"taking the King's shilling"
—he had to serve. In practice this meant that a captain short of
crew—and captains were always in this unhappy state—would
send out a dozen or so strong and reliable seamen under a lieutenant as a press-gang. Rowing ashore, usually after dark, and
armed with clubs and cutlasses, they would probably make their
way to an inn. Some men would guard the back door while the
lieutenant and the rest of the gang burst in through the front.
Any able-bodied man—whether a seafarer or not—sitting drinking
a glass of beer with his friends was liable to be seized; and even if
he argued that he was a farm-labourer with a wife and children to
keep, he would be carried off. Any argument could mean a bang
on the head with a club or the flat of a cutlass blade.

In the streets a man taking his wife or sweetheart home could be wrenched from her arms and dragged away; a yokel tired from the harvest field might be seized and bundled into a boat to be rowed out to the ship. The press-gang could board a merchantman and take off the best men; it could go to the local assizes, and the prisoners in the jail would be turned over to it. All debtors, before being sent to the Marshalsea or some other debtors' prison, were given the option of going to sea. An unrepealed law dating from the time of Queen Elizabeth decreed that "rogues, vagabonds and sturdy beggars shall be, and are hereby directed to be taken up, conducted, and conveyed unto HM Service at sea." Magistrates in courts near the seaports would send miscreants on board a warship with the request to the captain that they should not be allowed on shore again.[1]

Yet because jail-birds were pressed into the Royal Navy it must not be thought that the majority of these men were criminals in the modern sense of the word. In Nelson's day men were given extremely heavy sentences by judges and magistrates for even the most trivial offences—among those jailed were the poacher, the petty pickpocket, the smuggler, the man who had stolen a few pence because he was hungry and could not get work, and the debtor. The laws of George III's reign allowed a man to be hanged for stealing a handkerchief from another's pocket, and death, jail or transportation followed automatically for offences which today would often result only in a small fine or probation.

So the fact that the jails were emptied to help man the King's ships does not mean that a constant stream of hardened criminals left dank stone cells to infect the men already serving in the Navy: instead, it was a stream of young men who, for the most part, had committed very minor offences against society. The agile young poacher—who usually had plenty of initiative and a light tread—frequently made a good topman; the deft pickpocket soon learned to turn a neat splice.

To many men serving long jail sentences for trivial offences the prospect of being pressed into the Navy was the prospect of being given comparative freedom, for the prisons were a disgrace to society, even by the standards of Nelson's day. At that time it

[1] The pressing of allegedly British seamen from American ships was one of the main causes of the War of 1812 between Britain and America.

was usual for twenty prisoners at Newgate to be kept for twenty-four hours a day in a cell measuring twenty feet by fifteen; nearly twenty years later the Inspectors of Prisons condemned Newgate as "a monstrous place." Certainly no seaman lived on board His Majesty's ships in such conditions.

The hard core of the Navy consisted of men who had served as seamen all their lives in warships, merchantmen or fishing craft. They were tough, skilled, rough and honest men, and at a time when the Royal Navy was desperate for recruits it would be wrong to think that even the hardened criminal brought on board in any way lowered the standards of the regular seamen: on the contrary, the seamen very quickly raised the standards of the criminal. The fact that the raw recruit who had come on board thin and white-faced, verminous and hungry from one of His Majesty's jails, had been sent there for taking one of his squire's prime pheasants, mattered not at all to captain, bosun or seamen. What did matter was whether or not he would make a good seaman. The pickpocket who failed to break himself of his light-fingered habits quickly found that the seamen's own rough and ready justice helped him out and made him once again an honest man.

In addition, one must bear in mind that life in England in 1805 was, for the bulk of the population, hard and full of injustice. It is necessary to avoid falling into the trap of judging the conditions in the Navy, described in these pages, by the liberal standards of the welfare state. The seamen often found life hard, unpleasant and sometimes unjust; but hardness, unpleasantness and injustice were the common lot of seamen and landsmen alike. A captain might flog a seaman for a trifling offence; yet ashore a magistrate might condemn a man to death, jail for life or transportation for a comparable misdeed.

It should be mentioned that a man pressed into the Navy could, legally, appeal. The people and the courts were very much against impressment, and the naval officer knew that the courts would nearly always find against him should a pressed man have the knowledge and the time to appeal. As the naval officer could be prosecuted for wrongful impressment—and would get his knuckles rapped by the Admiralty as well—he nearly always gave up the man rather than face a court at all. However, a landsman pressed into a ship on the eve of sailing often had no time to exercise his constitutional right!

Once on board, the pressed men were required by regulations to be examined to see if they "have any hurts or diseases which may render them unfit to serve in His Majesty's Navy." Since there was always a desperate shortage of men, this regulation was not enforced very strictly, and certainly not more than the rule that only seafarers could be pressed. Having passed his perfunctory medical examination, the new recruit was then taken into the Navy.

On March 22, 1804, an Italian—one of many foreigners to serve on board the *Victory*—was sworn in as a member of the crew of Nelson's flagship. First of all he had to make and sign an attestation:

> I Gaetan Loyagalo, do make an oath that I am by trade a bricklayer, and to the best of my information and belief was born in Milan, and am entirely free from all engagements, and that I have no rupture nor was ever troubled with fits and that I am in no wise disabled by lameness or otherwise but have the perfect use of my limbs and that I have voluntarily enlisted myself to serve his Britannic Majesty King George the Third in his Royal Marine Forces during the present war under an agreement that I shall be discharged at the end of it and a passage free of expense to the Mediterranean.
>
> Witness present C. W. ADAIR, Captain, Inspecting
> Officer of Recruits for the Royal Marines
> As witness my hand this 22nd day of March 1804
> His
> GAETAN X LOYAGALO
> Mark

That done, the new recruit then took the oath of allegiance to "his Sovereign Lord King George the Third," promising to serve him faithfully "in defence of his person, Crown and dignity against all his enemies and oppressors whatsoever." Finally a certificate was drawn up, signed "Sworn before me on board HMS *Victory* this twenty-second day of March 1804, NELSON AND BRONTE," which said:

> These are to certify that Gaetan Loyagalo aforesaid aged 27 years 5 feet 10 inches high sandy hair grey eyes freckeled complexion came before me and declared he had voluntarilly enlisted himself to serve

his B. Majesty King George the Third in his Royal Marine Forces, he
is therefore duly enlisted and the second and third Articles of War
against mutiny and sedition are likewise read to him and he has taken
the oath of fidelity mentioned in the said Articles of War. . . .

So now Marine Loyagalo, handed his five guineas' bounty by
Captain Adair, was taken to the purser, who issued him with the
regulation suit of bedding, two "checquered" shirts and "a red
cloth coat, white cloth waistcoat and breeches, one shirt with one
black stock, one pair of shoes, a hat." The former bricklayer from
Milan was now to be paid eightpence a day. For that he could be
flogged to death or promoted, hanged or rewarded in the name of
the King he had sworn to serve.

Once a man was on board a warship he never knew when he
would again get ashore: it might be five or ten years before he was
paid off, and all that time his pay would be accumulating—with
deductions for clothes and tobacco—at the rate of 22s. 6d. a month
if he was rated a landsman or 25s. 6d. for an ordinary seaman.
But he would be lucky if he was paid off in cash—all too often he
would be given tickets instead, and they were very difficult to cash.
He would probably end up cashing them with some sharp rogue
who would give him anything from a half to three-quarters of its
face value.

With the crew on board at the beginning of a commission, the
first lieutenant (the senior of the lieutenants and second-in-command) would sort them out and, with the captain, allocate the
scores of jobs that had to be done continually, whether the ship
was under way, in port or in action. The experienced seamen who
were getting on in years were stationed on the fo'c'sle, to work at
the anchors, bowsprit and foreyards. Called fo'c'sle or sheet-anchor
men, they were, after the bosun's mates and gunner's mates, among
the most reliable in the ship. Then the topmen would be chosen.
These were usually young and active, because they had the most
dangerous job of all—working the sails above the lower yards,
where one slip could mean a plunge to death scores of feet below.
The topmen were divided into three divisions, one for each mast.
Since a ship's smartness was reputedly shown by how quickly her
topmen could set, furl or reef the sails and scramble down on deck

again, every captain's eye was on them, and they were usually hurried along by blows from a bosun's mate's starter or colt—a length of knotted rope.

The third group selected by the first lieutenant was the after-guard—usually sneered at by the fo'c'sle and topmen. Their job was working the braces (the ropes which hauled the yards round to trim the sails), the spanker, mainsail and lower staysails. They kept the after part of the ship clean and when in action they worked at the guns or trimmed the sails.

The fourth and largest group were the waisters, so called because they were stationed in the waist, the midship section between the fo'c'sle and the quarter-deck. They handled the fore- and main-sheets and kept the waist spotless. But because the waisters were generally a collection of landsmen and doltish seamen, they had plenty of other unskilled tasks such as looking after the pigs and sheep, pumping out the ship, and anything else the first lieutenant could devise.

The idlers formed the fifth group. They worked during the day but did not stand a watch at night, and included the butchers who slaughtered the livestock (and made sure there was plenty of swill on which to fatten them); the barbers who dressed the men's pigtails and tidied up the officers' wigs; the painters, the coopers who made and repaired the casks, the captain of the head, who looked after the crude lavatories, and the loblolly boys who helped the surgeon, and various others. Each man was issued with two hammocks, one being a spare. The hammocks were slung from the beams and each man was allowed a width of only fourteen inches. Slung side by side across the width of the ship, each slightly overlapped those forward and aft of it, like sardines in a tin. However, with the normal watch and watch system, every alternate hammock would be empty.

For meals the whole crew was divided up into messes consisting of up to eight men. Each mess sat at its own table slung from the deckhead between two guns. The table itself was normally kept hooked up between the beams overhead when not in use. Each mess would elect a cook whose job it was to collect the mess's provisions from the purser and take them along to the ship's cook in the galley, where they would be cooked—in water which was usually so bad that it was stagnant and stinking, its contents as interesting and lively as a village pond. Few people had stomachs strong enough to drink it, and while there was enough, men drank beer. This was, as Masefield describes it, "small beer, of poor quality, not at all the sort of stuff to put the soul of three butchers into one weaver." Every man was entitled to a gallon of beer a day, but when it ran out—as it usually did after a month at sea—the regulations laid down that instead he was to be issued with a pint of wine or half a pint of rum or brandy. If it had to be wine, then the sailors preferred white. Red was known as "black strap," while the favourite white, the Spanish Mistela, was known affectionately as "Miss Taylor." When the wine was gone, the sailors had rum or brandy.

If there was a shortage of any particular item on board, something else was substituted according to a set scale. In addition to the alternatives to beer already mentioned, four pounds of flour, for instance, were rated equal to four pounds of beef.

On paper the food ration issued was generous—but much of it was bad. It was laid down that everyone serving in one of His Majesty's ships should get a daily ration according to a specified table which was in fact a weekly menu as well. Thus Tuesday and Saturday were salt-beef days, while Sunday and Thursday were for pork.[2] The meat would probably have been in salt for several years before it was eaten, by which time, says Masefield, "it needed rather a magician than a cook to make it eatable. It was of a stony hardness, fibrous, shrunken, dark, gristly, and glistening with salt crystals . . . the salt pork was generally rather better than the beef, but the sailors could carve fancy articles, such as boxes, out of either meat. The flesh is said to have taken a good polish, like some close-grained wood."

Usually at least half a seaman's meat ration was fat, bone or gristle. The oatmeal issued as a corrective to "acid and costive humours" was called burgoo, or skillagolee, but under either name it was usually so rotten as to be almost uneatable and, after being cooked in ship's water, unbearable. Pea soup, issued on salt-pork days, was always a favourite meal; and another favourite among

2 The total weekly ration for a seaman was: biscuits, 7 lbs.; beer, 7 gallons; beef, 4 lbs.; pork, 2 lbs.; pease, 2 pints; oatmeal, 1½ pints; sugar, 6 ozs.; butter, 6 ozs.; cheese, 12 ozs., "together with an allowance of vinegar not to exceed half a pint to each man."

the men was Scotch coffee, which consisted of ship's biscuits burnt in the oven (thus killing and cooking the weevils) and then boiled in water until transformed into a thick liquid and finally sweetened with sugar. On Monday, Wednesday and Friday no meat was issued. The biscuits given to the men were invariably full of weevils—so much so, according to one source, that "the most common custom was to leave the creatures to their quiet and to eat the biscuits at night, when the eye saw not and the tender heart was spared." Altogether, it is not surprising that the men liked to chew tobacco. . . .

Every man in the crew had a series of jobs to do, depending on whether the ship was at anchor, under way or in action. He would be given a number when the ship commissioned—between 1 and 570, if there were that many men in the crew. By looking at his number on the ship's "General Quarters, Watch and Station Bill" he could see the tasks allocated to him. We can arbitrarily choose Number 88 in an 80-gun ship with 570 in the crew (the bill would vary from ship to ship, depending on the captain, but this particular one was used frequently). Our seaman would be a fore-topman and in the first part of the larboard watch (each of the two watches was divided into two parts) and the bill would also tell him that at general quarters[3] he was a sponger at Number 2 gun on the main deck. When boarders were called for he would be in the second division and would be issued with a cutlass and pistol, but not a pike, tomahawk or musket. He was not a fireman or pumper. For furling and loosing sails he worked on the fore-topsail yard. When the ship weighed anchor he would be down at the capstan. There were a dozen or more other jobs for him, and if he wanted to avoid having his ribs bruised by a bosun's mate's starter, he had to learn by heart what they were, so that he could go to his correct station in any eventuality.

Now for the day's routine—a Sunday. Once again it varied from ship to ship, but we will follow the one laid down to go with this particular watch bill. The starboard watch would have gone on deck at 8 p.m. the night before, and at midnight the bosun's mates would have gone to the hatchways and bellowed "Larboard

[3] Known in the Royal Navy today as "action stations." The original phrase is still retained in the United States Navy.

watch ahoy! Rouse out there, you sleepers!" To avoid the starters the men would roll smartly out of their hammocks, waking up on the way. Snatching up their clothes—if, in fact, they had undressed —they would head for the upper deck, leaving the fetid atmosphere of the lower deck to the starboard watch for the next four hours. At 4 a.m. the ungentle cries of the bosun's mates would rouse out the starboard watch after their brief respite, and they would rush on deck, instinctively side-stepping the starters, take off their shoes and roll up their trousers ready to holystone the deck. While some men rigged the pump, others would get out buckets and scrubbers and the more unfortunate would take up pieces of holystone—known as "prayer books." With the deck wetted and sand sprinkled over it, the men with holystones would go down on their knees and start scouring the sand into the deck, gradually getting it clean. Following behind them would be scrubbers, washing and brushing the sand into the scuppers and over the side. Finally came the swabbers, drying the decks with their swabs.

While the decks were being cleaned, other men would be polishing up the brightwork with brick dust and rags, taking care to keep ahead of the scrubbers who would wash away the dust. As dark gave way to daylight, the look-outs on deck would be sent up aloft to the masthead; then at 6.45 a.m. the bosun's mates would cry "All hands, up hammocks!" and each man would run down to the lower deck to lash his hammock into the shape of a long sausage—with the straw mattress, familiarly known as a "donkey's breakfast," and a couple of blankets inside—with the seven regulation turns of a lanyard.

"Muster and stow hammocks" came at 7 a.m., with all hands shouldering their hammocks and dashing up on deck to their respective divisions. There they would stow their hammocks in the nettings which formed a bulwark round the upper part of the ship, still under the watchful eyes of the bosun's mates, reinforced by quartermasters and midshipmen. Apart from keeping the lower deck clear during the day, the hammock stowage served as a protection when in action, the solid banks of canvas helping to stop grape-shot and musket balls from sweeping the decks. To protect the hammocks from the weather, long strips of canvas were placed over them and tucked well in. At 7.30 a.m. the upper deck would be spotless, the brightwork gleaming, hammocks stowed, and the log hove over the side to determine the ship's speed and the result noted down on a slate. The idlers, who had also been called at 4 a.m., would be busy. The cook would have lit the fire in the galley and the abominable burgoo would be bubbling with all the smell and steam of a witch's brew, the gruel cooking alongside the maggots for whom it had previously provided such a nourishing home. In other pots the Scotch coffee would be coming to the boil, the stagnant water rousing itself to blend with the burnt biscuits and charred weevils and to provide a hot, if not exactly nourishing, drink for the seamen. The Marines would have been busy cleaning muskets, polishing cutlasses (three feet long and curved, with a basket handle), tomahawks, which were small axes with spikes sticking out from the back of the blade, and half-pikes —ash handles with steel tips.

At 8 a.m. came the welcome pipe of "Hands to breakfast," and the men would troop down to their messes and rig the tables between the guns; when the mess cooks returned from the galley with the day's offering, they would spend the next half hour eating and reviling the cook.

At a few minutes before 10 a.m. the sweepers would make a last sally across the decks with their brooms; then at 10 a.m. precisely (9.30 on weekdays) all hands were called for divisions. The men would be newly shaved, their pigtails tidied, and smart in clean shirts; the Marines would be resplendent in their black, narrow-brimmed hats and red and white cockades, red tail coats, spotless white breeches, buttoned-up gaiters and brown shoes and with their crossbelts newly pipe-clayed.

The captain would inspect the men and then go round the whole ship, looking for a spot of grease on the deck, a trace of rust on a cannon, a speck of dirt on the cook's pots and pans. Some captains wore white gloves, so that an exploratory finger could always find if there was some dust at the back of a rack of half-pikes or behind a carronade slide. With the inspection over, the men were herded aft to the quarter-deck for divine service. There would be prayers, perhaps a couple of hymns helped along by the energetic sawings of a fiddler, and a short address. A good captain could learn a lot about the happiness or otherwise of his crew from the way they sang the hymns.

After church came the order to clear the decks and "Up spirits."

A fifer would play some cheery tune like "Nancy Dawson" and the Master's mate would stand by at the tub to issue the Royal Navy's liquid happiness. Mess cooks would grab their tin flagons to collect the share for their mess. The issue at noon would be a gill of pure rum mixed with three gills of water. With this inside him —plus any more he could scrounge or which was due to him as a gambling debt—the sailor "thought foul scorn of the boatswain's mate, and looked upon the world with charity." If too many of his mates repaid their debts he might, before Sunday afternoon was very old, find it hard to lie on the deck between the guns without holding on.

After dinner, as the midday meal was called, the watch on deck again swept up, but the watch below was free to sleep—on the deck, for the hammocks were still in the nettings, but beer, "black strap," "Miss Taylor" or rum softened the planks. They could also play chequers or—if they found a quiet enough spot out of the way of authority—throw dice or play cards, both of which were forbidden, and hazard their tots of rum against the mathematical laws of chance and the watchful eyes of the bosun's mates.

At 5 p.m. (the exact time varied with the ship's latitude and was usually an hour before dusk) the hands would be piped to supper, the third and last meal of the day, when the tough ship's biscuits and lively cheese would be washed down with a second ration of beer, wine or grog. Half an hour later a drum would beat to quarters and the men would run to their stations for battle. Guns would be cast loose and the ship's officers would carry out a detailed inspection.

Evening quarters were a dangerous time for those who had hoarded their noon issue of liquor so that they could add it to the supper issue: the master-at-arms would cast an experienced eye over the assembled men, and any that swayed more than the ship's pitch and roll warranted would provide material to be hauled, thick-headed and repentant, before the captain in the morning. On a weekday the men would exercise at the guns for half an hour after quarters, but on Sundays they were excused. As dusk fell the look-outs would be brought down from the mast-head and placed on deck, and at 8 p.m. "Down hammocks" would be piped. The men would collect their hammocks from the nettings and get down to the lower deck as fast as possible to sling them before "Ship's company's fire and lights out" was piped ten minutes later.

The day had ended: it was, as far as the Navy was concerned, a day of rest. The watches would change in monotonous regularity. From 5 p.m. in the evening the men would have nothing to eat until 8 a.m. the next morning. If there was rain or a heavy sea the water would probably drip through on to their hammocks. The great hawse-pipes, through which the anchor cables led, were at the forward end of their deck; in anything of a sea no plugs or oakum could stop the water getting in and sloshing back and forth along the deck, stirring up the livestock in the manger. The odours assaulting the nose on the lower deck of a ship-of-the-line

Reefing a topsail.

were an invisible maelstrom: to the reek from the manger, which in hot, rough weather, was like a farmyard midden, was added the stench of the bilges, of unwashed and perspiring humanity in unventilated quarters, and the pungent smell from wet clothing. It was in these conditions that men lived for years on end—spending a whole winter of Atlantic gales off Brest, or two years at sea in the Mediterranean and Atlantic, as Nelson had just done, without setting foot on shore. (A three-page drawing of the internal lay-out of the *Victory* is given facing p. 360.)

This was the price paid by the seamen to ensure that, ashore at least, "Britons never will be slaves." Yet the life was not without its advantages: under the harsh discipline, leading an extremely active life, the criminal was usually turned into a good seaman. And if the seaman of England was harshly treated afloat, the plebeian of England fared little better ashore: he could be hanged for more than two hundred offences, ranging from murder to sheep-stealing. The farm-hand "living in" was paid about £10 a year; his brother serving at sea as an ordinary seaman received £5 a year more, for which he hazarded his life as regularly as the farm-labourer had meals. Against that there was a life of excitement, some chance of prize money, comradeship—and the comforts of beer, rum or "Miss Taylor."

SEVEN

NAPOLEON SNUBBED

What fates impose, that men must needs abide;
It boots not to resist both wind and tide.

—Shakespeare

A S C H U R C H B E L L S boomed out the twelfth stroke of midnight
and men raised their glasses to toast the New Year of 1805, the
future for Britain seemed like a long dark tunnel with no hint
of its length and no sign of light at its end. Napoleon with his invasion fleet was apparently poised on the eastern flank of the
Channel. Holland, Switzerland and northern Italy were mere subject nations of France while Napoleon was threatening southern
Italy—endangering Britain's whole position in the Mediterranean—
and Turkey, which would open the East to him. Anticipating that
Spain would eventually come into the war on France's side, Pitt
had earlier ordered the home-coming Spanish treasure ships, bound
for Spain with silver from Montevideo, to be seized. Spain in turn
had declared war, bringing thirty-two ships-of-the-line to join
Napoleon's Fleet.

"Never, perhaps," wrote Nelson to the Queen of the Two Sicilies,
"was Europe more critically situated than at this moment, and
never was the probability of universal monarchy more nearly being
realized than in the person of the Corsican. . . . Prussia is trying
to be destroyed last—Spain is little better than a province of France
—Russia does nothing on the grand scale. Would to God these great
powers reflected that the boldest measures are the safest! They
allow small states to fall, and to serve the enormous power of
France, without appearing to reflect that every Kingdom which is
annexed to France makes their existence, as independent states,
more precarious. . . ."[1] Nelson was writing from his great strategic

1 These sentiments were equally as true for the periods before and after
the Second World War.

knowledge and insight, not because of a passing mood of depression, and in 1805, as in previous years, Britain's very existence depended on her control of the sea.

The great blockade of France's ports had begun in May, 1803, and had gone on ever since. Twenty-one battleships under Ganteaume were held in Brest by the ceaselessly watching ships of Admiral Cornwallis; five more battleships and five other warships under Missiessy were kept in Rochefort; fifteen Spanish battleships under Gravina were fitting out at Ferrol and Cadiz, and eleven more battleships and eight frigates, under Latouche Tréville and later Villeneuve, were penned in at Toulon by Nelson. Not that Nelson wanted them penned in: his great hope was that they would come out and fight. In the previous June he had written, "Do not think I am tired of watching Mr Latouche Tréville. I have now taken up a method of making him angry. I have left Sir Richard Bickerton, with part of the fleet, twenty leagues from hence, and, with five of the line, am preventing him cutting capers, which he had done for some time past, off Cape Sicie. . . . Some happy day I expect to see his eight [*sic*] sail which are in the Outer Road, come out. . . ."

Exactly a week after Nelson wrote that, the French admiral did in fact sail out of Toulon with eight battleships and six frigates. As Nelson said, they "cut a caper off Sepet, and went in again. I was off, with five sail of the line, and brought to for his attack, although I did not believe that anything was meant serious, merely a gasconade." That ended it as far as Nelson was concerned—until he saw Latouche Tréville's official report on the incident. Nelson, had, according to the French admiral, "recalled his ship and his two frigates, which were among the islands, and bore away. I pursued him until night; he ran to the south-east." Nelson was furious at this barefaced lie. To a friend he wrote: "If any Englishman has believed for one moment the story, I may, to my friend, say without fear of being thought arrogant, that they do not deserve to have me serve them; but I have kept Monsieur Latouche's letter; if I take him, I shall either never see him, or, if I do, *make him eat his letter.*"

But he was destined never to have the chance, for nine days later Latouche Tréville died. "He is gone, and all his lies with him," reported Nelson; "the French papers say he died in consequence of walking so often up to the signal post, upon Sepet, to watch us: I always pronounced that would be his death."

Napoleon's moves and counter-moves towards the end of 1804 and at the beginning of 1805 are an essential part of the campaign and battle of Trafalgar. On December 2, 1804, Napoleon and Josephine were crowned in the beautiful cathedral of Notre Dame—or rather, Napoleon lifted the golden laurel wreath before the Pope could reach it, and placed it on his own head. Napoleon was now at the height of his power. Professor Fournier, the Austrian historian and one of the most acute of Napoleon's biographers, writes that "Instead of the enthusiasm for Liberty which had inspired the armies of the Revolution, the soldiers were now possessed by the love of glory and a desire for distinguishing themselves and receiving distinctions. And the Emperor . . . began to talk to them of the Empire of Europe." Fournier adds: "In these schemes they seconded him willingly, and so the Republican army became Imperialist, and such it loyally remained as long as the *petit caporal* had even a gleam of victory."

Despite the cheers of his massed armies, the flattery of his generals and admirals, and the glitter of his court at the vast and beautiful Palais des Tuileries (shortly after Napoleon moved into the Palais it was noted that his court was "a more brilliant one perhaps than that of the unfortunate Louis XVI"), he still had to face the problem of England. He appears not to have been working to any long-term plan: this was because he was one of the greatest —and at first successful—opportunists in history. His Army of England, as we have seen, had been constantly drilling with its landing craft, and France was waiting for the master-stroke. Yet Napoleon hesitated once again. He had delayed in 1803 and 1804. What had he in mind for 1805?

He had spent eighteen months and millions of francs in preparing for the great *descente* for which all France waited. But now, at the beginning of 1805, was he looking for something which would avoid the necessity of his giving the possibly fatal order for the invasion to begin? A war on the Continent, for instance? Certainly this would give him a loophole. Austria, with the backing of Russia, was becoming restive, and his spies had already warned him that England was negotiating with Russia. His situation on the Continent, he realized, could become potentially dangerous. Some authorities claim that Napoleon never intended to invade; that the whole scheme was a gigantic bluff. But as that great historian Sir Julian Corbett has pointed out, "By the universal testimony of his relations, his most intimate friends and his most capable and best-informed enemies, he at this time believed he had escaped gracefully from having to attempt the invasion of England. . . . Austria, it seemed, was about to give him a pretext for escape without loss of prestige, but he had to justify to his Council the terrible cost which his pose had involved."

But according to Miot de Melito, who was a member, Napoleon told the Council: "For two years past France has been making the greatest sacrifices. A general war on the Continent would entail none greater. I now possess the strongest army, a highly developed military organization, and I am at present situated exactly as I would need to be if war should break out [on the Continent]. But in order to amass such forces in time of peace—20,000 artillery horses and complete baggage trains—I required a pretext which would allow all this to be prepared and collected without arousing the suspicions of the other continental powers. The plan of the invasion of England afforded this pretext." De Melito, who claims to have heard the speech, says Napoleon added: "For two years I have not been able to tell you this, but that nevertheless was my sole aim. You know it now and you see the explanation of many things. But we shall not have war, and I have just opened negotiations with the King of England."[2]

With Spain now in the war on his side he could count on another thirty-two battleships to back up his fleet, making him powerful enough to challenge Britain at sea—the only way he could make a challenge. But Spain had already warned him that, because Britain caught her unawares, the first twenty-five ships would not be ready for sea before March. Thus Napoleon could not make his challenge until the spring, but in the meantime he had to do something to keep Britain occupied until he resolved the Austrian problem. He therefore decided to make a peace offer to Britain, and at the

[2] Although the French Staff accepted de Melito as trustworthy it is curious that the biographies, memoirs and papers of people like Ney, Marmont and Davout—all of whom commanded corps—make no mention of the "pose"; and nor does Decrès, who should have been in a position to know.

same time launch a heavy attack on her rich sugar islands in the
West Indies, and also recapture those that Britain had taken.
This sudden assault, he guessed, would throw the merchants of
the City of London into a panic, and Pitt's ministry, which held
power by only a very slender majority, would probably topple
amid clamour for peace at any price. In addition, he thought, the
Royal Navy's strength would be drawn away from his Atlantic
coast in a hurried dash to the West Indies.

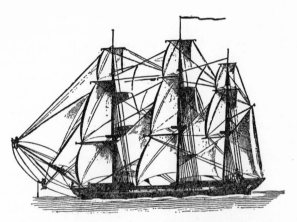

Taking soundings: the deep-sea lead is being heaved by
a man on the spritsail yardarm. A second man on the
jib-boom end holds a bight of the line while a third in
the mizen chains has the reel.

Napoleon's "direct negotiations with the King of England"
started on January 2, 1805. Proud of his month-old title of Emperor, he sent a letter not to the British Government but to the
old King, addressing him as "My dear Brother." Since he had been
called to the throne of France "by Providence and the suffrage of
the Senate, the people and the Army," Napoleon said, his "foremost and most earnest desire has been for peace."

Somewhat belying his earnest declaration were two sets of orders
sent off that same day. The first was to Missiessy at Rochefort, the
second to Villeneuve, who had taken over command of the fleet at
Toulon after Latouche Tréville's death. They were to take on
troops and sail independently for the West Indies, where they

were to conduct operations against the British and then return to Rochefort. At the same time Napoleon sent a sharp note to the Austrian Emperor, Francis, demanding to know why certain troop movements were being made and warning him against any breach of the peace.

Thus the first move in the train of events that was to lead directly and inexorably to the battle of Trafalgar began with Missiessy taking 3,500 troops on board. Rochefort was an extremely difficult port to blockade and for several reasons which we need not trouble with here, the British ships were not on their station when Missiessy sailed on January 11 in a snowstorm. His squadron was, however, spotted by a Royal Navy schooner, which was able to report his course. He had been at sea three days when, on January 14, Britain's reply to Napoleon's peace offer arrived in Paris. Addressed simply to "The Head of the French Government" —a deliberate insult which successfully infuriated the Emperor— and signed not by the King but by Pitt, it said Britain was not prepared to negotiate without consulting the other powers, particularly with the Czar, "who had always shown a warm interest in the integrity and independence of Europe." Once bitten—by the Treaty of Amiens—Britain was twice shy. Far from being ready to sue for peace she realized that there could be no peace in the world while Napoleon was alive.

EIGHT

THE EMPERORS' PLAN

*Dost thou not know, my son, with how little wisdom
the world is governed?* —Count Oxenstierna

VILLENEUVE had not been able to sail from Toulon until January 18—a week after Missiessy, and four days after Pitt's reply was received in Paris. But, like Missiessy, he was lucky. In a brisk north-westerly breeze he took his squadron to sea—and found, instead of Nelson waiting over the horizon to fall on him, only two British frigates. But strong winds turned into a gale, and in the darkness of his first night at sea Villeneuve was soon in trouble. His crews were little more than raw landsmen and there were 6,500 soldiers cluttering up the ships, adding their seasick contribution to the chaos and rapidly falling morale. By the time daylight came to the turbulent Gulf of Lyons, Villeneuve's telescope showed him a miserable picture: there were only four of the original eleven battleships still in company, struggling along with tattered sails, torn rigging and broken spars. He had covered only a few score of the five thousand-odd miles to the West Indies, and already one ship had lost her mainmast, another smashed her foreyard and a third had had one of her topmasts topple over the side.

Villeneuve gave up: he and the remains of his squadron were back in Toulon by the 21st, and to Decrès he wrote: "I declare to you that ships of the line thus equipped, short-handed, encumbered with troops, with superannuated or bad materials, vessels which lose their masts or sails at every puff of wind, and which in fine weather are constantly engaged in repairing the damages caused by the wind, or the inexperience of their sailors, are not fit to undertake anything. I had a presentiment of this before I sailed; I have now only too painfully experienced it."

Meanwhile Nelson, warned by his two frigates which both left the enemy Fleet on the 19th (why they both left together is not explained), combed the Mediterranean for Villeneuve. He thought the French might be heading for Naples or Sicily and slowly fought his way south in the teeth of the gale which had dealt Villeneuve such a blow. "I have neither ate, drunk, or slept with any comfort since last Sunday," he wrote. ". . . I consider the destruction of the enemy's fleet of so much consequence, that I would willingly have half of mine burnt to effect their destruction. I am in a fever. God send I may find them!"

Working to a strict plan of searching the areas where Villeneuve could do the most damage, Nelson eventually went as far as Egypt, but finding no trace of him, sailed back westward to Malta, where on February 19 he found that Villeneuve had been back in Toulon since January 21. "Those gentlemen are not accustomed to a Gulf of Lyons gale," he wrote, "which we have buffeted for twenty-one months, and not carried away a spar. I most sincerely hope they will soon be in a state to put to sea again." Three days at sea had been more than enough for Villeneuve, with his untrained crews and ill-conditioned ships, yet for eighty-four weeks Nelson's ships had defied those same storms in those very waters—often, as we have seen, in unseaworthy ships. Napoleon was furious at Villeneuve's failure. "The great evil of our Navy is that the men who command it are unused to the risks of command. What is to be done with admirals who allow their spirits to sink and resolve to be beaten home at the first damage they suffer?" he asked.

Something of an answer to Napoleon's exasperated comment on the leadership of the French Fleet can be gleaned by looking at the men who led the Royal Navy at this time. Head and shoulders above them all stood Nelson, the possessor of perhaps the most contradictory personality in British history. The legend of Nelson as the fearless fighter, the master strategist and tactician, and the greatest sailor-warrior in the Navy of great sailor-warriors, has tended to obscure the Nelson known to the men who fought with him, the women who loved him, and those of both sexes who met him yet rarely in the gay, etiquette-ridden and gossip-conscious salons that were the centres of London society.

By the standards of a welfare state, Nelson at any period in his life was an undersized adult weakling. "What," inquired his uncle, Captain Suckling, when asked to take the twelve-year-old boy into his ship as a midshipman, "has poor little Horatio done, who is so weak, that, above all the rest, he should be sent to rough it at sea?" Nor did the sea strengthen that thin body; in fact the sea, tropical sickness, and the wounds of war conspired only to shatter even further his fragile constitution. Physically and mentally Nelson is the odd man out in the gallery of great war leaders. His face had none of the dour sternness of purpose of that of "Old Jarvie," later Earl St. Vincent, who had grimly declared on St. Valentine's Day, 1797, before fighting the battle from which he took his title, that "A victory is very essential to England at this moment," and it had none of the steadfastness of Wellington's.

Instead of a square jaw, thin, firm lips and jutting chin, Nelson's face was narrow and half boyish, with sensitive lips forming a pouting mouth. The chin belied the strong will; in fact at first glance the head, with its careless hair and mobile, almost womanish features lined with pain and anxiety, might be that of a restless poet. A young midshipman who was destined to become William IV first met Nelson when he was twenty-four years old and commanding a frigate, and noted him as "the merest boy of a captain I ever beheld"; many years later Sir William Hamilton, meeting Nelson for the first time, referred to him as "a little man and far from handsome." Yet the personality emerging from that frail body is a contradiction of that associated with leadership, completely different from the calm, stern manner of St. Vincent and Wellington, who were men competent but cold, and brave but reserved, in the usual British tradition.

Nelson, "that cripple-gaited, one-eyed, one-armed little naval critter," was as emotional as a young woman; constantly moody and temperamental, he was one moment suicidally depressed and the next almost childishly elated. Of a race that prided itself on never revealing its feelings, he was a melodramatic and emotional exception. We will see from his letters how depressed he could become when Villeneuve proved so elusive, and how that depression affected him physically. From this his whole personality appears unstable—yet he rarely made a wrong decision, whether it was one long debated or suddenly arrived at in the heat of battle. It seemed as if he had two distinct personalities—the hot-blooded, hypersensitive and erratic one which manifested itself in his relations with people, and the ice-cold, steely, questing and unswerving personality which turned him into the most perfect human fighting machine ever seen, as brave and brilliant wielding a sword and leading a boarding party as when coolly handling a large fleet.

His extraordinary depression before battle is almost unbelievable. Yet his elation and bravery once battle started injected him with life: it is as if he only really lived at full capacity when his ears were deafened by the thunder of the guns, nostrils dilated with the smoke of powder and his remaining eye assaulted by the swirling panorama of massive ships pounding the enemy into bloody submission according to a plan previously conceived by his own brain. Then the pain and misery left that little body; all pettiness and melodrama dissolved.

His health greatly affected his mental outlook. Born a weakling, he was constantly ill when at sea. ("Dreadfully seasick," he wrote the year before Trafalgar; "always tossed about, and always seasick.") His health was ruined by fever in the West Indies, and sickness dogged him from then on. At Copenhagen the cold almost killed him; he broke down after his victory at the Nile—"I never expect to see your face again," he wrote to Jervis. When operating in the Channel off Boulogne his thin body was racked with spasms of perpetual coughing and seasickness and his head buzzed with toothache. Off Toulon while waiting for Villeneuve his muscles were knotted with rheumatism, he had a regular pain in the chest and "the constant sense of the blood gushing up the left side of my head." He appears to have had nervous dyspepsia almost without pause.

But these were not the moanings of a hypochondriac: when being given a pension in 1797 he had first to present a memorial outlining his service. "Your memorialist has been in four actions with the fleets of the enemy, in three actions with frigates, in six engagements against batteries, in ten actions in boats employed in cutting out of harbours, in destroying vessels, and in the taking of three towns. . . . He has assisted in the capture of seven sail of the line, six frigates, four corvettes, eleven privateers of different sizes, and taken and destroyed near fifty sail of merchantmen. [He] has been actually engaged against the enemy upwards of one hundred and twenty times, [and he] has lost his right eye and arm, and been severely wounded and bruised in his body. . . ." When that was written Nelson had just celebrated his thirty-ninth birthday; the Nile, Copenhagen and Trafalgar were yet to be fought.

While constantly complaining of illness he also retained an ironic sense of humour. "I have all the diseases there are," he once wrote, "but there is not enough in my frame for them to fasten on." To the future William IV he wrote after losing his arm at Santa Cruz, "I assure your Royal Highness that not a scrap of that ardour with which I served our King has been shot away!" And if one gets the impression that he made the most of his illnesses, one should remember that at Santa Cruz, shot down, with his right arm shattered and badly bleeding, Nelson was rowed back to the nearest ship, which was Thomas Fremantle's *Seahorse,* with Betsey—newly married—waiting anxiously on board for her husband to return from the landing beaches. Nelson, half unconscious and in urgent need of medical attention, refused to go on board and ordered that he was to be rowed to his flagship, the *Theseus.* Told his life was in danger, he said: "Then I will die rather than alarm Mrs Fremantle by her seeing me in this state when I can give her no tidings of her husband."

Alongside the *Theseus* he refused any help in climbing on board. "I have got my legs left, and one arm," and he scrambled up the ship's side, face white as a sheet, uniform covered in blood, and the shattered arm roughly tied up. Once on deck he ordered the surgeon to bring the instruments. "I know I must lose my right arm, and the sooner the better." Yet he could write words of self-pity to his beloved Emma which must have wrenched at her heart: "Nothing can be more miserable and unhappy than your poor Nelson," he wrote from off Toulon. "My heart is almost broken."

But Nelson could be petty, and there is often a hint of the shrewishness of a woman in his temper, usually where little things were concerned. He was a great friend of Captain Ball, yet when he first met him—in France during the brief period of peace in 1783—he was annoyed because Ball wore epaulettes, which were not part of an officer's uniform in the Royal Navy until several years later. "Two noble captains are here—Ball and Shepherd," he wrote acidly. "They wear fine epaulettes, for which I think them great coxcombs. They have not visited me, and I shall not court their acquaintance." Nelson met Ball again fifteen years later, when he came on board to report. "What," said Nelson sarcastically, "have you come to have your bones broken?" Less than a month later Nelson's ship lost her masts in a gale and her helpless hulk was being swept ashore. Ball, in the *Alexander,* immediately took the flagship in tow, and tried to get her out to sea. But there was a grave danger that both ships would be lost on the lee shore and Nelson ordered Ball to cast off the tow. The slow-moving, phlegmatic Ball refused, whereupon Nelson became extremely angry and ordered the tow to be cut, leaving himself and the flagship to their fate. Ball, however, carried on, and many hours later the flagship was saved. Nelson immediately went aboard the *Alexander* and, embracing the embarrassed Ball, declared: "A friend in need is a friend indeed."

It was Nelson's essential humanity which endeared him to his officers and men; hard-bitten seamen genuinely loved him. When he was ill they nursed him with all the tenderness they might have lavished on a woman. From the Baltic in 1801, when he was ill and irritated with the Admiralty, he wrote, "All the fleet are so truly kind to me that I should be a wretch not to cheer up. Foley has put me under a regimen of milk at four in the morning; Murray has given me lozenges; Hardy is as good as ever, and all have proved their desire to keep my mind easy." As one writer says, "That picture of one sea veteran administering warm milk to his admiral at four o'clock in the morning, and to another feeding him tenderly with lozenges, is amusing enough; but it shows more effectively than graver things could do the feeling Nelson inspired in his captains."

Warm-hearted with those he liked and respected, Nelson also had a tremendous loyalty—whether to a man, a ship or a fleet. Merely because it was his, then each was of the best. We have already seen his comment on the *Agamemnon* when he was given her to command. ("She is without exception the finest sixty-four in the Service.") So it was with the *Albemarle.* "Not a man or officer in her I would wish to change." His ships of the Mediterranean Fleet were "the best commanded and the best manned afloat." That warm loyalty was, of course, returned, and it was often returned in a similar, spontaneous and dramatized way. Thomas Troubridge, for instance, was a fine seaman with vast experience. He was heavily built and handsome, frank in manner and destined to be as good an administrator as he was a fighter. Jervis, at the battle of St. Vincent, watching the way Troubridge handled the *Culloden*, exclaimed: "Look at Troubridge! He tacks his ship into battle as if the eyes of all England were on him; and would to God they were!"

Yet this same Troubridge, upset at something Nelson had written, sat down and wrote: "Your letter has really so unhinged me that I am quite unmanned and crying. I would sooner forfeit my life—my everything—than be deemed ungrateful to an officer and a friend I feel I owe so much. Pray, pray acquit me . . . I pray your Lordship not to harbour the smallest idea that I am not the same Troubridge you have known me."

It is a great leader whose slightest word can make strong men weep—not because of the power he holds over their careers but because of the power he holds over their hearts. The gallant and wounded Captain Riou, reluctantly obeying Sir Hyde Parker's signal to withdraw from the action against the Trekroner Forts at Copenhagen, said bitterly, "What will Nelson think of us?" He then gave the order to cut the anchor cable—and was almost immediately killed by a cannon ball.

If it seems strange that Nelson's dying words were "Kiss me, Hardy," remember this was the Thomas Masterman Hardy, the massive, grave and kindly man from Dorset who, when the frigate *Minerve* was being chased by several Spanish battleships, lowered a boat and rowed after a seaman who had fallen over the side. The Spaniards were coming up fast and Nelson was faced with the danger that the *Minerve* would be captured before the boat could get back. However, he did not hesitate. "By God, I'll not lose Hardy! Back the mizen-topsail." The *Minerve* lay-to, motionless, while the boat caught up, and the nearest Spanish battleship, apparently bewildered by the tiny frigate's unexpected action, and probably fearing a trap, backed a topsail as well. This gave Nelson enough time to get Hardy and his boat's crew on board, and the *Minerve* escaped.

Nelson, of course, played the game of favourites in an age of favouritism, but apart from a few glaring exceptions each man deserved his loyalty. Each was an outstanding seaman, and each became Nelson's friend—one of his "band of brothers"—because he could and did fight the enemy like a demon, and because he could and did accept the kind of leadership Nelson offered, exploiting it to the full. Nelson's leadership was that of example and trust, accompanied with a warm smile—the rarest of all, the most easily abused, and yet, if followed, the most successful.

On February 1 a French ship sailed from Lorient bound for the West Indies with new orders for Missiessy, warning him that Villeneuve would not be joining him. Decrès told him that Villeneuve's squadron "is to have another destination" and Missiessy was to reinforce San Domingo and then sail back across the Atlantic to Rochefort. What was Villeneuve's new destination? Probably Napoleon had not made up his mind, though he ordered General Lauriston to disembark the troops which had been on board Villeneuve's ships. "You will receive an order to re-embark for elsewhere, for the season is past for your former destination," he wrote on February 5—the day he cancelled orders for a campaign against Austria, a cancellation forced upon him by the Austrian Emperor's placatory reply. Even now it is almost impossible to know what Napoleon had in mind.

At the Palais des Tuileries in the spring of 1805 most of the outward signs of the Revolution had gone. In place of boots men wore stockings and buckled shoes; elaborately wrought ceremonial swords replaced clumsy sabres. Men addressed each other as *"monsieur"* instead of *"citoyen"* and the Palais d'Égalité was once again known by its old name of the Palais Royal. Italian singers sang to the accompaniment of soft music to amuse the Emperor, and often he would fall quiet, as if in a daydream, and no one dared move until he recovered. Sometimes in Josephine's salon he would have the candles shrouded in white gauze, to cast an eerie light while he told ghost stories. On Sundays he would review a few thousand troops drawn up in the courtyard of the Palais, speaking to individual soldiers and hearing their complaints. While he grew more distrustful and more withdrawn from his generals and ministers, ancient Court posts were brought back into use as if Napoleon gloried in the splendours and routine that dated back to Charlemagne, and some aristocrats who had fled France at the Revolution flocked back to new posts at Court.

But if the Palais des Tuileries was a place where Napoleon lived in great splendour, it was also the place where he worked hard. Two or three secretaries were always at hand in his study, pens ready to fly across paper as their master dictated letters to kings and princes, orders to his generals and admirals, plans for new conquests. Maps hung on walls or lay unrolled on tables; the latest figures on the state of the Army, the Navy and the invasion flotillas were kept handy for instant reference. It was not unusual for Napoleon to work all night; indeed, when the English Ambassador left Paris just before war was declared again in 1803, Napoleon worked for three consecutive days and nights, keeping busy a relay of three secretaries at a time. "On the evening of the fourth day he took a warm bath to counteract his excitement, and remained in it for six hours, during which time he dictated important despatches. Finally he went to bed, giving orders to call him at three in the morning, so that he might see four or five couriers whom he was expecting." Each day he was up by seven in the morning, reading his own correspondence—and that of several other select people, many of them his ministers, which had been intercepted by his Postmaster-General. (He once boasted that a special department could decipher a coded letter, no matter what the language.) While he dressed, a secretary would read aloud various items from the newspapers. Breakfast, usually eaten alone and always hurriedly, followed. And then the real work of the day began.

So it was that on March 2, 1805, he made the third move in his great plan. The first move had been on February 27, when new orders were sent to Missiessy in the West Indies, cancelling the previous orders to return to France and instructing him to wait in the West Indies until the end of June for another French squadron and, if none came, to return to France. The second move, on the same day, had been to order Gourdon, at Ferrol, with four battleships (a fifth was in dock being repaired) and two frigates to be ready to join any French squadron which might arrive off the port to drive off the British ships and release him. Now, on March 2, the time had come for the third and most vital move. He had bathed, shaved and breakfasted, and he had read the correspondence. His secretaries were ready in the study, quills sharpened, inkwells full. The Emperor then began dictating one of the most fantastic orders he had ever given.

*Monsieur L'Amiral Ganteaume, vous appareillerez dans le plus
court délai possible avec notre escadre de Brest forte de 21 vaisseaux,
6 frégates et 2 flûtes . . . vous vous dirigerez d'abord sur le Ferrol
. . . vous ferez au contre-amiral Gourdon . . . le signal de vous
joindre.*

*Ayant ainsie rallié ces escadres, vous vous rendrez par le plus court
chemin dans notre île de Martinique . . .*

Ganteaume was to embark three thousand soldiers and take his
twenty-one battleships, six frigates, and two transports out of Brest
and sail for Ferrol. There he was to beat off the blockading British
ships and fetch out Gourdon's four battleships and two frigates,
and also the Spanish squadron. He was then to sail across the
Atlantic to Martinique, where he would find Villeneuve with the
Toulon squadron and Missiessy. . . . Once at Martinique he was
to join his own twenty-one battleships with Gourdon's four, Villeneuve's eleven and Missiessy's five, making a total force of forty-one
battleships and nineteen frigates, plus the Spanish squadron. He
was then to return to Europe immediately. Arriving off Ushant he
was to attack any British warships he found there and then sail on
to Boulogne, where he was to arrive between June 10 to July 10.

That was the main plan; but Napoleon knew his admirals—
especially Villeneuve—and allowed for eventualities. If Villeneuve
failed to turn up in the West Indies, he told Ganteaume, he would
still have more than twenty-five battleships, and after waiting thirty
days for Villeneuve, he should fight his way through to Boulogne.
If for any reason he had less than twenty-five, he was to sail back
to Ferrol, where he would find every available French and Spanish
warship waiting for him, and without going into port, he would
take them under his command and sail on for Boulogne. Napoleon
then drew up corresponding orders for Villeneuve. He was to sail
from Toulon direct to Cadiz, where he was to pick up a French
74 and the Spanish Admiral Gravina with as many of his fifteen
battleships as were ready. Then he was to sail direct to the West
Indies to join Missiessy and wait for Ganteaume, being ready to
sail immediately he arrived. So this was Napoleon's great plan—
for operations which, he ended his letter to Ganteaume, "will have
so much influence on the destiny of the World. . . ."

But seldom had operations been planned with so little regard for
what the enemy might do. Ganteaume was blockaded in Brest and

would probably have to fight his way out; so would Villeneuve and Gourdon. Ganteaume would have to raise the blockade at Ferrol and Villeneuve at Cadiz. There would be three separate groups of ships crossing the Atlantic and going to the West Indies; he also assumed that the British would not follow even one of them. And if Villeneuve was not at Martinique, Ganteaume was to wait thirty days; if Ganteaume did not arrive, Villeneuve was to wait forty days. In other words, there was to be a minimum wait at Martinique of a month, during which time he assumed the Royal Navy would have done nothing towards the destruction of these ships— an assumption which hardly corresponded with his plan that the Royal Navy should be led to the West Indies in a wild-goose chase.

In addition, Napoleon ignored a basic and age-old tenet of Britain's naval strategy: in a crisis, concentrate on the point of greatest danger. As at the time of the Armada, so now with the constant threat of invasion, the western approaches to the Channel were this focal point. With the Royal Navy holding the western approaches, Napoleon's invasion force could never sail, or if they did, the British squadrons would run up the Channel and destroy them. And for Napoleon's ships to be able to seize control of the Channel, they would have first to defeat the Royal Navy in the western approaches. "Against this fundamental strategy, imperturbably adhered to, all Napoleon's combinations were to be shattered," wrote Desbrière.

NINE

THE GREAT CHASE

*The advantage of time and place in all martial actions
is half a victory, which being lost is irrecoverable . . . .*
—Drake to Elizabeth I, 1588

THE EMPEROR's brave new plan soon started to go adrift. At
Brest, Ganteaume set to work getting his ships manned to their
full strength, taking on board stores, water, powder and shot. The
only thing he could not store was experience. A fortnight later an
impatient Emperor wrote spurring him on with the news that he
had not a moment to lose. "Do not forget the great destinies which
you hold in your hands. If you are not wanting in enterprise,
success is certain."

By March 24, Ganteaume was ready to sail and there was only
one snag: seventeen British battleships were waiting for him outside. It was impossible to sail without risking an engagement: what
should he do? The jerking arms of the telegraph swiftly sped the
question to Paris, but Napoleon's reply completely ignored the
situation. "A naval victory in these circumstances would lead to
nothing. Have but one object, to fulfil your mission. Go out without fighting." Three days later Ganteaume made a half-hearted
attempt to *"Sortez sans combat,"* but the seventeen British battleships soon persuaded him to return. By March 29 his ships were
safely moored up in harbour. And the next day, March 30, Villeneuve made his second attempt to leave Toulon with his eleven
battleships, some frigates and two brigs. The ships had enough
stores for six months, and they carried more than three thousand
soldiers under General Lauriston.

Once again Nelson was not waiting for Villeneuve outside
Toulon; instead two British frigates kept a watch. The reason for
this was that Nelson knew that with the frequent Gulf of Lyons

gales it was impossible to wait outside Toulon all the time, and in any case he wanted to destroy Villeneuve's squadron, not frighten it into staying in port. He knew that once the squadron sailed, it had but two courses open to it—to sail out of the Mediterranean into the Atlantic, or in the direction of Sicily, Sardinia and Egypt. In planning which to cover, he had to decide which was potentially the most dangerous and that was, of course, the route which led towards Egypt.

So Nelson waited off Sardinia, but before doing that he laid a trap. He left Toulon and sailed over to the Spanish coast, rattling the bars and making sure that his fleet was seen and reported to Villeneuve, reasoning that this would prevent the French admiral from sneaking along the Spanish coast—if he intended leaving the Mediterranean—and force him on a more easterly course, where Nelson would be waiting for him. If he was bound eastwards, Nelson was still in the best position. And this plan worked—at first. Villeneuve, sailing before dawn on March 30 and having heard that Nelson had been seen off Barcelona, sailed to the south, to pass outside the Balearic Islands. He wrote to Decrès, "May fortune fulfil the hopes which the Emperor has founded upon the destination of this squadron." Not that he knew the ultimate destination was Boulogne—Napoleon had not mentioned it in his orders, although his instructions to General Lauriston, which were to be opened only at sea, did.

The British frigates shadowed Villeneuve for a short time, and then went off to report to Nelson that the French Fleet was sailing south. But soon after they left, Villeneuve met a merchantman whose captain reported that Nelson, far from being off the Spanish coast, was south of Sardinia. Villeneuve immediately altered course and headed direct for the Strait of Gibraltar while Nelson covered the gap between Sicily and Tunisia, confident that Villeneuve's reported southerly course meant that he was bound for Egypt. He searched for three days, without success. By April 7 he was writing from between Sicily and Tunisia, "I am, in truth, half dead; but what man can do to find them out shall be done," adding, "but I must not make more haste than good speed," and leave Sardinia and Sicily or Naples open to capture. Nor would he search towards Gibraltar until his frigates could bring him definite news. He was covering the point of greatest danger, and although his excited body ("I can neither eat, drink or sleep") gave him no rest, his brain was as cold and calculating as always.

But on April 9, Captain Lord Mark Kerr, at Gibraltar, was startled to see Villeneuve's eleven battleships with attendant frigates and brigs go scudding past into the Atlantic. His own frigate *Fisgard* was being refitted, so he scribbled a note to Nelson, hired a brig and, putting one of his own officers in command, sent him off to the eastward to deliver it as quickly as possible. He set his own crew to work to get the *Fisgard* ready to sail and within four hours —leaving a launch, barge, an anchor, twenty-two tons of water in casks, and a lot of other equipment behind on the quayside—the frigate was at sea. Out in the Atlantic, however, there was no sign of Villeneuve, so Kerr decided to hurry northward with what news he had.[1]

Villeneuve had also been spotted earlier coming through the Strait by Sir Richard Strachan in the *Renown,* who immediately went about and headed for Cadiz to warn Vice-Admiral Sir John Orde, who was blockading the Spanish Admiral Gravina's squadron of fifteen battleships (only a few of which were ready for sea) with a force of four battleships. When the *Renown* came in sight flying the flags for a superior enemy fleet and firing guns to draw attention to her signal, Orde's ships were taking on stores from supply ships. The Admiral promptly cast off the transports and ordered them to head for the neutral waters off Lagos, in Portugal.

Meanwhile Villeneuve steered for Cadiz while Orde made up his mind what to do next. One thing was obvious—he was far outnumbered by Villeneuve's ships, and the French admiral had obviously come to bring out Gravina's squadron. What was more, Orde knew Ganteaume was preparing to sail from Brest. Considering that the combined French and Spanish fleet—which he estimated at nineteen or twenty battleships—could be at sea in forty-eight hours, Orde wrote to the Admiralty: "I think the chances are great in favour of their destination being westward where, by a sudden concentration of several detachments, Bonaparte may hope

[1] Corbett, in *The Campaign of Trafalgar,* is in error in saying that Kerr sailed from Gibraltar in the *Fisgard* the day *after* Villeneuve passed through the Strait. His letter of April 23, 1805, to Lord Gardner, makes this quite clear, as he is using nautical time. Also Nelson's letter to Marsden, dated May 1, says, "As the *Fisgard* sailed from Gibraltar on the 9th, two hours after the enemy's fleet from Toulon passed through the Strait . . ."

to gain a temporary superiority in the Channel, and availing himself of it to strike his enemy a mortal blow."

So, lifting his blockade of Gravina, he took his battleships north to reinforce the British fleet off Brest, which he regarded as the point of greatest danger. For this he was later strongly criticized and condemned.

Captain Lord Mark Kerr, in the meantime, had sped north. He warned one of the British fleet off Ushant on the way, sent a Guernsey privateer into Plymouth with a letter to the Admiralty, and sailed on to raise the alarm in Ireland.

Night was falling as Villeneuve sailed up to Cadiz, and he sent a frigate ahead to signal Gravina that the French battleship and the Spanish ships should sail at once. By the time darkness cut off the land he could see the French battleship, the *Aigle,* and several other ships getting under way, and he anchored his squadron. The anchor of his own flagship, the *Bucentaure,* was hardly down before news came that six Spanish battleships and a frigate would be joining him before midnight, but the dreadful picture of Nelson arriving on the scene like an avenging fury kept bothering him, and he sent his flag-lieutenant ashore to warn Admiral Gravina that "every minute was precious, that the enemy's Mediterranean squadron must be in pursuit and might effect a junction with the force that had blockaded Cadiz up till then and that it was essential to set sail for our destination."

By 2 a.m. next morning the French ships were on their way to Martinique with the Spaniards doing their best to catch up. By daylight only the *Argonaute,* Gravina's flagship, was in company. Villeneuve slowed down during the day and the following night, but daylight showed that only one more Spanish ship, the *America,* had joined. With four other Spanish battleships and a frigate still out of sight astern, Villeneuve's nerve or patience was exhausted. He ordered his ships to cram on sail. It "was not desirable to wait any longer," he wrote. The date was April 11. It was to be May 26 before the rest of the ships joined him—in Martinique.

On April 11 Nelson was off Palermo, in Sicily, a sad and bitter man. At 7 a.m. the day before one of his captains, Hallowell, arrived from Palermo with a report that General Craig's expedition —which unknown to Nelson was intended to operate with Russian forces in southern Italy—had sailed from England. This was the first news he had had of it and it completely changed the picture. The expedition would be an easy prey for Villeneuve. "I may suppose the French fleet are bound to the westward. . . . I am very, very miserable. . . ." So he set sail to the westward, but almost immediately ran into heavy weather and strong head winds which held him up for four days. On the 15th he was joined by a ship bringing more news of Craig's expedition—but still no word of it had come from the Admiralty. He had no idea of its whereabouts. Was it already in the Mediterranean? Had it already fallen foul of Villeneuve and been destroyed? Nelson had no means of knowing.[2] On the 16th he had just signed his name to a letter to the British Minister in Naples, complaining bitterly that the Admiralty had not warned him of Craig's expedition, when serious news arrived that startled him. He added a postscript to the letter: "Noon. A vessel just spoke says that on Sunday, April 7, he saw sixteen ships of war, twelve of them large ships off Cape de Gatte [Cape de Gata, on the Spanish coast south-west of Cartagena] steering to the westward, with the wind at the east. If this account is true, much mischief may be apprehended. It kills me, the very thought."

He decided to go first to Toulon, to make sure that the enemy was not once again returning to port, "and that is all I can tell at the present." If the French Fleet had left the Mediterranean he would go after them. He was still heading for Toulon when, on April 18, a frigate reported that a neutral ship had seen the French squadron go through the Strait of Gibraltar ten days earlier. Nelson rapidly recast his plans. He wrote, "I am going out of the Mediterranean after the French Fleet. It may be thought I have protected too well Sardinia, Naples, Sicily, the Morea [the southern part of Greece] and Egypt from the French; but I feel I have done right, and am, therefore, easy about any fate which may await me for having missed the French Fleet."

His main task had been to keep command of the Mediterranean, and now he decided to leave behind five valuable frigates and other ships "to protect our commerce and to prevent the French sending troops by sea," as he wrote to the Admiralty. By April 19— eight days after Villeneuve left Cadiz for the West Indies—Nelson

2 In fact it was still windbound in England.

had made hardly any progress against strong westerly winds. "My good fortune seems flown away," he wrote to Ball. "I cannot get a fair wind, or even a side wind. Dead foul!—dead foul!"

He wrote to Marsden that he was satisfied that the French Fleet were not heading for the West Indies "but intend forming a junction with the Squadron at Ferrol, and pushing direct for Ireland or Brest, as I believe the French have troops on board." Therefore he would bring his ships—"eleven as fine ships of war, as ably commanded, and in perfect order and in health, as ever went to sea"—up to the approaches to the Channel. But Nelson and his Fleet had many more days of thrashing to windward before they were clear of the Mediterranean. They did not arrive at Tetuan, on the south side of the Strait of Gibraltar, until May 4. While he was anchored there, restocking his ships with food and water, news came from Captain Otway, the Navy Commissioner in Gibraltar, that the general feeling was that Villeneuve had gone to the West Indies.

Nelson was both surprised and puzzled; his own evaluation led him to think that the French Fleet had gone north; now . . . To Otway he wrote grumbling that "I believe my ill-luck is to go on for a longer time." He could not run to the West Indies "without something beyond mere surmise; and if I defer my departure Jamaica may be lost. Indeed, as they have a month's start of me, I see no prospect of getting out time enough [sic] to prevent much mischief from being done."

As he turned over the possibility of the West Indies, the idea seemed to harden in his mind, and a possibility turned into a probability. To Dr. Scott, his chaplain, Nelson commented wryly, "If I fail, if they are not gone to the West Indies, I shall be blamed; to be burnt in effigy or Westminster Abbey is my alternative." He knew how fickle the Press and the public could be.

When the wind came round to the east Nelson gave the order to sail, and once through the Strait he steered northward towards Lisbon, keeping a sharp lookout for the frigate *Amazon*, which had earlier been sent to Lisbon in a last desperate attempt to get some reliable information about Villeneuve, amid the welter of rumours. Next day, May 7, Nelson was still without news. To Marsden he wrote, "If nothing is heard of them from Lisbon or from the frigates I may find off Cape St Vincent's [sic], I shall probably think the rumours are true, that their destination is the

West Indies, and in that case I shall think it my duty to follow them. . . ."

Early on the 9th the Fleet arrived under the cliffs of Cape St. Vincent. Nelson's ships still had not all the necessary stores on board, so they sailed on to Lagos Bay, where Sir John Orde's transports were still at anchor, and while Nelson waited for the *Amazon* his sailors worked like slaves filling their ships' holds. The *Amazon* arrived later with news from the American brig *Louisa*, of Baltimore, commanded by Peter Billings, who reported that a French fleet had arrived at Cadiz on April 9 and several Spanish battleships had sailed. Billings, who had just left Cadiz, said that three thousand Spanish troops, including a great number of cavalry, had been embarked "with great confusion." Seamen were scarce, and "were forced with great reluctance aboard the men-of-war."

That night, May 10, Rear-Admiral Donald Campbell is reported to have gone on board the *Victory* while Nelson's Fleet was still at anchor.[3] Campbell, a British officer employed by the Portuguese, who were using him to help improve their own Navy, is said to have told Nelson, in confidence, that the Combined Fleet was undoubtedly heading for the West Indies.

(The effect this visit had on Campbell's career was disastrous. The French and Spanish Ambassadors in Lisbon succeeded in forcing the Portuguese Government to sack him and he returned to England, where he died in poverty, neither the Admiralty nor the Government lifting a finger to help him.)

That night Nelson, in the great cabin of the *Victory*, reviewed all the factors in his mind. There was little chance now of getting any further information, and he had to decide what to do. Finally he made a decision. "My lot is cast," he wrote to Ball, "and I am going to the West Indies, where, although I am late, yet chance may have given them a bad passage and me a good one." To another friend he wrote, "Disappointment has worn me to a skeleton, and I am, in good truth, very, very far from well." Next day flags run up on the *Victory*'s signal halyards turned his decision into action. His ten battleships and three frigates, provisioned for five

---

[3] Some sources say Campbell went on board at Gibraltar, but since Nelson's mind was not then made up, this seems most improbable. The author has found no conclusive proof that Campbell gave information to Nelson.

months, laboriously weighed anchor and set sail. The chase was on, but Villeneuve had a thirty-one-day start. . . .

In London the Admiralty already knew, on the day Nelson sailed westward towards the setting sun, that the Combined Fleet's destination was almost certainly the West Indies, and the news of Villeneuve's break-out from Toulon could not have arrived at a worse time. On February 13, the commission set up to inquire into the state of the Navy issued a report showing various irregularities in the Navy's finances. The blame fell on the First Lord, Melville, who was a great friend of Pitt. This was just the sort of ammunition the Opposition was waiting for, and while Napoleon in Paris dreamed up his plans for the invasion of England, the Opposition in the Mother of Parliaments planned and schemed to overthrow Pitt and his Government. News that Missiessy had sailed to the West Indies added to the uproar and the debate in the Commons was fixed for April 8.

On that day, while Villeneuve neared the Strait of Gibraltar, constantly watching over his shoulder for Nelson, the Opposition had great sport in the Commons. Pitt fought bravely for Melville, but a vote of censure was put down. And despite all of Pitt's impassioned efforts, it was carried by one vote, that of the Speaker. Next day, as Villeneuve passed Gibraltar and Lord Mark Kerr hastened to get the *Fisgard* to sea, Melville resigned as First Lord. A jubilant Opposition forecast Pitt would soon follow, but they underestimated the Premier's courage. His enemy was Napoleon, not the Opposition, and he was going to carry on the fight. To fill Melville's post he turned, after some party squabbling, to the man who had been both Melville's unofficial adviser and also a kinsman, an eighty-year-old admiral who had never flown his flag at sea, but who was famous in the Service for his strict honesty and ability as an administrator. Admiral Sir Charles Middleton was not a Member of Parliament, so to get over that he was created Lord Barham. On April 21 he took over as First Lord against the wishes of the old King and many of Pitt's own Cabinet.

Two days earlier General Craig's expedition of seven thousand troops, embarked in more than forty ships and escorted by only two battleships, sailed from Spithead bound for Italy. Negotiations with the Czar had up to now been extremely difficult. To Pitt and his Cabinet it seemed that Russian demands were quite unrealistic. The temperament and outlook of the autocratic young Czar Alexander were far removed from those of Downing Street. But the one thing, apparently, that impressed the Czar brooding in the winter fastness of his palace at St. Petersburg was that Britain was prepared to send troops to Italy to fight side by side with a Russian force. So the little army which began its 2,500-mile voyage from Spithead, and which had to pass five ports holding sizable enemy squadrons—Brest, Ferrol, Cadiz, Cartagena and Toulon—contained Britain's hopes for the future. As it ran down the Channel and into the Bay of Biscay it passed two other ships heading north, the *Fisgard,* with the resourceful Lord Mark Kerr on board, taking the news to Ireland that Villeneuve was in the Atlantic, and the Guernsey lugger *Greyhound,* a privateer to whom Kerr had entrusted a letter to the Admiralty, and which was heading for Plymouth.

The news reached Barham at the Admiralty on April 25, four days after he took over his new office, and a fortnight after Villeneuve had left Cadiz. There was little in it to cheer him but, being a man with an immense knowledge of naval strategy, there was not much to alarm him. He already knew Villeneuve had been embarking troops at Toulon, and Pitt's spies had warned him to expect an attack on the West Indies. Barham therefore thought at first that Villeneuve would probably join Missiessy in the West Indies. A British squadron under Cochrane had already sailed to cover Missiessy. Working alone in his office near the Board Room, Barham drafted his first order. This was to Gibraltar, ordering the senior officer present to send two battleships to reinforce Cochrane in the West Indies if Nelson had not followed Villeneuve.

Two days later, on April 27, Barham had some doubts about Nelson's moves, knowing that he would most probably cast to the eastward first unless he had definite news that Villeneuve had gone westward to the Strait. So he decided to send part of the flying squadron under Collingwood direct to the West Indies. This would weaken the force off Brest under Lord Gardner (who had taken over from Cornwallis), but to make up for it the dockyards were working night and day to get more ships to sea. But before the orders to detach Collingwood reached him Gardner had re-

ceived some startling news: Villeneuve's sudden arrival at Cadiz
had caused Orde to fall back. Gardner therefore decided to use
his discretion and not send Collingwood to the West Indies until
further orders arrived from Barham.

As soon as Barham heard that Orde no longer guarded Cadiz
and that Villeneuve and Gravina had linked up, he realized that
Craig's expedition, on which so much depended, was sailing possibly to its destruction. The news was sent round to Number 10
Downing Street on April 29 to await Pitt's return from the House
of Commons. The Premier had had a terrible day: the Opposition
had set up a loud clamour over the report of the Navy Commission,
and in the rough-and-tumble put down a motion aimed at bringing
Lord Melville to trial. Pitt, a sick man, had fought back and the
motion was beaten. Melville was saved—temporarily.

When Pitt got back to Downing Street it was 2 a.m. on the
morning of April 30. He read through the papers waiting for him
—and realized they contained dreadful news. There was Barham's
report that Craig's expedition was in mortal danger, and also reports from one of his spies, who signed himself *"L'Ami,"* saying
that Villeneuve was probably heading for Jamaica, and a later one
saying that Napoleon was trying to divert the Royal Navy from his
real attack. The weary Pitt sat down to write a note to Barham
saying that "We must not lose a moment in taking measure to set
afloat every ship that by any species of extraordinary exertion we
can find means to man. . . ."

Later next day the old Admiral and the young Prime Minister
(whose forty-sixth and last birthday was but twenty-eight days off)
met and discussed plans. Then Barham went back to the Admiralty
to turn their decisions into orders. These aimed at three main
objectives—to save Craig's convoy from annihilation, to keep Ferrol
blockaded, and to block the western approaches should Orde's
guess that the Combined Fleet's destination was the Channel prove
correct. The key figure in Barham's consideration was, of course,
Nelson: Where was he? Had he gone to Egypt? News took a long
time to travel, and for this reason Barham's orders to the various
commands were complex and overlapping.

The main point that concerns this narrative is that Collingwood
was ordered to take Craig's convoy under his wing and escort it as
far as Cape St. Vincent. If he met Nelson, he was to place himself

under the Admiral's command. But if he discovered that Nelson had not followed Villeneuve to the West Indies Collingwood was himself to go in pursuit.

Although Barham had the situation well in hand, the rest of the country was far from calm. The *Morning Chronicle* spoke for many people when it said: "During the eight days which have just passed no one has slept in peace. Judge of the situation in which our Ministers have placed us when they have reduced us to hope that the French will content themselves with going to conquer our colonial possessions and ravage our settlements."

Admiral Lord Radstock wrote on May 13 to his son, whom he thought was still in the *Victory* but who had been transferred to the *Hydra,* "Where are you all this time? For that is a point justly agitating the whole country more than I can describe. I fear your gallant and worthy chief will have much injustice done him on this occasion, for the cry is stirring up fast against him, and the loss of Jamaica would at once sink all his past services into oblivion."

A week later he reported that "You may readily guess that your chief is not out of our thoughts at this critical moment. Should Providence once more favour him, he will be considered our guardian angel; but on the other hand, should he unfortunately take a wrong scent, and the Toulon Fleet attain the object, the hero of the 14th of February [the battle of Cape St. Vincent] and of Aboukir [the battle of the Nile] will be—I will not say what, but the ingratitude of the world is but too well known on these occasions."

Then, on June 4, the man of whom all Britain wanted news arrived at Barbados, and on the same day three letters which he had sent off a month earlier were delivered to Marsden at the Admiralty. They described his chase to Gibraltar, and said that he had now provisioned his ships for five months and was sailing for Barbados . . . Nelson had done it!

TEN

THE RENDEZVOUS

Now mark me how I will undo myself . . .
—Shakespeare (*Richard II*)

VILLENEUVE had arrived in the West Indies on May 16, and at
Martinique he settled down to wait for Ganteaume. Having missed
the latest instructions from France, Missiessy was on his way back
to Europe. It was not long before new orders from Napoleon began
to arrive. The Emperor, seeing that Ganteaume and his powerful
fleet were penned up in Brest, told Villeneuve, via General Lauriston, that he was sending Rear-Admiral Magon out to the West
Indies with two battleships from Rochefort. If, thirty-five days after
Magon's arrival, Villeneuve had not received any fresh orders and
he deemed it "proper and prudent" to return to Europe, he should
go to Ferrol. There fifteen French and Spanish battleships would
be waiting, and with this force—Napoleon estimated it at more than
fifty battleships—Villeneuve was to "enter the Strait of Dover and
join me off Boulogne." Villeneuve replied that he could not wait
for thirty-five days after Magon arrived—"I beg of you," he wrote to
Decrès, "to observe that the state of my stores absolutely forbids my
waiting until so remote a date."

Admiral Magon arrived in Martinique on June 4, bringing Villeneuve's fleet up to twenty battleships. But on that day another
fleet arrived in the West Indies. "At daylight saw Barbados bearing
west ten leagues. . . . At eleven received salutes of Rear-Admiral
Cochrane and Charles Fort . . . ," wrote Nelson in his private diary.

Villeneuve left Martinique on June 5, the day after Magon arrived, planning to attack some British-held islands to the north.
Instead, his fleet captured fourteen merchantmen—not a difficult
task, since they were escorted by only a 14-gun schooner. But from

prisoners Villeneuve heard some dreadful news: Nelson had arrived in the West Indies "with twelve or fourteen of the line."

The French did not know what to do next. "In this dilemma," he wrote, "I desired to confer with Admiral Gravina. I found him fully agreed as to the necessity of immediately making our way back to Ferrol, there to effect our junction [as Napoleon had ordered]. . . . I therefore determined for the greatest advantage to the state, to set sail for Europe." And on June 11, a week after Nelson's arrival in the West Indies, Villeneuve and his fleet were heading eastward.

Nelson had, in the meantime, searched first to the southward, owing to a mistaken report, and then come north again. On the 13th, two days after Villeneuve, he "sailed in my pursuit of the enemy," guessing they had gone back to Cadiz or Toulon. Just before he finally decided to sail for Europe Nelson wrote some letters. One, to Marsden at the Admiralty, said that when he finally returned to European waters he would "take their Lordships' permission to go to England, to try and repair a very shattered constitution." A postscript added fresh news which had just been received. "The French fleet passed to leeward of Antigua on Saturday last, standing to the northward . . . [and I] hope to sail in the morning after them for the Straits mouth." To a friend in London he wrote: "I have only a moment to say I am going towards the Mediterranean after Gravina and Villeneuve, and hope to catch them." And to the Duke of Clarence, he said: "My heart is almost broke, and, with my very serious complaints I cannot expect long to go on."

These and other letters were given to Captain G. Bettesworth, of the 18-gun brig *Curieux,* with orders that he was to sail straight to England and deliver them to the Admiralty. Nelson now knew he was close behind the Combined Fleet: the gap of thirty-one days between them had in fact been reduced to two days. On the 19th, when he was six hundred miles out into the Atlantic from Antigua, an American ship, the *Sally,* gave him the enemy's position. Nelson wrote to Marsden, "I think we cannot be more than eighty leagues [240 miles] from them at this moment, and by carrying every sail, and using my utmost efforts, I shall hope to close with them before they get to either Cadiz or Toulon."

Once again he was to be unlucky. He crossed Villeneuve's tracks one night and for the rest of the voyage back to Europe the Combined Fleet was to be to the north of him. But Captain Bettesworth of the *Curieux* had better luck: sailing a more northerly course because he was bound for the United Kingdom, he spotted the Combined Fleet. It was so far north that he realized it was bound for somewhere in the Bay of Biscay, and not the Strait of Gibraltar, as Nelson expected. Should he dash back to warn Nelson, or press on to warn Barham? Quite rightly he decided to sail on and warn the Admiralty. Nelson, however, was having second thoughts. He sent a frigate to warn the admiral blockading Ferrol to watch for the returning enemy; Captain Sutton, in the frigate *Amphion,* was sent ahead to Tangier to find out if the Combined Fleet had gone into the Mediterranean; later the *Amazon* was sent to search off Cape St. Vincent and Cadiz.

In the meantime Napoleon was busy changing his plans. Realizing that Villeneuve would not be able to wait thirty-five days in the West Indies, he ordered him to come back to Europe as quickly as possible, free the squadrons of Gourdon, Missiessy and Ganteaume, and get to the Channel—"the principal object of the whole operation is to procure our superiority before Boulogne for some days." However, if Villeneuve could not do all this, he was to go to Cadiz. Unfortunately for Napoleon, these orders arrived in the West Indies after Villeneuve had sailed. . . . In Rochefort, Commodore Allemand succeeded Missiessy and was told that if the British blockade lifted, he was to go to sea and wait for Villeneuve 120 miles west of Ferrol from July 29 to August 3.

The *Curieux* arrived at Plymouth on July 7 and Captain Bettesworth immediately rushed to London with Nelson's letters and his own news of sighting the Combined Fleet. As a result of this sighting, Barham straightway changed his plans. Previously he had reinforced Collingwood's weak force off Cadiz to make "a strong force at the very spot where they might be expected." Now here was Bettesworth reporting that the Combined Fleet was heading farther north. He therefore sent off orders reinforcing Calder's squadron and ordering it to patrol from 30 to 150 miles to the west of Cape Finisterre. These orders were written by the octogenarian

First Lord early in the morning a few minutes after waking and before he had time to dress. They were contained in half a dozen lines scribbled on a piece of paper, and they were quite sufficient.

On July 22 Villeneuve, with his twenty French and Spanish battleships, ran into Calder's fifteen battleships off Cape Finisterre. Beginning in the late afternoon, the battle lasted four hours in bad visibility. Calder captured two of Villeneuve's battleships and Villeneuve damaged several of the British ships. "A very decisive ac-

A barque.

tion," wrote Calder, who was to be court-martialled later for not doing his utmost to renew the battle. Villeneuve naturally saw it differently. "The enemy then made off. . . . He had had several ships crippled aloft, and the field of battle remained ours. Cries of joy and victory were heard from all our ships." But Calder prevented Villeneuve's going into Ferrol, and the next day Villeneuve decided to steer for Cadiz. Then bad weather sprang up and he changed his mind and ran in to Vigo. The Combined Fleet was back in port—and its troubles were only just starting.

Hopefully Nelson had sailed back across the Atlantic, praying that he would catch up with Villeneuve. On June 21 he wrote in his private diary: "Midnight, nearly calm, saw three planks, which I think came from the French fleet. Very miserable, which is very foolish." Nearly a month later, with the African shore close by, he wrote another entry: "Cape Spartel in sight, but no French fleet, nor any information about them—how sorrowful this makes me, but I cannot help myself!" Nelson finally anchored his fleet at Gibraltar on July 19. He wrote once again in his private diary on the 20th: "I went on shore for the first time since the 16th of June, 1803; and from having my foot out of the *Victory*, two years wanting ten days."

In a letter to Barham he said: "I have yet not a word of information of the enemy's fleet; it has almost broken my heart." But on July 25 a ship arrived with a Lisbon newspaper which told him about Bettesworth's glimpse of the Combined Fleet, and the position was so far north that Nelson guessed Villeneuve must have been making for the Bay of Biscay. He immediately sailed northward—running into strong head winds—to join the Brest fleet off Ushant. "I shall only hope, after my long pursuit of *my* enemy, that I may arrive at the moment they are meeting you; for my very wretched state of health will force me to get on shore for a little while," he wrote to Cornwallis, who was once again off Brest.

But, as we have seen, Nelson was too late: by the time he joined Cornwallis, Villeneuve was safe in Vigo. Then, worn out and with an ever-increasing sense of failure weighing him down, Nelson left his ships under Cornwallis's command and sailed for Portsmouth in the *Victory*, taking only the battered old *Superb*, commanded by Richard Keats, with him.

ELEVEN

TWENTY-FIVE DAYS

*I was only twenty-five days, from dinner to dinner,
absent from the* Victory. *In our several stations, my dear
Admiral, we must all put our shoulders to the wheel, and
make the great machine of the Fleet intrusted to our charge
go on smoothly.* —Nelson, 30th September, 1805

THE WIND was very light, and with irritating slowness the *Victory*
worked her way up the Channel. Daylight on August 17 showed
Portland Bill over on the port beam, with Weymouth Bay stretching away on the bow and farther ahead the heavy indistinct masses,
dark and menacing, in the chilly early mist, of St. Alban's Head
and Anvil Point.

A day earlier Nelson received the first news of how England had
reacted to Calder's action. Although worried about the reception
in England of his own failure to capture Villeneuve—he feared the
worst—he wrote to his friend Captain Thomas Fremantle that he
"was in truth bewildered by the account of Sir Robert Calder's victory, and the joy of the event; together with the hearing that *John
Bull* was not content, which I am sorry for. Who can, my dear
Fremantle, command all the success which our Country may wish?

"We have fought together [at Copenhagen], and therefore well
know what it is. I have had the best disposed fleet of friends, but
who can say what will be the event of a battle? And it most sincerely grieves me, that in any of the papers it should be insinuated,
that Lord Nelson could have done better. I should have fought the
enemy, so did my friend Calder; but who can say that he will be
more successful than another—I only wish to stand upon my own
merits, and not by comparison, one way or the other, upon the conduct of a brother officer."

The wind was still light as the day passed and it was dark by the time the *Victory* nosed past St. Catherine's Point and then, after losing the wind altogether, anchored off Dunnose Head. She was there for nearly six hours while Nelson waited impatiently, anxious to be on his way to Merton Place, where his beloved Emma was waiting for him.

In addition to being tired after two years and three months at sea, he was anxious at the reception that might be waiting for him, both from the crowds probably waiting at the quay and at the Admiralty, where Lord Barham was an almost complete stranger. He had all the misgivings that bedevil a long absence. There were, however, more delays. The *Victory* got under way just before dawn and sailed round to Spithead, but Nelson was not allowed ashore because there was yellow fever in Spain and Portugal, and the *Victory* had, of course, called at Gibraltar. Despite his protestations that there was no fever there "nor any apprehension of one" when he left, and that "neither the *Victory* nor the *Superb* have on board even an object for the hospital," he had to stay in the ship for another day—until the evening of the 19th.

By the time his barge reached the shore a large cheering crowd had gathered. After a courtesy call on the Commander-in-Chief, Nelson went along to the George, in the High Street, to wait for a postchaise. Rain was pouring down when finally he climbed into the carriage and the horses plunged forward up the London road. It was a wearisome journey through the night with raindrops streaming down the windows of the coach, but dawn brought Nelson his first sight for many months of the lush green fields. At 6 a.m., tired, cramped, dusty and yet excited, he reached Merton.

His home was a red-brick, two-storey house. A tributary of the River Wandle—Lady Hamilton called it "the Nile"—passed through the grounds and a previous owner had built an elaborate, Italian-style bridge across it. Many strange trees grew round the house and Virginia creeper climbed over the porch. And now his dreams had come true—he was back again, with Emma to welcome him. Soon they were laughing with their daughter Horatia, now four and a half and learning to play the piano.

His first day at Merton was spent quietly. Various members of his family were staying there, and apart from the uncertainty of his meeting with Barham, there was little to trouble him. He was a vice-admiral and viscount, and when he set foot in the streets the crowds cheered him for a popular hero. He loved a woman deeply and was deeply loved in return. The fact that the woman was not his wife did not damage that love; perhaps it made it more urgent.

At long last he had a home befitting his position—even though he still had to repay the money he had borrowed to buy it. Horatia had been born, and successfully passed off as his adopted daughter. The ruse did nothing to lessen his love for her. He knew he had the love and respect of his captains; his circle of friends was a large one.

For the next three weeks Nelson was to be busy discussing high policy with the nation's leaders, knowing his opinion was wanted and listened to with great interest. He knew, as will be seen, that his days were numbered; yet these few remaining days were perhaps the happiest of his life. He was a man consumed with zeal and ambition—ambition for his King and for his country. Now these emotions were being recognized and fulfilled. Although he had to die, he was to die content.

Next morning, August 21, he set off early for London with Emma. Whitehall was an hour's drive from Merton, and Emma left him at the Admiralty at 9.30 a.m., going on to her little house in Clarges Street.

It is unlikely that Nelson was looking forward to his meeting with Lord Barham when his carriage clattered through the narrow Whitehall entrance of the Admiralty. There is no doubt that Barham was, not unreasonably, suspicious of the vain and colourful young Admiral. Had Nelson's conduct in his long and fruitless chase of Villeneuve been all that it should have been? Could he be trusted once again with command in the Mediterranean during what were obviously going to be extremely critical days?

The shrewd old First Lord was certainly determined not to let Nelson's previous victories at the Nile and Copenhagen blind him to possible faults or errors of judgement. In fact Nelson had been greeted, on arriving in England, with a request that he forward journals for the First Lord's inspection. It was at that period an unusual thing to do, but typical of Barham's sensible, down-to-earth approach. From his chilly reply Nelson apparently read into the request a possible criticism of his conduct—a point about which he was already very sensitive, as we have seen—and he replied to

Marsden: "I beg leave to acquaint you that never having been called upon (or understanding it to be customary) as Commander-in-Chief to furnish their Lordships with a journal of my proceedings, none has been kept for that purpose, except for different periods the fleet under my command was in pursuit of the enemy . . . which I herewith transmit for the information of the Lords Commissioners of the Admiralty."

The happy result is reported by Nelson's biographers, writing only a short time after the event. Lord Barham "perused the whole narrative with an attention which enabled that Minister to form a more complete idea of the Admiral's professional character; and Lord Barham afterwards liberally declared he had not before sufficiently appreciated such extraordinary talents. This opinion of the noble Admiral's late proceedings was immediately communicated to the Cabinet, with an assurance from Lord Barham that unbounded confidence ought to be placed in Nelson; who was above all others the officer to be employed on the station he had so ably watched, and whose political relations he had so thoroughly understood." We have no reason to think that the biographers exaggerated, because every door in Whitehall was opened to Nelson. He saw Mr. Pitt and Lord Castlereagh almost immediately, and later reported to his friend Keats that both men "were all full of the enemy's fleet, and as I am now set up for a *Conjuror,* and God knows they will very soon find out I am far from being one, I was asked my opinion, against my inclination, for if I make one wrong guess the charm will be broken. . . . You will see [by] my writing tackle that I am not mounted as Commander-in-Chief."

The discussions he had with Pitt and Castlereagh during the next few days covered a wide range of subjects. Russia, after a lot of delaying, had just signed the new treaty and should already be marching through Austria. The time was rapidly coming for Craig's attack from southern Italy, although it was not yet known whether he had reached Malta. On the other hand the Neapolitan kingdom might give way to Napoleon before Craig arrived. Nelson's knowledge of the Mediterranean in general and the Kingdom of Naples in particular was invaluable, though his suggestions for securing Sardinia as a powerful base were less well received.

Nelson had many other calls to make and people to see. One visit was to Mr. Peddison in Brewer Street, off Regent Street. Mr.

Peddison was an upholsterer who had in his care Nelson's coffin. This was a gift from Captain Benjamin Hallowell, a burly Canadian with the build and face of a prize-fighter. A devoted friend of Nelson's—they had slept in the same trench at the siege of Calvi and fought together at Cape St. Vincent—he had, at the battle of the Nile, commanded the *Swiftsure*. After the French *L'Orient* blew up, part of her mainmast was brought on board. Hallowell (according to his brother-in-law, Rear-Admiral Inglefield), fearing the effect of all the praise and flattery being heaped on Nelson, ordered a coffin to be made from it. He gave instructions that nothing should be used which had not come from the mast. Nails and staples were made from metal fittings, and when the coffin was completed a piece of paper was pasted on the bottom saying "I do hereby certify that every part of this coffin is made from the wood and iron of *L'Orient,* most of which was picked up by His Majesty's ship under my command, in the Bay of Aboukir. *Swiftsure,* May 23, 1797—BEN HALLOWELL."

He then sent the coffin to Nelson with a covering letter: "My Lord, Herewith I send you a coffin made of part of the *L'Orient*'s mainmast, that when you are tired of this life you may be buried in one of your own trophies—but may that period be far distant, is the sincere wish of your obedient and much obliged servant, BEN HALLOWELL." Although the officers aboard the Admiral's flagship were appalled when they saw the coffin being brought on board, Nelson was delighted. Far from being disturbed by a constant reminder of his mortality, he had it placed upright, with the lid on, against the bulkhead of his cabin, behind the chair on which he sat at dinner.[1] It was finally removed after "the entreaties of an old servant" and ended up in Mr. Peddison's care at Brewer Street until its owner was ready for it.

Now, apparently having a premonition that he would shortly be making his last voyage, Nelson went to have a look at it and also give some more instructions. Made entirely of half-inch-thick planks of fir, the outside was covered in fine black cloth. Mr. Peddison's upholsterers had made a good job of the inside, which was padded with cotton and then lined with silk, the top being trimmed with a

---

[1] Nelson, seeing his officers looking at it one day, said: "You may look at it, gentlemen, as long as you please; but, depend on it, none of you shall have it."

quilting of mitred silk. The coffin was six feet long but narrow. Nelson inspected the upholstery and then told Mr. Peddison to have the wording of Hallowell's certificate of authenticity engraved on the lid, "for," he said, "I think it highly probable that I may want it on my return."

Among his many visits, both ministerial and macabre, Nelson found time to entertain a Danish author. Mr. Andreas Andersen Feldborg had met Nelson accidentally in Pall Mall and this led him to pay a call on August 26, when the Admiral had been at home at Merton for nearly a week. An erudite man who spoke fluent Russian, Feldborg had published a slim book on the battle of Copenhagen, which a year earlier had been translated into English and published in London. He had sent a presentation copy to the victor, and thanks to this urge to talk with him we can get a glimpse of Nelson at the height of his power and within a few weeks of his death, for Feldborg, under the pseudonym of "J. A. Andersen," was preparing another volume, finally published four years after Trafalgar. Called *A Dane's Excursions in Britain,* it describes his first visit to Merton.

"Merton Place is not a large, but a very elegant, structure; in the balconies I observed a great number of ladies, who I understood to be Lord Nelson's relations," he wrote. "Entering the house I proceeded through a lobby, which, among a variety of paintings, and other pieces of art, contained an excellent marble bust of the illustrious Admiral. . . . I was then ushered into a magnificent apartment, where Lady Hamilton sat at the window; I at first scarcely observed his Lordship, he having placed himself immediately at the entrance on the right. The Admiral wore a uniform emblazoned with different orders of knighthood; he received me with the utmost condescension.[2]

"Chairs being provided, Lord Nelson sat down between Lady Hamilton and myself, and having laid an account of the Battle of Copenhagen on his knee crosswise, a conversation ensued [of] which I strongly imprinted on my memory the following particulars." The conversation, according to Feldborg, was as follows, with Nelson saying:

---

[2] Feldborg uses the word "condescension" in the sense of "kindliness." Nelson's chaplain, writing after the Admiral's death, uses the word in the same way.

"It seems you have written an account of the Battle of Copenhagen, sir!"

"I have, my Lord."

"Well, sir! Since we did not fight the Danes from choice, I hope we are friends again."

"I trust so, my Lord, since the obstinacy of their resistance has so eminently tended to exalt the character of the Danes in the opinion of the British nation."

"I have found a passage in your account, which is not, perhaps, quite correct, sir." Nelson paused for some time, and then continued: "However, in the distribution of shadow, you would of course hold the pencil in a manner different from what an Englishman would have done."

Feldborg said he was going to publish in English a book on Denmark and Norway soon, and Nelson asked: "You intend to embellish the work with a portrait of the Crown Prince of Denmark? Come with me, and you shall see your Prince." The two men went upstairs, where Nelson pointed out a portrait. "Descending from the drawing-room, Lord Nelson paused on the staircase, the walls of which were adorned with prints of his Lordship's battles, and other naval engagements; he pointed out to me the Battle of Copenhagen, which was a tolerably correct engraving," commented Feldborg.

As frequently as he was able, the Dane closely observed the man who, on the eve of Good Friday four years earlier, had sailed past Kronborg Castle to attack nineteen ships and floating batteries off Copenhagen in a battle which broke up one of Napoleon's most cherished ambitions—a Northern coalition against Britain. Mr. Feldborg was impressed with what he saw: "Lord Nelson was in his person of a middle stature, a thin body, and an apparently delicate constitution. The lines of his face were hard; but the penetration of his eye threw a kind of light on his countenance which tempered its severity, and rendered his harsh features in some measure agreeable. His luxuriant hair flowed in graceful ringlets down his temples, and his aspect commanded the utmost veneration, especially when he looked upward. Lord Nelson had not the least pride of rank; but combined with that degree of dignity, which a man of quality should have, the most engaging address in his air and manners."

Another man whom Nelson met was Henry Addington, now Viscount Sidmouth, whose weak and vacillating premiership had been superseded by that of Pitt. "Lord Nelson surprised me yesterday in Clifford Street," Sidmouth recorded, "without my coat, just as I had undergone the operation of bleeding. He looked well, and we passed an hour together very comfortably."

The Admiral met a deputation from the committee of merchants of London trading to the West Indies. The merchants had unanimously agreed "That the prompt determination of Lord Nelson to quit the Mediterranean" in search of the French Fleet had been "very instrumental to the safety of the West India islands."

And he found time, in the evenings, for entertainment. Lady Bessborough reported the gossip from one dinner table to Lord Leveson-Gower: "Bess [Lady Elizabeth Foster] and Ca [Lady Exeter's son] din'd at Crawford's Tuesday to meet him. Both she and he say that so far from appearing vain and full of himself, as one has always heard, he was perfectly unassuming and natural. Talking of popular applause and his having been mobbed and huzza'd in the City, Lady Hamilton wanted him to give an account of it, but he stopped her: 'Why,' she said, 'you like to be applauded —you cannot deny it.' 'I own it,' he answered, 'popular applause is very acceptable and grateful to me, but no man ought to be too much elated by it; it is too precarious to be depended upon, and as it may be my turn to feel the tide set as strong against me as ever it did for me.'

"Everybody joined in saying they did not believe that it could happen to him, but he seemed persuaded that it might, but added: 'Whilst I live I shall do what I think right and best; the country has a right to that from me, but every man is liable to err in judgement. . . .' He says nothing short of the annihilation of the enemy's fleet will do any good. 'When we meet, God be with us, for we must not part again till one fleet or other is totally destroyed.' He hopes to be returned by Christmas. . . ."

Later she wrote: "Lord Holland says Lady Hamilton told the Fish [Mr. James Crawford] that if she could be Lord Nelson's wife for one hour she should die contented, and that he always invokes her in his prayers before action, and during the battle cries out very often, 'For Emma and England.' "

Nelson's favourite, Richard Keats, who had returned to England with the *Superb* at the same time as the *Victory*, soon arrived at Merton Place. He and Nelson walked through the grounds together, talking cheerfully as they skirted "the Nile" with its ornate bridge, and passed from the sunshine into the shade of the tall cedars of Lebanon. The two old friends were soon talking of naval battles. Nelson said: "No day can be long enough to arrange a couple of fleets, and fight a decisive battle, according to the old system.

The wheel and tiller: the tiller ropes go from the barrel of the wheel down to the tiller—a horizontal beam on the head of the rudder. In front of the men is the binnacle, containing the compass. The wheel would normally be double—the forward one is not shown.

"When *we* meet them [Keats was expected to be with him], for meet them we shall, I'll tell you how I shall fight them. I shall form the fleet into three divisions in three lines. One division shall be composed of twelve or fourteen of the fastest two-decked ships, which I shall keep always to windward, or in a situation of advantage; and I shall put them under an officer who, I am sure, will employ them in the manner I wish, if possible.

"I consider it will always be in my power to throw them into battle in any part I may choose; but if circumstances prevent their being carried against the enemy where I desire, I shall feel certain he will employ them effectually, and, perhaps, in a more advantageous manner than if he could have followed my orders.

"With the remaining part of the fleet formed in two lines I shall go at them at once, if I can, about one-third of their line from their leading ships."

Keats, describing the rest of the conversation, wrote: "He then said, 'What do you think of it?' Such a question, I felt, required consideration. I paused. Seeing it, he said, 'But I'll tell you what I think of it. I think it will confound and surprise the enemy. They won't know what I am about. It will bring forward a pell-mell battle, and that is what I want.' "

Richard Keats, although he was destined to miss the battle, appears to have been the first to have heard from Nelson his plan of attack, which he was to modify when he finally caught the Combined Fleet. The other person who heard his plan was Lord Sidmouth. Nelson went over to Richmond Park to see him several days after he knew he was to rejoin the Fleet. Sidmouth's biographer says, "His Lordship was accustomed in after years to relate to his friends interesting particulars of this interview. Among other things, Lord Nelson explained to him with his finger, on the little study table, the manner in which, should he be so fortunate as to meet the Combined Fleet, he purposed to attack them. 'Rodney,' he said, 'broke the line in one point; I will break it in two.' "[3]

---

[3] A tablet which Sidmouth later had inscribed and put on the table stated that Nelson said "he should attack them in two lines, led by himself and Admiral Collingwood [he had not mentioned Collingwood's name to Keats]; and felt confident that he would capture either their van and centre; or centre and rear."

TWELVE

NEW AT LAST

Happy thou art not;
For what thou hast not, still thou strivest to get;
And what thou hast, forgett'st.
　　　　　　　　　—Shakespeare (*Measure for Measure*)

THE NOISE of a dusty postchaise drawn by four horses clattering up the drive at five o'clock in the morning on Monday, September 2, warned Nelson—who was already up, shaved and dressed—either that urgent orders were coming from the Admiralty or, judging from the time, an important and unexpected visitor was arriving. It turned out to be a visitor—a tired man whose round and ruddy, sun-burned features with an incongruous aquiline nose were more those of a rich farmer than the naval captain that his creased uniform proclaimed him. And when he was ushered in, Nelson's face lit up, for he was Henry Blackwood of the *Euryalus*, at thirty-five years of age one of the greatest frigate captains the Navy has ever had, and whom Nelson knew had been watching the French.

As Blackwood gripped Nelson's left hand in greeting, the Admiral exclaimed: "I am sure you bring me news of the French and Spanish fleets, and I think I shall yet have to beat them!"

And that was, indeed, why Blackwood had called: searching for the enemy after the Combined Fleet left Ferrol and Corunna, he had found them off Cape St. Vincent and shadowed them. He had been chased but held on until he made sure the enemy had gone into Cadiz. Then, using every trick of seamanship he knew to keep the *Euryalus*'s sails drawing in fluky winds which strained every ounce of his patience, Blackwood hurried north to raise the alarm. Sixty miles from Cape St. Vincent he met Calder who, as soon as he heard Blackwood's news, sped south to join Collingwood's small force and slam the door on Cadiz.

Within ten days Blackwood had reached the jagged rocky outcrop at the western tip of the Isle of Wight so aptly named the Needles, but night was coming on—which meant the telegraph from Portsmouth to London could not be used—and the wind was falling away. The quickest way now of getting his news to London was to go himself. So he had taken the *Euryalus* into Alum Bay and anchored in the lee of the Needles. As soon as a boat was lowered he had been rowed across the Solent to Lymington Creek, as it was then called, and between the salt pans and mud flats flanking the river up to the village of Lymington, then sleeping on the edge of the New Forest. Hiring a postchaise and four—he later sent the Admiralty a £15 9s. bill for the journey—he was soon rattling northward into the gloomy New Forest, startling the sturdy wild ponies as they grazed beside the road and bound for the Admiralty by way of Merton.

His brief message to Nelson delivered, Blackwood climbed back into his carriage and the driver started off again. Nelson, left behind in the chilly house, had to break to Emma the news which she had been dreading to hear yet knew must one day arrive. There are several apocryphal accounts of that conversation which need not be repeated here, but she described her feelings two days later in a letter to Nelson's niece. "I am again heartbroken," she said, "as our dear Nelson is immediately going. It seems as though I have had a fortnight's dream, and am awoke to all the misery of this cruel separation. But what can I do? His powerful arm is of so much consequence to his country. . . . My heart is broken."

Nelson's exclamation at whatever reply Emma had made is, however, on record: "Brave Emma! Good Emma!" he said. "If there were more Emmas there would be more Nelsons." And within a short time the pair of them were in a carriage chasing up the London road after Blackwood, Nelson bound for the Admiralty and Emma, after leaving him there, for her house in Clarges Street.

Nelson knew beyond doubt that his hour had come. As he wrote later to his friend Davison, "I hope my absence will not be long, and that I shall soon meet the Combined Fleets with a force sufficient to do the job well; for half a victory would but half content me. But I do not believe the Admiralty can give me a force within fifteen or sixteen sail of the line of the enemy . . . but I will do my best; and I hope God Almighty will go with me. I have much to lose, but little to gain; and I go because it's right, and I will serve the country faithfully."

Lord Barham was in his little office at the Admiralty when Nelson strode into the hall, turned left past the small, bare waiting-room, where in a few weeks his body would be lying in Ben Hallowell's coffin for a brief few hours before the funeral at St. Paul's Cathedral, and up the narrow stairs. The old and white-haired First Lord and the young Admiral sat down to discuss plans upon which, quite simply, the whole safety and future of Britain depended; plans which could make history take a sharp turn; plans which could and would affect the future of the world for more than a century.[1] Fortunately, both men knew it. They were superb strategists and for once war plans were being made which paid no court to fickle chance, and which were not hurried half-measures drawn up by amateurs to placate an angry and alarmed Parliament nor desperate attempts to plug the breach after some ill-digested scheme dreamed up by ineffectual ministerial office-holders had inevitably gone awry.

Both Barham and Nelson knew they had a most formidable task before them. The over-all situation in Europe at this time, as far as British policy was concerned, was extremely delicate. The Czar had at last ratified the Anglo-Russian treaty—the despatch from St. Petersburg revealing this had arrived on August 22, and furthermore he was sending an army to help Austria. Austria in turn had said she would adhere to the Third Coalition, but first she wanted to try to mediate. At the same time the Russians were becoming impatient for action in southern Italy: their General Lacy was waiting for Craig to arrive, and London still did not know where Craig's convoy was. While they waited anxiously, they knew that Napoleon's emissaries were trying to frighten the Neapolitan Court. . . .

But Blackwood's news that Villeneuve was in Cadiz eased their

[1] If the Royal Navy lost control of the sea, then the Army could not have been transported to strike back at Napoleon; by the same token Napoleon would have been free to strike where he wished.

minds on one point: while at sea the Combined Fleet had been a powerful threat both to Craig and to British shipping returning from the four corners of the world. There was, for instance, the rich convoy from India, valued at £15 million, which was also bringing back a young major-general named Sir Arthur Wellesley, the future Duke of Wellington, but now thirty-six and fresh from his victories at Assaye and Argaon.

The precise problem now facing Barham and Nelson was how to deal with the new situation brought about by Villeneuve's move to Cadiz. Villeneuve had a total of thirty-three battleships in that port, while Allemand was at sea with four more battleships, and Ganteaume was still in Brest with twenty-one battleships. At this moment, on September 2, Calder was off Cadiz, adding his eighteen battleships to Collingwood's small force. Nelson had two bare alternatives—to force or lure Villeneuve to sail, and then fight a completely decisive action; or to blockade the Combined Fleet in Cadiz through the whole of the coming winter. How was he to get Villeneuve out of Cadiz? Ironically enough, the very weakness of the British fleet off Cadiz might do the trick by giving the French admiral enough courage to sail: yet that very weakness could possibly prevent Nelson from delivering the decisive blow that would, once and for all, put an end to Napoleon's threats at sea. While Nelson waited off Cadiz, Barham would send out every ship he could repair or refit, man and get to sea.

The first of many orders to leave the Admiralty after the two men started their task was telegraphed to Portsmouth to stop the *Victory* sailing, for she had just been ordered to join Cornwallis off Brest.

With Nelson resuming his role of Commander-in-Chief in the Mediterranean, which would include the Cadiz area, there came the question of which ships and officers he was to have. Once again Barham showed his admiration for Nelson's leadership. He gave him the latest edition of the *List of the Navy* containing the names of all its officers, and told him to choose whom he wanted. Nelson handed it back. "Choose yourself, my Lord, the same spirit actuates the whole profession; you cannot choose wrong." Barham then told him to dictate to his secretary, Mr. John Deas Thompson, the ships he wanted to join his squadron off Cadiz, and they would be ordered to follow him as soon as they were ready. "Have no scruple, Lord Nelson, there is my secretary. I will leave the room. Give your orders to him, and rely on it that they shall be implicitly obeyed by me." Nelson started dictating.

Later that same day an unconfirmed report reached London that Napoleon's Grand Army of England was breaking camp at Boulogne. It was only a report, but it held out hope. . . . Was the great invasion threat about to end?

The seven senior clerks at the Admiralty, who were paid between £350 and £800 a year, and the seventeen junior clerks, who received between £90 and £250, had on August 29 put in a claim for higher pay. It could not have been better timed, for between September 2 and September 6 they had to work like slaves preparing orders to set in motion Barham's and Nelson's decisions, and of course this came on top of their normal routine work.

Although Nelson had refused Barham's offer to choose his own captains, undoubtedly he did name at least a few. One was Captain Sir Edward Berry, a man who, coming from a poor family, had won command and fame with a pistol in one hand and a cutlass in the other. He was a fearless, desperate fighter, never happier than when leading hand-to-hand fighting across the decks of an enemy ship. He had little or no ability as a tactician or thinker, but fortune had smiled on his bravery. He had been with Howe on the "glorious first of June"; at Cape St. Vincent he had been on board Nelson's *Captain* when the battered 74 had captured two Spanish battleships with pistols and cutlasses, and he had led the party which took one of them, the *San Nicolas*. At the Nile he had been Nelson's flag-captain in the *Vanguard,* and it was into his arms that the wounded Nelson, blood streaming down his face, had reeled with the words: "I am killed. . . ."

Now, however, Berry was being neglected by the Admiralty and could not get a ship. As soon as Nelson had arrived at Merton, Berry wrote to him complaining of the treatment he had received. "A man's standing in the Service, and his *reputation* (and who has *not reputation* that has served with you?) all goes for nought," he had declared, expressing a wish that he could once again be at sea with the Admiral. A few days later, thanks to the news Blackwood had brought home, Nelson could satisfy Berry. He was to command the *Agamemnon*, which was considered by the French Admiral Allemand to be "England's fastest ship," and, as mentioned earlier, was one of the ships built by Henry Adams at Buckler's Hard.

Orders to place themselves under Nelson's command went out to Berry; to Henry Blackwood, commanding another of Adams's ships, the *Euryalus*; to Richard Keats and his *Superb*, which was now being hurriedly repaired at Portsmouth; to the faithful Hardy in the *Victory*; to the *Royal Sovereign*; and to the *Defiance*, which was in Portsmouth repairing the damage received in Calder's action against Villeneuve. Captain Philip Durham, who commanded the *Defiance*, had gone to the Admiralty and by chance met Nelson, who said, "I am just appointed to the command in the Mediterranean, and sail immediately. I am sorry your ship is not ready; I should have been glad to have you." This was quite enough for Durham: "Ask Lord Barham to place me under your Lordship's orders and I will soon be ready," he replied. Nelson agreed and promised to leave orders for him at Portsmouth.

The preliminary orders to the ships already mentioned (and to the *Ajax*, commanded by Captain William Brown, and the *Thunderer*, under Captain William Lechmere, both of whom had been with Durham in Calder's action and were now at Plymouth) were identical and brief and began with the time-honoured preamble:

> You are hereby required and directed to put yourself under the command of the R^t Honble Lord V^t Nelson, K.B. Vice Admiral of the White, and follow his lordship's orders for your proceedings.
>
> Given &c 5th September 1805.
>
> J. GAMBIER[2]
> P. PATTON
> GARLIES

And among the many other orders sent out and aimed at reinforcing the fleet off Cadiz was one to Lt. Lapenotiere. The little *Pickle* had been busy for the past few months operating off the French, Spanish and Portuguese coasts. Now she was at Plymouth having some repairs done. The order said:

2 Gambier, the First Sea Lord, was Barham's nephew and held the post before Barham's appointment. Vice-Admiral Philip Patton and Lord Garlies were also members of the Board of Admiralty.

You are hereby directed and required to put to sea in the gun vessel you command the moment she shall be ready, and wind and weather permit, and use your best endeavours to join Vice-Admiral Lord Viscount Nelson agreeably to the accompanying rendezvous; and having so done, put yourself under his command and follow his orders for your further proceedings.

The remaining days that Nelson spent in England were busy while he prepared for his last expedition. There were more orders to draft, and more talks with Ministers. On Thursday, September 5, the same day that the orders for the ships at Portsmouth and Plymouth were despatched, his steward, Henry Chevalier, and valet, Gaetano Spedilo, left Merton for Portsmouth and the *Victory* with Nelson's heavy baggage. On Friday, after Nelson returned from a visit to Downing Street to see Pitt, the Duke of Clarence arrived at Merton for the christening of the son of Colonel Maurice Suckling, Nelson's cousin.

On Saturday a letter arrived from Marsden saying that Nelson's orders were ready and asking him to call at the Admiralty to collect them. The Admiral went straightaway, to find that the First Lord had given him a free hand for all intents and purposes: he was to stop the enemy putting to sea from Cadiz, and protect the convoys in the Mediterranean. While at the Admiralty, Nelson wrote a short note to reassure Collingwood. "My dear Coll," he said, "I shall be with you in a very few days, and I hope you will remain second-in-command. You will change the *Dreadnought* for *Royal Sovereign,* which I hope you will like."

On the comparatively quiet Sunday all the Merton household headed by the Admiral (himself the son of a country parson) went off to the parish church of St. Mary the Virgin where the Reverend Thomas Lancaster took the service. Mr. Lancaster's feelings must have been very mixed. No doubt gratified to see the Admiral with his household and friends, he also knew that the great man was about to join the *Victory,* and he had agreed to take one of the vicar's younger sons with him as a volunteer. The subject of the sermon he preached has not been recorded.

Nelson was at the Admiralty again on Monday; on Tuesday he went over to Richmond Park to see Lord Sidmouth and, as already mentioned, to tell him his plan for fighting the Combined Fleet.

In the evening he went to the dinner with Mr. Crawford which Lady Bessborough has described. Wednesday was spent at the Admiralty issuing more orders, while Thursday was a day of official farewells. He also made his final visits to the Admiralty. One of the main reasons for this was his anxiety over a signal code, copies of which he wanted to take out to the Fleet with him.

Until quite recently the signals used by the Navy had consisted of ten flags representing the numbers one to nine and zero, plus flags for a substitute (so that the same number could be used twice) and "Yes" and "No." The *Signal Book for the Ships of War* at this time gave more than four hundred sentences, each of which was represented by two or three figures. Number 13, for instance, was "Prepare for battle," and Number 16 "Engage the enemy more closely." This was comparatively simple, but the code had to deal with every eventuality its compilers could think of—thus Number 280 meant "Send for fresh beef immediately," while 254 was "Fire ships are to prime and to be held in constant readiness to proceed on service," and Number 63 was "Anchor as soon as convenient."

The limitations of the system, where a group of two or three figures meant a whole sentence or order, are obvious: the orders the admiral could give to his fleet were limited entirely to the signals in the book. By 1805, when the signal book was only six years old, eighty additional orders had been written into it. But the effect was to shackle the admiral, for he could not order any manoeuvre unless it was "in the book." The system was not nearly flexible enough: it was as if a Frenchman were trying to write poetry in English using only an English tourists' phrase book containing less than five hundred phrases.

To overcome this problem, Sir Home Popham had produced a system where flags meant individual words. His first volume was called *Telegraphic Signals, or Marine Vocabulary.*[3] Containing nearly a thousand specially chosen words, it was a revolution in signalling—similar to giving the French poet a small dictionary in place of the phrase book. It meant that the admiral could signal his own words—and therefore original thoughts and ideas—to his fleet, within the limits of Home Popham's choice. To avoid con-

3 "Telegraph" in this sense, some thirty years before the invention of the electric telegraph, was used in the literal sense of writing at a distance.

fusion with the 1799 code, a Popham code signal would be indicated by a white and red preparative or telegraph flag.

Popham's code was not adopted immediately: for at least twelve years he produced the books privately and gave them away to his brother officers with the request that they try the code out. He issued a second part in 1803, and this added another thousand words, while part three, a little later, added a number of sentences and phrases. Even though the system had not been fully adopted by 1805, may warships had copies.

Nelson wanted to get enough copies of Home Popham's complete code to supply all his ships; they had been ordered from the printer, Mr. C. Roworth, of Bell Yard, Temple Bar, earlier, but had not yet arrived. When he got to the Admiralty the Admiral was disappointed. Sir John Barrow, the Second Secretary, wrote that in the morning Nelson had been "anxiously inquiring and expressing his hopes about a code of signals [Home Popham's] just then improved and enlarged. I assured him they were all but ready; that he should not be disappointed, and that I would take care they should be at Portsmouth the following morning."

Nelson then went off to say his official farewells to Pitt and Castlereagh, and it was while waiting to see the latter at the Colonial Office in Downing Street that he met an unusual man. He had been taken into the little waiting-room on the right of the hall. An Army officer was soon shown in—a man with a haughty air and a curt manner. The Army officer describes the meeting: "I found, also waiting to see the Secretary of State, a gentleman who from his likeness to his pictures and the loss of an arm, I immediately recognized as Lord Nelson. He could not know who I was, but he entered at once into conversation with me, if I can call it a conversation, for it was almost all on his side and all about himself, and in, really, a style so vain and so silly as to surprise and almost disgust me.

"I suppose something that I happened to say may have made him guess that I was *somebody,* and he went out of the room for a moment, I have no doubt to ask the office-keeper who I was, for when he came back he was altogether a different man, both in manner and matter. All that I had thought a charlatan style had vanished, and he talked of the state of this country and of the aspect and probabilities of affairs on the Continent with a good sense, and a knowledge of subjects both at home and abroad that surprised me equally and more agreeably than the first part of our interview had done; in fact he talked like an officer and a statesman."

Nelson had discovered that he was talking to none other than the victor of the Mahratta war, Major-General Sir Arthur Wellesley, who was destined to be the victor of Talavera, Salamanca and Waterloo, and better known in history as the Duke of Wellington. His recent safe arrival in England in the Indian convoy, mentioned earlier, was due, in part at least, to Nelson's actions in driving Villeneuve back to Europe and frightening him into inactivity.

"The Secretary of State," recorded Wellesley, "kept us long waiting, and certainly, for the last half or three-quarters of an hour, I don't know that I ever had a conversation that interested me more. Now if the Secretary of State had been punctual, and admitted Lord Nelson in the first quarter of an hour I should have had the same impression of a light and trivial character that other people have had, but luckily I saw enough to be satisfied that he was really a very superior man; but certainly a more sudden and complete metamorphosis I never saw."

After seeing Castlereagh and Pitt, Nelson was long overdue at Merton, where guests were waiting for him, but he made one final call at the Admiralty, which Barrow records: "In the evening he looked in upon me at the Admiralty, where I was stopping to see them [the signal books] off. I pledged myself not to leave the office till a messenger was dispatched with the signals, should the post have departed, and he might rely on their being at Portsmouth the following morning.

"On this he shook hands with me; I wished him all happiness and success, which I was sure he would command as he had always done; and he departed apparently more than usually cheerful."

Back at Merton, Lord Nelson's guests waited uncomfortably: there were Lord Minto, who thoroughly disliked Lady Hamilton, and Mr. James Perry, editor of the *Morning Chronicle*. They were not introduced until Lord Nelson and Emma arrived, two hours late, and Lord Minto then remembered without apparent embarrassment that the last time he had seen Perry he had jailed him for a libel on the House of Lords. Perry, in turn, bore no ill-will since Parliament was in those days easily libelled, and jail an accepted occupational hazard to those who reported and commented on the political activities and antics of their hereditary rulers and elected representatives.[4]

Lord Minto had an uneasy feeling when Lady Hamilton came into the room, eyes puffed and red from crying, that it was to be a strained and uncomfortable evening, and he was right. Sitting at the place of honour beside Lady Hamilton, he found her weeping. He reported, apparently shocked, that "she could not eat, and hardly drink, and near swooning, and all at table." Although it is unfortunate that his Lordship's appetite was probably affected, this was a somewhat arid judgement on Nelson's mistress. It is clear that the Admiral felt that he would die in the now nearly inevitable battle, and however much he tried, it is doubtful if he could hide this premonition from Emma, who almost certainly knew it instinctively. Nor did she have the comfort of being Nelson's wife, for he was being torn from her without their extremely happy union's being recognized by the outward symbol of legality, and to someone of Emma's background (she came from an obscure family and was reputed to have become Sir William Hamilton's wife after being cast off as a mistress by the aged envoy's nephew) this would be of great importance. As we have seen, she had already said that if she could be married to Nelson for an hour she would die content. The dinner guests departed early.

Friday, September 13, dawned at Merton and as usual Nelson was up early, long before the sun thought of dissolving the chilly autumn mist. The house was comparatively empty. His sister Susanna and her husband Thomas Bolton had left with their children and only his sister Catherine and her husband, George Matcham, and their young son remained in the house with the Admiral, Emma and Horatia. In the soft sunshine of an English autumn, taking his last stroll round the grounds of Merton, seeing the house, the graceful cedars, the quietly flowing river, and drink-

[4] The veneer of democracy in those days of "rotten boroughs" was spread very thinly: many boroughs with less than two thousand inhabitants regularly returned Members of Parliament while the great new industrial towns like Manchester and Birmingham with their teeming populations were not represented at all. Dunwich, which had been swallowed up by the sea, still had a Member. The rotten boroughs were often advertised for sale: indeed there were complaints that war profiteers, wanting to add a little tone to their newly acquired wealth, were bidding against each other and forcing the prices up.

ing in the quietness and beauty of a September day, he heard little Horatia's cheerful chattering. Perhaps he shook off the black thoughts which were creeping into his mind like a cold evening mist rising almost imperceptibly in a quiet spinney.

But the day was soon over. The sun set and Horatia was given her supper and put to bed, perhaps wrenching Nelson's heart as she kissed him goodnight. Dinner was served and it stuck in the throats of those eating it, for they felt as helpless to alter destiny as the warders keeping vigil over a prisoner in the condemned cell. The candles in silver candlesticks flickered as people moved about restlessly in the drawing-room, and the hands of the clock moved on with geometric precision and cold, remote inexorability. They all listened for the clatter of the coach, and ten o'clock of an autumn night had long struck before it arrived. Upstairs Nelson went quietly to the bedside of his daughter, conceived aboard the *Foudroyant* in the warm Mediterranean more than five years earlier. The little man knelt. Resting his head in his hand, he said a quiet prayer, and tiptoed out of the room and out of Horatia's life forever. Finally, having said farewell to a distraught Emma, kissed his sister Catherine goodbye, and shaken George by the hand with as much cheerfulness as he could muster, he walked to the carriage. Catherine and George were left to comfort Emma as the measured cadence of horses' hooves, overlaid with the rumble of the carriage wheels, died away in the distance.

In the solitude of the long night spent on the Portsmouth road Nelson had time for reflection. While the horses were being changed at Guildford he wrote in his private diary, in the upright, jerky writing that he contrived with his left hand, a prayer which gives a clearer insight into his feelings than anything else. "At half past ten, drove from dear, dear Merton, where I left all which I hold dear in this world, to go to serve my King and country. May the Great God whom I adore, enable me to fulfil the expectations of my country; and if it is His good pleasure that I should return, my thanks will never cease being offered up to the throne of His Mercy. If it is His good Providence to cut short my days upon earth, I bow with the greatest submission, relying that He will protect those so dear to me, that I may leave behind. His will be done. Amen. Amen. Amen."

At six o'clock next morning the carriage arrived at the George Inn, Portsmouth. Nelson, tired and stiff, went in to find his friend George Rose and a comparative stranger, George Canning, a brilliant orator and writer, a great friend of Pitt's and now the new Treasurer of the Navy. When breakfast was over, Nelson made some official calls and went back to the George, where by now an eager crowd had gathered. While Nelson talked with Rose, Canning and Hardy, the crowd and the clamour outside in the High Street increased and soldiers arrived to try to clear a way for the Admiral and his party. In an attempt to avoid the crowds, Nelson decided to board his barge at the bathing machines behind the Assembly Rooms on the front some half a mile away at Southsea, instead of using the sally-port steps at the end of the High Street.

However, as soon as he left the George by the back door for his last brief walk on English soil the people of Portsmouth gathered round him. Some cheered; others knelt before him in the dirty street and clasped their hands in prayer as he passed; many more stood unashamedly weeping. Whereas in London the crowds had cheered and jostled, joyful at being able to mob their hero, here in Portsmouth the people were more closely connected with the sea. In London the departure of a hero to join his ship and sail to meet the enemy presented the aspect of a carriage swaying off down a dusty street; here in Portsmouth it was a more urgent sight. From the Southsea beach they could see the *Victory* even now waiting at a single anchor across the Solent at St. Helen's, a brave sight with her black hull relieved by the yellow strakes, and her sails neatly furled on the yards.

Finally Nelson reached the sea, where his barge waited at the bottom of the steps. He paused while Hardy, Rose and Canning walked down and boarded the barge. The swirling mob of people surged forward as Nelson paused at the top of the steps and waved before following the others. (See illustration Number 1.) The crowd reached the edge of the parapet and became mixed up with the soldiers. An excited Army officer "who not very prudently upon such an occasion, ordered them to drive the people down with their bayonets, was compelled speedily to retreat; for the people would not be barred from gazing till the last moment upon the hero."

Nelson seated himself in his barge, the coxswain gave the order "Shove off," and within a few moments the crew were pulling at their oars, keeping perfect time, and the crowd redoubled its cheering. Nelson raised his hat, and turning to Hardy said: "I had their huzzas before—I have their hearts now."

Soon his barge was alongside the *Victory*, and his flag—white, with a red St. George's cross—was hoisted once again. To Marsden at the Admiralty Nelson wrote:

> You will please to acquaint the Lords Commissioners of the Admiralty that I arrived at Portsmouth this morning at six o'clock, hoisted my flag on board the *Victory* at this anchorage [St. Helen's] about noon. The *Royal Sovereign, Defiance,* and *Agamemnon* are not yet ready for sea, so that I must leave them to follow the moment they are complete. The ships named in the margin [*Victory* and *Euryalus*] only accompany me.

Rose and Canning had dinner with Nelson while the *Victory* prepared to sail. Next morning her log reported with stark brevity the beginning of Nelson's last voyage: "Sunday 15th. 8 a.m. weighed and made sail to the S.S.E. *Euryalus* in company." Once again the wind was foul, and by next day the two ships had got only as far west as Portland. Nelson wrote to a friend: "My fate is fixed, and I am gone, and beating down Channel with a foul wind."

On September 17 he wrote to Emma, dating his letter off Plymouth, "Nine o'clock in the morning, blowing fresh at W.S.W. dead foul wind."

> I sent, my own dearest Emma, a letter for you, last night in a Torbay boat, and gave the man a guinea to put it in the post-office. We have a nasty blowing night, and it looks very dirty. I am now signalizing the ships at Plymouth (*Ajax* and *Thunderer*) to join me; but I rather doubt their ability to get to sea. However, I have got clear of Portland, and have Cawsand Bay and Torbay under the lee. I intreat, my dear Emma, that you will cheer up; and we will look forward to many, many happy years, and be surrounded by our children's children. God Almighty can, when he pleases, remove the impediment. My heart and soul is with you and Horatia. I got this line ready in case a boat should get alongside.

However, he was unlucky, and added to the letter next day.

> I had no opportunity of sending your letter yesterday, nor do I see
> any prospect at present. The *Ajax* and *Thunderer* are joining; but it
> is nearly calm, with a swell from the westward. Perseverance has got
> us thus far; and the same will, I dare say, get us on.

He remembered that the vicar of Merton would probably be
worrying about his young son, now experiencing his first few days
at sea.

> Thomas seems to do very well, and content. Tell Mr Lancaster
> that I have no doubt that his son will do very well. God bless you, my
> own Emma! I am giving my letters to Blackwood to put on board the
> first vessel he meets going to England or Ireland. Once more, heavens
> bless you! Ever, for ever, your NELSON AND BRONTE.

And to Rose he wrote a letter with a typical ring:

> I shall try hard and beat out of the Channel, and the first northerly
> wind will carry me to Cape St Vincent, where nothing be wanting on
> my part to realize the expectations of my friends. I will try to have a
> motto, at least it shall be my watchword, *"Touch and Take."* I will
> do my best; and if I fail at any point I hope it will be proved that it
> was owing to no fault of, my dear Mr Rose, your very faithful friend,
> NELSON & BRONTE.

On Thursday the *Victory*, with the *Euryalus, Ajax* and *Thunderer* in company, took her departure from the Lizard, following
in the wake of Drake when he went off to "Singe the King of
Spain's beard" at Cadiz in 1587; of the gallant Sir Richard Gren-
ville who sailed in the *Revenge* to meet a brave death at "Flores,
in the Azores," and of Raleigh who went to find El Dorado. So
Nelson sailed on to meet his destiny with open arms but with
occasional half-ashamed backward glances. He was willing to ac-
cede to the need for his death, and would gladly exchange his life
for England's safety, if his life was to be the price exacted for
England's past mistakes in the war against the French. It was as
if he was reconciled to the fact that his personal happiness was
always to be fleeting, and as if he knew that in this last and greatest
battle he would be the victor, but also the victim. Death had its

sting—that Emma and Horatia would not have him to shelter them. Mercifully he would never know the depths to which Emma would be left to sink. But he was to die in good company; this was in many ways a compensation. There may be a few Judases, he was to say, but in fact there were none. No one did less than was expected of him, and most did more.

A brig.

THIRTEEN

"IT IS TREASON!"

When the sea was calm all boats alike
Show'd mastership in floating.

—Shakespeare (*Coriolanus*)

BEHIND the bare report that Blackwood had brought to Merton on September 2, that the Combined Fleet had put into Cadiz, was a series of catastrophes for both Napoleon and Villeneuve. As we have seen, the orders that the Emperor had sent to Villeneuve in the West Indies—that he was to return to Europe and, with the Rochefort, Ferrol and Brest squadrons, "procure our superiority before Boulogne for some days"—arrived after the French admiral had sailed for Ferrol. After running into Calder and finally putting in to Vigo, Villeneuve found no new orders waiting for him. He despatched a tale of woe to Decrès in Paris. "Urgent, irresistible necessity has obliged me to put in to Vigo," he wrote, "misfortunes in an ever-increasing progression have accumulated on this squadron." In another letter he listed those misfortunes—one ship had lost her main-topmast, another had 200 men on the sick list and water on board for only five days, three others each had more than 150 sick, and every other ship had between 60 and 120 sick.[1]

Nevertheless, he worked swiftly: the ships were watered and all the sick crammed aboard the *Atlas,* which he proposed to leave behind with two Spanish ships "which cannot manoeuvre with the squadron and seem made to compromise everything." Then after warning Gourdon at Ferrol that he was to do his utmost to join,

[1] Compare with the conditions of Nelson's ships on their return from the West Indies: the Admiral wrote from Gibraltar on July 20 "The squadron is in the most perfect health, except some symptoms of scurvy, which I hope to eradicate by bullocks and refreshments from Tetuan."

ne sailed again. But on arriving at the entrance to Ferrol and Corunna—with Admiral Gravina and two Spanish ships already in the narrows leading to Ferrol—he met a boat which came alongside with orders from Napoleon. They prohibited him from putting in to Ferrol. Instead he was, with the Rochefort and Brest squadrons, to "make himself master of the Strait of Dover, were it only for four or five days."

Decrès, in a covering letter, added an important point: the Emperor had anticipated that in certain circumstances "the situation of the Fleet would not allow of our carrying out his designs which would have so great an influence on the fate of the world; and in this case alone the Emperor desires to assemble an imposing array of forces in Cadiz."

Gravina and his two Spanish ships had not been able to anchor off Corunna in time and had gone up to Ferrol. Villeneuve followed to have a talk with Gravina, and both men decided that Napoleon's new plan was dangerous. Gravina said he was quite ready to follow Villeneuve, but in the sixty days since the Combined Fleet had left the West Indies the English had had time to receive warning. "As we are getting out of this place they will be able to give us battle and provide us with a second fight before our approach to Brest," he said.

And once again Villeneuve took up his pen to write to Decrès. Had he made a fast Atlantic crossing, defeated Calder, joined with Ganteaume at Brest "and enabled the great expedition to take place," he said, "I should be the foremost man in France. Well, all this should have happened—I do not say with a squadron of fine sailors—but even with very average vessels . . . two north-easterly gales damaged us because we have bad sails, bad rigging, bad officers and bad seamen. The enemy have been warned, they have been reinforced, they [i.e., Calder] have dared to attack us with numerically inferior forces, the weather favoured them. Unpractised in fighting and fleet manoeuvres, in the fog each captain carried out but one rule, that of following his next-ahead; and behold us the laughing-stock of Europe."

On August 6, with eight English battleships reported waiting outside, Villeneuve wrote to Decrès, "I am about to set out but I do not know what I shall do. . . ." Four days later he worked out of the bay with four French and eight Spanish battleships, but his troubles were far from over: the north-east wind dropped before the last three Spanish ships were clear, and the Fleet had to anchor. As if the element of farce was to enter into everything connected with Villeneuve, "All the ships, French and Spanish, ran aboard each other in anchoring." Finally, on August 13, the Combined Fleet of twenty-nine battleships (eighteen French and eleven Spanish) sailed, heading westward. It is difficult to know exactly what was in Villeneuve's mind. He may have intended to sail for Brest and the Channel, but Gravina's Chief-of-Staff, Rear-Admiral Escaño, wrote in his journal: "We sailed for Cadiz."

That evening, according to Villeneuve, some battleships were sighted at 6 p.m., followed next day by a report of fourteen more, then eight others. Ironically enough it is now known that the only battleships in the area were probably French—those of Commodore Allemand, to whom Villeneuve had sent the frigate *Didon* with orders to meet him off Brest.

The rest of the day was uneventful. During the night Allemand's squadron again passed close but unseen. The 15th was a busy day for Villeneuve's frigates, which searched neutral ships and sank a British merchantman. Then in the evening one of them reported sighting a ship with another in tow. Although Villeneuve did nothing about identifying them, they were in fact the British *Phoenix* towing the *Didon,* which she had captured after a bitter fight in which 70 of the French ship's crew of 370 had been killed. Captain Baker of the *Phoenix* had thus brought to nought Napoleon's plan for Villeneuve to link up with Allemand's Rochefort squadron. Without the *Didon*'s despatches from Villeneuve, Allemand was without information or new orders. The Combined Fleet and Allemand were destined never to meet, and Allemand, like a latter-day Flying Dutchman, was left roaming the seas.

Another British ship, Captain Griffith's *Dragon,* also played her part in deciding Villeneuve's destiny. Griffith boarded a Danish merchantman and said, quite casually, that his ship was part of a fleet of twenty-five British battleships. Later on Griffith sighted a strange fleet, and then saw a French frigate boarding the Danish merchantman. Had the Danes seen any British ship? Indeed they had, the Danes told the Frenchmen, reporting Griffith's visit and the "intelligence" that his ship was part of a fleet of twenty-five battleships.

This news was hurriedly relayed to Villeneuve, who immediately assumed that Captain Griffith's imaginary fleet was one sent out to chase him. During the rest of that night, however, he continued steering towards the first rendezvous arranged for Allemand—although he had more than a suspicion that the ship seen under tow earlier was the *Didon*.

That evening, August 15, two days after he left Corunna, Villeneuve made his great decision, based on two factors—the eight ships sighted on the 13th[2] and the threat he thought existed from the Dane's report of Captain Griffith's "fleet" of twenty-five British battleships. Villeneuve was well aware of the proviso in his orders allowing him to go to Cadiz; as night fell a signal from his flagship, the *Bucentaure*, turned the Combined Fleet southward, heading for Cadiz.

Since August 2 Napoleon had been waiting at Boulogne, frequently riding up and down the beach on his famous horse Marengo. Events were moving fast. On August 5, he heard that Nelson was back in Europe, and two days later news reached him that Villeneuve had left Vigo for Ferrol. His plan was apparently beginning to mature. Along the French coast facing England his great army was waiting, led by a formidable array of warriors. Marshal Davout commanded the right wing at Ambleteuse; Soult had the centre at Boulogne; Ney had the left wing at Etaples, and the advance guard at Wimereux was under Lannes. Yet while Napoleon and his look-outs stared up and down the Channel watching for the squadrons of Villeneuve and Ganteaume to come sailing up, the alliance between England, Russia and Austria was, as we have seen, growing stronger each day. Napoleon was beginning to have to face both ways—eastward to Austria and Russia and westward to Britain.

Where was Villeneuve? For several days the Emperor ranted and raged; then on August 22 he heard that Villeneuve and the Combined Fleet had sailed from Ferrol on August 13. The fact that he had not yet appeared off Brest, explained Decrès, was because the wind was foul. However, Napoleon was not convinced

2 Villeneuve made no attempt to identify these as friendly or enemy; they were probably Allemand's, and in any case would have been no match for Villeneuve's twenty-nine battleships.

and gave instructions in case Villeneuve had gone to Cadiz. They had a familiar ring—he was to reinforce his Combined Fleet with the six battleships in Cadiz and others in Cartagena and "proceed up to the Channel." But this brought an agonized wail from Decrès, who believed that if Villeneuve had gone to Cadiz the great invasion scheme should be abandoned. He wrote on August 22 (two days after Villeneuve had, unknown to the Minister, arrived in Cadiz) imploring Napoleon not to associate the Spanish ships with the French squadron's operations. "If your squadron is at Cadiz," he wrote, "I implore you to look upon this occurrence as a decree of destiny, which is reserving it for other operations. I implore you on no account to order it to come round from Cadiz to the Channel, because if the attempt is made at this moment it will only be attended with misfortune.

"In truth, sire," he declared, "my situation is becoming too painful. I reproach myself for not knowing how to persuade your Majesty. I doubt if one man alone could. . . . And to be candid, a Minister of Marine overawed by your Majesty in those matters which concern the sea, is serving your Majesty ill and is becoming a cipher. . . ."

But Napoleon now apparently had no further patience to waste on Villeneuve. The day after Decrès made his plea, the Emperor wrote to his Foreign Minister, the lame and brilliant aristocrat Talleyrand, a man who successfully combined debauchery with diplomacy, who was as cultured as he was rakish, and who had that invaluable asset for a politician, the ability to survive when one régime crumbled and was replaced by another.

His Emperor, who had made the pilgrimage to Aix-la-Chapelle to worship in his fashion at the tomb of the great Frankish emperor Charlemagne, said that in the following April he would find a hundred thousand Russians—supplied with British equipment—in Poland; up to twenty thousand Englishmen in Malta, and fifteen thousand Russians in Corfu. "I shall then find myself in a critical situation. My decision is made." That decision was to declare war on Austria. His Army of England, camped on the cliffs before him, was to become once again the Grand Army. Breaking camp and marching swiftly and secretly across Europe, it would deal the impertinent Austrians a crushing blow before they realized what was happening and, so Napoleon planned, before they had time to attack him.

Yet apparently Napoleon did not entirely wash his hands of Villeneuve. "If he follows his instructions, joins the Brest squadron, and enters the Channel, there is still time; I am master of England," he told Talleyrand. On the other hand, if his admirals hesitated he would have to "wait for winter to cross with the flotilla." In the meantime he would "replace my war battalions with my third battalions, which will still give me a sufficiently formidable army at Boulogne." Although Talleyrand was to draw up the declaration of war against Austria, it was to be kept secret for the time being. Napoleon then started drafting the first orders which would start his Grand Army marching towards Austria. On the 24th the routes to Vienna were decided; on the 25th he dictated the detailed orders for the whole forthcoming Austrian campaign— with its victories of Ulm and Austerlitz. By August 29 the Grand Army was tramping eastward, leaving the Channel coast behind it. And in the harbours hundreds of transports began to rot.

On September 1, as Blackwood arrived off the Isle of Wight on his way to Merton with the news that Villeneuve had reached Cadiz, Napoleon at Boulogne received the identical information. The next day, when Nelson followed Blackwood to the Admiralty, Napoleon left the seashore that now mocked him. For three days after receiving the information—while he was on his way to Paris, and after he arrived—the Emperor was silent on the subject of Villeneuve. However, he soon made up for it. "Admiral Villeneuve," he wrote to Decrès on September 4, the day the clerks at the Admiralty worked overtime on Nelson's orders, "has filled the cup to overflowing. . . . It is treason beyond all doubt. . . . Villeneuve is a scoundrel who must be dismissed from the service in disgrace . . . he would sacrifice everything to save his own skin. . . ."

FOURTEEN

RATTLING THE BARS

The fathers have eaten sour grapes, and the
children's teeth are set on edge.—Ezekiel, XVIII, 2

ON SEPTEMBER 14, the day that Nelson boarded the *Victory* off
St. Helen's to sail for Cadiz, Napoleon drew up the orders for
Villeneuve which were to lead directly to the battle of Trafalgar,
the greatest victory yet won by British arms. From then on the
Royal Navy would be the most powerful force afloat for more than
a century and a quarter.

Twelve days earlier, Villeneuve had reported that there were
eleven British battleships off Cadiz, although a further twenty-
three were reported from Lisbon to be steering south. Napoleon's
new orders for Villeneuve were based on the fear of what General
Craig's tiny expedition might do when it linked up with the
Russians in southern Italy. The Emperor saw this British and
Russian move as an attack on his "soft under-belly," and a threat
to his Austrian campaign. To crush it he finally abandoned his
Channel venture and ordered Villeneuve to sail the Combined
Fleet into the Mediterranean. He was to go to Naples, land the
troops he had on board, and then take the Fleet back to Toulon.
. . . But there was one snag: although Villeneuve reported only
eleven British battleships off Cadiz, the situation had changed
considerably by the time Napoleon's orders were drafted. Calder
had been reinforced, and now twenty-six of the Royal Navy's battleships were waiting.

Decrès forwarded the Emperor's orders to Villeneuve on September 16 with a covering letter which contained this strong hint
to the man the Emperor now regarded as a coward: "I cannot too

highly recommend you, M. *L'Amiral,* to seize the first favourable opportunity to effect your departure; and I repeat my most earnest wishes for your success." Yet Decrès did not tell Villeneuve the most vital news of all, that Napoleon, having on September 14 ordered Villeneuve to sail for Naples, had decided next day to sack him and place Admiral Rosily in command of the Combined Fleet.

Rosily was told of his new appointment on the 18th, and on the same day Decrès sent him Napoleon's orders, saying, "It is the Emperor's intention that you should proceed in all haste to the port of Cadiz." And whereas Villeneuve's orders said he was to sail for Naples immediately, the orders to Rosily gave the new Commander-in-Chief a loop-hole—if "insuperable obstacles" were found, he was to "cause either the whole Fleet or several divisions to leave port whenever the weather permits," to rattle the bars, keep crews active, and "put an end to this blockade which is an insult to the flags of the two Powers." Four days after Villeneuve's orders had been despatched a curt letter was written telling him "His Majesty the Emperor and King has just appointed Vice-Admiral Rosily to the command of the naval forces assembled at Cadiz and has given orders that you are to proceed to Paris in order to give an account of the campaign on which you have been recently employed." Oddly enough this letter was not immediately sent off to Cadiz: instead it was given to Rosily to deliver person-ally to Villeneuve, even though he was not leaving until the 24th. As we shall see later, reports that he was sacked were to reach Villeneuve through unofficial channels and drive him to such a desperate act that the letter never reached him.

In Paris the Emperor packed his bags and on September 23 left the city; by the 26th he was in Strasbourg, and his five great armies—three from Boulogne, one from Holland and one from Hanover—were marching across Europe. By October 5 all were poised within twenty miles of the Danube, ready to strike the Austrians a crippling blow. The Austrian General Mack, imagin-ing the Grand Army still on the seashore at Boulogne, had decided not to wait for his new Russian allies, and pushed ahead with seventy thousand men across the River Inn into Bavaria on Sep-tember 8. By the 14th he reached Ulm, where he planned to hold the French, taking up the defensive role beloved of the Austrian

Army which, though brave, was tangled in red tape and unsuited to mobile warfare.

Napoleon, by transferring his Grand Army secretly from the Channel to the Danube before the Russians could get their troops to Ulm, had the chance to fling two hundred thousand tough, highly trained veterans against seventy thousand troops officered by elegant, highly cultured and highly inefficient amateurs. On October 7 Napoleon struck his blow. By the 17th General Mack (of whom Nelson had warned the Duke of Clarence less than two months earlier, "if Your Royal Highness has any communication with Government, let not General Mack be employed, for I know him to be a rascal, a scoundrel, and a coward"[1]) was surrounded. By the 20th—the day the Russians were to have joined him on the River Inn had he stayed there—he had surrendered. It was the eve of Trafalgar. At Ulm Napoleon had scored his first victory of the Austrian campaign.

In the great Spanish port of Cadiz, conditions for Villeneuve were about as bad as they could be. The newly arrived Combined Fleet was in a poor state and he had hardly got the ships anchored before he fell ill with "bilious colic," a stomach upset which had troubled him at sea and which was probably brought on by worry. For eleven days he waited for some word from Decrès or Napoleon, but none came. "My Lord," he wrote to Decrès, on September 2, "I was awaiting the arrival of a courier from your Excellency every minute, in the supposition you could but too clearly surmise that the Fleet has put in to Cadiz. The lack of funds, the poverty of the port, the great requirements of the ships, and those of the crews, increase in proportion to the time passing and to the season that is approaching."

The "lack of funds" which he mentioned had soon reached almost farcical proportions. Villeneuve wanted cash to provide supplies for some seventeen thousand men for at least fifty days, plus the normal daily rations, but as soon as he arrived in Cadiz, the French Agent-General, le Roy, warned that he had no money and his credit was exhausted. The French Ambassador in Madrid tried

[1] Nelson's comment on General Mack dates from the Admiral's days in Naples, when Mack was sent to command the Neapolitan Army.

to get money from the Spanish Government, but it was in the midst of a financial crisis and, the Ambassador reported, had not "the flimsiest of credit." The Ambassador had himself been "obliged to glean from all the bankers in order to get the money for the couriers that I despatch." The Inspector of Artillery refused to supply any powder or shot unless it was paid for with cash, until direct orders came—very late—from Madrid.

Apart from supplying the ships with food, powder and shot, it was a massive task to get them ready for sea again. The frigates were all short of sails; one battleship needed a new main yard, another had lost her rudder head, a third had a broken bowsprit, and a fourth had damaged her sternworks in a collision. Two others were leaking badly and several more needed various vital repairs.

Not only were the ships sick; the crews were decimated by illness. On September 2 Villeneuve reported that he had 1,731 seamen in hospital, 311 more had deserted since he originally left Toulon, and altogether he was short of more than 2,000 men. Later this deficit totalled 2,207, of whom 649 were in hospital in Cadiz. Fortunately for Villeneuve, the French Ambassador in Madrid finally managed to get some help from a French banker, who lent some cash and paid various bills.

The Spaniards were in no better condition regarding their ships. One of Gravina's battleships had been left behind in Ferrol, and three more at Vigo. There should have been six fresh battleships waiting for him in the roads at Cadiz, but in fact there were only four, and two of these were useless and had to be replaced. The Spanish Navy suffered from the same weakness that troubled the Royal Navy, the difficulty of getting seamen to man the ships. Recruiting, says Desbrière, "was too often the result of sweeping in beggars, vagabonds and common-law prisoners, owing to the scarcity of enlisted seamen. In this respect the English were hardly better, but long cruises and a terrible discipline had transformed the bad material—too often recruited by force—into splendid topmen and gunners. The inferiority of the Spaniards in this respect was manifest; their guns, served by untrained sailors under the direction of artillerymen from land—but little practised themselves and altogether insufficient in number—were to exercise but poor effect." This was "still further lessened by the singular predilection—which, moreover, the Spanish shared with the French—for aiming at the rigging in preference to the hulls of their opponents; thus wasting their ammunition for a problematical result."[2]

Villeneuve, reporting to Decrès on the Spanish squadron, said: "It is very distressing to see such fine and powerful ships manned with herdsmen and beggars and having such a small number of seamen."

Moreover, there were no extra men available in Cadiz: the press-gangs roamed the streets, looking particularly carefully for the hardy fisherman. But Cadiz, like the rest of Andalusia, had already suffered the ravages of yellow fever. Those not struck down by the disease were already serving or had managed to hide. This forced Gravina to pay off the worst and slowest of his ships and use the crews to reinforce the fifteen best ships. With the eighteen French battleships, this gave the Combined Fleet a strength of thirty-three.

But Gravina was still short of men, and the only solution was to draft soldiers on board: they could at least man some of the guns, freeing trained seamen for the more skilled tasks. The troops were drawn from some of the most famous units in Spain, among them a battalion of the Regimiento de Cordoba, which was sent aboard the *Santissima Trinidad* and *Argonauta*, and battalions from the Regimiento de Soria, Regimiento de Africa and Regimiento del Corona which joined the *San Juan Nepumuceno, Neptuno* and *San Francisco de Asis*. These men were to fight at Trafalgar even as their forebears fought the British from the decks of ships of the Armada in 1588: the Regimiento de Africa, for instance, then named the Tercio de Sicilia, had men on board the *Nuestra Señora del Rosario* which Sir Francis Drake himself had brought to action in Torbay, and the rest were in the Duke of Medina Sidonia's flagship *San Martin*.

It was against this background that Villeneuve worked hard to get his ships ready for sea. Equally busy was General Lauriston, who commanded the French troops aboard the ships and who had been sending reports to the Emperor which were highly critical of Ville-

[2] The French Navy's habit of firing at their enemy's rigging was probably a hangover from privateering. When chased by a more powerful ship, a privateer often escaped because a lucky shot damaged her opponent's rigging. But in a pitched battle—particularly against the British, whose trained seamen quickly repaired damage to masts and rigging—it was damage to the hull that decided the issue.

neuve. On September 16 he wrote to Napoleon that "Reports from Tangiers, which Admiral Gravina regards as being very reliable, state that Admiral Nelson, with six more line-of-battle ships, is to arrive directly to take command."

Meanwhile Villeneuve, still preparing the Combined Fleet to carry out Napoleon's orders to go to the Channel, was reporting regularly to Decrès. "We have seen twenty-four or twenty-five line-of-battle ships, of which seven are three-deckers, appear off this bay. . . . I await the Emperor's [latest] orders with great anxiety, and I count the minutes and hours until they arrive," he said. When the last two Spanish ships were ready "and I have a fair wind to put to sea with both squadrons, we shall set sail to carry out the Emperor's orders." These orders were that he should take the initiative against the enemy whenever possible. The second set of instructions, ordering him to Naples, were still on their way from Paris, taking many days to cross the rugged countryside.

The courier bearing them finally arrived in Cadiz on September 27. The watchword for the Naples expedition, Napoleon said, was "L'audace et la plus grande activité." This stirring phrase did little to bolster up Villeneuve's morale, and the orders were a good example of Napoleon's lack of understanding of the best way of using his Fleet. Bearing in mind that at this time it was only at sea that he could bring Britain to battle, he now proposed using the major part of his available Fleet to carry out a comparatively unimportant landing. He was cheerfully hazarding some thirty-three battleships—there would have been more if crews had been available—to land four thousand troops.

Thus Pitt's plan for sending Craig and his tiny expedition of six thousand men to Naples was beginning to have an importance out of all proportion to its size or power. Its mere existence posed so real a threat in the Emperor's eyes that he was apparently willing to sacrifice his Fleet to defeat it.

There is no doubt that he let the Combined Fleet sail knowing that it might well be annihilated. His orders of September 14 were admittedly based on the report that there were only eleven British ships off Cadiz, but by the 20th—three days before he left Paris for Strasbourg—he knew that there were by then some twenty-seven battleships waiting off Cadiz. Orders took under a fortnight to pass between Paris and Cadiz, so from September 20 he had more than a fortnight to cancel or delay the order to sail for Naples, since Villeneuve did not sail until twenty-nine days after Napoleon had found out the British strength. Yet the Emperor did nothing.

In Cadiz itself the French and Spanish admirals received the order without fuss. Gravina read his copy on board the *Principe de Asturias* and straightaway had himself rowed across to see Villeneuve in the *Bucentaure*, where he told him that the fourteen battleships under his command were "absolutely ready to set sail, and to accompany the Imperial Fleet anywhere." Villeneuve in turn reported to Decrès—in four letters written on the same day, September 28—that "the captains in command will realize from the position and strength of the enemy before this port that an engagement must take place the very same day that the Fleet puts to sea." Then he wrote with a sudden burst of confidence: "The Fleet will see with satisfaction the opportunity that is offered to it to display that resolution and daring which will ensure its success, revenge the insults offered to its Flag, and lay low the tyrannical domination of the English upon the seas.

"Our Allies will fight at our side, under the walls of Cadiz and in sight of their fellow citizens; the Emperor's gaze is fixed upon us."

But the news he sent in the last of the four letters, written at midnight, must have tempered his earlier elation. "I have just been informed that the enemy squadron has just been joined by three sail of the line—one of which is a three-decker—coming from the west. There are now thirty-one line-of-battle ships well known to be in these waters."

The three ships were the *Victory, Ajax* and *Thunderer*.

Tacking: with the wind coming from the right, the left-hand ship is on the starboard tack. She turns (*centre sketches*) head to wind and then pays off on the larboard, or port, tack.

FIFTEEN

THE NELSON TOUCH

The golden rule is that there are no golden rules.—Shaw

NELSON had passed Lisbon on September 25 while Napoleon's orders to the sick and harassed Villeneuve and to Gravina were still being carried over the hot and dusty roads of France and Spain. Thinking that he could lure the Combined Fleet out of Cadiz only by letting them think that there was but a small British force blockading them, he also tried to ensure that his own name would not scare the enemy into staying in port. He therefore wrote to Collingwood, giving the letter to Henry Blackwood to take on ahead in the *Euryalus,* with the request "if you are in sight of Cadiz, that not only no salute may take place, but also that no Colours may be hoisted, for it is as well not to proclaim to the enemy every ship which may join the Fleet." Perhaps realizing that neutral ships with prying eyes might be in the vicinity, he added a postscript, "I would not have any salute even if you are out of sight of land." And in his private diary that night he recorded: "At sunset the captain of the *Constance* came on board. . . . The enemy's fleet had not left Cadiz the 18th of this month, therefore I yet hope they will await my arrival."

Saturday, September 28, brought a fresh north-westerly breeze in the morning and the *Victory,* with the *Ajax* and *Thunderer* in company, ran before it across Cadiz Bay. The breeze almost fell away during the late afternoon, and once again Nelson wrote in his private diary: "In the evening joined the Fleet under Vice Ad[l] Collingwood, saw the enemy's fleet in Cadiz amounting to thirty-five or thirty-six sail of the line."

The effect on the Fleet of his arrival was instantaneous. Captain Edward Codrington of the *Orion* wrote to his wife Jane: "Lord Nelson is arrived. A sort of general joy has been the consequence,

and many good effects will shortly arise from our change of system."
One of these, Codrington hoped, would be a little more social life
in the Fleet: he found Collingwood a dull fellow.

The next day was Sunday, September 29, and Nelson's birthday:
he had been born forty-seven years earlier, the sixth child and fifth
son of the Rector of Burnham Thorpe, in Norfolk. It was an appropriate day to take over command of the Fleet from Collingwood.
And one of Nelson's first visitors was in fact Collingwood, whose
barge brought him over from the *Dreadnought* to the *Victory* at
7 a.m.

It is almost impossible to imagine two more different men. Cuthbert Collingwood was now fifty-five, of medium height, thin, with
a small head and a round face. In a crowd he would pass without
notice except for his penetrating blue eyes, and his thin lips, which
betrayed a firm and unruffled character. His hair was powdered and
worn in a pigtail; his square-cut coat had a stiff, stand-up collar
and what were now unfashionably long skirts, over blue knee-
breeches and white stockings. A weary man now, his thoughts were
constantly turning to Morpeth, in his native Northumberland,
where his wife Sarah had waited so long for his return. He had
married her just fifteen years earlier, and they had two daughters—
Sarah, now thirteen and named after her mother and grandmother, and Mary Patience, a year younger. Most of his married
life had been spent at sea, yet fewer men longed more urgently
for home. A week before Nelson's arrival he had written: "How
happy I should be, could I but hear from home, and know how
my dear girls are going on! Bounce [his dog] is my only pet now,
and he is indeed a good fellow: he sleeps by the side of my cot,
whenever I lie in one, until near the time of tacking, and then
marches off, to be out of the hearing of the guns, for he is not
reconciled to them yet. I am fully determined, if I can get home
and manage it properly, to go on shore next spring for the rest of
my life; for I am very weary."

Tragically enough, although he was not to die until five years
after Trafalgar, Collingwood was doomed never to see England
or his family again: succeeding to the command on Nelson's death,
he was left at sea despite his protestations over the years that followed. Commenting on how he had been forgotten the year after
Trafalgar, he wrote: "Fame's trumpet makes a great noise, but the

notes do not dwell long on the ear." His thoughts turned on "those delightful blackbirds whose morning and evening song made my heart gay."

"Tell me," he wrote to Sarah, "how do the trees which I planted thrive? Is there shade under the three oaks for a comfortable summer seat? Do the poplars grow at the walk, and does the wall of the terrace stand firm?" And at the prospect of his wife moving house he regretted losing "those beautiful views" from Morpeth, which he was in any case never to see again, "and even the rattling of that old wagon that used to pass our door at six o'clock on a winter's morning had its charms." He wished he was with his wife and her sister "that we might have a good laugh. God bless me! I have scarcely laughed these three years."

This was the heart of a man who had gone to sea at the age of eleven and led a party of seamen at Bunker Hill at twenty-four. Strangely enough he had, for many years, followed in Nelson's footsteps: when Lt. Nelson was promoted out of the *Lowestoft,* Lt. Collingwood succeeded him; when Commander Nelson of the *Badger* was promoted to post captain in command of the *Hinchinbrooke,* Lt. Collingwood was promoted to Commander and given the *Badger.* When Nelson left the *Hinchinbrooke,* Collingwood was promoted to post captain, and took over command. And at Cape St. Vincent, when Nelson hauled out of the line in a desperate attempt to head off the enemy, followed by Troubridge in the *Culloden,* Collingwood in the *Excellent* immediately went to his aid. A strict and stern disciplinarian, he nevertheless ruled his ships and later a fleet with a light hand: as mentioned earlier he hated flogging and rarely used the cat-o'-nine-tails. His ships were famous for the fitness of their crews, and Nelson when taking over command reported to the Admiralty that the fleet was "in very fair condition and good humor."

Nelson's first day in command was a busy one. After meeting Collingwood and receiving from him the various unexecuted Admiralty orders, he proposed changing the whole system of blockade. By shifting his entire fleet over the horizon he would take it out of the sight of the prying eyes of the French and Spanish lookouts whose telescopes pointed westward from the San Sebastian Tower at Cadiz.

By staying some fifty miles to the west he could watch over the

Combined Fleet whether it went north to the Channel, south to Gibraltar or west into the broad Atlantic. More important, he would be sufficiently far off-shore that a westerly gale would not force him to run before it through the Strait of Gibraltar and into the Mediterranean with his unwieldy three-deckers, leaving the stable door open for the Combined Fleet to bolt before he could get back on station again. Nelson also realized that famine in Cadiz itself might well drive the Combined Fleet to sea, and he approved of Collingwood's decision to seize the neutral coasters— most of them Danish—which were trying to take supplies into the blockaded port, and send them off to the prize court at Gibraltar.

On this first day nearly all his captains, wearing their best uniforms with swords at their sides, left their ships and were rowed across to the *Victory* to meet their new Commander-in-Chief. It might be thought that most of these men were simply renewing their acquaintanceship with Nelson—that they were already tried and trusted members of his "band of brothers," who knew from past experience that he was a leader to be loved and trusted. But this was far from being the case. Of the twenty-seven British battleships which were to fight at Trafalgar—and several of them had not joined at this stage—only five belonged to Nelson's own Mediterranean Fleet. One had joined in the West Indies, and the other twenty-one were sent out from the Channel Fleet. Only eight of the twenty-seven battleship captains had previously served with Nelson. One of the two who had been with him since 1803 was Thomas Hardy, his own flag captain. Only five had commanded their ships since 1803; only five had previously commanded a battleship in action. Thus Nelson had but twenty-two days to get to know those nineteen captains who had never previously served with him. In that time he had to gain their confidence, let them see how he reasoned and what he expected—so that they could read his thoughts—and train them as a fleet.

One by one the captains clambered up the ship's towering black-and-yellow sides and went on board through the entry port abreast of the mainmast on the middle deck. Forward and aft of them the great 24-pounder guns, gleaming black on carriages painted with yellow ochre, ran in even lines down each side the full length of the ship. (See drawing facing page 360.)

Turning aft, the captains walked a few feet to the ladder leading
up through the hatchway to the upper deck. Once there they
turned aft to Nelson's cabins. The first of these was the dining
cabin, and walking through they came to his day cabin. This ran
the width of the ship, and light streamed in through the windows
built right across the raking stern. The deck of the cabin, covered
in canvas painted with a black-and-white chess-board pattern, was
cambered, and the thick beams overhead followed the same curve
so that each side of the cabin seemed to sag away from the centre
line. A large table dominated the cabin; several armchairs were
scattered about, among them a particularly deep one, leather-
covered, which was Nelson's favourite. It was very narrow so that
it held his slim body comfortably, and on each side there was a
pocket into which he could slip papers.

Incongruous among the finely carved pieces of furniture and the
paintings on the bulkheads (among them one of Horatia, a dumpy
little girl in a high-waisted dress) were two 12-pounder cannon,
one on each side. The solid wooden wheels of the carriages reached
nearly to a man's knee; the blocks (pulleys) of the side-tackles were
twice as thick as a man's fist, and above the guns, between the
beams overhead, were more tackles for opening the gun ports. Most
of the cabin was painted in pale green and buff, but grey and
yellow were used to pick out some of the woodwork; and the deep
rich browns of the polished furniture made the yellow ochre on
the gun carriages look dull and heavy, as if emphasizing how out of
place they were in such surroundings. The sun sparkling on the
sea surging and rippling under the *Victory*'s massively ornate stern
reflected up through the windows and made dancing patterns on
the white deckhead; the slow, easy movement of the ship caused
the thick oak timbers which made up her huge bulk to move a
fraction of an inch, so that they groaned as if in protest. The
distant shouts of orders, the occasional slap of canvas and the air
of controlled bustle all gave the ship life and movement.

One by one the captains were announced and strode into the
cabin to grip Nelson firmly by his left hand, and also wish him a
happy birthday. Among them were a handsome Scot, George Duff
of the *Mars,* and John Cooke of the *Bellerophon* (both of whom,
like their Admiral, had but another twenty-two days to live), and

Israel Pellew of the *Conqueror,* one of the finest sailors Cornwall
ever produced, and younger brother of the famous Lord Exmouth.
Nelson had a special word for Edward Codrington, of the *Orion,*
who had not heard from his wife Jane for some time. "He received
me in an easy, polite manner," Jane was told by a proud husband,
"and on giving me your letter said that being entrusted with it by
a lady, he made a point of delivering it himself."

And when Fremantle of the *Neptune,* whose Betsey had been expecting another baby, came on board Nelson greeted him warmly
and immediately asked: "Would you have a girl or a boy?"

"A girl," replied Fremantle, who already had two boys.

"Be satisfied," said Nelson, and gave Fremantle a letter. It was
from Betsey's sister Harriet and told him that he had a new daughter whom Betsey was proposing to call Christine.

Nor were there only captains present: apart from Collingwood
there was also Rear-Admiral the Earl of Northesk, another Scot,
who was flying his flag in the *Britannia,* and who was to be third-
in-command at the battle. The fourth admiral, Louis, was still close
off Cadiz with the *Canopus.*

Very soon the cabin was echoing to the sound of their voices,
and the talk was young men's talk, for few of them had reached
their mid-forties. Codrington was thirty-five, Duff and Cooke were
forty-two, Hardy, commanding the *Victory,* was thirty-six, while
Charles Tyler of the *Tonnant* was at forty-five one of the oldest
present.

Nelson was well pleased with the way he was received: indeed,
the Fleet's reception, he wrote later, "caused the sweetest sensation
of my life. The officers who came on board to welcome my return
forgot my rank as Commander-in-Chief in the enthusiasm with
which they greeted me. As soon as these emotions were past I laid
before them the plan I had previously arranged for attacking the
enemy; and it was not only my pleasure to find it generally approved, but clearly perceived and understood." And to Lady Hamilton he described it more jubilantly: "When I came to explain to
them the *Nelson Touch* it was like an electric shock. Some shed
tears, all approved—'It was new—it was singular—it was simple!'
and, from Admirals downwards, it was repeated—'It must succeed
if ever they will allow us to get at them! You are, my Lord, sur-

rounded by friends, whom you inspire with confidence.' Some may
be Judases; but the majority are certainly much pleased with my
commanding them."

Unfortunately none of the officers present left a description of
what Nelson said when he explained his plan, and this has caused
a lot of misunderstanding to historians ever since. In addition to
describing what he intended to do, he later issued a Memorandum
to all senior officers and captains, and the way he fought the battle
varies from what he laid down in the Memorandum. This led
many people to suppose that in the heat of the moment, with the
Combined Fleet in front of him, he completely abandoned his
plan in his excitement and fought what at best could be called a
free-for-all. However, the answer seems to be that at this meeting
with the captains he so inculcated them with his own ideas that
they knew what to do, and the subsequent Memorandum was
simply an *aide-mémoire*. When other captains joined fresh from
England they too were told verbally the basic plan. (The contents
of the Memorandum will be dealt with later and are given in full
in Appendix III.)

The discussion on strategy and tactics over, Nelson was able to
play the role of genial host. His steward, Henry Chevalier, was
hard at work taking bottles from the circular wine cooler, uncork-
ing them and pouring drinks for the thirsty captains, who were
perspiring freely in the uncomfortable tightness of high, stiff collars
and cravats. When the time came for them to go back to their
ships, fifteen of them received invitations to stay to lunch with
Nelson and the rest were promised invitations for the following day.

Next day, Monday, presented several new and varied difficulties
for the attention of the Commander-in-Chief. By now Henry Blackwood in the *Euryalus,* and the *Hydra,* were off Cadiz as the new
in-shore squadron, but the *Hydra* had left the Admiral with a
human problem. Her lieutenant had deserted his ship and run
away in Italy with a ballet dancer from Malta. He had left a series
of unpaid debts behind him—his father reckoned between £200
and £300—and was "very probably in prison." Now Nelson sat
down to try and sort out the mess. He wrote to Captain Sotheran,
commanding the *Excellent,* in Naples harbour, asking him to try,
with the help of the British Embassy, to trace the lieutenant. The

lad's father would pay the accumulated debts, Nelson said, "and if now a few more [pounds] are necessary to liberate the youth, I will be answerable. All we want is to save him from perdition."

Then there was the problem of Vice-Admiral Sir Robert Calder. That officer was, this very day, writing to Marsden at the Admiralty demanding an inquiry into his conduct against Villeneuve's Fleet on July 22. He had just "learnt with astonishment yesterday by the ships just arrived, and by letters from friends in England, that there has been a most unjust and wicked endeavour to prejudice the public mind against me as an officer." His decision to ask for an inquiry seems to have been based on a talk with Collingwood and Nelson—of whom he had previously been reckoned an enemy. Now he was asking that Captain William Brown of the *Ajax*, Captain William Lechmere of the *Thunderer*, and Captain Durham of the *Defiance*, who were with him in the action, should be allowed to return home with him as witnesses. The *Defiance* had in fact not yet joined the Fleet. Nelson was touched by Calder's anguish and reported to Lord Barham, "It will give your Lordship pleasure to find, as it has me, that an inquiry is what the Vice-Admiral wishes. . . . Sir Robert felt so much, even at the idea of being removed from his own ship which he commanded, in the face of the Fleet, that I much fear I shall incur the censure of the Board of Admiralty." He then went on to explain why. He felt he could not insist on Calder's leaving the *Prince of Wales* for a smaller ship for the voyage home, and although he could ill afford the loss of such a powerful, 98-gun ship, "I trust that I shall be considered to have done right as a man, and to a brother officer in affliction—my heart could not stand it, and so the thing must rest."

There were plenty of other letters to write that Monday morning, and his secretary, Mr. John Scott (not to be confused with the *Victory*'s chaplain, the Reverend Dr. Alexander Scott), was kept busy. There was a gentle reproof to be sent to Rear-Admiral Knight ("I was only twenty-five days, from dinner to dinner, absent from the *Victory*. In our several stations, my dear Admiral, we must all put our shoulders to the wheel, and make the great machine of the Fleet intrusted [*sic*] to our charge go on smoothly"); to Lt.-General Fox at Gibraltar, saying that if the enemy "know of our increased numbers we shall never see them out of Cadiz"; to his old

friend Ball at Malta, grumbling that "I know not a word of Sir
James Craig or his troops, or what they are going about, except,
as the man said of the parson, 'he preached about doing good.' "
And among several other letters he signed was one to his old friend
Alexander Davison. "Day by day, my dear friend, I am expecting
the [enemy] Fleet to put to sea—every day, hour, and moment;
and you may rely that, if it is within the power of man to get at
them, that it shall be done; and I am sure that all my brethren look
to that day as the finish of our laborious cruise. The event no
man can say exactly; but I must think, or render great injustice to
those under me, that, let the Battle be when it may, it will never
have been surpassed. My shattered frame, if I survive that day, will
require rest, and that is all I shall ask for.

"If I fall on such a glorious occasion," he wrote, "it shall be my
pride to take care that my friends shall not blush for me. . . . My
mind is calm, and I have only to think of destroying our inveterate
foe."

By 1.30 in the afternoon, the captains who had not lunched with
Nelson the previous day came on board the *Victory*. They included
Thomas Fremantle, George Duff and Edward Codrington ("What
our late Chief [Collingwood] will think of this," he wrote to Jane,
"I don't know; but I well know what the fleet think of the difference; and even you . . . will allow the superiority of Lord Nelson
in all these social arrangements which bind his captains to their
admiral"). It was a jovial lunch:[1] gusts of laughter frequently
rattled the thin, elm-wood bulkheads, and the steward Chevalier
was busy at the wine cooler, broaching bottles and filling glasses
while Nelson and his captains drank bumpers, toasting victory, the
King, and Emma. The *Victory*'s own band played, and soon the
time came for the captains to return to their ships. Nelson, however, asked Fremantle to stay—"to see a play that was performed
by the seamen on board the *Victory*," as the young captain later
told Betsey. "I assure you it was very well conducted, and the voice
of the seaman, who was dressed in great form and performed the
female part was entertaining to a degree."

Nelson went to bed that night in his long, narrow cot, which hung

[1] Nelson usually breakfasted early, had "dinner" at about 2 p.m. and supper
at about 7 p.m.

from the deckhead. Its hangings had been embroidered by Emma, and he quickly fell asleep as it swung gently with the roll of the ship. But he woke at 4 a.m. with "one of my dreadful spasms, which had enervated me." "However," he wrote next day to Emma, "it has entirely gone off, and I am only quite weak. The good people of England will not believe that rest of body and mind is necessary for me. . . . I had been writing seven hours yesterday; perhaps that had some hand in bringing it upon me."[2]

Some of the other captains also found that waiting off Cadiz was not a very healthy occupation. Fremantle, telling Betsey that "I shall be outrageous if you do not christen my new tittler by the name of Louisa. I have taken such an aversion to Christine that I shall be sick and melancholy," grumbled about his rheumatism. However, at the moment the weather was so hot that he slept with the stern windows and the doors of his cabin open, and this seemed to do the rheumatism some good. He found half a pint of wine made him heavy and dozey, but fortunately the spruce beer he had taken aboard the *Neptune* "turns out famous, I drink it all day." Indeed, since he stopped drinking wine and stuck to spruce beer, "I have not had so much bile."

Over in the *Mars* the big and burly Captain George Duff was a happy man. His thirteen-year-old son Norwich had joined the ship a few days earlier and it was becoming quite clear to the proud father that the boy was making good progress. "He seems very well pleased with his choice of profession," Duff wrote home to his wife Sophia at 30, Castle Street, Edinburgh, where a Raeburn portrait[3] showed the fair-haired captain looking down from the wall with clear eyes and a friendly smile. Duff was a good example of a man who lived and died for the Royal Navy. He had been born in the little port of Banff, on the north-east coast of Scotland, into a family descended from the old earls of Fife. His mother had died within six weeks of his birth, and the whole of his childhood was spent, when not in his father's study with a private tutor, scampering among the sailing ships in the little harbour half a mile from the town, or playing with boats on the River Doverean which ran near his home on its way to the sea. Young George listened to the tales

2 Beatty, the surgeon, diagnosed these spasms as indigestion. They might well have been attacks of nervous dyspepsia.
3 See illustration Number 14.

the sailors told—there were many sailors along this stretch of the coast—and his imagination did the rest. He dreamed of going to sea like his great-uncle Robert, who was already a commodore. His father disapproved, but the boy, at the age of nine, stowed away on board a small merchant ship which arrived at a neighboring port before he was discovered. His father, a sensible man, then relented and the tutor was ordered to change the curriculum to one more suited to a prospective sailor. At thirteen George joined great-uncle Robert in the *Panther*. By the time he was sixteen he had fought in sixteen actions.

The arrival of young Norwich and his cousin Thomas on board the *Mars* brought the muster of Duffs up to four, because Thomas's elder brother Alexander was an acting lieutenant, being too young to take his lieutenant's examinations. Thomas and Alexander were sons of Lachlan Duff, of Park. Also in the *Mars* was a boy from Banff whom Norwich knew well, Midshipman T. Robinson. The *Mars* was something of a family ship, for another of the lieutenants, Benjamin Patey, had his fifteen-year-old nephew George on board as a midshipman. Benjamin was one of ten sons of a Royal Navy gunner.[4]

Tuesday, October 1, found the crews of most of the ships in the British Fleet hard at work with scrapers, paint pots and brushes. The *Victory*'s hull was painted in the Nelson style—in black with three horizontal yellow bands or strakes. Each yellow strake was at the same level as a tier of gun-ports, but the port lids were painted black on the outside so that with the lids closed they gave a chequer-board effect. This looked smart and impressive and, what was more important, it was the Nelson style. Individual captains were quick to emulate it, and although many of them probably had to foot the paint bill themselves, they did it willingly. It was a proud Fremantle who reported to Betsey from the *Neptune* (which was, he pointed out, "only a foot shorter than the *Victory* and appears much larger upon deck") that "we are all busy scraping our ships' sides to new paint them in the way Lord Nelson paints the *Victory*."

Nelson himself, lying in his cot in the *Victory*, was weak and

---

4 Nine of them joined the Royal Navy. One of the gunner's grandsons became an admiral, another a rear-admiral and a third a captain.

weary after the "dreadful spasm" during the night, but he got up early as usual to attend to the day's business. His valet Gaetano helped him wash, shave and dress; then Chevalier served his breakfast. After that there was the usual crop of letters. To Emma he wrote of his reception from the Fleet; to Lord Castlereagh he wrote of the enemy. Colonel Congreve's new rockets might, if they had a range of one and a half miles, do execution among the ships of the Combined Fleet, then lying abreast of the town of Cadiz, which was itself on a narrow spit of land jutting into the bay; but he thought "we have a better chance of forcing them out by want of provisions: it is said hunger will break through stone walls—ours is only a wall of wood."

In the afternoon the little schooner *Pickle* joined Nelson's Fleet after a fairly fast passage out from Plymouth. She had taken seven days to reach Cape St. Vincent and just over a day from there to rendezvous with the Fleet.

Collingwood came over to the *Victory* to have a quiet meal with his old friend: at lunch the previous two days Nelson's dining cabin had been full of his captains; now the two admirals were able to talk freely.

Although Nelson was sure that the Combined Fleet faced a famine, he was worried about his own supply situation, which was far from good. The Fleet needed more than eight hundred bullocks (these had to come from Tetuan, on the African coast inside the Strait of Gibraltar) and a transport laden with wine each month, and a lot of fresh water. He therefore decided to send small groups of his ships to Gibraltar and Tetuan, starting with Admiral Louis and the battleships *Canopus*,[5] *Queen, Spencer, Tigre* and the *Zealous* (which had just come out from England to find her mainmast sprung and rotted in several places) and the frigate *Endymion*, which had also joined the Fleet with a sprung mainmast. Louis and his flag-captain, Charles Austen, who was in command of the *Canopus* and one of Jane Austen's three sailor brothers,[6] were not very pleased at the idea of being sent away at this time. The two

---

[5] The *Canopus* was formerly the French 80-gun battleship *Le Franklin*, captured at the battle of the Nile.

[6] Charles Austen later became a rear-admiral; Herbert was a captain, and Francis eventually became an admiral of the Fleet and was also knighted.

of them dined with Nelson in the *Victory* just before leaving, and when the time came to return to the *Canopus,* Louis said: "You are sending us away, my Lord—the enemy will come out, and we shall have no share in the battle."

"My dear Louis," replied Nelson, "I have no other means of keeping my Fleet complete in provisions and water, but by sending them in detachments to Gibraltar. The enemy will come out, and we shall fight them; but there will be time for you to get back first." To reassure Louis, Nelson added: "I look upon *Canopus* as my right hand; and I send you first to insure your being here to help beat them."

With Blackwood in the *Euryalus,* and the *Hydra* watching every movement of the Combined Fleet from close in to Cadiz, Nelson needed a string of ships stretching from the look-out frigates across the fifty-odd miles to the westward where the Fleet waited, so that as soon as the *Euryalus* ran up a flag signal it could be repeated from ship to ship until it reached the *Victory* fifty miles away. To provide this link Nelson needed at least three more ships. He had no other frigates available and had already appealed to the Admiralty for more. To Castlereagh he had also written: "I have only two frigates to watch them, and not one with the Fleet. I am most anxious for more eyes, and hope the Admiralty are hastening them to me. The last fleet was lost to me for want of frigates; God forbid this should." The only thing he could do now was to use three battleships. He chose the *Mars, Defence* and *Colossus,* and a delighted Duff found he was to command this little squadron. To Sophia he wrote that he could manage only a short letter because "since *I am Commodore* I have not much time during the day, and am ready for my nap as soon as I can in the evening." Later, grumbling that Admiral Louis would presumably soon return and "deprive me of my honours" by taking over the command of the advance squadron, Duff said of Nelson: "He is so good and pleasant a man, that we all wish to do what he likes, without any kind of orders. . . . Even this little detachment is a kind thing to me, there being so many senior officers to me in the Fleet."

Blackwood was warned by Nelson of "the importance of not letting these rogues escape us without a fair fight, which I pant for by day, and dream of by night." Four more frigates were expected soon, and two would be sent to help him. "In fresh breezes easterly[7] I shall work up for Cadiz, never getting to the northward of it; and in the event of hearing they are standing out of Cadiz, I shall carry a press of sail to the southward towards Cape Spartel and Arrache [i.e., the North African coast]." He added, "I am confident you will not let these gentry slip through our fingers, and then we shall give good account of them, although they may be very superior in numbers."

With so much work to do, the days passed quickly. On Thursday, October 3, a sharp letter was sent to Lord Strangford, the British minister in Lisbon, about the churlish treatment of British war-ships in Lagos by the Portuguese Government. When a vessel went there for food and water, as provided for by treaty, "She seems placed under the direction of the consul of one of our enemies and very improper language is held by our enemies to the British officers and seamen and inducements held out to them to desert. The enemy's consul then directs that only so many cabbages, or bullocks, or sheep shall go on board—and, at his will and pleasure, so much water." To this degradation, declared Nelson, no nation can submit. He was certainly not going to allow any French or Spanish consul to say, "You English shall either wear a dirty shirt, or go without water to drink."

He wrote to the Earl of Northesk that "It is likely to be a very fine day, therefore will you do me the favour of dining on board the *Victory*. Your captain [Bullen] I shall of course expect with you." The Earl treasured this letter and sent it home to his wife at Rosehill, near Winchester, as an indication of Nelson's friendliness. On the back of the letter he also wrote a brief message—"*Do not pay the duty for the wine that comes home in the Prince of Wales* [Calder's flagship, due to sail for England in a few days] till I tell you."

On Friday, October 4, the little cutter *Entreprenante,* com-manded by Lt. Robert Young, joined the Fleet. Next day the wind went round to the east and Nelson sent the *Pickle* to help Black-wood's two frigates off Cadiz. "The French and Spanish ships have taken the troops on board," he wrote to Barham, "and it is said

---

[7] This was the wind with which the Combined Fleet could sail.

they mean to sail the first Levant wind."[8] The enemy ships in the Spanish port of Cartagena, inside the Mediterranean, had hoisted their topsails and, Nelson concluded, "it looks like a junction."

By Sunday the wind was in the east, and with the Combind Fleet embarking troops Nelson was a very anxious man. The clash seemed to be imminent. "I verily believe," he wrote to George Rose in London, "the country will soon be put to some expense for my account, either a monument, or a new pension and honours; for I have not the very smallest doubt but that a very few days, almost hours, will put us in battle; the success no man can ensure, but the fighting them, if they are to be got at, I pledge myself." He was equally anxious while he waited for more reinforcements to arrive. "It is, as Mr Pitt knows, annihilation that the country wants, and not merely a splendid victory of twenty-three to thirty-six—honourable to the parties concerned, but absolutely useless in the extended scale to bring Bonaparte to his marrow-bones: numbers can only annihilate."

On Monday the 74-gun *Defiance*, commanded by Captain Philip Durham, arrived from England to join Nelson's Fleet. It will be remembered that he served with Calder in the action of July 22 against Villeneuve, and he held very strong views about it. After the action, Calder had thought it necessary to bring his squadron to, in order to cover the captured ships, and both the British and the enemy spent the night repairing damage. Next morning Durham in the *Defiance* had been ordered to take his station between the two fleets. He did this fully expecting the action to be renewed, his biographer wrote. He signalled to Calder, "You can weather the enemy," but there was no reaction from the flagship. Villeneuve's fleet then started to draw away, and Durham signalled "The enemy increase their distance." Still there was no reply, and a desperate Durham made a final signal, "Am I to keep sight of the enemy?" To which Calder replied by recalling him to take his station in the line. Aware of the consequences of Villeneuve's escape, Durham called his officers together and told them to "be particular in their journals, as that was not the last they would hear of that affair." His words were prophetic, for no sooner had he boarded the

---

8 A Levanter is a strong easterly wind blowing out of the Mediterranean.

Victory two and a half months later to report to his Commander-
in-Chief than Nelson greeted him with: "Durham, I am glad to
see you, but your stay will be very short, for Sir Robert Calder sails
tomorrow, and takes with him all the captains who were in his
action, to give evidence at his court-martial. I am very sorry
to part with you, but you will have to leave your ship under the
command of your first lieutenant: but go on board the *Prince of
Wales* and settle that with Sir Robert. The wind is at the north-
east; the enemy will be out. . . ." Durham took the hint: he had
been more than thankful for the chance meeting with Nelson at the
Admiralty several weeks before which led to his being in the
Fleet, and he was in no mood to be thwarted by Calder, having got
so close to Cadiz and so obviously near to a battle.

Leaving the *Victory,* Durham went across to the *Prince of Wales,*
where he found Captain William Brown, who had left the *Ajax*
under the command of his first lieutenant, John Pilford, and
Captain William Lechmere, who had left the *Thunderer* under the
command of Lt. John Stockham. Both captains were apparently
quite willing to return home with Sir Robert Calder, but Durham
asked to see the Admiralty order. When he discovered that it said
the captains were to go home to England to give evidence only if
willing, he told Sir Robert he was certainly not willing, and at the
same time he refused to sign a public letter applying for leave to
quit his ship. With that gesture he took his farewell, climbed back
into his boat and returned to the *Defiance.*[9] His biographer makes
it quite clear that Calder was probably better off without Durham's
presence at the court-martial since he would have given evidence
unfavourable to the Admiral.

The *Royal Sovereign,* freshly repaired, joined the Fleet from
England on Tuesday, and she brought further problems for Nelson.
Secret orders from the Admiralty, enclosing a letter from Lord
Castlereagh, told him that in addition to dealing with the Com-
bined Fleet off Cadiz he was to cover Craig's operations in the
Mediterranean, and that in the event of hostilities on the Conti-

9 The *Defiance* took on board 750,000 Spanish dollars before leaving England.
As soon as it appeared the Combined Fleet was preparing to sail Durham
asked Nelson what should be done with the money. "If the Spaniards come
out, fire the dollars at them," replied His Lordship, "and pay them off in
their own coin!"

nent—which were virtually certain—Craig's men might be used on the coast of Italy. With a small convoy due to sail from Gibraltar for Malta with reinforcements for Craig, it meant Nelson's force of battleships would be even further denuded: the convoy would have to be guarded against any sally by enemy ships from Cartagena.

To a friend Nelson wrote on this same day, October 8: "I have 36 sail of the line looking me in the face; unfortunately there is a strip of land between us, but it is believed they will come to sea in a few days. The sooner the better. I don't like to have these things upon my mind; and if I see my way through the fiery ordeal, I shall go home and rest for the winter." And even as Nelson wrote those words, events reached a crisis aboard Villeneuve's flagship anchored in Cadiz.

Wearing: with the wind coming from the left, the left-hand ship is on the larboard tack. She turns (*centre sketches*) away from the wind, which crosses her stern, and comes round until she is on the starboard tack.

SIXTEEN

COUNCIL OF WAR

But I'll endeavour deeds to match these words.
    —Shakespeare *(Troilus and Cressida)*

WE HAVE SEEN how Napoleon's orders for Villeneuve to sail for
Naples had arrived in Cadiz on Friday, September 27, two days
before Nelson took over command of the British Fleet off the
port, and how on Saturday, Villeneuve reported that the troops
would embark within a day or two. On Monday as Villeneuve
paced up and down on board the *Bucentaure,* he was a lonely man,
prey to many emotions. He knew he had little or no sympathy
from the Emperor; Decrès was clearly doing his best, but he had
to obey Napoleon. His own flag officers, Rear-Admiral Magon
and Rear-Admiral Dumanoir, were not, apparently, giving him
the support he expected. The French and Spanish captains were
saying openly that they stood very little chance against the British.
In addition friction was growing between the French and Spanish
squadrons. French sailors were being murdered in the streets;
stories that the French had treacherously abandoned the two
Spanish warships in the action of July 22 against Calder were
spreading through Cadiz, and there were many people only too
willing to believe them.

Already extremely anxious at the reported strength of the British
fleet awaiting him over the horizon, he now knew that at last
Nelson had arrived, and the knowledge that the almost legendary
figure of that terrible fighter was poised a few leagues away to
the westward almost unnerved him.

The wind had stayed in the west—foul for getting the Combined
Fleet out of Cadiz; then later on Monday afternoon (the day
Durham arrived in the *Defiance* and refused to go back with
Calder) it went round to the north-east. At last they could leave.

Villeneuve made his decision, and within a few minutes the signal for the Combined Fleet to prepare to put to sea was run up aboard the *Bucentaure*. At once there was a great deal of bustle aboard all the ships: captains were called from their cabins, first lieutenants gave orders which called all hands, and men went to the capstans to get ready to heave up the anchors. Then more flag hoists were run up from the *Bucentaure*: the order was cancelled. The Fleet would not now sail after all.

Next day Villeneuve wrote his excuses in a letter to Decrès and contradicted himself. "In my impatience to carry out the Emperor's orders," he said, "heeding neither the strength of the enemy nor the condition of the greater number of the ships in the Combined Fleet, I desired yesterday to take advantage of an easterly breeze on which the Fleet could work out, and I made the signal to prepare to sail, but the wind having blown a gale from this quarter and being therefore diametrically opposed to the course that I was to shape, I was not able to carry out my design."

That much was quite clear: the breeze had increased so much that it threatened a Levanter, so that the wind which took him out of Cadiz would prevent his getting through the Strait of Gibraltar. But then, as if that was not a good enough reason for not sailing, he added another—which contradicted his first sentence. "Nevertheless I could not turn a deaf ear to the observations which reached me from every side, as to the inferiority of our force in comparison with that of the enemy, which is at the present time from thirty-one to thirty-three line-of-battle ships, of which eight are three-deckers, and a large number of frigates; to put to sea in such circumstances has been termed an act of despair which is not consonant with the prestige of the Allied cause . . . an action on the very day of our leaving port was inevitable; that to hope for a favourable issue of an action at the mouth of the harbour with crews such as those in our ships and more especially in those of His Catholic Majesty, would be a strange self-deception."

So Villeneuve that Tuesday morning called a council of war of all the flag officers of the Combined Fleet and the senior captains. They totalled fourteen men, of whom seven were French and seven Spanish. Those fourteen men who sat down in Villeneuve's cabin on board the *Bucentaure* were to bear the responsibility for the Combined Fleet's success or failure against the British. At their head was Villeneuve, now aged forty-one, who had fought at the Nile and was later to be described by a British officer as "a tallish, thin man, a very tranquil, placid, English-looking French-man."[1] One of his ancestors had fallen at the side of Roland in the pass of Roncesvalles; another had charged beside Richard Coeur-de-Lion in Palestine. The Admiral himself was a Knight of Malta—the ninety-first member of the family to belong to the order—and had gone to sea when very young. He was one of the few members of the nobility who did not leave the Navy at the Revolution. Like Collingwood, Villeneuve thought longingly of his wife and his home among the pine trees in Provence. Like Collingwood he was never again to see his village of Bargemon; he was not to hear the song of the cicada, nor feel the sun rising over the Alps to warm and ripen the peaches and the melons. Instead he was to meet his death, apparently, at the hands of the Emperor he now tried to serve.

Rear-Admiral Dumanoir le Pelley, Villeneuve's second-in-command, was thirty-five; his family was one of the wealthiest on the Cotentin peninsula and his background was that of the rolling green hills of the Calvados country. Like Villeneuve, he had served the King yet survived the Revolution, and he owed much of his promotion to Murat, who escaped from Egypt at the same time as Napoleon in a frigate commanded by Dumanoir.

The third-in-command of the French Fleet was an impetuous —almost reckless—Breton, Rear-Admiral Magon. His full name, de Magon Clos-Doré, showed he was of noble birth, and like his two superiors he had first served in the Navy under the King. He now had little but contempt for Villeneuve; indeed he was reported to have got into such a rage when Villeneuve did not renew the action against Calder on July 22 "that he stamped and foamed at the mouth." While he paced furiously up and down aboard his own ship, Villeneuve's flagship passed and Magon "gave vent to furious exclamations, and flung at him in his rage whatever happened to be at hand, including his field-glass and even his wig."

The senior French captain at the council of war was Cosmao-

---

1 Collingwood described him as "a well-bred man, and I believe, a good officer: he has nothing in his manners of the offensive vapouring and boasting which we, perhaps too often, attribute to Frenchmen."

Kerjulien, round-faced, burly and grave; a Breton who was perhaps one of the finest captains in the French Navy. He had run away to sea at the age of twelve and had been in action many times. The other three Frenchmen were Captains Maistral, Lavillegris and Prigny, who was Villeneuve's Chief-of-Staff.

The Spaniards were led by Don Federico Gravina, a grandee of old Spain, with the right to put on his hat in the Presence Chamber of the King. Now forty-nine, he had been at sea since he was twelve and he was the most highly regarded officer in the Spanish Navy. His second-in-command was Vice-Admiral don Ignatio Maria de Alava, fifty-one years old, grey-haired and round-faced, who had fought with Gravina at the siege of Gibraltar. The third Spanish flag officer was Rear-Admiral don Baltazar Hidalgo Cisneros, who had commanded the *San Pablo* at the battle of Cape St. Vincent. The other Spaniards present were Rear-Admiral don Antonio de Escaño, who was Gravina's Chief-of-Staff, Commodore don Rafael de Hore, Commodore Galiano, and Commodore Enrique MacDonell.[2]

Villeneuve, dressed in a long-tailed uniform coat, green corduroy breeches with a two-inch wide stripe down each side, and half-boots with sharp toes, opened the council of war by saying that the Emperor's instructions were that the Combined Fleet should weigh at the first favourable opportunity and that "wherever the enemy should be encountered in inferior strength they must be attacked without hesitation in order to force them to a decisive action." From various sources—the Spanish Ambassador in Lisbon, an agent at Tangiers, look-outs and coastal craft—it had been discovered that the British had between thirty-one and thirty-three battleships. Would everyone, Villeneuve asked, "be so good enough as to give his opinion upon the situation in which the Combined Fleet is placed?"

In the discussion that followed the Spanish were at an advantage: unlike the French they had talked it over among themselves before they boarded the *Bucentaure*. Some of the French officers at first declared that there was no doubt about the proposal to

2 Commanding the *Rayo*, he was in fact an Irishman, born in Ireland of Irish parents and christened Henry. He had joined the Spanish Regimiento de Hibernia—originally raised from Jacobite refugees in Spain—to fight against Britain during the American war, and later transferred to the Navy.

sail: the result would be the rout of the British and "the conse-
quent ease" of carrying out their orders to make for Naples.

The Spanish officers replied simply that they agreed with Rear-
Admiral Escaño, their Chief-of-Staff, since they had all discussed the
situation. And Escaño,[3] reporting his own remarks later, wrote that
he asked the French "whether in the circumstances—the English
having twenty-five to thirty ships at the harbour mouth—it were
preferable to leave port or to receive an attack at anchor." He
made several comments on "the difference between the skilled
seamanship of those [British] who had been at sea with their
squadrons without the least intermission since 1793 and those who
had spent eight years without putting to sea, pointing out to the
Spanish that they were not able to rely on their short-handed unskilled seamen."

He concluded: "Superior orders cannot bind us to attempt the
impossible, as nothing would serve as an excuse in the event of
a disaster, which I see to be inevitable if we weigh."

The impetuous Breton, Rear-Admiral Magon, immediately
leapt up, angry and red in the face, to contradict Escaño. He spoke
so hotly that he very soon upset the Spaniards. The sensitive and
punctilious Commodore Galiano interrupted angrily, demanding
that Magon withdraw several expressions concerning the Spanish,
and within a few moments there was uproar in Villeneuve's cabin
as several other Spaniards joined in the demand that Magon
retract. Magon, on the other hand, loudly refused. Finally Admiral
Gravina stood up and, quieting them all, requested that they vote—
without any further arguing—on the question: should or should not
the Combined Fleet put to sea considering that it had not a superiority of force to make up for its inherent inferiority. Villeneuve
took a vote—and the majority verdict of the French and Spanish
senior officers was that they should stay at anchor. After a brief
discussion about forming a defence flotilla in case Nelson should
attempt to attack the Fleet in Cadiz itself, the men present signed
the minutes of the meeting and the council of war broke up.

All present recognized, the minutes said, that the Combined
Fleet was for the most part badly manned and that several of the
ships had not even been able to exercise their crews at sea. "They

[3] See Notes, p. 371.

are by no means in a state to render the service in action of which they will be capable when they are organized." They concluded with a paragraph which can hardly have expressed their true feelings, but which was a sop to Decrès and the Emperor: "In all these observations, the officers of the two nations composing this assembly have borne witness to the desire that they will always feel of going out to engage the enemy, whatever his force, as soon as His Majesty desires it. . . ."

On the day the turbulent council of war was being held aboard the *Bucentaure*, Nelson was, as we have seen earlier, writing that "I have 36 sail of the line looking me in the face." Later in the day he sat down at his desk in the great day cabin aboard the *Victory*, took up his pen and started to write laboriously with his left hand. Heading it with the two words "Secret" and "Memorandum," and paying scant regard to punctuation, he wrote:

"Thinking it almost impossible to bring a Fleet of forty Sail of the Line into a Line of Battle in variable winds thick weather and other circumstances which must occur, without such a loss of time that the opportunity would probably be lost of bringing the Enemy to Battle in such a manner as to make the business decisive.

"I have therefore made up my mind to keep the fleet in that position of sailing (with the exception of the First and Second in Command) that the order of Sailing is to be the Order of Battle, placing the fleet in two Lines of Sixteen Ships each with an advanced Squadron of Eight of the fasting [sic] sailing Two decked ships which will always make if wanted a Line of Twenty four Sail, on which ever Line the Commander in Chief may direct.

"The Second in Command will in fact command his line and" he wrote, then crossed out the last six words, put a comma after "will" and continued, "after my intentions are made known to him, have the entire direction of His Line to make the attack upon the Enemy, and to follow up the Blow until they are Capturd or destroy'd."

Nelson was writing his famous Memorandum, "The Nelson Touch," which his secretary, John Scott, was to correct. Describing how Collingwood's division was to break through the enemy line about the twelfth ship from the rear and his own would break through about the centre, he emphasized that "the whole impression of the British Fleet" must be to overpower a part of the enemy line, from two or three ships ahead of their Commander-in-Chief—whom he supposed would be in the centre—to its rear. In this way the whole of the British Fleet (which he estimated at about forty ships) would be concentrated on half the Combined Fleet. The rest of the enemy ships would take some time to re-form and join in the battle.

"Something must be left to chance," he wrote; "nothing is sure in a sea fight beyond all others, shot will carry away the masts and yards of friends as well as foes, but I look with confidence to a victory before the van of the Enemy could succour their friends." (He then crossed out the last word and substituted "Rear," adding that his ships would be "ready to receive their Twenty Sail of the Line, or to pursue them should they endeavour to make off. . . .")

He then went on to give his plan in greater detail. John Scott was kept busy for the rest of the day and much of the night supervising the many copies which had to be made of the Memorandum and distributed next day to the captains throughout the Fleet.

That night Nelson wrote in his private diary: "Fresh breezes easterly. Received an account from Blackwood, that the French ships had bent[4] their topgallant sails. Sent the *Pickle* to him, with orders to keep a good look-out. Sent Admiral Collingwood the Nelson Touch. At night wind westerly."

Next day, Thursday, October 10, he wrote to Collingwood: "The enemy's fleet are all but out of the harbour—perhaps, this night, with the northerly wind, they may come forth, and with the westerly sea breeze tomorrow go into the Mediterranean." But he was disappointed: as we have already seen, the council of war had decided otherwise. This Thursday was another busy day for John Scott: Nelson sent fourteen standing orders "to the respective captains" in the Fleet, and they covered subjects ranging from sending in copies of their logs to vouchers for bullocks, lemons and onions, muster books, returns of killed and wounded, shortening sail at night because of sudden gales, and an order concerning the colours that ships were to wear. At this time admirals, vice-admirals and rear-admirals were designated of the blue, the white, or the red. Nelson was a vice-admiral of the white and the ships

---

[4] Sent the sails up the mast and secured them to the yards ready for use.

in his division would wear the white ensign. Collingwood, however, was a vice-admiral of the blue, and his division would normally wear the blue ensign. Now, however, Nelson ordered, "When in presence of an enemy, all the ships under my command are to bear White Colours, and a Union Jack is to be suspended from the fore-topgallant stay."

A further letter went to Blackwood, keeping vigil off Cadiz: "Keep your five frigates, *Weazle* and *Pickle,* and let me know every movement. I rely on you, that we can't miss getting hold of them, and I will give them such a shaking as they never yet experienced: at least I will lay down my life in the attempt. We are a very powerful fleet and not to be held cheap."

On the 11th he began a letter to Emma which he continued on the 12th. He told her that a mutual friend, Captain Sutton, was being invalided back to England. "Ah, my beloved Emma," he wrote, "how I envy Sutton going home; his going to Merton and seeing you and Horatia. I do really feel that the twenty-five days I was at Merton was the very happiest of my life. Would to God they were to be passed over again, but that time will, I trust, soon come, and many, many more days added to them." He added to the letter on the 13th, "I am working like a horse in a mill, but never the nearer finishing my task, which I find difficulty enough in getting and keeping clear from confusion, but I never allow it to accumulate. *Agamemnon* [from England] is in sight, and I hope I shall have letters from you, who I hold dearer than any other person in this world, and I shall hope to hear that all our family goes on well, at that dear, dear cottage. . . ."

More ships were coming out to reinforce his Fleet. In addition to the *Royal Sovereign,* which joined on the 8th, the *Belleisle,* commanded by Captain William Hargood, arrived on the 10th. Two frigates which arrived on the 11th were sent on to Gibraltar to help escort the convoy. When the *Agamemnon,* one of the ships built at Buckler's Hard, was signalled, Nelson slapped his thigh and exclaimed with glee, "Here comes Berry; now we shall have a battle!"

Sir Edward Berry had indeed only just avoided a battle with Allemand, who was still at sea with his battleships, a constant threat to Nelson's communications. Berry reported that he had run into Allemand's force and had been chased, a three-decker getting within gun-shot on the weather quarter and an 80-gun ship on the lee. He had had to pump fresh water over the side and cut away a boat to lighten the ship, and had only escaped after a seventy-mile dash, after which Allemand had recalled his ships. Allemand's ships also chased the British frigate *L'Aimable*, which made an equally skilful escape. A twelve-year-old midshipman who was on board wrote an uninhibited letter to his mother, saying:

> I hope you are all well at home and I am sure will be very glad to hear from me, but you were very near losing me on the 10th of this month, for we were chased by the French Squadron and were very near being come up with, but we cut away two of our boats and one anchor and hove two or three hundred shot overboard. . . . We were so deep we could not sail [fast] until we staved in nine butts of water and pumped it out, and cut the boats adrift. Besides all, there was a very heavy squall came, and we had all sails set [and] were very near going down. She laid down on her beam ends for several minutes. . . . Do not fret about me, for if you cared no more for the French than I, you would care very little about them. Give my love to father, brothers and sisters. Success to William and his rabbits. Dear Mother, I remain, your ever affectionate son, CHARLES.

Calder left for England in the *Prince of Wales* on October 13, the same day that the *Agamemnon* arrived and next day the *Africa*, commanded by Captain Henry Digby, joined the Fleet. The little *Africa*, with 64 guns and a crew of only 490, was the smallest battleship on either side in the battle and was commanded by one of the most successful of captains. The third of the Dorset captains at Trafalgar (Hardy, and Bullen of the *Britannia* were the other two), he was the eldest of three sons of the Dean of Worcester. Going to sea at the age of thirteen, he was later very fortunate with prize money: he was only twenty-nine when, with three frigates, he captured two Spanish ships carrying three million dollars. Each captain received £40,130. Digby had also captured twenty merchant ships, and by the time he was thirty he had received £57,000 in prize money, adding another £6,000 in the next six years. But he was as brave as he was successful: despite her size, the little *Africa* was to tackle the biggest ship in the world, the 130-gun *Santissima Trinidad*.

These October days were now passing quickly, with the Fleet

constantly taking on stores from transport ships. Nelson's plans for the battle were made; it only remained to wait patiently for the enemy to make the first move, and to hope that they did so before the winter gales came whirling in from the Atlantic. The crews of the British ships had little trouble in keeping themselves amused. In the *Britannia*, for instance, the Earl of Northesk's flagship, there was a flourishing amateur dramatics group which had been putting on shows regularly from the time the ship first arrived off Cadiz. The producer was Second Lieutenant L. B. Halloran, of the Marines, whose father, Dr. Halloran, was also on board the *Britannia* as chaplain and secretary to Lord Northesk. The Admiral always lent his fore-cabin for the performances, but they had become so popular it was impossible to get both audience and stage into the fore-cabin. Lord Northesk agreed to the forward bulkhead of the cabin's being taken down, leaving the cabin open to the main deck. Thus the audience could sit on the main deck looking aft into the cabin, which would be the stage. The doors on either side leading aft into the Admiral's day cabin were useful as the stage exits. Previous performances—including *Lord Hastings, Miss in Her Teens, The Siege of Colchester* and *The Mock Doctor* —had whetted everyone's appetite for *Columbus, or a World Discovered,* to be performed on October 9, the day Nelson's Memorandum was delivered on board. Mr. Adams, the Master's mate, had proved an excellent artist and he had painted the scenery which the carpenter had proudly built in his spare time. A large play-bill was prepared which announced: "In the course of the performance will be two splendid processions—a view of the Interior of the Temple of the Sun with a Grand Altar burning incense, etc.—Grand Hymn of Priestesses etc.—Towards the close of the play the Destruction of the Temple by an Earthquake accompanied by Thunder, Lightning and Hail Storms!! With the rescue of Cora from the ruins by Alonzo!!" For several days beforehand the cast had been busy, when off watch, learning their lines. Lt. Wilson was to be the High Priestess of the Sun, with other parts being taken by various other officers, with the midshipmen acting as "priestesses and ladies." Lt. Halloran was also busy putting the finishing touches to a short play he had written called *The Village* which, with *Catharine and Petruchio,* was scheduled for performance a few days later.

In the late afternoon the stage hands—there were always plenty of volunteers—took the bulkheads down, set up the scenery under the direction of Mr. Adams, trimmed the lanterns which were to act as footlights and, after supper, brought up forms from the mess decks and chairs from the wardroom for the audience to sit on. The play-bill had announced "Doors to be open at 6.30. To begin at 7." The crew were in their places promptly at 6.30, the lucky ones getting seats on the forms, the less fortunate squatting on the guns. The officers sat down in the chairs and waited while, in the Admiral's cabin, the cast donned wigs made from teased-out ropes' ends, rouged their faces with red lead, and dressed themselves in clothes skilfully adapted from their workaday rig. Finally Lord Northesk and Captain Bullen made their appearance and sat down in two chairs in the centre of the front row.

At this moment, fifty miles to the eastward, Villeneuve was waiting on board the *Bucentaure* in Cadiz; a few score miles to the north an officer was riding *à franc étrier* for Paris, taking the council of war's decision to Decrès, travelling day and night, pausing only to change horses and, if he had time, snatch a meal, but frequently having to eat in the saddle. Nelson now could only wait. Close in to Cadiz Henry Blackwood watched with the *Euryalus,* and in company were four other frigates (*Naiad,* under Thomas Dundas, *Phoebe,* commanded by the Hon. Thomas Bladen Capel, *Sirius* under William Prowse, and the *Amazon* under command of Captain William Parker), the schooner *Pickle,* and the 16-gun brig *Weazle.* Out to sea, just in sight of the *Euryalus,* and forming the first link in the chain which stretched to the Fleet waiting some fifty miles to the westward, was Captain George Hope with the 74-gun *Defence.* To the west of him Berry waited with the 64-gun *Agamemnon* and beyond him Captain James Morris tacked and wore the *Colossus.* The last link was Captain George Duff, with the *Mars.*

"Touch and Take," Nelson said, was to be his motto; but for the time being it might well have been "Watch and Wait." And while he waited he wrote in his diary. The entry for Wednesday, October 16, said: "Moderate breezes, westerly. All the forenoon employed in forming the fleet into the Order of Sailing . . . in the evening fresh gales. Enemy as before, by signal from *Weazle.*" Next day he wrote, "Moderate breezes, north-westerly. Sent the *Donegal* to Gibraltar to get a ground tier of casks . . . at midnight the wind came round to the eastward." And on Friday: "Fine weather, wind easterly; the Combined Fleets cannot have finer weather to put to sea."

Early on Saturday morning the British Fleet was sailing in two divisions, the one to windward led by Nelson and the other to leeward by Collingwood. Several flag signals were made by the *Victory* to the captains of certain ships asking them to lunch that day and telling them to signal their reply. At the same time Nelson wrote to Collingwood, ending his letter with: "What a beautiful day! Will you be tempted out of your ship? If you will, hoist the 'assent' and *Victory*'s pendants." A boat took this letter across to Collingwood in the *Royal Sovereign*. While he was reading it and before he had time to send his reply, the *Victory* signalled to the *Bellerophon*, which was the fourth ship in Collingwood's division, to close. Captain Cooke had just had time to order the *Bellerophon* to make more sail before she hauled up to windward when his first lieutenant, William Cumby, spotted that the nearest look-out ship, the *Mars*, was flying a hoist of flags from her mast-head. Putting his telescope to his eye he read them—a yellow diagonal cross on a blue background; blue, white and blue vertical stripes, and a flag divided diagonally in white and blue: the signal 370.

"I immediately reported this to Captain Cooke," Cumby wrote later, "and asked his permission to repeat it. The *Mars* at that time was so far from us that her topgallant-masts alone were visible above the horizon; consequently the distance was so great for the discovery of the *colours* of the flags that Captain Cooke said he was unwilling to repeat a signal of so much importance unless he could clearly distinguish the flags himself, which on looking through his glass he declared himself unable to do.

"The very circumstances of the importance of the signal, added to my own perfect conviction of the correctness of my statement founded on long and frequent experience of the strength of my own sight, induced me again to urge Captain Cooke to repeat it, when he said if any other person of the many whose glasses were now fixed on the *Mars* would confirm my opinion he would repeat it. None of the officers or signalmen, however, were bold enough to assent positively, as I did, that the flags were number 370, and I had the mortification to be disappointed in my anxious wish that the *Bellerophon* should be the first to repeat such delightful intelligence to the Admiral.

"Soon afterwards, the *Mars* hauled the flags down, and I said, 'Now she will make the distant signal 370.' "[5] The sharp-eyed and thwarted Cumby added: "She did make the distant signal 370 as I had predicted; this could not be mistaken and we were preparing to repeat it, the *Mars*'s signal was answered from the *Victory,* and immediately afterwards the dinner signal was annulled and the signal given for a general chase." The reason for Cumby's anxiety over signal Number 370 was shown by its meaning given on page 9 of the *Signal Book for the Ships of War:* "The Enemy's ships are coming out of port, or are getting under sail."

[5] Distant signals were used when distances were so great that colours of flags could not be distinguished, or when the wind blew the wrong way (i.e., directly towards or away from the ship to which the signal was made). They consisted of various flags and shapes hauled up at different mastheads, the combination of shape and mast giving the meaning. Those for 370 were a flag, a ball and a pendant.

A topsail schooner—the *Pickle* had this rig.

SEVENTEEN

SIGNAL NUMBER 370

Had I but serv'd my God with half the zeal
I serv'd my king, he would not in mine age
Have left me naked to mine enemies.
> —Shakespeare (*Henry VIII*)

VILLENEUVE was now a man for whom the future held little promise. On October 15 he heard from Bayonne, on the Franco-Spanish border, that Vice-Admiral Rosily had passed through on his way to Cadiz. At the time this report was not alarming, because although Rosily was at the top of the vice-admirals' list he had not been to sea for a dozen years or more, and was often employed by Decrès and Napoleon for various administrative missions. The unfortunate Rosily, bearing the secret orders which sacked Villeneuve and put himself in command of the Combined Fleet, was having a rough time. The journey from Paris to Bayonne presented no difficulties, but the first lap from there to Madrid started off badly. There was only one carriage in Bayonne and the owner made Rosily pay heavily for it. The coach travelled very slowly, and it took Rosily eleven days ("halting at inns where with difficulty I found a bed and leaving at one or two in the morning," he complained to Decrès) to cover the 300 miles across the Pyrenees to Madrid.

Even in the capital his troubles were by no means over. The French Ambassador warned him that he would not be able to travel by postchaise over the remaining 450 miles to Cadiz because there would be no horses for the carriage. From Madrid to beyond Cordoba—more than 250 miles—he could not be given a mounted escort. Instead, to defend him from "a considerable gang of bandits" lurking along forty-five miles of road beyond Cordoba he would have to collect an escort of militia in the town who would march on foot beside him. He expected to reach Cadiz in ten days, he wrote to Decrès from Madrid on October 12.

Although the real reason for Rosily's journey was being kept as secret as possible, rumour travelled a good deal faster than the Admiral, and within a few hours of learning that he had passed through Bayonne, Villeneuve heard reports that Rosily was in fact coming to take over command of the Combined Fleet. Apparently he regarded them as true, and in any case it was now quite clear to him that, whatever Rosily's mission, Decrès and the Emperor were deliberately keeping him in ignorance of it, and that in itself was significant. Swiftly, and without telling anyone, Villeneuve made his plans. His orders from the Emperor to sail at once to Naples still held good, and if he had carried them out before Rosily arrived he could not be blamed—and his honour would be satisfied. His order of battle, showing how the ships were divided into three squadrons with two further squadrons of observation, had been distributed on October 6, before the council of war.

His final instructions to the Combined Fleet—Villeneuve's equivalent of "The Nelson Touch"—was an extraordinary document. It showed that he had in fact correctly guessed the way Nelson would attack and, what is more, he had guessed it ten months to the day before Nelson carried it out. It might be asked why he had not, during that time, attempted to work out a method of countering it; but in fact there was no real defence. It was as if Villeneuve were being forced to behave like a mesmerised rabbit which knows it will be killed by the stoat but is rendered powerless to do anything. Villeneuve's final instructions consisted, in fact, of a re-issue of the last few paragraphs of the general directions given to his captains many months earlier (the originals were dated December 21, 1804) when preparing to leave Toulon. They dealt first with signals, and then said: "I by no means propose to seek out the enemy; I even wish to avoid him in order to proceed to my destination. But should we encounter him, let there be no ignominious manoeuvring; it would dishearten our crews and bring about our defeat." He described what the Combined Fleet was to do if the British were to leeward, and emphasized that "any captain who is not under fire will not be at his post; any whose next ahead or next astern is closer than he to the enemy will not be doing his duty and a signal recalling him to his post will be a reflection on his honour." And if the British attacked from to windward, the Combined Fleet would meet them in a close-formed line of battle.

He then wrote the paragraph which showed he had penetrated Nelson's mind. "The enemy will not confine himself to forming on a line of battle parallel with our own and with engaging us in an artillery duel, in which success lies frequently with the more skilful but always with the more fortunate; he will endeavour to envelop our rear, to break through our line and to direct his ships in groups upon such of ours as he shall have cut off, so as to surround them and defeat them." Having got as far as this, Villeneuve offered no defensive measure to combat it. Instead he wrote: "In this case, a captain in command must consult his own daring and love of honour far more than the signals of the Admiral, who being perhaps engaged himself and shrouded in smoke, may no longer have the power of making any. Here again it is a case of repeating that a captain who is not under fire is not at his post."

He rounded off the instructions with some wishful thinking. "Nothing in the sight of an English Squadron should daunt us . . . they are worn out with a two years' cruise; they are not braver than we and have infinitely less feeling of enthusiasm and patri-otism. They are skilled in seamanship; in a month's time we shall be as skilful. Finally, everything unites to give us the firm hope of the most glorious victories and of a new era for the seamen of the Empire."

With his final orders in the hands of all the French and Spanish captains, Villeneuve's first step was to plan a night attack by a squadron of seven battleships under Magon on Blackwood's five frigates waiting outside Cadiz. With Nelson's "eyes" captured, Magon would then be able to reconnoitre to see where the British Fleet was and what was its strength. If Magon's report was favour-able, the Combined Fleet would sail immediately. Once again Villeneuve had to wait for a favourable easterly wind and a moonless night. On Wednesday evening, October 16, there was a westerly gale which by Thursday morning had dropped to a moderate breeze and veered to north-west. Would it continue to veer? Villeneuve waited, and by midnight it had gone round to the east. Next morning (as Nelson wrote "The Combined Fleet cannot have finer weather to put to sea"), Villeneuve sent orders across to Magon: he was to sail with his force that night.

But by this Friday evening, before darkness fell, a message arrived in Cadiz. It came from Algeciras, the Spanish frontier town overlooking Gibraltar, and had been passed up the coast from one look-out post to another. The British convoy which had been waiting at Gibraltar had at last sailed with an escort of four battleships, while a fifth battleship was at Gibraltar with her mainmast out, and a sixth was steering up the Strait to anchor in the port.[1] Realizing that Nelson's fleet had now been weakened by six battleships, Villeneuve knew he had to seize this chance. He called on Gravina and told him he had made up his mind to sail the next day.

Back on board the *Bucentaure* a series of signal flags was soon fluttering at the mast-head. The first, according to the Spanish ship *Montañes,* ordered the removal of the guns from the long-boats, which had been armed so that they could patrol the entrance to Cadiz. The second hoist ordered each ship to summon its crew on board. This, according to Major-General Contamine (who had just taken over command of the troops from Lauriston) filled the men "with the most ardent desire to give battle; our invalids, soldiers and sailors forsook the hospitals; they rushed to the quay in crowds to embark." The next signal told every ship to send an officer on board the flagship to receive orders, and this was followed by the order to hoist in the boats and to be ready to weigh anchor. But Villeneuve did not attempt to get to sea under the welcome cover of darkness.

He had written to Decrès earlier in the day saying that he had given Magon orders to sail with his squadron next morning to drive off the frigates and carry out a reconnaissance, and that if all was well the Fleet would follow. Then he added: "I am informed that Vice-Admiral Rosily has arrived at Madrid; the com-

[1] The convoy consisted of the forty-nine transports taking reinforcements to Craig which sailed from Gibraltar on October 17, the day before the news reached Villeneuve and the same day that Louis received orders to take his four battleships and escort the convoy past Cartagena. The fifth battleship was the *Zealous,* whose mainmast was to be replaced, and the sixth the *Donegal,* which was going in for water.

mon report is that he is coming to take over the command of the Fleet; undoubtedly I should be delighted to yield him the foremost place if I am permitted to occupy the second; it is due to his seniority and his abilities, but it would be too terrible to me to lose all hopes of having an opportunity of showing that I am worthy of a better fate."

Next day, Saturday, broke with a clear sky and the wind variable, little more than a balmy breeze. Between 5 a.m. and 6 a.m. Villeneuve hoisted the signal for the ships to sail, but the individual captains seem to have been far from clear whether this was intended only for Magon, the frigates or the whole Fleet. Magon's flagship, the *Algésiras*, hove up her anchor, set sail and managed to catch a breeze which took her out of Cadiz, followed by the *Achille*. The frigate *Hermione* was less fortunate and lost the breeze altogether, so Commander Mahé ordered the boats to be put over the side to tow the ship out.

Although some of the battleships and frigates managed to sail out or use their boats for towing before the young flood tide became too strong, the majority of the Combined Fleet did not have enough breeze to warrant their weighing anchor. Gravina's flagship, the *Principe de Asturias*, Villeneuve's *Bucentaure* and the great 130-gun *Santissima Trinidad* stayed where they were. The *Montañes* spent an hour trying to work her way through the tangled mass of ships, many of which had their sails set with boats rowing ineffectually ahead at the end of anchor cables, looking like captive water-beetles. By the evening the only battleships which had managed to get out were Magon in the *Algésiras*, the French *Neptune, Héros, Argonaute, Achille, Duguay-Trouin* and the Spanish *Bahama*. With them were the frigates *Hermione, Themis* and *Rhin*. Once outside, Magon ordered his motley squadron (only two of them actually belonged to his division) to form line of battle, while Villeneuve was forced to order the ships left in Cadiz to anchor. By 10 p.m., to Magon's annoyance, the breeze faded away until his ships barely had steerage way. He tried to keep them together, but in the darkness they lost each other and two of them anchored for the rest of the night off Rota. Thus, as far as the Combined Fleet was concerned, Saturday, October 19, drew to a close. All this time the British ships had kept discreetly

to seaward. And now Villeneuve knew the alarm had been raised
What would Nelson do?

Long before daylight that Saturday morning Henry Blackwood
and his little squadron had been keeping their usual vigil, tacking
back and forth watching the five miles between Cadiz and Cape
San Sebastian on the south side of the anchorage and Rota on the
north side. They were so close in, wrote Midshipman Hercules
Robinson of the *Euryalus*, "as to see the ripple of the beach and
catch the morning fragrance which came off the land." Day after
day the routine had been the same. At 3.30 a.m. on this day the
Euryalus reached the Rota end of the bay with the rest of the
squadron in company and prepared to tack to get the wind on
the other side and sail back again.

"Ready ho!" called a voice from the quarter-deck, clear and
sharp in the night air. "Put the helm down."[2]

The wheel was eased over so that the frigate's bow began to
swing across the wind, pointing directly towards Cadiz for a
moment as it came round.

"The helm's a'lee!"

Up forward the men working in the darkness let go the headsail
sheets so that the sails lost the wind and did not stop the ship's
swing. In a few moments she had come so far round that the wind,
instead of hitting the great square sails at right angles, blew along
their edges, making the canvas flutter and flap instead of arching
with its thrust.

"Off tacks and sheets!"

Men scrambled to new positions, throwing some ropes off their
cleats, hauling on others and preparing to trim the sails. The
ship's bow was now almost pointing into the wind.

"Mainsail haul!"

Quickly men hauled sheets and tacks so that the sails, now
hanging loose and fluttering from the yards, would be ready to
receive the wind as the bow swung across and brought it on to
the other side.

---

[2] The actual wording of orders tended to vary from ship to ship: there were
no standard instructions laid down by the Admiralty, and the only attempts
at standardization were made by individuals who wrote and published seamanship books.

"Let go and haul!"

They braced the great yards smartly round, the sails filled and the *Euryalus* heeled over slightly on the other tack, heading for San Sebastian and Cadiz, with canvas taut and bulging, the sea creaming under the bow and gurgling under the stern. The man at the wheel continually glanced at the compass, his face faintly lit by the reflection of the oil lamp in the binnacle, and then peered at the leech of the sails. Frederick Ruckert, the *Euryalus*'s Master, filled in his log. "At 3.30 tacked ship. Moderate and clear. Out 2nd reef, set foresail and spanker. At 4. ditto weather. Squadron in company. At 5.30, tacked. Sebastian NE, about 4 miles. . . ." Very slowly the sky lightened over the land, the dark grey transmuting itself to a faint pink. The sails overhead, the deck under foot, the wind-rippled sea and the next man's face slowly began to take on their own colours albeit, with the sun still well below the horizon, pale and washed out.

Closer in-shore, Captain William Prowse in the *Sirius* was aiming his telescope at one ship of the Combined Fleet and then another as they swung, like grotesque swans, at anchor in the roads and inside the protective peninsula on which Cadiz stood. His eye ran from mast to mast; then he gave an order which the signal midshipman and signalman went scurrying to execute. Flags were bent on to the halyards and the blocks squealed as, hand over hand, the signalman hoisted them up, each group forming a word in Sir Home Popham's telegraphic code. Over in the *Euryalus* Midshipman Bruce read them off, conscious that every ear on the quarterdeck waited on his words: "249—'enemy'—354—'have'—864—'their' —875—'top'—756—'sails'—986—'yards'—1374—'hoisted.' "

It was 6.04 a.m., and men's pulses quickened as the sun climbed higher over the land, shortening the shadows. Yet on board the frigates the shipboard routine continued as if nothing had happened. The look-outs were now at the mast-heads, hammocks were lashed up and stowed in the nettings round the upper decks; in the galleys the cooks stoked up the fires while the crews kept their fingers crossed that breakfast would be prepared before the captains ordered the drummers to beat to quarters—an order which meant, among other things, that the galley fires would be doused. The minutes sped by and warmth came into the sun. From all the frigates and the *Pickle* and the *Weazle,* telescopes watched the enemy. Were there men climbing the rigging of those northern-most ships like spiders up a web?

There was a slight movement, just visible to Prowse in the *Sirius,* in the upper parts of the masts. Suddenly the topsails were let fall, and they could see the wrinkles in the canvas disappearing as the sheets were hauled. Then the masts moved slowly against the backcloth of the land as the ships got under way, coming slowly round to the north-west, towards the entrance of the anchorage and the broad Atlantic. The signal midshipman quickly went to work, and farther out to sea Midshipman Bruce in the *Euryalus* read off the next signal: "370—'Enemy's ships are coming out of port, or getting under sail.' "

Blackwood had several things to do now. He ordered Bruce to signal the *Phoebe* to go to the westward and repeat signals be-tween the *Euryalus* and the *Defence,* the first link in the chain of ships stretching out to where Nelson waited. Peter Parker in the *Weazle* was ordered to sail immediately to warn Rear-Admiral Louis that the enemy were coming out (Blackwood assumed he would be at Gibraltar or Tetuan), and Signalman Soper hauled up one last cryptic signal to speed Parker on his way: "Make all pos-sible sail with safety to the masts." By this time the *Phoebe* was heading westward, like a blackbird squawking in the hedge, towards the *Defence,* firing three-minute guns and flying the signal that the enemy were coming out of port. Blackwood then ordered Dundas in the *Naiad* to take up a position between the *Euryalus* and the *Phoebe,* ready to pass on further signals. The *Sirius* was left close in to Cadiz with the *Euryalus* farther out. The *Defence* soon repeated the long-awaited warning to the *Agamemnon.* She passed it on to the *Colossus,* who signalled it to the last link, the *Mars.* From the *Mars,* as we have already seen, it reached the *Victory* without the *Bellerophon*'s being able to get the credit for being the first to spot and repeat it.

Nelson had reacted quickly by making a signal to the Fleet for "General chase south-east," his plan being to steer immediately for The Gut, as the Strait of Gibraltar was known, to cut off the Combined Fleet and prevent its sailing through into the Mediter-ranean. In addition Nelson hoped to meet Louis; he did not know that Louis had been delayed, and instead of being on his way back from escorting the Malta convoy, was still sailing eastward with it.

In a faint wind the British Fleet slowly made its way to the south-east, each ship with its yards braced hard up to catch every scrap of breeze. At noon Nelson went down to his cabin and sat once again at his desk to write two letters, one to each of the people he loved and longed for so dearly.

Victory, October 19th, 1805, Noon, Cadiz, E.S.E. 16 leagues

My dearest beloved Emma, the dear friend of my bosom. The signal has been made that the Enemy's Combined Fleet are coming out of port. We have very little wind, so that I have no hopes of seeing them before tomorrow. May the God of Battles crown my endeavours with success; at all events, I will take care that my name shall ever be most dear to you and Horatia, both of whom I love as much as my own life. And as my last writing before the Battle will be to you, so I hope in God that I shall live to finish my letter after the Battle. May Heaven bless you prays your

NELSON & BRONTE.

He put the letter away in his desk. He was to make one more addition to it. He still had another letter to write, and it was to Horatia.

My dearest Angel, I was made happy by the pleasure of receiving your letter of September 19th, and I rejoice to hear that you are so very good a girl, and love my Dear Lady Hamilton who most dearly loves you. Give her a kiss for me. The Combined Fleets of the Enemy are now reported to be coming out of Cadiz; and therefore I answer your letter, my dearest Horatia, to mark to you that you are ever uppermost in my thoughts. I shall be sure of your prayers for my safety, conquest and speedy return to dear Merton, and our dearest good Lady Hamilton. Be a good girl, mind what Miss Connor says to you. Receive my dearest Horatia, the affectionate parental blessing of your Father.

NELSON & BRONTE

At 3 p.m. Captain Morris's *Colossus,* the ship beyond the *Mars* in the communication chain, came hurrying up, all sails set and firing guns to draw attention. From her mastheads flew another series of signals reporting that the enemy's fleet was at sea. Unfortunately this information, following the report that they were leaving port, was only partly accurate.

Blackwood, in the meantime, had continued watching the enemy ships as they slowly worked their way out of the Bay. By 10 a.m. the breeze had shown every sign of fading right away, and by noon had carried out its threat. The *Euryalus* and *Sirius* wallowed and drifted, sails hanging limply from the yards like so much old and much-patched laundry. In the entrance to Cadiz the enemy ships had been in the same plight.

Blackwood had taken the opportunity to go down to his cabin and wrote a letter to his wife:

> What think you, my own dearest love? At this moment the enemy are coming out, and as if determined to have a fair fight; all night they have been making signals, and the morning shewed them to us getting under sail They have thirty-four sail of the line and five frigates. Lord Nelson has but twenty-seven sail of the line with him; the rest are at Gibraltar, getting water. Not that he has not enough to bring them to close action; but I want him to have so many as to make this the most decisive battle that was ever fought, and which may bring us lasting peace and all its blessings.
>
> Within two hours, though our fleet was sixteen leagues off, I have let Lord N. [*sic*] know of their coming out, and have been enabled to send a vessel to Gibraltar, which will bring Admiral Louis and the ships there.
>
> At this moment (happy sight) we are within four miles of the enemy, and talking to Lord N. by means of Sir H. Popham's signals, though so distant, but reached along by the rest of the frigates of the Squadron.
>
> You see dearest, I have time to write to you, and to assure you that to the latest moment of my breath, I shall be as much attached to you as man can be. It is odd how I have been dreaming all night of carrying home despatches. God send me such good luck. The day is fine, and the sight magnificently beautiful. I expect before this hour tomorrow to carry General [*sic*] Decrès[3] on board the *Victory* in my barge, which I have just painted nicely for him.

As evening came on Nelson formed the "Advanced Squadron" visualized in his Memorandum by putting eight of his fastest ships under the command of that appreciative Scot, Captain George Duff in the *Mars*. They were to burn lights during the night and some of them were to keep to the eastward and maintain contact with

---

[3] The British Fleet had heard as early as October 9 that Villeneuve was to be superseded, and it was assumed that Decrès would take command.

Blackwood's frigates. The three slow ships of the British Fleet, the 100-gun *Britannia* and the two 98-gun ships *Prince* and *Dreadnought*, were ordered to "take station as convenient."

While Nelson was under the impression that all the enemy had sailed, the position at midnight was that most of the French and Spanish ships were still at anchor in Cadiz. Outside, the *Achille* and *Bahama* were at anchor off Rota, while Magon's other five battleships were scattered to the north-west of Cadiz, with the frigates well up to windward. Blackwood with the *Euryalus, Sirius* and *Phoebe* were close by to seaward. Beyond them, forming the link with the main fleet which was now some twenty-five miles west of Cadiz and steering for The Gut, were the *Defence*, then the *Colossus* and finally, nearest to Nelson, the *Mars*.

A letter Codrington of the *Orion* wrote in the evening gives a good description of the day:

> How would your heart beat for me, dearest Jane, did you but know that we are now under every stitch of sail we can set, steering for the enemy. . . . We have now a nice air, which fills our flying kites and drives us along four knots an hour [*sic*].
>
> I trust by the morning we shall be united and in sight of the enemy. As to my coming out of the battle alive or dead, that is the affair of chance and the little cherub: but that I shall come out without dishonour is my affair; and yet I have but little apprehension about the matter, so great is my confidence in my ship, and in our excellent Admiral.
>
> It is not, my dear Jane, that I am insensible to the value of life with such a domestic circle as I belong to: no, my heart was never more alive to the sacrifice than at this very moment. But life in such a situation as this, even with the delightful prospect of returning to pass years in the society of a wife and children whom I love with a religious reverence, is really but a secondary consideration. . . .
>
> I feel a little tired; and as I have now nothing to do but keep the ship's head the right way, and take care that the sails are well trimmed, in readiness for the morning, I shall even make that over to the officer of the watch and go to my cot; nor do I think I shall sleep the worse for my cabin being only divided from the quarter-deck by a boat's sail. [The bulkheads had been removed because the ship was expecting to go into action.] And so, dear, I shall wish thee once more a good night, and that thy husband's conduct in the hour of battle may prove worthy of thee and thy children.

Overhead, the sky which had in the later afternoon speckled its blue dome with white feathery mares' tails, gave its silent warning of the promise of bad weather.

Dawn on Sunday, October 20, brought with it dull weather: thick cloud masked the sun, and what wind there was came up from the south. About 6 a.m. Villeneuve once again ordered the Combined Fleet to weigh anchor and make for the open sea. Shortly after 7 a.m. the *Bucentaure* hoisted a signal ordering the ships to clear for action and prepare for battle. By 8 a.m. all the ships were under sail except the Spanish *Rayo,* commanded by the Irishman, MacDonell. Lt. Taillard's little brig *Argus,* which had been given the task of acting as whipper-in, set her topsails and tacked patiently back and forth. Finally Taillard had a boat lowered and sent across to ask MacDonell what was delaying him. The Irishman answered that he had a lot of anchors to raise, but he would soon be ready.

Ashore, the quays and roads overlooking the anchorage were now thronged with people—many of them in tears—to bid the Combined Fleet farewell. Mothers and fathers, wives and sweethearts of many of the Spanish crews queued outside the Iglesia del Carmen, the old sailors' church, to be admitted in relays; at the high altar of the Oratorio de San Felipe Neri, Archbishop Utrera spent the day on his knees pleading with his God for the safety of the great ships.

By 10 a.m. the weather was rapidly worsening; the wind went round to the south-west and increased, bringing heavy seas and rain squalls. One of the first orders Villeneuve gave that morning when he got outside was for his fleet to reef. And the wind was foul for the Strait of Gibraltar, the very course he wanted to steer. . . . The *Argus,* having at last seen the *Rayo* on its way, hurried out of Cadiz to report to Villeneuve that all was well.

Villeneuve had great trouble in getting the Combined Fleet, consisting of thirty-three battleships, five frigates and two brigs, into some semblance of formation. He ordered the Fleet to sail on a course of west-north-west, which was about the closest even a well-handled battleship could steer to the wind. Raw seamen, hastily trained while the ships were at anchor, were now having to scramble aloft and lay out on yards swaying upwards of a hundred and fifty feet above sea level with strong winds tearing at them and trying to fling them off. The thick, stiff canvas flogged and thrashed as they tried to tie reef points, tearing the nails from their fingers and stripping off the skin. The result was that several of the ships sagged off to leeward of the main fleet; and in the midst of the confusion a man fell overboard from the *Bucentaure*. She immediately signalled this to her next-astern, the *Redoutable*, commanded by Lucas. He at once hove-to, had a boat lowered, picked up the man and got under way again with the minimum delay.

At about noon Villeneuve signalled his fleet to form itself into three columns—a disposition which meant that only one column could fire at the enemy without the risk of hitting its own ships. Once again there was confusion as the ships manoeuvred to get into position. They still had not managed to do so when the wind suddenly swung round to the west. If Villeneuve kept the Fleet on the same tack it would be forced up to the north—the opposite course to the one for the Strait. So he ordered the Fleet to go about, to bring the wind on to the starboard side and thus steer southward. But ordering a half-formed fleet to tack was a dangerous business, and as he saw his ships milling around the *Bucentaure*, falling astern or sagging down to leeward, giving the appearance of a flock of startled sheep, he must have known in his heart that the dice was loaded against him.

Blackwood's frigates stayed on the edge of the horizon, watching every move, yet Villeneuve himself still had no news of the whereabouts of Nelson's Fleet until six o'clock in the evening, when the *Achille* reported sighting eighteen ships in the distance. The French admiral, frightened of the consequences of meeting Nelson with the Combined Fleet in three columns, promptly ordered it to form line of battle. The result was something approaching chaos, because the ships still had not formed into three columns and they could not sort themselves out before night came down. The *Achille* later reported that a ship would take station as soon as she saw three or four ahead of her in the darkness. Thus it was with his ships moving southward in a vast, unco-ordinated mass, lights showing from ports and through the tiers of windows in the stern galleries, that

Villeneuve spent Sunday night. Round the fleet, hidden in the
darkness, the British frigates watched in silence.

Nelson was cheerful enough at first, because he did not have to
worry about ships manned by raw sailors and tardy and unskilful
captains. Steering south-east during the night, by dawn on Sunday
morning the British Fleet was some dozen miles off Cape Trafalgar
and thirty miles from the narrowest part of the Strait of Gibraltar.
The weather had changed for the worse, as we have already seen, and
with daylight coming anxious eyes searched all round the horizon
for a sight of the enemy. Codrington of the *Orion* gave vent to his
feelings in another letter to Jane which he wrote before breakfast:
"All our gay hopes are fled; and, instead of being under all possible
sail in a very light breeze and fine weather, expecting to bring the
enemy to battle, we are now under close-reefed topsails in a very
strong wind with thick rainy weather, and the dastardly French we
find returned to Cadiz. . . ."

Nelson's cheerfulness quickly disappeared. Strong winds, rough
seas and heavy rain which cut visibility down to a few hundred
yards, was just the weather—as Codrington had realized—to send
the Combined Fleet scurrying back to Cadiz with broken topmasts,
torn sails and seasick crews. The Admiral knew that, had Villeneuve sailed on, the Combined Fleet would now be very near, and
that was quite clearly not the case. And it was equally clear that the
British Fleet could not stay off Cape Trafalgar under present conditions lest a storm blow up. He was probably making up his mind
to take the Fleet to the north-west, back the way they had just
sailed, when the *Mars,* closely followed by the *Defiance, Defence*
and *Phoebe,* signalled that the enemy was to the northward. So at
6.20 a.m. on Sunday morning Nelson gave the order for the Fleet
to wear and sail back to the north-west.

What had happened was that the British Fleet had arrived too
early: Nelson, understanding from the frigates on Saturday morning that the whole of the Combined Fleet had sailed, had promptly
headed for the Strait, but as we have already seen, only a few
enemy ships, led by Magon, had succeeded in getting out that day.
And it was not until ten minutes after Nelson ordered the Fleet to
retrace its steps this Sunday morning that Villeneuve, still in the
Cadiz roads, had hoisted the signal for the Combined Fleet to sail.

Collingwood was now invited to the *Victory,* and Duff, Morris and Hope were told to drop to leeward with their ships so that they could support Blackwood's frigates.

However, the bustle of organizing the Fleet did not interrupt the shipboard routine: it was Sunday, and at nine o'clock the Reverend Dr. A. J. Scott, as the *Victory's* Master noted briefly in his log, "performed Divine Service." It was uncomfortable for the crew, with the ship rolling and rain squalls sweeping the deck. Just after the service began the *Agamemnon* passed on a signal to the *Victory* from the *Euryalus* which began to correct the somewhat distorted picture of the enemy's strength and position: thirteen of the enemy had left Cadiz, and the rest had their yards hoisted and were about to follow.

By noon the British Fleet was south-west of Cadiz, steering west-north-west, and unknown to Nelson the Combined Fleet, having now successfully emerged from port, was twenty-five miles away to the north attempting to steer a similar course. Above all else, Nelson was anxious to know whether there was a chance of Ville-neuve's doubling back into Cadiz. Fortunately Henry Blackwood must also have realized this: signalling to the *Sirius,* "I am going to the Admiral, but return before night," he reached the Fleet by 3 p.m. and twenty minutes later on board the *Euryalus* Midshipman Bruce and his signalman, Soper, were busy with a new signal: "The enemy appears determined to push to the westward: thirty ships." "And that," the Admiral wrote later in his private diary, "they shall *not* do if in the power of Nelson & Bronte to prevent them. At 5 telegraphed Captain B., that I relied upon his keeping sight of the enemy."

That Sunday afternoon the Admiral walked up and down the weather side of the poop, watching the ships, hearing Lt. Pasco reading off the signals they made, fitting the scraps of information together in his mind like a man doing a jig-saw puzzle. He had already said to both Hardy and Dr. Scott that "The 21st of October will be our day." Now, to a group of young midshipmen standing near him, he said with a smile: "This day or tomorrow will be a fortunate one for you young men." It was a grim jest, but one they understood: heavy casualties in the Fleet, especially among the lieutenants, would mean promotion to acting rank for some fortunate midshipmen.

Nelson's night orders for the watch on the enemy were drawn up so that Blackwood with two frigates would keep in sight of the enemy, passing signals to two other frigates. They in turn would link with the *Defence,* which would keep in touch with the *Mars,* the last ship in the chain to the *Victory.* The signals for the night were: "If the enemy are standing to the southward, or towards the Strait, burn two blue lights together, every hour, in order to make the greater blaze. If the enemy are standing to the westward three guns, quick, every hour."

Yet even though Nelson was, without being able to see his opponent's moves, playing a most intricate game of chess upon which the fate of Britain—indeed, of freedom itself—depended, he still had time to remember the smaller details which contribute to victory. Midshipman Richard Roberts recorded it thus: "*Victory* tellegraphed [sic] to the *Africa* to paint the hoops of her mast yellow." The signal was also made to the *Belleisle,* because she too had her mast-hoops painted black. Nelson knew that this was a French custom, and in the thick smoke of battle the colour of the mast-hoops might well be the only way of identifying a ship before pouring a broadside into her.

Earlier in the day Nelson had added a few more sentences to his letter to Emma, describing the day's events: "In the morning we were close to the mouth of the Strait, but the wind had not come far enough to the westward to allow the Combined Fleets to weather the shoals off Trafalgar; but they were counted as far as forty sail of ships of war, which I suppose to be thirty-four of the line and six frigates. A group of them was seen off the Lighthouse of Cadiz this morning, but it blows so very fresh and thick weather, that I rather believe they will go into the Harbour before night. May God Almighty give us success over these fellows, and enable us to get a peace."

By Sunday evening, however, he was fairly sure that the enemy were not going into Cadiz for the night, and at supper he commented to those sitting at his table: "Tomorrow I will do that which will give you young gentlemen something to talk and think about for the rest of your lives, but I shall not live to know about it myself." He added that he expected to capture from twenty to twenty-two enemy ships.

So Sunday, October 20, drew swiftly to a close. At 5 p.m. the

Naiad reported that the Combined Fleet was at last steering to the south. Nelson did not want to get too close, in case Villeneuve was frightened back into port. He therefore signalled that the Fleet would go on to the starboard tack at the close of the day, putting them into a commanding position, ten miles to windward and five miles ahead of the enemy, ready to counter any move Blackwood's frigates might report. At 8.30 p.m. the order for the Fleet to come on to the starboard tack and thus sail south was given. One ship missed the signal—the little *Africa,* commanded by Digby. She continued sailing north.

Everything was now ready. The fact that the enemy had stayed at sea in the heavy weather instead of turning back made Nelson certain that there would be a battle on the morrow. His Fleet was concentrated up to windward, with the frigates down to leeward watching Villeneuve's every move and lighting flares or firing guns.

Aboard the *Britannia,* Lord Northesk and Captain Bullen had supper with the officers but did not linger long over the port. As soon as they had gone back to their cabins the officers and men went to work taking down the bulkheads and stowing them in the holds, and clearing the ship for action. "We, however, all went to rest at our usual hours," wrote Lt. Halloran, "having only hanging screens instead of cabins." Monday was going to have a different climax from the one he and his fellow amateur actors had planned. Lord Northesk, at forty-six a quiet, stolid and efficient officer, went back to his cabin after supper and wrote to his wife, dating the somewhat clumsily phrased letter:

> *Britannia,* off Cadiz at 10 o'clock p.m. Oct 20 1805
>
> My dearest wife,
>
> We have every hope of bringing the enemy to action; if I should not survive the glorious day; take care of yourself and my dear children and I beg you may have one [he then crossed out "one" and wrote "two" above it] thousand pounds after my death for your own use and at your own disposal beside what I left you by will—made in Scotland and at Battle—Believe me ever to have been your affectionate husband, NORTHESK.

He folded and interleaved the sheet, heated some black sealing wax and dropped a blob on to the paper. Then he pressed his seal on to it and wrote on the outside simply: "Countess of Northesk."

In the *Neptune,* young Midshipman William Lovell, little guessing that one day he would become a vice-admiral, was excited. "All hearts towards evening beat with joyful anxiety for the next day, which we hoped would crown our anxious blockade labours with a successful battle," he wrote. "When night closed in, the rockets and blue lights, with signal guns, informed us that the inshore squadron still kept sight of our foes, and, like good and watchful dogs, our ships continued to send forth occasionally a growling cannon to keep us alert, and to cheer us with a hope of a glorious day on the morrow."

As far as the frigates were concerned, Midshipman Robinson felt that at least the *Euryalus* had done her share: "When we had brought the two fleets fairly together we took our place between the lines of lights, as a cab might in Regent Street, the watch was called and Blackwood turned in quietly to wait for the morning."

An hermaphrodite brig.

EIGHTEEN

"PREPARE FOR BATTLE"

O, that a man might know
The end of this day's business ere it come!
But it sufficeth that the day will end,
And then the end is known.
—Shakespeare (*Julius Caesar*)

ON MONDAY, October 21, men of many nations waited with ill-concealed impatience for the dawn, but it seemed reluctant to lighten the black of night to the eastward, as if unwilling to begin such a dreadful day. In the darkness, the British Fleet tacked and then sailed slowly northward, more than thirty miles from Cape Trafalgar. In-shore of them, some fifteen miles away, the Combined Fleet was on an almost opposite course, heading south-east and dogged by Blackwood's frigates. They, like dark phantoms on the edge of a dozing man's consciousness, lit two blue flares from time to time which bathed their ships in an eerie light, bringing disquiet to many French and Spanish hearts.

In the *Victory* a Marine sentry, hot and sticky in short scarlet jacket and white pipe-clayed crossbelts, white breeches and gaiters, shifted the weight from one foot to the other as he stood guard over Lord Nelson's cabin, and hidden away in some dark corner within earshot the Admiral's steward, Henry Chevalier, snatched some sleep. Inside the cabin Nelson's slender body was resting, lying in the narrow cot slung from the deckhead, half hidden by the hangings which Emma had embroidered. The cot swung from side to side as the *Victory* pitched and rolled in the heavy swell which was welling up in the darkness under an otherwise calm and breeze-dappled sea.

Two decks below and farther forward, the men who were off watch slept in a fetid atmosphere, their hammocks swinging in unison, their snores punctuating the creaking of the timbers. There were Richard Collins, of Philadelphia, now twenty-one years old, who had been press-ganged into the Royal Navy and transferred to the *Victory* two years earlier, and William Thompson, from the same town, who was a volunteer. Hans Yaule, a Swiss, had been twenty when his ship brought him to the Thames and he was seized by the press-gang. A Frenchman whose name was put down on the *Victory*'s muster list as John Packett—the nearest the English ear could approximate to his pronunciation— came from Le Havre (better known then as Havre-de-Grace). Now, at forty-five, a press-ganged able seaman, he was about to fight his own countrymen. Samuel Lovett, born forty years earlier at Portsmouth, America, had suddenly found himself press-ganged at Portsmouth in England, and hustled aboard the *Victory*. Stromblo Milligue, a Sicilian from Messina, was a volunteer, as was another Frenchman, John Dupuis, of Nantes. The press-gang had also caught Matthew Miers, a German from Hamburg, and Dominick Dubine, from Italy. William Sweet, of New York, had been in Nelson's flagship for a year and a day—he had been brought on board on October 20, 1804.

The *Victory* was a cosmopolitan ship: of the 663 officers and men (excluding Marines and boys) mustered four days earlier, there were 441 English, sixty-four Scots, sixty-three Irish, eighteen Welshmen, three Shetlanders, two Channel Islanders and one Manxman. Of the seventy-one foreigners who volunteered or were press-ganged, twenty-two were Americans, seven Dutch, six Swedes, three Frenchmen, two Danes, three Norwegians, one Russian, three Germans, two Swiss, two Portuguese, four Italians, four Maltese and two Indians, while one man was African and nine came from the West Indian islands.

The 441 Englishmen on board came from many parts of the country. Included among them were more than a hundred from London, and twenty-seven from Kent. Twenty-four were Devonians, but only six Cornishmen; fifteen were, like Nelson, from Norfolk and twelve came from Suffolk, while Hampshire contributed twenty and Northumberland, Lancashire and Yorkshire eighteen each. Essex and Lincolnshire each sent nine, and Oxfordshire and Herefordshire a dozen, while Durham—reflecting perhaps the number of its men who went into the coasting trade from its flourishing ports and were seized by the press-gangs—sent seventeen. The youngest of the *Victory*'s crew was Johnny Doag, aged ten and rated "boy, first class." Four others were only twelve, and six but a year older. And also on board—although none of the crew knew it—was a woman dressed as a man. She was the wife of one of the four Maltese seamen.

Now, whether they were white or coloured, British or foreign, they had taken the oath, each swearing to be true to his Sovereign Lord King George the Third and to "serve him honestly and faithfully in defence of his person, Crown and dignity against all his enemies and oppressors whatsoever." Whether they heeded or even understood that oath, they were now—like their fellow seamen in the other twenty-six battleships of the British Fleet—being borne along in the great wooden ship towards a battlefield where death waited to look them over. Having long since ceased to be masters of their fate—the press-gangs, their oath and the Articles of War had seen to that—they waited, in their hammocks or on watch, to become heroes or cowards, corpses or cripples. Living a life little removed from slavery, fed with food rather more suited to swine, rarely given leave to go ashore, and having frequently been snatched up while going about their lawful occasions on land, they would meet the enemy shouting defiance, showing raw bravery and fighting like fiends, proud of their hour of glory.

Looking back on the scene from more than a century and a half away, one might be forgiven for musing that by contemporary standards the food and the system might well have produced men who were sick and sullen, mutinous and cowardly. Instead, strange material and unpromising circumstances were about to be forged by the Royal Navy into a great British tradition.

In each of the British ships as they continued steering northward in the darkness before Monday's dawn, a faint light from the binnacle lit the compass and reflected in the helmsman's face as he stood sure-footed at the wheel easing the spokes this way and then that, using a mixture of craft and guile to keep his ship on course. Overhead the great yards creaked and groaned (the *Victory*'s main yard was more than a hundred feet long); the massive, arching sails occasionally gave prodigious flaps as an extra large swell rolled the ship and the to-and-fro movement of the masts snatched the wind out of the canvas. The ropes of the sheets and braces grumbled to themselves as they rendered through numerous blocks before reaching their respective cleats, and the slings and trusses which held up the yards and kept them close to the masts creaked in sympathy. The slow roll tried to shift the guns; the breeching and tackles added their murmur as the carriages pulled and strained against the ropes fixed to eye-bolts in the ship's side.

Then the ships suddenly came to life. The bosun's mates with their shrill pipes—which earned them the nickname of "Spithead Nightingales"—soon had the men lashing up their hammocks and stowing them in the nettings on the upper deck. And over to the eastward, almost imperceptibly, a small band of blackness on the horizon diluted into grey and began to spread outward and upward. In his cabin Nelson scrambled awkwardly from his cot and began to wash, while Chevalier brought him a hot drink. The breeze was showing signs of becoming fitful, but the sea still creamed away from the cutwater at the bow in lazily folding waves and swilled under the stern, acting invisibly against the rudder as it bubbled aft to become the wake. Gradually the ship moved from its black world into the greyness of morning twilight. From the quarter-deck of each ship, the long, smoothly rounded crests of the swell-waves could now be distinguished, rippling like shadows across the otherwise calm sea. As it grew lighter the waves seemed to grow bigger, but this was a common optical illusion.

In the *Victory* a small figure with an empty sleeve[1] stepped up the weather ladder on to the poop, and everyone already there automatically moved respectfully over to the lee side. Nelson was wearing his usual threadbare frock coat, with his orders of knighthood embroidered on the left breast. They were, as always, tarnished from the salt air and spray. His sword had been taken down from the rack in his cabin but left lying on a table.

The first sight of the enemy is perhaps best described by an able seaman in the *Victory*, J. Brown, born twenty-three years earlier in Waterford and writing to "Mr Thos Windever, at the

---

[1] Nelson did not usually wear a black patch over his eye—except in the popular imagination. None of the authentic portraits show one (see Abbott's, illustration Number 2) and since there was no disfigurement to the eye it was not necessary. He did wear a shade attached to his cocked hat to help shield his good eye from strong light. The shade can be seen on the actual hat of the effigy in Westminster Abbey.

Sign of the blue bell new Albs Street Liverpool." With scant regard to punctuation he wrote: "At day light the french and Spanish Fleets was like a great wood on our lee bow which cheered the hearts of every british tar in the *Victory* like lions Anxious to be at it. . . ."

Dawn had given way to what young Hercules Robinson in the *Euryalus* called "a beautiful misty sun-shiny morning," with the sea like a mill-pond, apart from the ominous ground swell rolling in from the Atlantic. And Midshipman Badcock in Fremantle's *Neptune* described the scene years later when he was himself an admiral: "The sun rose, which, as it ascended from its bed of ocean, looked hazy and watery, as if it smiled in tears on many brave hearts which fate had decreed would never see it set."

On board the *Royal Sovereign* Collingwood's servant, Smith, had gone into the Admiral's cabin at daylight and found him already up and dressing. "Have you seen the French Fleet?" Collingwood asked. Smith replied that he had not. "Then look out at them," said Collingwood; "in a very short time we will see a lot more of them." In recalling that morning Smith wrote: "I then observed a crowd of ships to leeward; but I could not help looking with still greater interest at the Admiral, who, during all this time, was shaving himself with a composure which quite astonished me." After dressing with particular care Collingwood went up on deck. He saw Lt. John Clavell wearing high leather boots. "You had better put on silk stockings as I have done," the Admiral observed, "for if one should get a shot in the leg, they are so much more manageable for the surgeon."

Nelson, standing on the poop of the *Victory*, surveyed the enemy ships silhouetted to leeward against the lighter eastern sky and apparently making their way towards the Strait. Although to leeward, as he intended, they were not as he had pictured, "in the line of battle ready to attack"; instead they appeared to be in no formation at all, simply a mass of ships scurrying southward. However, with this light wind it would be several hours before they could be brought to action. In the meantime it was now light enough for the British ships to see the *Victory*'s flag signals, and Nelson set about putting his own Fleet in order. Up to then it had been in a loose formation and at 6.10 a.m., before the sun had risen over Cape Trafalgar to the eastward, Nelson gave instructions to Lt. Pasco to hoist the signal for the Fleet to form the order of sailing in two columns. Signal Number 72 was run up, and the ships of the Fleet quickly hoisted the answering pennant and prepared to get into station astern either the *Victory* or the *Royal Sovereign,* depending upon their division.

Nelson had two main concerns, now that he had spotted his quarry. Keeping the weather gage was the first, allowing his Fleet to manoeuvre much more freely and disguise until the last moment exactly where it would attack the enemy (preventing Villeneuve from reinforcing any part of his line, since he would not know where the blow would fall); the second was to cut off the enemy from their bolt-hole of Cadiz which, for all the manoeuvring since they sailed, was still only a bare twenty-five miles away to the northward. If Nelson sailed to the east-north-east he would both stay up to windward *and* cut them off, and at 6.13 a.m. a second signal was run up aboard the *Victory:* to bear up and sail large on an east-north-easterly course. (Sailing large meant that the wind was free—abaft the beam.) Then, at 6.46 a.m., he made one more order to the Fleet—to come round two points to starboard and steer due east.

Now Nelson's column was heading towards the rear of the enemy's line and Collingwood's, a mile away to the south, was heading for the van. Nelson may well have guessed that Villeneuve would eventually turn back to the north, towards Cadiz, and this order to steer east, although it was made five and a quarter hours before the first British ship fired a shot at the enemy, was the last manoeuvring signal he had to give to the Fleet as a whole.[2]

The *Victory*'s signal lieutenant was having a busy time. Nelson regarded the signal lieutenant's job as a very important one, and had given it to John Pasco, who was senior lieutenant. He then appointed a junior officer to take over what should have been Pasco's job of being first lieutenant, choosing John Quilliam, who was fifth in seniority.[3] This switching round had annoyed Pasco

[2] For those who are concerned that Nelson did not attack exactly according to his Memorandum, the fact that the Fleet as a whole sailed for five and a quarter hours without further manoeuvring signals, shows that the captains knew all along exactly what was expected of them, and that the Memorandum was regarded only as an *aide-mémoire.* For the signal to bear up, see Notes, p. 372.

[3] Quilliam was a Manxman who had been pressed into the Navy.

considerably, and he had a very legitimate grievance. After a successful action it was usual to promote the first lieutenant who was, of course, normally the senior. Under Nelson's system, however, the senior might receive no recognition, but the lucky junior would. Pasco was waiting to point this out to Nelson, but had up to now been unable to find an opportunity.

More than twenty minutes before the order to steer east was given, Pasco had been ordered to hoist the signal for which the Fleet had been waiting with ill-concealed impatience for many weary months. It was Number 13—"Prepare for battle." "Flagship signals 'Prepare for battle,'" the signal officers in various ships reported to their captains. Immediately the order "Clear for action!" was shouted from the quarter-decks. Bosun's mates ran to the hatchways, their pipes sounding the call like a chorus of angry birds. At once the men went to work.

In the *Victory*, Lt. Quilliam detailed off parties of men to go round and finish off the already partly completed task of clearing away the bulkheads forming the cabins. If they were hinged at the top they were swung up horizontally to the deckhead and secured out of the way, making a false ceiling; if they were not hinged they were knocked down section by section and carried below into the hold. In this way the decks were opened up from one end of the ship to the other: a man standing at the after end of Nelson's cabin against the stern windows could now look right through to the forward end of the fo'c'sle, past the mizenmast where it came through the deck, past the elm-tree pump which was hollowed from a solid tree and past the mainmast and the foremast. He could see fifteen 12-pounder guns ranged uniformly along each side of the ship, and the shot, like black beads, stowed in the racks round the hatchways.

The men took the furniture—chairs, tables, a cot and desk—from Captain Hardy's cabin under the poop and carried it carefully down four ladders to the orlop, from where it was lowered into the holds. Most of the Admiral's furniture was left for the time being until he had given his special instructions, but the few pieces of furniture and sea chests in the lieutenants' cabins were dragged below. On the mess decks the tables now slung up on the deckhead between the guns were taken down and stowed in the hold together with the forms on which the men sat. All this was done not to protect the furniture but the men: a shot hitting a bulkhead or a piece of furniture would shatter it into scores of splinters—sharp slivers which could kill or wound a man almost as effectively as grape-shot or musket balls. All wooden ladders not needed in action were unshipped and taken below, rope ladders being fitted in their place; leather fire buckets were moved away from the ship's side and placed near the centre-line.

While Quilliam's men cleared the ship below decks, William Willmet, the *Victory*'s bosun, collected his mates and some seamen to carry out Article VII in *Regulations and Instructions* relating to the boatswain's duties—"When the ship is preparing for battle, he is to be very particular in seeing that everything necessary for repairing rigging is in its proper place, that the men stationed to that service may know where to find immediately whatever may be wanted."

The first task for Willmet and his "Spithead Nightingales" was to make sure that the great yards on which the sails were set would not come crashing down on to the deck, where they would do untold damage. The thick rope slings were reinforced with chains. Extra sheets and braces were rove in case those in use should be shot away, and by exercising a little cunning much of the rigging could be arranged so that if some was cut the rest would take the strain of holding up masts and yards. Grappling irons (large grapnels) were secured to ropes and hung from the lower yard-arms or ranged along the bulwarks ready to be hooked to an enemy ship to clutch it in a lethal embrace. The boats stowed amidships would be left, but the quarter boats would be towed astern in action, where they would be comparatively safe from shot and would not get in the way of the guns. Axes were placed round the upper deck where they could be snatched up by men to cut away wreckage. Splinter nets were slung between the masts.

The surgeon, William Beatty, went down to the cockpit amidships on the orlop with the two assistant surgeons, and the loblolly men who acted as nursing orderlies. As soon as the ship was in action the purser, Mr. Walter Burke, would join them to bear a hand, and the *Victory*'s chaplain, Dr. Scott, would be there to help comfort the men. The cockpit was a dark and cheerless place, lit only by a few dim lanterns and now cleared of everything except for a few forms and tables which stood starkly in the middle of the open space like altars. This was, indeed, where the wounded men would be offered up to Beatty's skill: limbs would be amputated without anaesthetics—other than perhaps a stiff tot of rum—and with the loblolly men holding down the unfortunate and writhing victim. A couple of tubs would soon be rolled along and put by the table ready, as the men termed it, for the "wings and limbs" that accumulated as Beatty went about his gruesome work.

Forward in the cable tier, on the same deck, men were wrestling with the massive rope anchor-cables (each twenty-four inches in circumference) to make as level a surface as possible; awnings and spare sails would then be laid out flat on top, and here wounded men would lie awaiting their turn to be treated. To avoid favouritism it was a strict rule that the wounded were attended to in the same order that they were brought down to the cockpit or cable tier. It was a fair rule in the sense in which it was intended; in practice, however, it meant that many of the badly wounded— especially those who had lost limbs—died from loss of blood before their turn came.

The gunner, Mr. William Rivers, and his mates, went to the main and the two hanging magazines, the most carefully protected parts of the ship. Built below the water-line, where they could be quickly flooded in case of fire, their bulkheads were lined with felt and no lanterns were allowed inside. To provide light there were small light rooms with glass windows built on to the side of the magazines. Lanterns placed in the light rooms showed a dim light without any danger of fire. With the lanterns lit, Rivers and his mates put on soft leather or felt slippers—the nails in ordinary shoes or boots might kick up sparks—before unlocking the doors and going inside. Ranged on the deck in the magazines were hundreds of cartridges, which were simply flannel bags filled with gunpowder. The largest were for the thirty 32-pounders, the biggest guns in the *Victory* which, because of their weight, were kept on the lower deck. With a distant charge[4] they could fire a 32-pound shot, which was nearly six and a half inches in diameter, more than a mile. At a range of about three hundred and fifty

4 There were three types of charges—"distant," for maximum range and labelled with black paint, containing ten pounds eleven ounces of gunpowder; "full," marked in blue and holding eight pounds of powder; and "reduced," marked in red and with six pounds of powder.

yards the shot would penetrate at least three feet of solid oak and six feet of fir.

In peace or war, fire was the great enemy in a wooden ship, and in action the main danger was that loose grains of gunpowder, falling along the passageways or on to the decks round the guns, would be ignited by a spark. To guard against this the planking of the gun decks and passageways would be washed down with water before the ship went into action. Now, while Rivers and his mates were checking over the charges, making sure there were also plenty ready in the two smaller hanging magazines on the orlop, other men were letting down screens of thick flannel which would be soaked with water immediately the drummer beat to quarters. There were holes in the screens through which the charges would be passed from the magazine to the powder monkeys, whose task was to carry them to the guns.

On the gun decks fire screens were being let down and match tubs dragged to each gun. Although the guns would generally be fired by flintlocks, slow-burning matches—lengths of loose-laid rope steeped in nitre, which burnt at the rate of about an inch an hour—had to be kept ready. Since they were a fire risk, they were kept in the match tubs, which were casks filled with water. The lid of each tub was perforated with several holes, and the burning end of the match was thrust down through one of them, hanging over the water. It was thus ready for the gun captain. Should his flintlock fail to produce a spark, his second-in-command would snatch a match from the tub, blow on it to make it glow, and then press it on to the priming powder when the gun captain gave the order.

Spare casks of water with swabs beside them were placed round the decks. The water could be used to douse a small fire, or the men could snatch a quick drink and sluice their faces to refresh themselves during the action. Other casks by the guns were for soaking the sponges which would be rammed in after each firing to clean out any burning residue in the barrels.

Each gun captain—the leader of a gun team—had gone to his guns at the order to clear for action to make sure that all the items of equipment (with the exception of flintlocks and other items which the gunner, Mr. Rivers, would issue when the drummer beat to quarters) were ready and secured to the deckhead: the sponge on its stiff rope or wooden handle; the worm—a spiral of metal, like a spring, on a similar rope or wooden handle, which cleared out anything the sponge missed; the rammer, used for pushing home the cartridge, wad and shot; and the handspikes used to lever the carriage round bodily to train the gun. Each captain checked the breeching, a thick rope securing the gun to the ship's side and preventing it from recoiling too far, and the gun-tackles which were used to pull the gun up to the ship's side after loading, so that the muzzle was poking out through the port, ready for firing.

Mr. William Bunce, the *Victory*'s carpenter, and his mates, went down to their storerooms to get out the shot plugs, which would bung up any holes that the enemy's shot might tear in the *Victory*'s hull. The plugs were cone-shaped pieces of wood, of various sizes and covered with oakum and liberally spread with tallow. They could be pushed into the smaller shot holes and hammered home. For the bigger, more jagged holes, sheets of lead and salted hides were put ready, along with nails and hammers to secure them. The carpenter also had to make sure the ship could still be steered if the tiller or wheel were smashed by an unlucky shot. Relieving tackles and rudder tackles had to be hooked on ready for immediate use; the spare tiller was in position, waiting to be shipped on the rudder head should the standard one be shattered. (See picture of a wheel and tiller on page 126.)

While the specialists were methodically working through the pre-arranged and frequently practised drill for preparing a huge ship like the *Victory* for battle, dozens of men—rated landsmen, ordinary seamen, Marines and volunteers, many of whom had never heard a gun fired in anger—were scrambling up the ladders dripping with perspiration, cursing with what little breath they had left inside them, carrying extra shot. Rings of rope called "garlands" were in position behind the guns and into them the men rolled the shot, an extra ten or dozen for each gun, in addition to those nestling like innocent black eggs in the racks.

Other men dragged the fire engine into position. Listed in the ship's inventory as "Engine, Water," it was a rectangular wooden tank perched incongruously on four small, thick wheels, with the mechanism sticking up in the middle and looking like an ordinary pump stolen from some village square. Jutting from the sides like large claws were four handles which, worked up and down vigorously by as many men as could crowd around, sent water spurting from the long brass nozzle fitted on a swivel at the top of the pump.

While the tank of the engine was being filled with water from buckets and the small wash-deck pumps, the Marines under Captain Adair were being inspected. The whole aim of training the Marines, according to the drill book, had been "to teach them the air of a soldier and drive out the clown." The rows of serious faces, stiff backs and well-oiled muskets showed Adair had succeeded. While he marched the detachments away, the master-at-arms, Mr. William Elliott, who was the ship's policeman, walked along the decks keeping an eye on the hundreds of men, conscious that few gave him glances which conveyed any fondness. The lieutenants supervised the decks for which they were responsible; the excited midshipmen dashed here and there, carrying messages or supervising men old enough to be their fathers.

In every ship the men were waiting for the staccato rattle of the drum beating to quarters, a tattoo which surprised some because they found they were not frightened, and sickened others because it left them craven. It showed many men to be fearful at heart yet for all that brave, because they were more frightened of revealing their fear than they were frightened of fear itself.

In the *Euryalus,* out ahead of the Fleet, Blackwood went down to his little cabin. He was now thirty-five and had been in the Navy since he was eleven years old. He had risked death several times before while fighting the French, and now, as Nelson was about to signal for the captains of his frigates to come on board, Blackwood added to his previous letter to Harriet: "The last 24 hours has [*sic*] been most anxious work for me; but we have kept sight of them, and at this moment bearing up to come into action. Lord N. 27 sail of the line. French 33 or 34. I wish the six we have at Gibraltar were here. My signal just made on board *Victory;* I hope, to order me into a vacant line of battleship. [*Ajax* and *Thunderer* were, since their captains went back with Calder, under the command of their first lieutenants.] My dearest Harriet, your husband will not disgrace your love or name; if he dies, his last breath will be devoted to the dearest best of wives. Take care of my boy; make him a better man than his father."

Blackwood then went down over the side of the *Euryalus* into his boat, to be rowed across to the *Victory,* but in the meantime another captain was also writing a letter to his wife. In the *Mars* George Duff wrote:

> My dear Sophia, I have just time to tell you that we are just going into action with the Combined [Fleet]. I hope and trust in God that we shall all behave as becomes us, and that I may have the happiness of taking my beloved wife and children in my arms. Norwich is quite well. I have, however, ordered him of [sic] the quarterdeck. Yours ever, and most truly,
>
> GEO. DUFF

He had made four blots on the paper before he folded and sealed the letter, addressing it to "Mrs Duff, Castle Street, Edinburgh." He then placed it in his desk where—for the hope he expressed to Sophia was never realized—it was found after the action and sent home with a poignant letter from Norwich who, at the age of thirteen, had to write to his mother and tell her she was a widow.

Blackwood arrived on board the *Victory* to find Nelson "in good, but very calm, spirits." The young frigate captain congratulated his Admiral on the approach of the moment he had so often and so long wished for, and received the reply: "I mean today to bleed the captains of the frigates, as I shall keep you on board until the very last minute." The four frigates were in fact his messengers: if he wished for last-minute instructions to be given to another ship which were too complicated for flag signals, he could always send it by frigate. Blackwood had not been on board the *Victory* more than a few minutes when a shout made everyone look towards the enemy. The three masts of each of the enemy ships—for the hulls still could not be seen above the horizon—appeared to be getting closer together and the sails were at the same time broadening: the enemy was turning away. Then the sails began to narrow and the masts appeared to draw apart.

Villeneuve had ordered his fleet to wear. Like a line of marching soldiers doing an about-face, they came off their southerly course and headed up to the north. What had been the rear ship now became the leader. Instead of heading boldly southward towards the Strait of Gibraltar, the Combined Fleet was now sailing back towards Cadiz. Although he had anticipated that they would probably do this, Nelson was far from pleased. With the Combined

Fleet in its present position or any farther to the north, the shoal-strewn and dangerous coast between Cape Trafalgar and Cadiz was close to leeward, a dreadful trap for any ships crippled in battle, particularly since the weather was obviously going to get a great deal worse and a westerly gale was brewing. Had the French and Spanish ships continued sailing southward they would be bringing the Strait of Gibraltar under their lee, providing an escape route into the Mediterranean for damaged ships.

Nelson, still on the poop, then gave instructions for the removal of various items of furniture and personal belongings in his cabins. He warned the men to be very careful when they took down the portrait of Lady Hamilton from the bulkhead. "Take care of my Guardian Angel," he said. But before they cleared away all the furniture he left the poop and went down to his day cabin, where he knelt at his desk—the chairs had already been removed. Through the stern windows of the great cabin he could see his ships strung out astern, some behind the *Victory,* others astern of the *Royal Sovereign.* The weak sun sparkled off the water, reflecting through the windows on to the deckhead above him. He took a pen and started writing in his private diary.

> At daylight saw the Enemy's Combined Fleet from East to E.S.E.; bore away; made the signal for Order of Sailing, and to Prepare for Battle; the Enemy with their heads to the Southward: at seven the Enemy wearing in succession. May the Great God, whom I worship, grant to my Country, and for the benefit of Europe in general, a great and glorious Victory; and may no misconduct in any one tarnish it; and may humanity after Victory be the predominant feature in the British Fleet. For myself, individually, I commit my life to Him who made me, and may his blessing light upon my endeavours for serving my country faithfully. To Him I resign myself and the just cause which is entrusted to me to defend. Amen. Amen. Amen.

While he had been writing this prayer Lt. Pasco had come down to the cabin with a message, fully intent on seizing the opportunity of telling the Admiral that he regarded himself as very unfortunate, on such an occasion, "to be doing the duty in an inferior station, instead of that to which his seniority entitled him." But Pasco was disappointed. "On entering the cabin," he wrote later, "I discovered his Lordship on his knees writing. He was then penning that beautiful prayer. I waited until he rose and communicated what I had to report, but could not at such a moment disturb his mind with any grievances of mine."⁵ As soon as Pasco had made his report and left the cabin Nelson took a sheet of paper and started writing a codicil to his will. "October the twenty first, one thousand eight hundred and five, then in sight of the Combined Fleets of France and Spain, distant about ten miles," he wrote, and went on to list the "eminent services of Emma Hamilton, widow of the Right Honourable Sir William Hamilton," for which she had received no reward "from either our King or Country." "Could I have rewarded these services," he wrote, "I would not now call upon my Country; but as that has not been in my power, I leave Emma Lady Hamilton, therefore, a legacy to my King and Country, that they will give her an ample provision to maintain her rank in life. I also leave to the beneficence of my country my adopted daughter, Horatia Nelson Thompson; and I desire she will use in future the name of Nelson only. These are the only favours I ask my King and Country at this moment when I am going to fight their Battle. May God bless my King and Country, and all those I hold dear. My relations it is needless to mention: they will of course be amply provided for." Nelson sent for Hardy and Blackwood to come down and witness his signature.

After signing, the three men went back on deck again, and a few minutes later Hardy decided the time had come for all the men in the *Victory* to go to their battle stations.

"Mr. Quilliam," he called, "send the hands to quarters." The acting first lieutenant glanced round for the bosun and for the drummer, who was standing on the quarter-deck with his heavy drum slung over his shoulder.

"Mr. Willmet! Hands to quarters! Drummer—beat to quarters!" Within a few seconds the staccato beat of the drum, to the tune of "Heart of Oak," reverberated across the upper deck, through the hatchways and down to the gun decks. Up and down the drummer

---

⁵ Pasco's delicacy cost him dear: Quilliam, fifth in seniority, who acted as first lieutenant in place of Pasco, was promoted to captain after the battle; but Pasco, with his protector dead, was promoted only to commander. The three other lieutenants senior to Quilliam suffered in the same way. Pasco says he went to Nelson's cabin "About 11 a.m.," but it might have been earlier. Nelson, likewise, was mistaken in saying that the enemy wore at 7 a.m.: the *Redoutable* wore then to get into position, but the Fleet was not ordered to wear until about 8 a.m.

paced, conscious that he held the stage for a brief few moments. Doom-da-doom-da-da-doom—"Heart of Oak are our ships. . . ." Willmet and his mates ran to the hatches to sound their shrill pipes.

"All hands to quarters! All hands to quarters! Rouse out there and look alive! All hands to quarters!"

The decks looked like a suddenly disturbed ant-hill, but behind the apparent chaos of running men there was order. Fifty men were heading for the twelve 12-pounders on the quarter-deck (four of them in Hardy's cabin), while twenty more made for the fo'c'sle to handle the two 68-pounder carronades. One hundred and fifty were running to the thirty 12-pounders on the upper deck (four of them in Nelson's cabins) and nearly two hundred for the twenty-eight 24-pounders on the middle deck. The thirty 32-pounders on the lower deck had more than two hundred men to load and fire them. Another fifty men and boys went to the magazines and the passage-ways to fill or pass cartridges and ten more were needed in the cockpit to help the surgeons and loblolly men.

Those whom the watch bills ordained should also have small arms ran to the arms stands or gunner's store to collect their weapons—pistols, cutlasses, pikes, tomahawks or muskets—before going to their guns. Lieutenants, usually two to a deck, one commanding the forward part and one aft, went to their quarters. The captain of each gun fitted on the lock, made sure its flint was a good one and checked the trigger-line—a lanyard which would allow him to fire the gun while standing well back out of reach of the recoil. His priming wire was tucked in his belt and a powder horn was hung up on the deckhead. The powder monkeys had to run to the magazine scuttles. They carried the cartridges in special cases, and by now Marine sentries were guarding the fore and after hatches. Their orders were to allow no one up or down unless he was an officer, midshipman or powder monkey. To prove he was a powder monkey, a man or boy had to show his cartridge case as he reached the hatch. Any man trying to force his way through the hatchway would be assumed to be deserting his post and the sentries could shoot him. While the guns' crews assembled at their stations the Marines in their scarlet jackets were clumping to the quarter-deck and to the poop where, under the eagle eye of their sergeants, they assembled in neat and orderly lines, muskets at their sides, bayonets at their belts.

In the galley the cook had doused his fire as soon as he heard the first clatter of the drum. On all the decks men with buckets were flinging water over the fire screens while others were sluicing the decks. Others sprinkled sand to give a better grip for the men's feet. Most of the seamen were now stripped to the waist. Many had narrow bands of cloth which they would bind round their heads, covering their ears, to lessen the deafening effect of the guns firing, and also to prevent the salty perspiration running into their eyes.

Every gun was short of men. The ship's complement normally allowed full crews only for the two guns on one side. The 32-pounders, weighing nearly three tons, needed fourteen men to fire them, according to the drill books, but there were only seven. To make up for the shortage the men ran from side to side as each broadside was required. As the men fell in at their respective guns the loader and the sponger went to the muzzle and took out the tompion, the plug which sealed the barrel when the gun was not in use. While they were doing that, others were hauling on a tackle, raising the port lid which came up like a vertical trap-door, letting sunlight stream in. For a few moments the effect on the lower decks, previously only dimly lit by the flickering fighting lanterns, was blinding. The inside of the lids and the woodwork round the ports were painted red, but not for aesthetic reasons: in action, splashes of blood would not show. With the squeal of the port-lid tackles, the movement of the men round each of the guns ceased to be an apparently aimless and disorganized fussing: instead they settled down into a rhythmic tempo.

The lieutenants, seeing the tompions out of each of the guns and the port lids up, started the stream of orders which had in past months been used so frequently in practice. Each of the lieutenants put a speaking-trumpet to their mouths.

"Load!"

Each powder monkey slipped a bulky cartridge out of the carrying case and gave it to the assistant loader, who quickly took a couple of paces and handed it to the loader as if it was a hot potato. The loader, standing by the muzzle, slid the cartridge into the barrel. The sponger took up the rammer and pushed the cartridge home, giving it a couple of sharp blows to bed it in. Because the gun would not be fired for a while, a wad was rammed in before the shot, but once the ship was in action this would not be necessary. Then the shot was handed to the loader, who tipped it into the barrel. He then helped the sponger ram it home. Another wad followed and that too was rammed in. As soon as the gun was loaded the men stood back, waiting for the next order.

"Run out!"

All the crew except the captain and powder monkey grabbed the gun-tackle falls and hauled. The gun rumbled out until the forward edge of the carriage was hard up against the ship's side and the muzzle projected through the port.

"Prime!" bellowed the lieutenants.

The gun captain thrust the priming wire into the vent so hard that it made a small hole in the flannel covering the cartridge. He then pulled out the wire and slipped a thin tube—in effect a fuse made of a quill—into the vent, and poured some gunpowder into the pan of the lock.

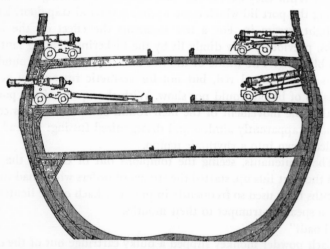

A section through a two-decker. The upper left gun is in position for firing, but breeching and tackles are not shown. The gun below has the train-tackle fitted. The upper right gun is secured against recoil; the one below is secured for sea.

The *Victory*'s guns were now prepared. Since it was unlikely that firing would start for some time, the flintlocks would not be cocked. The lieutenants reported that their decks were ready. For another hour there was little for the men to do. The midshipmen, pistols tucked in their belts, waited at the hatchways ready to run messages for the lieutenants. Mr. Elliott, the master-at-arms, strode round deck after deck, his eyes, sharpened by many years of looking upon the weakness and shortcomings of man, casting about, watching for trouble.

From the flagship's decks Nelson could see the Union Jack flying from the fore-topgallant and main-topmast stay of each of the British ships, as if waving defiance.

Lt. Quilliam reported to Captain Hardy on the quarter-deck that the ship was ready for action. More than eight hundred men in the *Victory* were at general quarters. Midshipman Richard Francis Roberts's *Remark Book* noted the next thing that concerned the sailors and Marines waiting at the guns, in the magazines, and on deck. "At 11—Dinner and grog."

NINETEEN

"BRITONS, STRIKE HOME!"

Take therefore no thought for the morrow; for the morrow shall take thought for the things of itself. Sufficient unto the day is the evil thereof. —St. Matthew VI, 34

W I T H the unruffled majesty of swans the British battleships sailed down towards the Combined Fleet drawn up across their course. The four frigates and the *Pickle* and *Entreprenante* were ranged on the larboard side like attendant cygnets. Some of the slower battleships already had studding sails at the end of their yards. It seemed incredible that so much canvas could be set. Leading the straggling windward column was the *Victory*. Just astern of her was the *Téméraire*, nicknamed then the "Saucy" *Téméraire*—the prefix "Fighting" was not to be coined for another thirty-four years, when Turner sent his famous painting to the Royal Academy.

An Essex man, Captain Eliab Harvey, commanded the 98-gun ship, which was one of the few with an almost complete crew. She had an official complement of 738, and when the whole crew had mustered the previous day they totalled 718. Of these, 220 were Irishmen, fifty-three Scots and thirty-eight Welshmen. Of the Englishmen, nearly a third were Devonians. Like the *Victory*, she had a number of foreigners on board.[1]

Next astern of the *Téméraire*—although the British Fleet was far from being in precise formation—was the *Neptune*, commanded by Thomas Fremantle. One of the midshipmen serving on board was William Badcock, who regarded Betsey's husband as "a clever, brave and smart officer." Now aged seventeen, Badcock had been in the

[1] There were sixty-six altogether, and among them were twenty-eight Americans, nine Germans, six Swedes, five Portuguese, three Frenchmen and three Spaniards.

Navy for seven years. After several cutting-out expeditions and actions in the Mediterranean, followed by a winter of Atlantic storms while blockading Brest, he was excited at the prospect ahead of him this Monday morning. "It was my morning watch," he wrote. "I was midshipman of the fo'c'sle, and at the first dawn of day a forest of strange masts was seen to leeward. I ran aft and informed the officer of the watch. The captain was on deck in a moment. . . . Our ship had previously prepared for battle, so that with the exception of stowing hammocks, slinging the lower yards, stoppering the topsail sheets, and other minor matters, little remained to be done. . . .

"The old *Neptune,* which was never a good sailer, took it into her head to sail better that morning than I ever remember to have seen her do before."

Close astern of the *Neptune* were the *Leviathan* and the *Conqueror.* The latter was commanded by Captain Israel Pellew, a name already famous enough to bring Cornishmen flocking to join his ship as volunteers. Pellew was a gunnery expert, and knowing the French ships would be full of soldiers, with sharp-shooters in their tops, had ordered his Marines below out of the way of musket balls until they should be needed.

Astern of the *Conqueror* came the *Britannia.* The Earl of North-esk and Captain Bullen were on her quarter-deck and the crew were at general quarters. They had had their breakfast by 8 a.m. and an hour later the rhythmic thumping of the drum had sent them to the guns. Now they were getting bored, and Lt. Halloran, the amateur actor, was delighted to hear them amusing themselves by repeating scraps from a prologue he had recited at a previous performance. The favourite lines seemed to be:

> We have great guns of tragedy loaded so well,
> If they do but go off they will certainly tell.

Halloran was stationed at the after-most gun on the larboard side of the lower deck, and he chatted with Midshipman Tompkin. Now and again they scrambled past the muzzle of a gun, looking out through the port to see how near they were to the Combined Fleet.

The commanding officer of the *Ajax,* just astern, could be forgiven any nervousness he felt over his responsibilities. He was Lt.

John Pilfold, whose captain had gone back to England with
Calder. When Lt. Ellis, of the *Ajax*'s Marines, was sent below about
this time with orders he was "much struck with the preparations
being made." Some of the men, stripped to the waist, were sharpen-
ing their cutlasses. Others were polishing the guns "as though an
inspection were about to take place, instead of a mortal combat,
while three or four, as if in mere bravado, were dancing a horn-
pipe; but all seemed deeply anxious to come to close quarters with
the enemy. Occasionally they would look out of the ports and
speculate as to the various ships of the enemy, many of whom had
been on former occasions engaged by our vessels."

The impetuous Sir Edward Berry in the *Agamemnon* followed
the *Ajax,* and close to him was the *Orion.* Codrington was just
about to order his crew to dinner, and was himself looking forward
to a leg of cold turkey which had, with commendable forethought,
been prepared by his steward. "We were," he reported, "all fresh,
hearty and in high spirits." The panorama stretched out before
him, with eight ships of his own division preceding the *Orion* and
heading for the waiting enemy with all sail set, was impressive. "I
suppose no man ever before saw such a sight as I did," he wrote,
"or rather as we did, for I called all my lieutenants up to see it."[2]

A considerable distance behind the *Orion* was the *Prince,* commanded by Captain Richard Grindall. She was a 98-gun ship and
really belonged to the head of Collingwood's division, but she had
been forced to shift a topsail and this, combined with the fact that
she was a very slow ship at the best of times, made her lag behind
to become involved in the rear of Nelson's division.

The men of the *Minotaur,* next astern of the *Prince,* were standing to their guns after hearing a rousing speech from Captain
Mansfield. The ship had cleared for action by 8 a.m., and before
beating to quarters he had every available man assembled on the
quarter-deck. Standing at the break of the poop and facing forward, he could see each man's face. Behind them, in perspective
beyond the bowsprit and irregularly spaced, were ten British battleships. Beyond, their hulls now visible over the rim of the horizon,
were the enemy ships ranged like a sea wall protecting a flat shore.

2 The view that Codrington had later, when the battle started, is vividly
portrayed by Harold Wyllie's painting, which is reproduced as illustration
Number 16.

"Men," Mansfield said loudly, "we are now in the sight of the enemy"—the seamen began a ragged cheer, but he held up his hand for silence—"whom there is every probability of engaging; and I trust that this day, or tomorrow, will prove the most glorious our country ever saw.

"I shall say nothing to you of courage: our country never produced a coward. For my own part I pledge myself to the officers and ship's company not to quit the ship I may get alongside of till either she strikes or sinks—or I sink.

"I have only to recommend silence and strict attention to the orders of your officers. Be careful to take good aim, for it is to no purpose to throw shot away. You will now, every man, repair to your respective stations, and depend, I will bring the ship into action as soon as possible." He paused a moment, and then cried: "God save the King!"

The men promptly cheered him: blunt words, a short speech and a rousing finish appealed to them. Mansfield watched them dismiss, and perhaps he wondered how many of the grinning, eager faces would answer at the next muster. The cheers carried across the water to the next ship astern, the *Spartiate,* commanded by Captain Sir Francis Laforey. She was the last in Nelson's division and there was one ship missing, the *Africa,* which had lost sight of the Fleet the previous night.

Blackwood's *Euryalus* was up on the larboard side of Nelson's division, and the men on board of her had perhaps the best view of all the Fleet. Hercules Robinson wrote: "How well I remember the ports of our great ship hauled up, the guns run out, and as from the sublime to the ridiculous is but a step, the *Pickle,* schooner, close to our ship with her boarding nets up, her tompions out and her four guns (about as large and formidable as two pairs of Wellington boots), 'their soul alive and eager for the fray,' as imposing as Gulliver waving his hanger [sword] before the King and Queen of Brobdingnag."

Although Nelson's division was steering for the enemy in some semblance of a column, Collingwood's ships, following a signal from him that they were to form on the larboard line of bearing, were sailing with each successive ship out on the starboard quarter of her next ahead. The slower ships were dropping astern and the

Neptuno
Scipion
Intrepide
Formidable
Mont-Blanc
Duguay-Troui
Rayo
S. Francisco de.
S. Augusti
Héros
S. Trinidad
Bucentaur
Redoutable
S. Just
Neptune
S. Leandro
Indomptable

Africa

Euryalus   Victory
Neptune   Téméraire
Britannia   Leviathan
Ajax   Conqueror
Agamemnon
Orion
Prince
Minotaur
Spartiate
Thunderer
Dreadnought
Defence   Defiance
Swiftsure
Polyphemus

Royal Sovereign
Belleisle
Mars
Tonnant
Bellerophon
Achille   Colossus
Revenge

S. Ana
Fougueux
Monarca
Pluton
Algésiras
Bahama
Aigle
Montañes Swiftsure
Argonaute
Argonauta

S. Ildefonso
Achille

Noon

P. de Asturias
Berwick
San Juan de Nepomuceno

CHART No. 2

Trafalgar: the opening round. The British ships are shown in black.
The wind was westerly—i.e., from the left of the chart.

Royal Sovereign was drawing ahead. Newly arrived from England, her coppered bottom was still clean, but many of the others were foul with months' accumulation of weed and barnacles which, particularly in the present light winds, slowed them up considerably.

On board Collingwood's flagship young Midshipman Thomas Aikenhead had just stowed in his sea chest a letter to his family living at Portsea, Hampshire, and his will. "We have just piped to breakfast," he wrote. "Thirty-five sail, besides smaller vessels, are now on our beam, about three miles off. Should I, my dear parents, fall in defence of my King, let that thought console you. I feel not the least dread in my spirits. Oh my parents, sisters, brothers, dear grandfather, grandmother and aunt, believe me ever yours!

"Accept, perhaps for the last time, your brother's love; be assured I feel for my friends, should I die in this glorious action—glorious, no doubt, it will be. Every British heart pants for glory. Our old Admiral [Collingwood] is quite young again with the thought of it. If I survive, nothing will give me greater pleasure than embracing my dearest relations. Do not, in case I fall, grieve—it will be to no purpose. Many brave fellows will no doubt fall with me on both sides. Oh! Betsey, with what ardour I shall, if permitted by God's providence, come to England to embrace you all!" And as he had saved another £10 since he had written his will, he added a note to his letter: "Do not be surprised to find £10 more—it is mine." Despite his brave words, perhaps he did have a presentiment that he would not survive the battle, for he was one of the two midshipmen killed in the flagship.

Admiral Collingwood had, after breakfast, walked round the various decks, talking to the seamen. Coming across a group of men who had been brought over with him from the *Dreadnought* when he transferred to the *Royal Sovereign,* he paused for a moment. They were all, like Collingwood, from the Newcastle area. "Today, my lads," he said, "we must show those fellows what the 'Tars of the Tyne' can do!" To a group of officers he remarked: "Now, gentlemen, let us do something today which the world may talk of hereafter."

The *Royal Sovereign* was the nearest ship to the enemy line, but seeing the *Victory* up to the northward setting studding-sails, Lt. Clavell (wearing the silk stockings that Collingwood had earlier advised) asked permission for the *Royal Sovereign* to set hers.[3] Collingwood saw the danger of carrying the unspoken competition with the *Victory* too far, and also was finding himself so far ahead that he would have to fight on his own for longer than was sensible. "The ships of our line are not sufficiently up for us to do so now," he said, "but you may be getting ready." Clavell gave the necessary orders.

Astern and to starboard of the *Royal Sovereign* was the *Belleisle,* commanded by William Hargood. She was a powerful two-decker, captured from the French ten years earlier, and her band was playing as she bore down towards the enemy. Earlier she had gradually caught up the *Tonnant,* her next ahead which should have been close to the *Royal Sovereign,* but had been unable to keep up. To Hargood's delight he was signalled to change places with her. As the *Belleisle* forged ahead, Hargood ordered the band to play "Rule, Britannia," and not to be outdone, Captain Tyler ordered the *Tonnant'*s band to reply with "Britons, Strike Home!" Putting his speaking-trumpet to his lips, Tyler called to Hargood from the quarter-deck: "A glorious day for old England! We shall have one apiece before night!"

Aboard the *Belleisle,* with the band thumping away with more enthusiasm than skill, the young officers were now considerably more cheerful. Their earlier feelings are described by Lt. Paul Harris Nicolas. "The officers now met at breakfast; and though each seemed to exult in the hope of a glorious termination to the contest so near at hand, a fearful presage was experienced that all would not again unite at that festive board. One was particularly impressed with a persuasion that he should not survive the day, nor could he divest himself of this presentiment, but made the necessary disposal of his property in the event of his death. The sound of the drums, however, soon put an end to our meditations, and after a hasty and, alas, a final farewell to some, we repaired to our respective posts."

Captain George Duff had been trying to give his ship wings. Every stitch of canvas was set: studding-sails hung out over the water at the end of the yards, and Duff tried every trick he knew

---

[3] Studding-sails (also known as stunsails or steering sails) were additional sails set on booms which were extensions of the yards. They can be seen clearly in Harold Wyllie's painting, illustration Number 9.

to add even a fraction of a knot of speed. The reason for this was that Nelson had just signalled direct to Duff, ordering the *Mars* to lead the lee column. The *Prince* should have been ahead, but, as we have seen, she was shifting a topsail and had dropped several miles astern. Now, a plain hint to Collingwood to drop back, Duff was ordered to go ahead and thus be the first to break through the enemy line. But Duff could not manage to overtake the *Royal Sovereign*, and Collingwood was certainly not reducing canvas to slow down—in fact he was just about to let Lt. Clavell set the studding-sails.

Duff, sword at his waist, a massive figure on the quarter-deck, was helpless. The descent on the enemy was turning into a race between Nelson and Collingwood. He fingered the ram's horn snuff-box in his pocket and then, clasping his hands behind him, looked up at the sails yet again. They were set perfectly: there was nothing that could be done to improve them. At that moment, a few minutes after Duff had answered Nelson's signal, Lt. Clavell on the quarter-deck of the *Royal Sovereign* gave an inquiring look at Collingwood, who nodded. Clavell promptly went over to Captain Rotheram, who was commanding the flagship, and said that the Admiral desired him to make all sail. Rotheram gave the orders to rig out and hoist away the studding-sails, and over on the starboard quarter a disappointed Duff watched the flagship begin to draw ahead. His chance of the honour of leading the British Fleet and being the first to break the enemy's line had now gone for good.

The *Tonnant*, which had been forced to drop back, was one of Nelson's trophies from the battle of the Nile. As a prize she had been brought back to England, repaired and given a new figure-head (Jupiter hurling a thunderbolt). Now, under Tyler, her band playing such tunes as "Britons, Strike Home!" and "The Downfall of Paris," she steered down to assault her erstwhile owners. The *Tonnant*'s third lieutenant has left an amusing picture of some of his fellow officers. The surgeon, Mr. Forbes McBean Chevers, who had been with Howe at the "glorious first of June," was clever, dapper and irritable, fond of ethics, etymology and the blue pills which worked remarkable cures with costive seamen; the assistant surgeon was a tall, gangling Scot, his head filled with the *Pharmacopoeia*, bleeding, blistering and gallipots. The sixth lieutenant was fond of gaming and grog, while the seventh, who liked coining new words, was not much of a seaman. The senior of the Marine lieutenants read novels and fancied himself with the ladies, while the Purser was very regular with his accounts and played the flute. The third lieutenant himself, Frederick Hoffman, had fought in eighteen boat actions and one siege, been wounded in the head and deafened in one ear, twice had yellow fever and once been captured by the French. Now the whole of the *Tonnant*'s crew waited patiently for a small portion of cheese and half an allowance of grog to be issued. That, today, was to be their dinner.

The *Bellerophon*—the "Billy Ruff'n" which led Howe's fleet to victory on the "glorious first of June" and single-handed fought the French flagship *L'Orient* at the Nile—was the next in Collingwood's division. In Howe's action a Scotsman had commanded her and fallen wounded; at the Nile an Irishman commanding her had also been badly wounded. Now the Englishman commanding her, John Cooke, was about to be killed and a Welshman was to take over command. Captain Cooke had first gone to sea at the age of eleven. Now happily married, with an eight-year-old daughter, and for the past sixteen months—thanks to a recent legacy—owner of a large estate at Lower Donhead, in Wiltshire, he had always had one hope: to serve under Nelson. To be in a general engagement with that admiral would, he declared, crown his military ambition. With his ambition about to be achieved he now stood on the quarter-deck talking to Cumby, his first lieutenant, Edward Overton, the Master, and Captain William James Wemyss, commanding the Marines.

Near them was a young midshipman with a slate in his hand, busy reading off signals from the flagship. He was John Franklin, now aged nineteen, the ninth child and fifth son of a prosperous draper of Spilsby, in Lincolnshire. The boy destined to become world famous as an Arctic explorer was untidy and round-faced, with a hot, generous temper, and a curiously earnest manner.

With the bandsmen on board the *Bellerophon* thumping at their drums and sawing away with gusto at their fiddles and the fifers getting red in the face, "one would have thought that the people were preparing for a festival rather than a combat," one of the midshipmen wrote later, "and no dissatisfaction was expressed, except at the state of the weather, which . . . prevented our quickly nearing the enemy." One seaman, glancing through the port at the Combined Fleet on the horizon, spat. "What a fine show them ships will make at Spithead!" And with a piece of chalk several of the men wrote on their guns: "*Bellerophon*—Death or Glory."

Lt. Cumby, describing the day's events aboard the *Bellerophon* up to now, wrote later: "I was aroused from my slumbers by my messmate, Overton, the Master, who called out, 'Cumby, my boy, turn out; here they are all ready for you, three and thirty sail of the line close under our lee, and evidently disposed to await our attack.'

"You may readily conclude I did not long remain in a recumbent position, but sprang out of bed, hurried on my clothes and, kneeling down by the side of my cot, put up a short but fervent prayer to the great God of Battles for a glorious victory to the arms of my country, committing myself individually to His all wise disposal and begging His gracious protection for my dear wife and children, whatever His unerring wisdom might see fit to order for myself.

"This was the substance and, as near as memory will serve me, the actual words of my petition, and I have often since reflected with a feeling of pride how nearly similar they were to what our immortal leader himself committed to paper as his own prayer on that occasion. . . ."

As usual, Cumby had breakfast with the Captain in his cabin under the poop deck. As soon as they finished eating Cumby prepared to leave, conscious that as first lieutenant he had a lot to do. But Cooke "begged me to wait a little as he had something to show me, when he produced and requested me to peruse, Lord Nelson's private Memorandum addressed to captains relative to the conduct of the ships in action, which having read he enquired whether I perfectly understood the Admiral's instructions.

"I replied they were so distinct and explicit that it was quite impossible they could be misunderstood; he then expressed his satisfaction, and said he wished me to be made acquainted with it, that in the event of his being 'bowl'd out' I might know how to conduct the ship agreeable to the Admiral's wishes. On this I observed that it was very possible that the same shot which disposed of him might have an equally tranquillizing effect upon me, and under that idea I submitted to him the expediency of the Master (as being the only officer who in such case would remain on the quarter-deck) being also apprised. . . .

"To this Captain Cooke immediately assented, and poor Overton, the Master, was desired to read the Memorandum, which he did. And here I may be permitted to remark *en passant* that, of the three officers who carried the knowledge of this private Memorandum into action, I was the only one that brought it out [alive]. . . .

"At eleven o'clock, finding we should not be in action for an hour or more, we piped to dinner, which we had ordered to be in readiness for the ship's company at that hour, thinking that Englishmen would fight all the better for having a comfortable meal, and at the same time Captain Cooke joined us in partaking of some cold meat, etc., on the rudder head, all our bulkheads, tables, etc., being necessarily taken down and carried below."

Away to the westward were the rest of the ships of the British Fleet. Among them were the *Colossus,* a 74 commanded by Captain James Morris; the *Achille,* under Captain Richard King; and the *Revenge,* whose captain, Robert Moorsom, was a gunnery expert. A long gap separated the next ship, the *Defiance,* whose commanding officer, Durham, was thankful he had been bold enough to refuse to go back to England for Calder's court-martial. The *Defiance*'s carpenter was making a mental note of the items already thrown overboard—he would have to put them in his report after the battle. One sheep pen, eight wardroom berths, four tables, four hen coops, an arms chest . . . there would be a lot more for his list before the day was out. The three ships following the *Defiance* were almost abreast of each other—the *Swiftsure, Dreadnought* and *Polyphemus.* And the last two ships were the *Thunderer* and *Defence,* quite close to the last ships of Nelson's division.

There remained now only the little 64-gun *Africa,* smallest of Nelson's battleships, which had lost the Fleet the night before. She had now appeared to the northward, sailing down towards the British Fleet and passing close to the leading ships of the Combined Fleet. (See Chart No. 2 on page 228.) Digby had, after losing touch, seen the French Fleet's signals during the night and taken up "a station of discretion." It put him in a dangerous position, and a signal from the *Victory* was soon to test him and his ship's company.

TWENTY

PERDIDOS!

If the trumpet give an uncertain sound, who shall prepare
himself to the battle? —Romans XIV, 8

SHORTLY after dawn the look-outs in the French frigate *Hermione* had spotted the British Fleet up-wind to the westward. They had counted the number of enemy ships and immediately signalled to Villeneuve: "The enemy in sight to windward," firing a gun at the same time to summon attention. The French and Spanish ships were sailing southward, as we have already seen, silhouetted against the rising sun and in some disorder. Villeneuve immediately signalled to the frigates to reconnoitre the enemy, and once again ordered the Fleet to form line of battle.

The four divisions forming the Combined Fleet were the squadron of observation, under the Spanish Admiral Gravina[1] in the *Principe de Asturias,* whose position was supposed to be to windward of the Fleet and thus available to reinforce the line anywhere it was threatened; the van squadron under Vice-Admiral Alava, in the *Santa Ana,* which was to lead the line; the centre squadron under Villeneuve in the *Bucentaure* which would be in the middle, and the rear squadron, under Rear-Admiral Dumanoir in the *Formidable.* Thus the first ship of Alava's van squadron, the *Pluton,* should have been leading the line to the south, while the last ship in Dumanoir's squadron, the *Neptuno,* should have been at the end of it to the north. It was to these positions that, in very

1 Gravina's ADC was Don Miguel Ricardo de Alava, nephew of Rear-Admiral Alava of the *Santa Ana.* When Spain left Napoleon's side in 1808 he joined the patriot army, later serving as an ADC to the Duke of Wellington. Sent in 1814 as Spanish Minister Plenipotentiary to Holland, he was at Wellington's headquarters for the battle of Waterloo. He later became the Spanish Ambassador in London.

light winds and a heavy swell, thirty-three battleships of the Combined Fleet tried to scramble when Villeneuve signalled them to form line of battle on the starboard tack. They had very little chance of succeeding.

As far as manoeuvring was concerned the Combined Fleet was worse off than the British because the swell was coming in on their beam, making them roll badly; in addition, with the wind also on the beam they had far more difficulty in keeping their sails filled, because the swaying masts flung the wind out of the canvas. While the three other squadrons tried to get themselves into some semblance of a line, Admiral Gravina ordered his dozen ships of the squadron of observation to take up a position ahead of the main body of the Combined Fleet, instead of staying up to windward, putting the *San Juan Nepomuceno* at the head of the line. This had not been ordered by Villeneuve, and for the moment he did nothing about it, but it was to have a great effect on the battle.

At 7.30 a.m. Villeneuve was in a difficult position. "The enemy squadron," he reported, "which had very soon been discovered to be composed of twenty-seven sail of the line, appeared to me to be standing in a body for my rear, with the double intention of attacking it advantageously and of cutting off the retreat of the Combined Fleet on Cadiz." To the south-east—on his larboard bow —lay the Strait of Gibraltar. With the wind westerly at least some of his ships would be able to escape after the battle into the Mediterranean and make for Cartagena or Toulon. But there were six other British battleships in that area, he already knew, and there was a chance they might be able to intercept. Cape Trafalgar and its line of dangerous shoals lay twelve miles away to the eastward; Cadiz, his port of refuge, lay astern to the north. Every moment that passed meant he was drawing farther away from it and at the same time Nelson was nearer to cutting off the line of retreat.

Villeneuve finally made up his mind: he would turn about and steer towards Cadiz, "my sole object being to protect the rear from the projected attack of the entire enemy force." As we have seen, by wearing together the ships would "about turn" in the line, so that the *Neptuno* to the north, which had been the last ship in the line, would now be the leader, and the *San Juan Nepomuceno,* which had been the leader, would bring up the rear.

When he saw the signal Commodore Churruca, commanding the *San Juan Nepomuceno* and one of the most capable and brave of the Spanish officers, turned to his second-in-command. *"Está la escuadra perdita,"* he said. "The Fleet is doomed. The French admiral does not understand his business. He has compromised us all!"

Churruca had sailed with a heavy heart. Before leaving Cadiz he had told his nephew, who was serving in the *Nepomuceno* as a volunteer: "Write to your friends that you are going into a battle that will be desperate and bloody. Tell them also that they may be certain of this—that I, for my part, will meet my death there. Let them know that rather than surrender my ship I shall sink her." Churruca was not a coward: he was a realist, and he had no faith in Villeneuve's ability. Such an evolution as Villeneuve had just ordered, he declared, was bound to throw the Fleet into confusion, and in the light wind it would take them all morning to re-form. In this estimate he was not far wrong. Since the Combined Fleet had not had time to form properly on the starboard tack, it was quite obvious there would be chaos when it was ordered to wear round and head in the opposite direction.

It was like telling a mixed group of new recruits on parade for the first time, some truculent and some keen, to fall into single file while on the move, and while they were walking to their positions ordering them to about-face and, still walking, get into line. Some ships sagged off to leeward, unable or unwilling to get into position, while others moved ahead to take their place; more, several places from where they should be, just scrambled into the line wherever they could find a gap. Then, to add to the confusion, a light wind came up from the south-west and, reaching the rear ships first, bunched them up. Thus, like an unruly mob trying to form a queue to go to its own execution, the Combined Fleet formed line of battle.

Desbrière, commenting on Villeneuve's decision to stand in for Cadiz, wrote that he "seemed to be seeking the possibility of taking refuge in that port. But it was a dangerous temptation to offer to his Fleet and little calculated to inspire all present with the desperate energy requisite. Moreover . . . his order, at the time that it was given, could no longer have the result of assuring the retreat of the whole Fleet in that direction.

"This is certain at any rate, the action was about to be fought off a very dangerous lee shore and in conditions which would render the situation of the disabled ships critical if the lowering weather broke up altogether. Nelson was not to be mistaken, and the order to anchor, which he was to give later, at the very minute when he was breathing his last, shows plainly what peril he foresaw for all those who were to be crippled in the action."

The order which Villeneuve gave at 8 a.m. for the Fleet to wear was finally completed—inasmuch as his thirty-three ships were steering in roughly a northerly direction—by 10 a.m., but there were large gaps in the line. At about 10.15 a.m. (the time, as usual, varies in the reports of individual ships) Villeneuve signalled to the leading ship, the *Neptuno,* to hug the wind, and the others to follow in succession. By this, Villeneuve was simply trying to get his line formed properly—the leading British ship was only some five miles away on his larboard beam by now, and the Combined Fleet's line had formed into a huge half moon, the centre sagging away from the advancing British. But in hugging the wind the leading ships slowed up, and those astern dropped farther to lee-ward. In addition Villeneuve now apparently saw from the *Bucentaure* that Gravina and his squadron of observation were sailing down into the wake of what should have been the last ship in the line, instead of staying up to windward ready to strike where needed. The French Admiral promptly signalled him to keep up to windward "so as to be at hand to cover the centre of the Fleet, which appeared to be the point on which the enemy was desirous of concentrating his greatest effort." But it was too late. Gravina could never get back into such a position in time.

Churruca, whose ship was now the last in Gravina's squadron and therefore the most southerly of all, had been standing on his quarter-deck, telescope to his eye, watching the *Bucentaure* and waiting patiently for Villeneuve to make the signal for the move which Churruca considered would foil Nelson's attack. "Our van will be cut away from the main body and our rear will be over-whelmed. Half the line will be compelled to remain inactive," he declared. "The French admiral does not—will not—grasp it. He has only to act boldly, only to order the van ships to wear round at once and double on the rear squadron. That will place the enemy between two fires." But the signal never came. Churruca snapped his telescope shut. *"Perdidos!"* he muttered, and stalked across the quarter-deck. *"Perdidos! Perdidos!"* He then ordered all available hands to be turned up on deck. Sending for the chaplain he told him: "Father, perform your sacred office. Absolve the souls of these brave fellows, who know not what fate this battle may have for them!" The chaplain stepped forward. The men bared their heads, muttering the responses in the short service. Then Churruca walked to the quarter-deck rail and faced them. "My sons," he cried, "in the name of the God of Battles I promise eternal happiness to all those who today fall doing their duty.

"On the other hand," he added ominously, "if I see any man shirking I will have him shot on the spot. If the scoundrel escapes my eye, or that of the gallant officers I have the honour to command, rest assured of this, that bitter remorse will dog the wretch for the rest of his days, for so long as he crawls through what may remain of his wretched existence." He paused for a moment and then called for three cheers for His Catholic Majesty. The men hustled back to their guns and once again the fifes and drums struck up bravely.

The British ships were now drawing very close. With their studding-sails set and hanging out on the ends of the already wide yards, they looked as if they had wings; indeed, with what little breeze there was behind them, they did have wings, by comparison with the Combined Fleet which was trying to hug the wind.

"I made the signal to commence the action as soon as within range," wrote Villeneuve. The Imperial Eagle, borne by Midshipman Donadieu and Midshipman Arman, who had been ordered to guard it throughout the forthcoming battle, was paraded round the deck by Villeneuve, followed by his flag-captain, Magendie, Major-General Contamine, who was commanding the troops, and the rest of the *Bucentaure*'s officers.

"It is impossible," wrote Magendie, "to display greater enthusiasm and eagerness for the fray than was shown and evinced by all the officers, sailors and soldiers of the *Bucentaure,* each one of us putting our hands between the Admiral's and renewing our oath upon the Eagle entrusted to us by the Emperor, to fight to the last gasp; and shouts of *'Vive l'Empereur, vive l'Amiral Villeneuve'* were raised once more." He adds: "We returned to the upper works and each of us resumed our post; the Eagle was displayed at the foot of the mainmast."

The intrepid little Captain Lucas—he was only four feet four inches tall—in the *Redoutable* was close astern of the *Bucentaure*, so close in fact that a little later someone hailed him several times from the *Bucentaure*'s stern gallery that he was about to run aboard the flagship. "Actually," Lucas wrote afterwards, "the *Redoutable*'s bowsprit did graze her taffrail, but I assured them they had nothing to fear." Like the crew of the flagship, the men of the *Redoutable* were rousing themselves and being roused to vast heights of patriotic fervour compared with the rather brief speeches being delivered by some of the captains aboard the British ships. Lucas reported: "I laid the *Redoutable*'s bowsprit against the *Bucentaure*'s stern, fully resolved to sacrifice my ship in defence of the Admiral's flag. I acquainted my officers and crew, who replied to my decision by shouts of '*Vive l'Empereur! Vive l'Amiral! Vive le Commandant!*' repeated a thousand times.

"Preceded by the drums and fifes that I had on board, I paraded at the head of my officers round all the decks; everywhere I found gallant lads burning with impatience to be in the fray; many of them saying to me, 'Captain, don't forget to board!' "

For all his rather flamboyant literary style, Lucas almost certainly commanded the best-trained crew in the whole Combined Fleet. His men had cried "Don't forget to board!" for a good reason: Lucas's ideas "were always directed towards fighting by boarding." He said that "I so counted upon its success that everything had been prepared to undertake it with advantage: I had had canvas pouches to hold two grenades made for all captains of guns, the crossbelts of these pouches carrying a tin tube containing a small match.

"In all our drills, I made them throw a great number of pasteboard grenades and I often landed the grenadiers in order to have them explode iron grenades; they had so acquired the habit of hurling them that on the day of the battle our topmen were throwing two at a time.

"I had a hundred carbines fitted with long bayonets on board; the men to whom these were served out were so well accustomed to their use that they climbed halfway up the shrouds to open a musketry fire.

"All the men armed with swords were instructed in broadsword practice every day and pistols had become familiar arms to them. The grapnels were thrown aboard so skilfully that they succeeded in hooking a ship even though she was not exactly touching us." Even allowing for Lucas's exaggerations—and they become clearer when he describes how the *Redoutable* engaged the *Victory*—Villeneuve must have regretted not having more captains like him.

The 130-gun *Santissima Trinidad* was an impressive sight. Her huge sides were painted in alternate bands of red and white; her figurehead, as befitted the largest ship in the world, was an imposing white-painted carving of figures representing the Holy Trinity, from whom she took her name. She had a crew of 1,048 and one of them, going into action for the first time, wrote later:

"Early in the morning the decks were cleared for action, and when all was ready for serving the guns and working the ship, I heard someone say: 'The sand—bring the sand.' A number of sailors were posted on the ladders from the hatchway to the hold and between decks, and in this way were hauling up sacks of sand . . . they were emptied out on the upper decks, the poop and the fo'c'sle, the sand being spread about so as to cover all the planking. The same thing was done between decks. My curiosity prompted me to ask a lad who stood next to me what this was for. 'For the blood,' he said very coolly. 'For the blood!' I exclaimed, unable to repress a shudder. I looked at the sand—I looked at the men who were busily employed on this task—and for a moment I felt I was a coward."

So the ships of the Combined Fleet waited. For the moment the drums and fifes were playing; the French Tricolour or the yellow-and-red flag of Spain was flying. In every Spanish ship a large wooden cross, solemnly blessed by the chaplains, now hung from the boom and over the taffrail. Villeneuve wrote: "I did not observe a single man daunted at the sight of the formidable enemy column, headed by four three-deckers which bore down on the *Bucentaure*." Commander Bazin, second-in-command of the 74-gun *Fougueux* (whose crew was owed sixteen months' pay) wrote: "Captain Baudouin had the colours and the French pendant hoisted and fired the whole broadside at the foremost ship; from that minute the action commenced vigorously on both sides. . . ."

In the *Victory*, after Hardy and Blackwood had witnessed Nelson's will, the Admiral was getting very impatient. Looking at the Combined Fleet spread out ahead of him he remarked to Blackwood: "They put a good face on it." But he quickly added: "I'll give them such a dressing as they never had before!" He then grumbled at the nearness of Cape Trafalgar to leeward. At that moment Blackwood, realizing that the *Victory*, being at the head of the division, would bear the brunt of the enemy's fire, pointed out respectfully to Nelson the value of his life, particularly in the battle about to begin. "I proposed hoisting his flag in the *Euryalus*, whence he could better see what was going on, as well as what to order in case of necessity," Blackwood wrote, "but he would not hear of it, and gave as his reason the force of example; and probably he was right.

"My next object, therefore, was to endeavour to induce his Lordship to allow the *Téméraire, Neptune* and *Leviathan* to lead into action before the *Victory* . . . after much conversation, in which I ventured to give it as the joint opinion of Captain Hardy and myself, how advantageous it would be to the Fleet for his Lordship to keep as long as possible out of the Battle, he at last consented to allow the *Téméraire*, which was then sailing abreast of the *Victory*, to go ahead." Nelson had smiled significantly at Hardy when he said: "Oh, yes, let her go ahead." Blackwood, however, seems to have missed the implied "if she can!"

Then, according to Blackwood, the Admiral hailed Captain Harvey in *Téméraire* to tell him to go ahead, but he was too far away to hear. He therefore sent Blackwood over in a boat to pass the order. But if Blackwood thought Nelson was going to stand back and let someone else lead him into battle, he was mistaken. "On returning to the *Victory*," the young frigate captain reported, "I found him doing all he could to increase rather than diminish sail, so that the *Téméraire* could not pass the *Victory*." Blackwood then managed to get Hardy on his own and tell him that he ought to warn the Admiral that unless he shortened sail the *Victory* would stay ahead, but Hardy had been with Nelson for a long time and he refused as, says the *Victory*'s surgeon, "he conceived his Lordship's ardour to get into battle would on no account suffer such a measure."

Nelson, when chatting to Blackwood a little later, asked him what he would regard as a victory. "Considering the handsome way the enemy are offering battle," Blackwood replied "their apparent determination for a fair trial of strength, and the nearness of the land, I should think that if fourteen ships are captured it would be a glorious result." Nelson looked up at the burly prince of frigate captains, a gleam in his one remaining eye, "I shall not, Blackwood, be satisfied with anything short of twenty."

Nelson, Hardy, Blackwood and Quilliam all trained their telescopes on the row of French and Spanish ships from time to time, trying to discover in which ship was the enemy commander-in-chief—whom Nelson wanted to capture himself. But none of them was then flying an admiral's flag.

About this time Lt. John Yule, commanding on the *Victory*'s fo'c'sle, saw that the starboard lower studding-sail was not set properly. He immediately ordered it to be taken in and reset. Unfortunately for him Nelson saw the sail being lowered with Yule standing by supervising it, and misunderstanding the young lieutenant's motive he scolded him angrily for reducing sail without orders from the captain.

A little earlier Nelson had gone round the various decks, chatting with the men as they stood to their guns, warning them not to waste a single shot. Seaman Brown, part of whose colourful letter we have already seen, described it thus: "Lord Nelson went round the decks and said My noble lads this will be a glorious day for england who ever lives to see it I Shant be Satisfied with 12 ships this day as I took at the Nile So we piped to dinner and ate a bit of raw pork and half a pint of wine."

Several of the *Victory*'s officers had been very worried over the fact that the very large stars of the various orders embroidered on Nelson's frock coat would make him—with the one arm—a most conspicuous and tempting target for sharpshooters. Beatty suggested that the Admiral should be asked to cover up the stars with a handkerchief, but Dr. Scott, the chaplain, and John Scott, Nelson's secretary, did not agree. Such a request, they observed, would have no effect: knowing him so well they realized that he would be extremely annoyed with anyone who suggested any change in his dress for this reason. Beatty was not put off by this: he said he would take the opportunity of mentioning it to the Admiral when he made his sick report for the day. "Take care, Doctor, what you are about," warned John Scott. "I would not be the man to mention such a matter to him." Beatty stayed on deck as long as he could, waiting to take his chance; but Nelson was always occupied.

The wind was falling lighter than ever. According to Midshipman William Rivers, who was on deck, Nelson was afraid that if the wind dropped any more he might have to round up and open fire on the enemy at long range. The guns had been double-shotted and this was effective only at short range. But, Rivers reported, Nelson "desired me to acquaint the officers to load with *single* shot." The rolling of the ship had been lifting and slatting the sails when Rivers started off on his mission to the lieutenants on each of the gun decks, but by the time he returned the breeze had become steadier and he "found the sails asleep."

A few minutes later Nelson, looking first at the *Royal Sovereign* over on the starboard beam and then at the Combined Fleet, said to Hardy: "We shall have some warm work, and that pretty close." He looked round the bulwarks of the *Victory,* seeing the black canvas cloths which covered the hammocks in the nettings. A sudden thought struck him. "Send young Rivers down with a few hands to get up and spread the white hammock cloths, and let them be well saturated."

The bustle aboard the flagship was quietening down now: with all preparation made for battle, the main task was to keep the ship sailing as fast as possible. This fell to Thomas Atkinson, the Master. He was a very experienced man, having served at the Nile, commanded a boat at the siege of Acre, and been Master of the *Elephant* under Nelson at Copenhagen. The Admiral had a high regard for him—back in England Atkinson's young son rejoiced in the Christian names of Horatio Nelson, a tribute to the Admiral who had been only too willing to be the child's godfather.

For Nelson there were still some signals to make. As we have seen, he intended to break through the enemy's line somewhere about the thirteenth or fourteenth ship and then harden in sheets and braces to sail up to attack the van and prevent its coming down to help the rest of the Combined Fleet. By chance the thirteenth ship was the *Bucentaure,* with Villeneuve on board, although Nelson did not know this, and at the moment the *Victory* was heading for the twelfth ship, the *Santissima Trinidad.*

Nelson had already told Collingwood by signal what he proposed doing—"I intend to push through the end of the enemy's line to prevent them from getting into Cadiz." Now, with the nearest enemy ships less than two miles ahead, the Admiral walked up and down on the poop with Blackwood. He was completely controlled, but he seemed poised like a coiled spring. Turning to Blackwood he said: "I'll now amuse the Fleet with a signal. Do you not think there is one yet wanting?" "I think the whole of the Fleet seem to understand very clearly what they are about," answered Blackwood.

But Nelson was already walking across to where Pasco and his signalmen were waiting. He ordered a signal to be made to the *Africa*—sailing towards them over on the larboard beam near the head of the enemy's line—to "Engage the enemy more closely," and another to the Fleet, to "Prepare to anchor after the close of day."

Then he said: "Mr. Pasco, I wish to say to the Fleet, 'England confides that every man will do his duty.' " He added: "You must be quick, for I have one more to make, which is for Close Action."

Pasco thought for a moment, mentally searching through Sir Home Popham's telegraphic vocabulary. Then he replied: "If your Lordship will permit me to substitute 'expects' for 'confides' the signal will soon be completed, because the word 'expects' is in the vocabulary, and 'confides' must be spelt." "That will do, Pasco, make it directly," Nelson said hurriedly. The signalmen swiftly bent the flags on to the halyards and hoisted them.[2] Nelson then said to Pasco, "Make the signal for Close Action, and *keep it up.*"

Turning away to Hardy and Blackwood he remarked: "I can do no more. We must trust to the great Disposer of all events, and the justice of our cause. I thank God for this great opportunity of doing my duty." As he spoke two flags were being run up—the Numbers 1 and 6: "Engage the enemy more closely."

Then they looked over on the starboard beam, to where the *Royal Sovereign,* well ahead of the rest of the line, was now within a few hundred yards of what seemed to be a solid wall of enemy

2 The signal is as follows: Telegraphic flag and then—253 (England) 269 (expects) 863 (that) 261 (every) 471 (man) 958 (will) 220 (do) 370 (his) 4 (D) 21 (U) 19 (T) 24 (Y).

Some confusion has, in the past, been caused because in numbering the letters of the alphabet Popham put "I" and "J" together, and "V" before "U."

ships. Suddenly a row of glowing red dots rippled down their sides. It wanted a few minutes to noon: the *Fougueux* had launched her first broadside at Collingwood's flagship, and the battle of Trafalgar had begun.

"See how that noble fellow Collingwood carries his ship into action!" exclaimed Nelson. In the *Royal Sovereign* Collingwood turned to Rotheram and remarked quietly: "What would Nelson give to be here!"

A little earlier some of his officers, appalled at seeing that Rotheram intended to go into action in a gold-laced hat and heavy gold epaulettes, a fine target for enemy sharpshooters, had asked him to change into something less conspicuous. "Let me alone!" growled Rotheram in reply. "I've always fought in a cocked hat and always will!"

Throughout the Fleet the reaction to Nelson's rousing signal was varied. Some ships, however, probably did not receive it. In the *Bellerophon* it was read off by Midshipman Franklin, and immediately reported to Captain Cooke who, realizing what Nelson had meant in making it, promptly went round the decks, where the men were waiting impatiently at the guns, and read it to them. With the sound of their cheers ringing in his ears he strode back to the poop. Captain Durham of the *Defiance* turned up all hands, read the signal and was answered with cheers. "Everything then being ready—matches lit—guns double-shotted with grape and rounds, and decks cleared—we piped to dinner and had a good glass of grog."

The *Neptune*'s crew heard of the signal and gave a cheer, and in the *Britannia* it was "joyfully welcomed." In the *Ajax*, Lt. Ellis, told to tell the sailors on the main deck, began with the quartermaster who, without any more ado, assembled the men with: "Avast there, lads, come and hear the Admiral's words." Ellis repeated Nelson's signal, but at first the men did not appreciate it, "for there were murmurs from some, whilst others in an audible whisper murmured, 'Do our duty? Of course we'll do our duty! I've always done mine, haven't you? Let us come alongside of 'em and we'll soon show whether we'll do our duty.'" Nevertheless, they soon started cheering—"more from love and admiration of the Admiral," says Ellis, "than from a full appreciation of his signal." The *Polyphemus*'s men, hearing the signal, gave three cheers and received three in reply from the *Dreadnought* on their starboard beam.

The *Royal Sovereign* opened fire on the enemy, as we shall see later, exactly at noon. Fifteen minutes later the first of the enemy ships opened fire at long range at the *Victory*. But those ships were rolling: the swell waves coming in on the larboard beam gathered them up and rolled them over to starboard. They righted themselves as the crests passed beneath, and then rolled to larboard on the backs of the waves which then moved on to the eastward, to crash along the rocky shore of Cape Trafalgar.

The inexperienced French and Spanish gunners peering down their sights had the same view as a man glancing up at the blue sky and then deliberately lowering his gaze to the sea twenty yards off the ship's side and then looking up skywards again. Their task was similar to a man with a pistol sitting in a rocking chair and trying to shoot a tumbler off the mantelpiece at the far end of the room. For the first few broadsides they were about as successful, but the shooting served a good purpose, because it tended to steady the men—and not only in the enemy ships.

The time had now come for Nelson to send Blackwood back to the *Euryalus* and Prowse to the *Sirius* (the other two frigate captains appear to have left earlier). On their way, said Nelson, they were to tell all the captains of the battleships (i.e., those of Nelson's division) that he was "depending on their exertions; and if by the mode of attack prescribed they find it impracticable to get into action immediately, they may adopt whatever they think best, provided it leads them quickly and closely alongside an enemy."

The three men stood at the forward end of the quarter-deck of the *Victory*. From ahead, like thunder before a summer storm, came the rumble of the French and Spanish guns, and the hiss of shot passing overhead. Prowse said goodbye to his nephew Charles Adair, the *Victory*'s captain of Marines, for the last time.

Blackwood took Nelson's hand. "I trust, my Lord, that on my return to the *Victory*, which will be as soon as possible, I shall find your Lordship well, and in possession of twenty prizes." Nelson looked at Blackwood, and his presentiment of death must have been gripping him now. "God bless you, Blackwood, I shall never speak to you again."

TWENTY-ONE

NELSON IS SHOT

When without stratagem
But in plain shock and even play of battle,
Was ever known so great and little loss
On one part and on the other? Take it, God,
For it is none but thine.

—Shakespeare (*Henry V*)

T H E *Victory* was sailing in the faltering breeze at the speed of a dawdling child. With the *Téméraire, Neptune, Leviathan* and *Conqueror* following close astern, she seemed to the French the sharp and vicious end of a massive wedge driving down on to them with the ponderous and crushing inevitability of a glacier.

There were four enemy ships directly ahead. Captain Poulain, commanding the northernmost, the 74-gun *Héros,* gave orders to try the range, and from the *Victory* they could see red flame spitting from her gun ports, and almost immediately smoke wreathed up, blurring her outline. The huge *Santissima Trinidad,* just astern of her, followed. Like pebbles in the distance the shot splashed up well short of the *Victory.* Then the third ship, the *Bucentaure,* fired a few ranging shots. They too fell short.

Two or three minutes passed. "Starboard a little," ordered Hardy, and Atkinson, the Master, repeated it to the quartermaster. The *Victory* had for a short while come up to larboard, as if making a feint, but now she came back on course. On each of the gun decks the lieutenants put their speaking-trumpets to their lips. Perspiration trickled down naked backs. There was no laughing and joking now, for each man was alone with himself.

"Make ready!"

The second captains at the guns leapt to the flintlocks and a series of metallic clicks showed that they had cocked them. The

gun captains, standing six or seven feet behind the guns holding
the trigger-lines which linked them to the flintlocks, crouched
down with right knees bent and left legs flung out a pace to the
side. They looked down the glistening barrels but at the moment
there was only the sea and an empty horizon in their sight.

Again the *Bucentaure* fired a few rounds. The *Victory* was just
over a mile away and they fell short. A few moments elapsed and
the other ships again fired. The men on the *Victory*'s upper deck
heard some shots whirr overhead. Then they saw a hole suddenly
appear in the main-topgallant sail: a clear indication to the enemy
that they were now in range. The desultory firing stopped. There
was a minute of awful silence.

Suddenly the fear-sharpened outlines of the French ships blurred
and in their place were rolling banks of flame-tinged yellow smoke:
nearly two hundred guns, the full broadsides of the *Héros, Santissima Trinidad, Bucentaure* and *Redoutable,* had fired. Before the
sound of their discharge reached the *Victory* an invisible hail of
death smashed into her: solid shot plunged through the hull, throwing out a hail of great splinters which cut men down like invisible
scythes; straining ropes were slashed, whiplashing like elastic; holes
pock-marked the sails. Men grunted and sat down abruptly with
death inside them; others fell shrieking, stumps of limbs pumping
blood on to the scrubbed decks. When the enemy guns stopped—for
a moment—vomiting their grotesque mixture of round-shot and
grape, livid flame, noise and smoke, it seemed incongruous that the
weak sun still shone, that the sails still flapped with lazy majesty,
ropes creaked through blocks with easy familiarity, and the sea
continued to murmur its quiet song under bow and stern.

Again the enemy guns coughed their vicious death . . . and
again, and again. Nelson's secretary, John Scott, was talking to
Hardy when suddenly an invisible hand flung him to the deck,
dead. Captain Charles Adair, commanding the Royal Marines on
the quarter-deck, called a seaman and attempted to carry away the
body before Nelson noticed, but the Admiral walked across.

"Is that poor Scott that is gone?" Adair replied that it was. "Poor
fellow!" said Nelson. Then he and Hardy paced up and down the
quarter-deck talking with the easy unconcern of two diplomats
walking of a summer's morning along Whitehall.

Again the enemy's guns fired. A double-headed shot spun into the group of red-coated Marines drawn up on the poop and eight of them collapsed to the deck. Seeing this, Nelson called to Adair: "Disperse your men round the ship." But for this order they would have cleared the sharpshooters from the enemy's tops—and perhaps saved Nelson's life.

Hardy glanced at his heavy gold watch. It was of curious design, with the hours marked in Roman numerals and the minutes in Arabic. Barely 12.20 . . . they had been under fire less than five minutes. A shot cut through four rolled-up hammocks in the nettings, smashed away part of the launch as it lay on the booms, hit the fore-brace bitts on the quarter-deck and whined between the two men. A splinter from the bitts hit Hardy's left foot, tearing away the ornate buckle of the shoe.

Both men stopped instinctively. Nelson glanced up questioningly at the massive Hardy; he in turn looked down at his Admiral. Each feared the other had been wounded. Nelson smiled. "This is too warm work, Hardy, to last long."

Again the enemy guns rumbled. A shot smashed the *Victory's* wheel, and for a moment she was out of control. Quilliam and Atkinson ran down to the gun room to organize emergency steering, using the tackles which had already been hooked on to the tiller when the ship cleared for action. Suddenly there was a crash high above the poop as a shot cut into the mizen-topmast and sent it toppling down. Forward the foresail—it was almost new—began to flap. More than two hundred feet of it had been torn from the yard and it hung down in shreds over the fo'c'sle. Within five minutes each of the studding-sails had been ripped from the booms; every other sail in the ship was pocked with holes. The *Victory* was like a bird with its wings clipped. Thirty men had been carried wounded out of the sunlight and down to the half-darkness of the cockpit for Beatty to attend to them; twenty more were beyond reach of his skill.

Now the *Victory* was only a few hundred yards from the enemy: within a short while she would be able to bring her broadsides to bear.

She was heading for the space between the stern of *Santissima Trinidad* and the bows of *Bucentaure,* but Hardy saw the gap closing as the *Bucentaure* slowly moved ahead. Nor did there seem enough room to pass astern of the *Bucentaure* because Captain

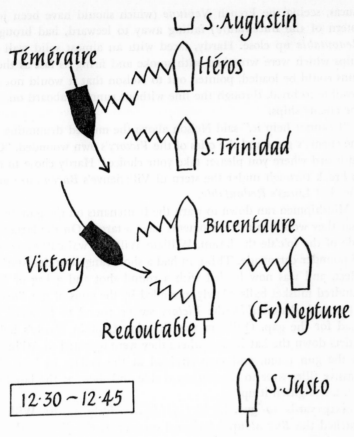

S. Augustin

Téméraire

Héros

S. Trinidad

Bucentaure

Victory

(Fr) Neptune

Redoutable

S. Justo

12·30 ~ 12·45

DIAGRAM 1: The *Victory* sailing down to break the line, under fire from *Bucentaure, Redoutable* and French *Neptune*. At 12.40 *Téméraire* engages *San Augustin* and *Héros*. It should be noted that this and successive diagrams are not to scale. Zigzag lines indicate gunfire.

Lucas, seeing the French *Neptune* (which should have been just astern of the *Bucentaure*) falling away to leeward, had brought *Redoutable* up close. Hardy, faced with an almost solid wall of ships which were wreathed with smoke and firing as fast as their guns could be loaded, pointed out to Nelson that it would not be possible to break through the line without running aboard one of the enemy ships.

"I cannot help it," said Nelson above the muffled drumming of the enemy's guns and the cries of the *Victory*'s own wounded. "Go on board where you please: take your choice." Hardy chose to try to break through under the stern of Villeneuve's *Bucentaure* and ahead of Lucas's *Redoutable*.

Midshipmen ran down to warn the lieutenants on the gun decks that they would in a few moments have a target. On the larboard side of the fo'c'sle the bosun, William Willmet, waited beside the 68-pounder carronade. This gun had a short range but devastating effect, and was now loaded with a round shot and a keg of five hundred musket balls. Slowly, pounded by the guns of the *Bucentaure* and *Redoutable,* the *Victory* swung round to larboard to head for the gap. Quilliam was shouting Captain Hardy's helm orders down the hatchways, where they were repeated to Atkinson in the gun room, and men strained at the tackles to haul the massive tiller over to the starboard side and then, at the last moment, straighten it up.

Sixty yards to go . . . fifty yards . . . forty yards: Willmet watched the *Bucentaure*'s larboard quarter as the *Victory* slowly steered to cross her stern. He could see the lozenge-shaped escutcheon painted in horizontal bands of blue, white and red; the sun reflected on the windows of the stern cabins—the upper ones of Magendie's quarters, those below of Villeneuve. The great Tricolour hung limp over the taffrail.

Hardy was taking it very close. Thirty yards . . . now the *Victory*'s great long bowsprit was overlapping the *Bucentaure*'s stern . . . twenty yards, and Willmet took the strain on the trigger-line and gave a last-minute adjustment to the spiral elevating screw. Ten yards . . . Willmet realized that in a moment or two he would almost be able to reach out and grasp the Tricolour . . . five yards.

Down on the gun decks the captains were crouching over their sights, and taking up the strain on their trigger-lines; the lieutenants, snatching quick glances through the ports, in a moment sprang back clear of the gun muzzles.

Suddenly Willmet's right hand jerked back: the thunder of the carronade gave way to the terrible clatter of the shot and five hundred musket balls smashing through the *Bucentaure's* flimsy stern, fanning out to sweep the lines of guns, cutting down in swathes the mass of Frenchmen working them. But almost before Willmet's carronade had finished its short recoil the guns on the decks below were firing into the *Bucentaure's* stern as, one by one, they came to bear. From the *Victory's* decks they could hear the wild screams of the wounded and dying. The smoke from the guns blew back into the ports and set the men coughing; up on deck clouds of dust from the shattered woodwork of the French flagship flew across to cover Nelson's and Hardy's coats.

As the *Victory* passed through, still rolling in the swell, the end of her main yardarm caught the vang of the *Bucentaure's* gaff and ripped it away. But waiting beyond the *Bucentaure* was the French *Neptune*: as soon as the *Victory* was clear she poured a broadside into the British flagship and quickly set a jib to run ahead in case the *Victory* tried to board. Her broadside did much damage to the *Victory's* foremast and bowsprit; several shot smashed through the bow planking and others damaged her anchors and spritsail yards.

Hardy, however, had decided to get alongside the *Redoutable*, now on his starboard side, and ordered the helm to be put over. While the men at the larboard guns quickly sponged out and reloaded with two or three shot to each gun, the starboard gun captains waited for the *Victory* to come round far enough for them to fire their first broadside. In a moment or two they could see Lucas's ship. The captains jerked their trigger-lines and the full starboard broadside smashed into the *Redoutable*. Willmet, who had run across to the starboard carronade, fired it down on to the French sailors massed on the enemy's decks. The *Redoutable* shut most of her lower-deck gun ports and then the two ships crunched together, but as they bounced apart again the *Victory's* topmast studding-sail boom irons hooked on to the *Redoutable's* fore-topsail and held the two ships together.

Down below in the *Victory* the lieutenants were yelling themselves hoarse in the half-darkness. Clouds of smoke meant that they could not see farther than a couple of guns away, and the men worked almost instinctively: sponge—in with the cartridge —ram it home—in with the shot—ram—in with a wad and ram—another shot—ram—wad and ram—cock the lock; everyone then jumps well back; there is a jerk on the trigger-line and the gun flings back, flame and noise spurting from the muzzle and a little "huff" of flame coming from the vent-hole to burn the beams overhead.

While all the *Victory*'s starboard guns pounded the *Redoutable,* the larboard guns kept on firing at the *Bucentaure* as she drifted away, and some of them managed to fire into the stern of the *Santissima Trinidad.* The *Bucentaure* had suffered dreadful damage from the *Victory*'s momentary assault. As Nelson's flagship approached, Villeneuve had ordered Magendie to prepare to board, but Hardy's sudden turn under his stern had caught him unawares.

"The swell, which made our ships roll, lessened the accuracy of our aim," Major-General Contamine wrote, "and a dense cloud of smoke, that the calm prevented from dispersing, often forbade our seeing anything round us."

Villeneuve, as soon as he had an indication of what Nelson proposed doing with his division, had hoisted a belated signal. It was not the one for which Churruca had earlier waited in vain—for the van to wear round and help the rear. With the line being broken by both British divisions, Villeneuve hoisted a signal which ordered "all those ships, which by their actual position are not engaging, to take any such as will bring them as speedily as possible into action." But Dumanoir and his ships ahead, for whom the order was really intended, sailed majestically on to the northward.

Meanwhile Captain Lucas's well-trained sharpshooters perched in the tops of the *Redoutable* kept up a hail of musket fire down on to the *Victory*'s decks. Down below most of the French guns were silent, but the *Victory*'s guns were being constantly run out —their muzzles almost touching the French ship's side—and fired. It seemed likely that the *Redoutable* might be set on fire by the flash of their discharge, and such a blaze would be a danger to the *Victory* as well. So at the *Victory*'s guns men stood by with buckets

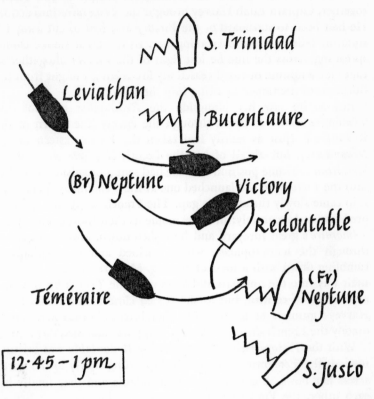

S. Trinidad

Leviathan

Bucentaure

(Br) Neptune

Victory

Redoutable

Téméraire

(Fr) Neptune

S. Justo

12·45 – 1 pm

DIAGRAM 2: At 12.45 *Victory* rakes *Bucentaure* and, 12.50, runs aboard *Redoutable*, both ships drifting to leeward. British *Neptune* rakes *Bucentaure*. French *Neptune* and *San Justo* open fire on *Téméraire*.

of water, and as each gun fired they flung the water out of the port to stifle any flames.

While the *Victory* and the *Redoutable* fought it out, locked together, Captain Eliab Harvey brought the *Téméraire* into action. He had been to starboard of the *Victory* and had to cut away his studding-sails to avoid overtaking her. In the great smoke clouds spreading across the line he lost sight of the *Victory* altogether so that "for a minute or two I ceased my fire fearing I might from the thickness of the smoke be firing into the *Victory*."

But as he saw her alongside the *Redoutable* he took the *Téméraire* round to break through the enemy line astern of the *Redoutable* (just as Hardy had taken the *Victory* astern of the *Bucentaure*); but ahead of her the French *Neptune* was waiting and, from the same position that she had sent a broadside smashing into the *Victory*, so she launched one at the *Téméraire* as Harvey's ship came slowly through the gap. The French *Neptune*'s gunners fired fast and accurately: in a few moments their shots cut away the *Téméraire*'s great foreyard and it crashed down. More shots sliced through the main-topmast, which buckled and then collapsed, tumbling down with a mass of rigging. More round-shot punched their way into the foremast and bowsprit. The *Téméraire* was now almost out of control, but as she passed close to the *Redoutable*, Harvey's gunners fired broadside after broadside into her. Immediately the French ship's lower-deck gun ports slammed down shut.

With the *Victory* lashed alongside, the *Redoutable* was drifting towards the *Téméraire* as Harvey's ship swung slowly to the north across her bows. A collision was unavoidable and they finally hit each other, the French ship's bowsprit crashing over the British ship's deck just forward of the mainmast. Immediately Harvey ordered his men to lash it, thus holding the two ships in position. Now they could rake the *Redoutable* with their larboard broadside, but the enemy could not reply. Again and again their shot smashed into the French ship's unprotected bows, hurling guns off their carriages, slashing rigging and sails, tearing up deck planking, and cutting down the French seamen and soldiers so that the dead were lying in heaps.

In the meantime the *Redoutable*'s sharpshooters were wreaking great execution on the *Victory*'s decks. "At one time," wrote Seaman Brown, "they would have sunk us only for the Timmera

(1) Nelson leaves England for the last time, boarding his barge at
Southsea to join the *Victory. From the painting by Gow*

(2) Nelson.
From the portr
by Abbott

(3) Sir Henry
Blackwood,
the "prince of
frigate captains."
From the
portrait by
Hoppner

(4) Collingwood.
*From the painting
by Howard*

(5) Nelson's Hardy.
*From the painting
by Abbott*

(6) Rear-Admiral Magon.

(7) Captain Lucas,
commanding the
French *Redoutable*.

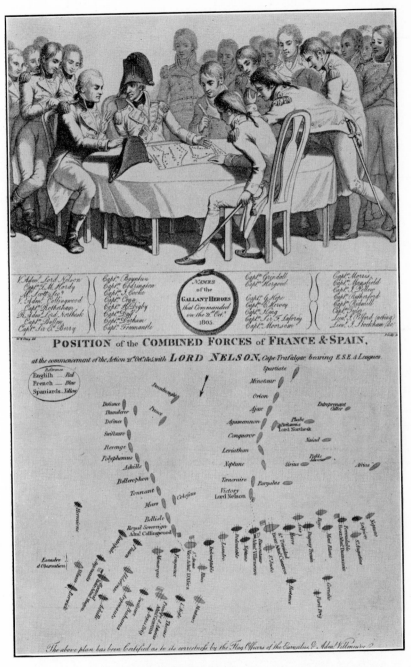

(8) Nelson with his captains, explaining the plan of attack before
Trafalgar. *From a print, with a diagram of the battle, dated
January 9, 1806*

(9) The *Victory*, studding sails set, sails down to break the enemy line. The *Téméraire* is on the left. On the extreme right is Blackwood's frigate *Euryalus* and, in the distance, the schooner *Pickle*. *From the painting by Harold Wyllie*

(10) Into battle: the gun deck of a line-of-battle ship, from a painting by Harold Wyllie. The man with his arms outstretched is the gun captain, pulling the trigger-line.

(11) The *Belleisle* breaks the enemy line. From left to right the ships are the French *Fougueux*, *Belleisle*, French *Indomptable*, the Spanish flagship *Santa Ana*, and Collingwood's flagship *Royal Sovereign*. From an engraving of the

(12) The *Santa Ana* at bay: the Spanish flagship is in the centre with the *Royal Sovereign* almost hidden in the smoke on her starboard side. The three-decker on the left is intended to be the *Dreadnought*, although she was never in that position. *From the painting by Oleo de Cortellini*

(13) "Crippled but unconquered" — the rescue of the *Belleisle*.
From the painting by W. L. Wyllie, R. A.

(14) Captain George Duff, who was killed in the battle while in command of the *Mars. From the painting by Raeburn in possession of the Misses Duff*

(15) Captain Digby's view from the deck of the *Africa* as he sailed into the battle. *Detail from the painting owned by Lord Digby*

(16) Captain Codrington's view of the battle from the deck of the *Orion* at about 2 p.m. This painting by Harold Wyllie shows, from left to right, the *Britannia*, Spanish *S. Trinidad*, British *Neptune*, *Leviathan*, French *Bucentaure* (dismasted and heeling to starboard), *Conqueror*, *Victory* (heeling to port), French *Redoutable*, *Téméraire*, French

(17) The *Victory* at the close of day. Harold Wyllie's painting shows seamen at work repairing action damage to masts, sails and rigging while the sky and swell give silent warning of the approach of a great gale.

(18) The death of Nelson. The main figures, from left to right, are Lt. Yule, Midshipman Francis Collingwood, Nelson's valet, Gaetano, Dr. Scott (with his hand on Nelson's chest), Burke (with his arm around the Admiral), Chevalier (in white shirt), and Dr. Beatty, who is holding Nelson's hand. *From the painting by Devas*

(19) The Schooner *Pickle* arrives off Falmouth with Collingwood's despatches announcing the victory at Trafalgar. *From the painting by W. McDowell*

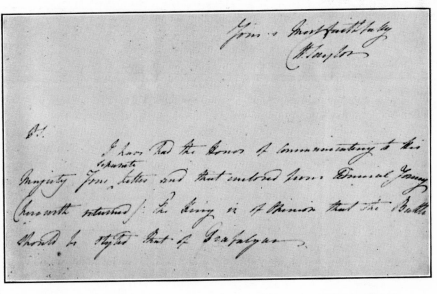

(20) Part of a letter written by the King's secretary to William Marsden, Secretary of the Admiralty. The last few words read: "The King is of opinion that the Battle should be styled that of Trafalgar." *Original letter in the possession of C. Marsden, Esq*

(21) The great storm after the battle: British, French and Spanish ships fight for their lives within sight of Cadiz, which can be seen on the left of the picture. *Detail from the painting owned by Lord Digby*

[*Téméraire*] took the firy [*sic*] edge of us the repaiting [*sic*] frigate could not see us for fire and smoke from 12 o'clock until two they thought we was sunk but instead of what we were giving Johnny Craps their breakfast. . . ."

The *Victory*'s lieutenants in charge of her guns realized that there was a grave danger of their shot going clean through the French ship and hitting the *Téméraire* on the far side. They therefore shouted to the gun captains on the middle and lower decks to depress their guns so that the shot would go downward.

Down in the cockpit the wounded were being brought down in a never-ending stream. Dr. Scott, the chaplain, horrified at the dreadful suffering of many of the men, was almost demented by what he saw in the faint light of the fighting lanterns, but he went round to crouch at the side of each man, doing what he could to comfort him.

Lt. William Ram, a twenty-one-year-old Irishman, was carried down desperately wounded from a shot which had smashed up through the deck at his feet. One of the surgeons tied tourniquets to stop the bleeding, but Ram suddenly realized that he was dying. Impatiently he ripped the tourniquets off so that he bled to death more quickly. The sight of this so upset the frenzied Scott that he ran up the hatchways, now stained with blood, to the upper deck. There he found little relief: a pall of smoke and dust hung so thickly that he could only just make out the figures of Nelson and Hardy walking up and down.

But tragedy was about to strike on board the British flagship. Nelson and Hardy were regularly pacing up and down a twenty-foot stretch of the quarter-deck between the shattered wheel and the hatchway. They had reached to within two or three feet of the hatch and Nelson turned to the left. Hardy took another pace and also turned—to see Nelson on his knees, trying to support himself with his left hand. Before he could reach him, Nelson's one arm gave way and he collapsed. In a moment Hardy was crouching over him. "I hope you are not severely wounded, my Lord?" he inquired anxiously.

"They have done for me at last, Hardy," Nelson gasped.

"I hope not!"

"Yes," said Nelson, "my backbone is shot through."

Hardy called to a Marine sergeant nearby, Sgt. Secker, and two seamen. They ran over and knelt down at Nelson's side. "Take the Admiral down to the cockpit immediately," ordered Hardy. Gently they lifted the stricken man in their arms, and stepped the few paces to the hatchway leading down to the upper deck. Somehow Nelson managed to use his one arm to take out a handkerchief and place it over his face, so that no one should recognize him as he was carried below.

Many others had been wounded at about this time by the musket balls of the French sharpshooters and the blast of the grenades, and Secker and the two seamen had to take their turn as they shuffled down to the upper deck, trying to avoid jolting Nelson. From the upper deck they gently manoeuvred him down to the middle deck and then to the gun deck. As they reached the bottom of each ladder they had to be careful because on either side of the hatchway there were guns, and they were still being fired as fast as they could be loaded. Finally they left the daylight behind as they scrambled down the last ladder to the orlop, and then slowly made their way past the wounded sitting or lying about on the deck. Several of the wounded men recognized Nelson from the decorations on his coat.

"Mr. Beatty!" they cried. "Mr. Beatty! Lord Nelson is here!"

"Mr. Beatty! The Admiral is wounded!"

Beatty, his clothes soaked in the blood of the men he was tending, was already heavy-hearted from the number of wounded all round him and especially from the death of Lt. Ram, who had been a great friend.[1] Then above the bedlam of groans and cries punctuated by the rumble of the 32-pounders on the deck above being run out, and the crash of them firing, he heard the agonized call: "Mr. Beatty! Quickly! The Admiral is wounded!"

He turned, and in the gloom he saw three men, bent down because of the lack of head room, stumbling along towards him, carrying a small figure. A handkerchief over the face slipped away, and he saw it was Nelson. His premonition, expressed earlier to the two Scotts, had come true. He ran the last few steps and Burke, the purser, who had also heard the urgent calls, joined him. Quickly they took the Admiral from the arms of the seamen and

---

[1] Some reports say that Lt. Ram was wounded after Nelson; but Beatty's account makes it clear that this was not the case.

carried him towards the midshipmen's berth. One of them tripped and stumbled, but managed to avoid falling.

"Who is that carrying me?" asked Nelson.

"Beatty, my Lord, and Burke," said the surgeon.

"Ah, Mr. Beatty! You can do nothing for me. I have but a short time to live: my back is shot through."

In the near-darkness Beatty could feel the Admiral's blood-soaked coat, but he said: "I hope the wound is not as dangerous as your Lordship imagines."

The overwrought Scott, who had been giving lemonade to the wounded in another part of the cockpit after his brief glimpse of the holocaust on the upper deck, suddenly appeared, grief-stricken at the sight that met his eyes and wringing his hands in anguish. "Alas, Beatty, how prophetic you were!" he exclaimed.

They bore Nelson to an empty space on the larboard side, just forward of the after hanging magazine, and put him down gently on a rough mattress, his back against one of the massive frames of the ship's side. Swiftly Beatty and Burke slipped off his coat —an easy task since he had but one arm—shirt and the rest of his clothes, and drew a sheet over him. While they were doing this Nelson said to Dr. Scott in a quiet voice: "Doctor, I told you so. Doctor, I am gone."

Apparently convinced that he would die within a few minutes he added, after a short pause, "I have to leave Lady Hamilton, and my adopted daughter Horatia, as a legacy to my country."

Beatty was by now ready with his surgical instruments. He felt the pulse. Overhead the 32-pounders crashed and rumbled; the frame against which Nelson rested his back shivered and vibrated with the shock of battle as Lucas's *Redoutable* also fought a losing struggle for life. A fighting lantern was hung from a beam overhead and Beatty assured Nelson he would not put him to much pain in trying to discover the course of the musket ball. The more Beatty gently probed the more he realized its hopelessness. The ball had plunged deep into the chest and was now probably lodged in the spine. He bent over Nelson and explained this to him.

"I am confident my back is shot through," said Nelson.

While Burke held him forward, Beatty examined the narrow back; but there was no mark of a wound.

"Tell me all your sensations, my Lord," requested Beatty.

"I feel a gush of blood every minute within my breast," said Nelson. "I have no feeling in the lower part of my body . . . breathing is very difficult and gives me very severe pain about the part of the spine I am sure the ball has struck—for I felt it break my back. . . ."

Beatty heard the Admiral list his symptoms with a sinking heart: they confirmed his suspicions. He wrote later: "These symptoms, but more particularly the gush of blood which his Lordship complained of, together with the state of his pulse, indicated to the surgeon himself the hopeless situation of the case: but till after the victory was ascertained and announced to his Lordship, the true nature of his wound was concealed by the surgeon from all on board except Captain Hardy, Dr Scott, Mr Burke and Messrs Smith and Westemburg, the Assistant Surgeons."

Twenty-year-old Midshipman George Westphal was carried down now after being wounded in the head and set down on the deck near Nelson. Someone, wanting to make him a pillow, seized a coat which had been flung down and rolled it up, not noticing the blood-stained orders of knighthood embroidered on its breast. Westphal, born in Lambeth of an old Hanoverian family, little knowing he would survive to be promoted to post captain and receive a knighthood, settled his throbbing head on his Admiral's coat and waited patiently for the surgeon.

The upper decks of the *Victory* now looked like a slaughter-house, thanks mainly to the sharpshooters and grenade-throwers hiding in the *Redoutable*'s tops. Smoke swirled like thick fog on a moor, blinding men and making them cough and splutter. Casualties were so heavy that the crews of the dozen 12-pounders on the quarter-deck had to quit: they were sent below to reinforce the upper-, middle- and gun-deck guns.

Soon the massive figure of Hardy striding about with his telescope under his arm, Captain Adair, the red-jacketed Marine, and one or two other officers were the only men left alive on deck. The seamen who had escaped were busy carrying their wounded comrades down to the cockpit. At the same time the *Redoutable*'s big guns had almost stopped firing, and this led the *Victory*'s gunners to think she was about to surrender, so they too stopped firing.

This led to an extraordinary misunderstanding, because the

sharpshooters in the *Redoutable*'s tops shouted down to their officers that the *Victory*'s decks had been swept bare and, coupled with the silence of the guns which had been tearing their ship to pieces, Lucas drew the wrong conclusion. At the same time Hardy and Adair called up Marines and seamen from below to get ready to take possession. Arming themselves with pistols and pikes, muskets and tomahawks, they streamed up the hatchways into the smoke and ran to the bulwarks.

Captain Lucas, describing the *Redoutable*'s point of view, wrote: "At last the *Victory*'s batteries were not able to reply to us; I perceived that they were preparing to board, the foe thronged up on to their upper works.

"I ordered the trumpet to sound (it was the recognized signal to summon the boarding parties in our exercises). They came up in such perfect order with the officers and midshipmen at the head of their divisions that one would have said that it was only a sham fight.

"In less than a minute the upper works were covered with armed men who hurled themselves on to the poop, on the nettings and into the shrouds; it was impossible for me to pick out the most courageous."

There followed an imaginative touch: "Then there began a furious musketry fire in which Admiral Nelson was fighting at the head of his crew; our fire became so greatly superior that in less than fifteen minutes we had silenced that of the *Victory;* more than two hundred grenades were thrown aboard her with the most marked success, her upper works were strewn with the dead and wounded, and Admiral Nelson was killed by the fire of our musketry." (This in fact refers to the beginning of the battle, but Lucas was preparing to make a very exaggerated claim.)

"Almost immediately the upper works of the enemy ship were deserted and the *Victory* ceased absolutely to engage us; but it was difficult to get aboard her owing to the rolling of the two ships and to the superior height afforded by her third deck.

"I gave orders to cut away the slings of the main yard and to lower it to serve as a bridge. Midshipman Yon and four seamen succeeded in getting on board the *Victory* by means of the anchor and informed us that there was not a soul on her decks; but at the moment when our brave lads were just hurling themselves after them the three-decker *Téméraire*—who had doubtless perceived that the *Victory* had ceased fire and would inevitably be taken—ran foul of us to starboard and overwhelmed us with the point-blank fire of all her guns."

Once Hardy and Adair had called up men from below, the French attack was quickly beaten off, but nineteen officers and men were killed and twenty-two wounded. Captain Adair was standing on the *Victory*'s gangway encouraging his men when he was killed by a musket ball in the back of the neck.

The arrival of the *Téméraire* soon changed the picture. "It would be difficult to describe the horrible carnage caused by the murderous broadside of this ship," wrote Lucas. "More than 200 of our brave lads were killed or wounded. I was wounded at the same instant but not so seriously as to prevent me from remaining at my post.

"Not being able to do anything more on the side next the *Victory* I ordered the rest of the crew to go below promptly and to fire into the *Téméraire* with those starboard guns which had not been dismounted in the shock of the collision with this ship."

However, the *Redoutable*'s sharpshooters kept up their fire on the decks of both British ships. In the *Victory,* the midshipman who had hoisted Nelson's "England expects" signal, John Pollard, had been the first man on the poop to be wounded, a shot through the bulwarks flinging up a heavy splinter which gashed his right arm. He had tied up the wound and carried on. Later, alongside the *Redoutable,* a musket ball had knocked the telescope from his hand, and then a bullet hit him in the thigh, smashing a watch in his fob pocket. Some time after Nelson had been shot, Pollard's attention had been drawn to three men in the *Redoutable*'s mizen-top—whence the shot had come. The top was about twenty feet above the *Victory*'s poop, and the men kept bobbing up from behind a strip of canvas, firing their muskets and then crouching to reload. Pollard picked up a musket from a dead Marine lying nearby and fired back, an old seaman named King bringing him fresh ammunition. While he was having his duel with the sharp-shooters, another midshipman, Francis Collingwood, a boy from Greenwich and no relation to the Admiral, arrived and had a shot before going on to carry out another task. Doggedly Pollard waited for the sharpshooters to show themselves again. One stood up, levelling his musket, but Pollard ducked behind the bulwark while King helped him to reload. He waited and suddenly the second Frenchman appeared. Pollard fired, and he too dropped behind the canvas. The third Frenchman, however, dodged behind the mast, and he fired before Pollard. King dropped dead, shot between the eyes, and the Frenchman tried to scramble down the rigging. But Pollard fired once again and the Frenchman fell to the deck.

By now the *Téméraire*'s broadside had given the *Redoutable* a terrible hammering. "Our ship was so riddled," wrote Lucas, "that she seemed to be no more than a mass of wreckage.

"In this state the *Téméraire* hailed us to strike and not to prolong a useless resistance. I ordered several soldiers who were near me to answer this summons with musket shots, which was performed with great zeal." But it was a hopeless gesture. Lucas describes the damage to the *Redoutable*. "All the stern was absolutely stove in, the rudder stock, the tiller, the two tiller sweeps, the stern-post, the helm port and wing transoms, the transom knees, were in general shot to pieces; the decks were all torn open by the fire of the *Victory* and the *Téméraire;* all the guns were shattered or dismounted by the shots or from these two ships having run us aboard.

"An 18-pounder gun on the main deck and a 36-pounder carronade on the fo'c'sle having burst, killed and wounded many of our people; the two sides of the ship, all the lids and bars of the ports were utterly cut to pieces; four of our six pumps were shattered as well as all our ladders in general, in such a [way] that communication between the decks and upper works was extremely difficult.

"All our decks were covered with dead, buried beneath the debris and the splinters from different parts of the ship. A great number of wounded were killed on the orlop-deck. Out of the ship's company of 643 men we had 522 disabled, 300 being killed and 222 wounded . . . in the midst of this horrible carnage the brave lads who had not yet succumbed and those who were wounded, with whom the orlop-deck was thronged, still cried 'Vive l'Emperor! We're not taken yet; is our Captain still alive?' "

There was little point in holding out any longer. "I only awaited

the certain knowledge that the leaks which the ship had sprung
were so considerable that it could not be long before she foundered,
in order to strike."[2]

Lucas had no sooner ordered the colours to be hauled down
than the mizenmast from which they were flying collapsed across
the *Téméraire*'s poop.

Some fires had broken out aboard the *Redoutable* and, without
bothering to send a lieutenant from the *Victory* to take possession
of her, Captain Hardy ordered Midshipman Collingwood and
Midshipman David Ogilvie, with a Marine sergeant-major and
eight or ten hands, to go aboard the French ship and put them out.
They could not step from one vessel to another because of the
tumble-home—the sides of the ships curved in towards the upper
decks like a brandy glass—so they went aft and found that one of
the two boats which the *Victory* had been towing astern was still
there. They hauled in the painter, scrambled down from a stern
port, rowed the few yards to the *Redoutable*'s stern and climbed
aboard through an open port. To their surprise they were well
received by the French.

For the moment it was comparatively quiet in the *Victory*. She
had, as already mentioned, lost her mizen-topmast at the beginning
of the action. Her fore- and mainmasts and their yards, main-topmast, fore- and maintops, bowsprit and jib-boom were all badly
damaged; her sails were in shreds and the rigging cut to pieces,
while the hull was badly damaged. More than fifty officers and
men had been killed, and more than a hundred wounded.[3]

Hardy now wanted to get the *Victory* clear of the *Redoutable*
and he set men pushing her off with fire booms. A few moments
earlier, just after the two midshipmen had left for the French
ship, a lieutenant, hearing the *Téméraire*'s guns firing on the other
side, looked out of a gun port aft and saw another French two-
decker lying close on the *Téméraire*'s starboard side. A few minutes
later he could read the name of the stern. It was the *Fougueux*.

For the moment, however, we must pass on to see the fate of the
Bucentaure, Villeneuve's flagship.

[2] By contrast, the *Téméraire*'s log dismisses the action in two dozen words.
[3] The *Victory*'s official returns listed seventy-five wounded, but Beatty says
that a further twenty-seven men reported themselves wounded after the returns
were made up.

TWENTY-TWO

THE BROADSIDES

So much bravery and devotion deserved a better fate, but the moment had not yet arrived when France will have her naval successes to celebrate together with her victories upon land. . . . —Villeneuve to Decrès

THE *Victory*, by firing her shattering broadside into the *Bucentaure* and then crashing alongside the *Redoutable*, forcing her off to leeward, had prised a big gap in the enemy line. As we have seen, the *Téméraire* could not take advantage of it in time and was forced to go round under the *Redoutable*'s stern, but the third ship in Nelson's division, Thomas Fremantle's *Neptune*, could and did.

The *Neptune*'s band had been playing bravely as the enemy's guns started the overture to their thunderous symphony; Fremantle found the excitement, as he wrote later to Betsey, "entirely drove away the bile" which had been troubling him, and he was a proud man as he stood on the quarter-deck, the band striking up "Rule, Britannia" and "Britons, Strike Home!" and bringing answering cheers from the *Téméraire* ahead and the *Leviathan* on the quarter. "During the whole of the time we were going down into action and being raked by the enemy," wrote Midshipman Badcock, "the whole crew, with the exception of the officers, were made to lie flat on the deck to secure them from the raking shots, some of which came in at the bow and went out at the stern. Had it not been for [this] precaution many lives must have been sacrificed."

Fremantle watched the *Victory* rake the *Bucentaure* and then run alongside the *Redoutable,* and he immediately decided to go through the gap. (See Diagram 2 on page 255.) "We put the ship's helm a'starboard and the *Neptune* passed between the *Victory* and the *Bucentaure,* with which ship we were warmly engaged," noted Lt. Andrew Green, Fremantle's signals officer. Villeneuve's flagship was still reeling from the *Victory*'s treble-shotted broadsides—Villeneuve himself described them as "exceeding deadly and destructive"—when Fremantle took the *Neptune* right across her stern. On the gun decks the lieutenants were shouting themselves hoarse. "Make ready! . . . Don't fire until your guns bear!"

Through the gun ports the crouching gun captains saw first the horizon and then the *Bucentaure*'s damaged stern apparently rising and falling as the *Neptune* rolled her way along in the swell. One after another the gunners tugged the trigger-lines: in succession the treble-shotted guns belched smoke and flame, and flung back in recoil.

This hail of nearly a hundred and fifty shot pouring in through the *Bucentaure*'s stern flung almost every remaining 24-pounder gun off its carriage, the crews collapsing where they stood, cut down by solid shot or splinters. On the deck below more than half the men serving the 36-pounders were killed. On board the *Neptune* Fremantle ordered the Master to bring the ship round to larboard, and as she swung the whole broadside once again smashed into the French flagship. She appeared a pitiful sight now, and while the *Neptune*'s gunners loaded once again the French ship's captain, Magendie, reeled and fell, wounded by a splinter.

Villeneuve ordered Lt. Joseph Daudignon to go aft and take over command, and at the same time he told the men left alive on the upper works to get below to the 24-pounder guns. The *Neptune* fired another broadside and Fremantle peered through the smoke, casting about for another victim.

Just ahead and slightly to starboard of the *Bucentaure* was the great *Santissima Trinidad*, her red-and-white topsides gleaming through the clouds of smoke, her topsails, topgallants and royals set and, more important, heading away from the *Neptune* so that Fremantle would be able to sail across her unprotected stern and—just as he had done with the *Bucentaure*—give her a devastating raking broadside while being immune from her guns. After a final broadside at the French flagship, the *Neptune* slowly advanced on the *Santissima Trinidad*. Once again the gunners had a good target in their sights as Fremantle steered to within less than a hundred yards to rake her. Leaving the *Neptune* hammering away at the *Santissima Trinidad*, we must again return to the *Bucentaure,* now

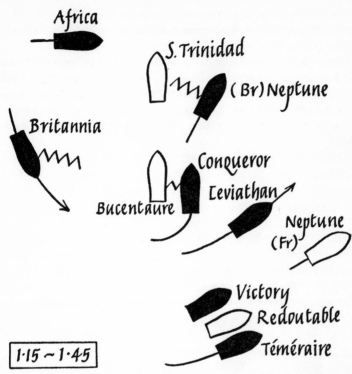

Africa

S. Trinidad

(Br) Neptune

Britannia

Conqueror

Leviathan

Bucentaure

Neptune
(Fr)

Victory

Redoutable

Téméraire

1·15 ~ 1·45

DIAGRAM 3: British *Neptune* luffs up and engages *Santissima Trinidad*.
1.15 *Conqueror rakes Bucentaure* and, 1.25, goes alongside, 1.25 *Téméraire* alongside *Redoutable; Britannia* opens fire on *Bucentaure; Africa* approaches *Santissima Trinidad*.

experiencing the last stages of attacks which were to leave her utterly helpless and a floating tomb.

The fourth ship in Nelson's line, Bayntun's *Leviathan*, followed through the gap in the wake of the *Neptune*. Half hidden in the smoke he found the *Bucentaure* and, like Fremantle, he took his ship across her stern, fired off a raking broadside, came round slightly to larboard to get off another broadside, and then looked for another opponent. (See Diagram 3 on page 267.) The *Neptune* was taking care of the *Santissima Trinidad* just to the northward, and Bayntun spotted a French 80-gun ship to the eastward on his starboard bow. She too was named the *Neptune* and had, as mentioned earlier, been firing into the *Téméraire* as Captain Harvey battled with the *Redoutable*. But the sight of the *Leviathan* steering towards him was apparently too much for the French *Neptune*'s captain, who promptly fled to leeward. Bayntun turned his ship away to the north-east and raked the *Santissima Trinidad*. (See Diagram 4 on page 272.)

He then saw several more French ships in the distance to the north and headed for them. They appeared to be turning back towards the battle (they were, in fact, Dumanoir's squadron) and Bayntun was pleased at the idea that he would be able to take his pick, for there were at least eight of them, apart from one or two other enemy ships which one might be forgiven for thinking were trying to avoid action.

While the *Victory* and *Téméraire* were tackling the *Redoutable*, the British *Neptune* was fighting the *Santissima Trinidad* and the *Leviathan* was trying to find herself a victim, the 74-gun *Conqueror*, under Israel Pellew, fifth in Nelson's line, arrived at the gap. (See Diagram 3.) Captain Pellew immediately took his ship under the stern of the *Bucentaure* as his three predecessors had done. "Previously to this," wrote one of his lieutenants, Humphrey Senhouse, "all the firing had been mere child's play to us, but now a cannonading commenced [at the *Bucentaure*] at so short a distance that every shot flew winged with death and destruction."

And he did not exaggerate. More than thirty treble-shotted guns, the whole of the *Conqueror*'s larboard broadside, smashed in through the *Bucentaure*'s stern. A few minutes earlier Villeneuve, his ship nearly battered to pieces and, with the hard-pressed *Santissima Trinidad*, cut off from the rest of the Combined Fleet, had ordered one more attempt to be made to get Dumanoir's van squadron into action to try to save the day. Signal Number 167 ("The van division to wear together"), which should make Dumanoir turn back, was hoisted. Then the *Conqueror*'s broadside tore into the ship, overturning the remaining guns and trapping more men. Several shot splintered the mizenmast and it began to topple; others cut through the mainmast just above the upper deck, and that too began to fall, taking Villeneuve's last signal to Dumanoir with it. Slowly, as if reluctant to spoil the symmetry of the flagship's outline, both masts collapsed over the starboard side, wreckage and torn canvas covering many of the gun ports.

Pellew luffed the *Conqueror* round to larboard and brought-to on the *Bucentaure*'s quarter. By this time his guns were again loaded and run out, and the gun captains paused a moment, looking down their sights and waiting until the *Conqueror* rolled to larboard to bring their guns to bear. Aboard the *Bucentaure* the end was very near. Lt. Daudignon, who had taken over when Magendie was wounded, was himself hit, and Villeneuve sent down to the lower deck for Lt. Fournier, who was commanding the guns there. Fournier came up on deck to find the foremast crashing over the side. The *Bucentaure,* with the collapse of her foremast, had no colours flying, so Midshipman Donadieu secured the Eagle of the Empire to his body and stood on the upper deck. Villeneuve, amid the thunder of the *Conqueror*'s broadsides and the thud and crash of the shot biting home, lamented bitterly to Prigny, his Chief-of-Staff, "that he was spared amidst so many balls, grape and splinters." His lamentations were cut short by Prigny's collapsing at his side, hit in the right leg by a splinter flung up from a shot.

The last minutes of his command are described by Villeneuve: "I had kept a boat lowered, foreseeing the possibility of being dismasted, with the intention of going aboard another vessel. As soon as the mainmast fell I gave orders for it to be made ready, but whether it had been sunk by shot or crushed by the falling of the masts, it could not be found.

"I had the *Santissima Trinidad,* which was ahead of us, hailed to know if she could send a boat and give us a tow. I had no reply; this ship was herself engaging vigorously with a three-decker [*Neptune*] that was firing into her quarter.

"In the end, surrounded by the enemy ships which had congregated on my quarters, astern and abreast to leeward; being power-less to do them any injury, the upper works and the 24-pounder gun deck being deserted and strewn with dead and wounded; the lower-deck guns dismounted or masked by the fallen masts and rigging; the ship isolated in the midst of the enemy, lying motion-less, and it being impossible to make any movement, I was obliged to yield to my fate and put an end to a slaughter already vast, which was from henceforward useless." A white handkerchief was waved at the *Conqueror* in token of surrender. Fournier had the Eagle, which had been broken into pieces by now, flung over the side—"not wishing that the relics should provide a trophy for the enemy." Both Villeneuve and Magendie (who had come back on deck after having his wound dressed) were mistaken in the number of ships engaging them in the last few minutes, and the only other ships which fired a broadside into the *Bucentaure* just before she surrendered were the *Britannia,* next astern of the *Conqueror,* and the *Agamemnon.* The officers in the *Britannia* saw a white handkerchief being waved from the remains of the lar-board gallery and went on to join the attack on the *Santissima Trinidad.*

Pellew was impatient to be on his way. Apparently realizing that there was still some hard fighting ahead, he did not want to weaken his own ship by putting a large prize-crew aboard the *Bucentaure.* He sent for Captain James Atcherley, commanding the *Conqueror*'s Marines. Without knowing that it was the French Commander-in-Chief who had just surrendered—for Villeneuve's flag had not been flying for some time—he ordered Atcherley to take a few men and receive the *Bucentaure*'s surrender.

Atcherley hurriedly called up a Marine corporal, two other Marine privates and a couple of seamen. The *Conqueror*'s cutter was lowered and six men climbed in and rowed across to the *Bucentaure.* Atcherley scrambled on board and made his way past groups of wounded and heaps of dead French sailors to the quarter-deck. As soon as they saw his blue hat and bright red coat, with its white sash and gold epaulettes, three French officers slowly walked over towards him. Their leader was a tall, thin-faced man in the uniform of an admiral—a long-tailed coat with a high collar and greenish-coloured corduroy trousers with a wide stripe down each side.

"To whom," said Villeneuve in good English, proffering his sword, "have I the honour of surrendering?"

"To Captain Pellew of the *Conqueror*," replied an over-awed Atcherley.

"It is a satisfaction to me," Villeneuve said courteously, "that it is to one so fortunate as Sir Edward Pellew that I have lowered my flag."

Atcherley looked startled. "It is his brother, sir."

"His brother? What, are there two of them? *Hélas!*"

The short and fat, jocund-looking man at Villeneuve's side, who had already been taken to England twice before as a prisoner, shook his head philosophically. "*Fortune de la guerre*," said the bandaged and bloodstained Magendie. The officer wearing the uniform of a general in the Grand Army, Contamine, kept silent. Atcherley politely suggested that they had better keep their swords and surrender them to an officer of a higher rank than himself, and asked if they would excuse him for a few minutes.

Leaving them waiting on the quarter-deck, he went quickly down to the magazines with the two seamen, picking his way over the bodies (for the *Bucentaure* had suffered more than two hundred and fifty killed and wounded). Suddenly, out of the gloom, a man lunged at them with a sword. One of the two seamen struck back with his cutlass and the man, his head nearly severed from his body, fell to the deck. He had been a Briton, one of eighteen who had deserted from the Royal Navy ships at Gibraltar, crossed into Spain and ended up in Cadiz as welcome reinforcements for the *Bucentaure*'s crew. The men had been kept together and during the battle they had served two of the lower-deck guns. Now, as traitors, the survivors inevitably faced being hanged from the yardarm.

Having locked up the magazines and put the keys in his pocket, Atcherley went back up on to the quarter-deck and asked Villeneuve, Contamine, Magendie and two of Villeneuve's aides to accompany him. The wounded Prigny, who was below, did not go with them: instead he stayed on board—and later helped recapture the ship from the British prize-crew. As he led his captives down to the cutter waiting alongside, Atcherley saw that Captain Pellew had gone on with the *Conqueror*, so he looked round for the nearest British ship. This was the *Mars*, and he ordered his

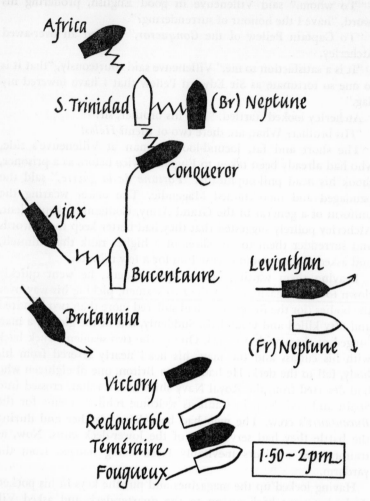

DIAGRAM 4: *Victory* gets clear of *Redoutable.* **Leviathan** engages French *Neptune,* which bears away. *Conqueror* goes ahead to rake *Santissima Trinidad. Africa* luffs and opens fire on *Santissima Trinidad.*

men to row for it. In a few minutes her surprised commanding officer, Lt. William Hennah (for Captain Duff, as will be related later, had been killed), was receiving the sword of Vice-Admiral Pierre Charles Jean Baptiste Sylvestre de Villeneuve, commanding the Combined Fleet of France and Spain.

The *Santissima Trinidad*, putting up a brave and lonely fight ahead of the surrendered *Bucentaure*, was now fighting the *Neptune* on her starboard quarter, and the *Conqueror* which, fresh from her assault on the *Bucentaure*, had just come up on her windward side. Their combined broadsides smashed into the great ship and the effect was almost instantaneous: several shot bit into the massive mizenmast below decks like axes, and slowly it toppled over the side, taking the red-and-yellow flag of Spain with it. More shot cut into the mainmast, which creaked and swayed. Too many shrouds had been cut away to give it much support and the weight of the huge yards slung on it proved too much. Like a great branch-laden tree it crashed down, collapsing over the larboard side. The sails, almost shredded, hung down over the gun ports; the men who had been perched in the tops with muskets were catapulted into the water, where their cries for help went unheard or unheeded.

"Gave three cheers," noted Lt. Green, "she [*Santissima Trinidad*] then paid off and brought us nearly on her lee beam."

"Her immense topsails had every reef out," wrote one of the *Conqueror*'s officers. "Her royals were sheeted home, but lowered; and the falling of this majestic mass of spars, sails and rigging plunging into the water at the muzzles of our guns, was one of the most magnificent sights I ever beheld."

By now the little 64-gun *Africa* had joined the fray. As mentioned earlier, she had been coming down from the north to rejoin Nelson. On her way she had passed the eight ships of Dumanoir's van squadron and despite the fact she was the smallest battleship in the action, she exchanged broadsides with them. Finding the largest battleship in the action, the *Santissima Trinidad*, Digby luffed up, brought-to on her weather bow and began firing broadsides into her. (See Diagram 4 opposite.) The *Britannia*, in passing, had also given her a broadside which, wrote Lt. Halloran, "shattered the rich display of sculpture, figures, ornaments and inscriptions with which she was adorned. I never saw so beautiful a ship."

The *Santissima Trinidad,* flying the flag of Rear-Admiral Cisneros, and commanded by Commodore de Uriarte, had fought bravely. At the beginning of the battle she had been one of the ships which had poured devastating broadsides into the *Victory* as she came to break the line, but the arrival of Fremantle in the *Neptune* had been the beginning of her defeat. The British three-decker's broadsides had soon killed or wounded every man on the upper deck with the exception of her captain. Rear-Admiral Cisneros was hit and carried below; grape-shot moaned in through gun ports and shot-holes to freeze men for an instant in grotesque poses before they dropped dead. "Blood ran in streams about the deck, and in spite of the sand, the rolling of the ship carried it hither and thither until it made strange patterns on the deck," says a Spanish account.

The broadsides of the *Neptune* and the *Conqueror,* helped by the *Africa,* were hitting home in the ship's most vulnerable part —her underwater sections. Shorn of her masts, the *Santissima Trinidad* was rolling considerably in the swell, and first one side and then the other of her weed-stained hull would show above water, and shot would crash in from the British guns. Before the Spanish carpenter's mates could get the shot plugs in position and hammered home, water was flooding across the hold. Men sent to the pumps were cut down by grape-shot and splinters; others who went to take over collapsed at the next broadside.

A splinter hit Commodore de Uriarte in the head and knocked him unconscious; the second-in-command, Lt. Oleata, was also wounded within a few moments. He managed to drag himself down to the cockpit to report personally to Cisneros that the ship was "unmanageable, being totally dismasted, a large part of the guns out of action and the rest unable to fire on account of the decks being encumbered with masts, rigging and sails, with many shot holes between wind and water [i.e., on the water-line] and the decks strewn with dead and wounded."

Cisneros sent his only surviving aide, Don Francisco Basurto, to give fresh orders to the third-in-command; he was to continue the action as long as possible and not to strike before consulting with the surviving officers who were still at their posts. When the third-in-command, who had been below, arrived on the upper deck he saw that further resistance would be useless. The rest of the officers agreed. But how were they to surrender? There was no mast left, not even a stump, from which a white flag could be flown. Someone discovered a British flag and ran to the gangway waving it.

At last the guns of the *Neptune* and *Conqueror* stopped firing. Lying in heaps, trapped under gun carriages, caught by falling masts and yards, or dragged to one side in the cockpit because the overburdened surgeons reached them too late, were more than two hundred dead Spanish seamen and soldiers; and more than a hundred others were wounded. Fremantle and Pellew then both saw that Dumanoir's van squadron was less than two miles away, coming down southward, towards them, as if to join in the battle. They could see Bayntun's *Leviathan* boldly steering northward to meet the enemy, and they too followed.

Digby in the *Africa* had not seen the flag waved from the *Santissima Trinidad*'s gangway, but as she had stopped firing he assumed she had surrendered and ordered Lt. John Smith to go across in a boat and take possession. Smith went over, scrambled on board and made his way through the wreckage to the quarterdeck, where a Spanish officer met him. Smith asked him if his ship had struck. Despite the previous flag-waving which had led to the *Neptune*'s and *Conqueror*'s ceasing fire, the Spaniard pointed to Dumanoir's squadron, by now drawing closer, and replied, "No, no!" Smith, who had only a boat's crew with him, left and rowed back to the *Africa*, where Digby was preparing to join the *Neptune* and *Conqueror* and deal with the ships that the Spaniard had used as a reason for changing his mind about surrendering.

In the gloom of the *Victory*'s cockpit Nelson was half-lying, half-sitting on the deck, his back against a thick oak frame. It was the only position that gave him any relief from the gnawing pain in his chest, and Dr. Scott and Burke, the purser, squatted down on either side, supporting him. They were soon joined by Chevalier and Gaetano, Nelson's servants, who were anxious to help their master.

The lanterns with their flickering candles swayed, casting eerie shadows which were lengthened and then shortened with the ship's roll. Beatty and his two assistant surgeons hurried from one wounded man to the next, arms scarlet with blood, occasionally ordering someone to be carried to the table to have a limb sawn off. There were groans from some men; screams came from others. More, who had been waiting for the surgeons to reach them, were strangely silent, for death had already stopped their pain.

There were faint cheers from the decks above. "What is that?" asked Nelson. "Why are they cheering?" Lt. Pasco, lying wounded nearby, raised himself on his elbow. "Another enemy ship has struck, my Lord."

Nelson settled back, apparently well satisfied. Occasionally, when particularly bad spasms of pain twisted his emaciated body, he would gasp, "Fan, fan," and Burke or Scott would wave a cloth in front of him, the cooling air seeming to give him relief. Then he would whisper, "Drink, drink," and they would give him sips of lemonade, or wine and water. Frequently he would ask how the battle was going, his voice revealing his apprehension. Burke and Dr. Scott used every argument they could think of to relieve the dying man's anxiety. Burke, trying to comfort him, said: "The enemy are decisively defeated, and I hope your Lordship will live to be yourself the bearer of the joyful tidings to our country."

But Nelson, who had seen a man fall and break his back in the *Victory* only a month earlier and had often questioned Beatty in detail about the man's symptoms (for he had taken thirteen days to die) was not to be fooled by such well-meant but clumsy words.

"It is nonsense, Mr. Burke," he gasped, "to suppose I can live: my sufferings are great, but they will soon be over." Scott, over-wrought and heartbroken, exclaimed: "Do not despair of living, my Lord," and added, "I trust that Divine Providence will restore you once more to your dear country and friends."

"Ah, Doctor!" replied the Admiral. "It is all over; it is all over."

For some time Nelson had been very worried about Captain Hardy. Beatty had sent several messengers to fetch him, but the burly Hardy had his hands full dealing with the *Redoutable* alongside, and during the worst of the fighting dared not leave the quarter-deck, although his heart was heavy. Nelson became more and more impatient and anxious about the friend who had served him so faithfully. "Will no one bring Hardy to me? He must be killed: he is surely destroyed!" A few minutes later Midshipman Richard Bulkley, whose father had served with Nelson twenty-

five years earlier in the San Juan expedition, arrived fresh from
the quarter-deck, where he had been acting as aide to the Captain,
with a message for Beatty from Hardy.

"Circumstances respecting the Fleet require Captain Hardy's
presence on deck," he said, carefully repeating the message and
probably over-conscious of the drama of the occasion, "but he will
avail himself of the first favourable moment to visit his Lordship."

Nelson overheard the message and asked who had brought it.
"It is Mr. Bulkley, my Lord," said Burke.

"It is his voice," murmured the Admiral, and raising his voice
said to Bulkley: "Remember me to your father. . . ."

The "circumstances respecting the Fleet" which now detained
Hardy were the ships of Dumanoir's squadron which, as we have
seen, had finally turned and were at last sailing down from the
north, apparently about to enter the battle. Hardy was carrying
Nelson's burden on his shoulders: from the moment the Admiral
had fallen wounded, Hardy had in fact been acting as Commander-
in-Chief. The *Regulations and Instructions* laid down that if the
Commander-in-Chief fell his flag was to be left flying "till the
Battle is ended, and the Enemy is no longer in sight," but the
officer next in command was to be told immediately and was to
go on board the flagship and take over. This took time and until
it happened the responsibility was Hardy's.

By now a new assailant had crashed alongside the *Téméraire*.
Nelson had been wounded about 1.15 p.m. and it will be
recalled that the *Victory* and *Redoutable*, lashed together, had the
Téméraire come alongside, with her mizen and main-topmasts and
foreyard down, at about 1.25 p.m. The fourth ship to join the
fray, at about 1.45 p.m., was the *Fougueux* (see Diagram 4 on
page 272), commanded by Captain Baudouin. She was a French
74-gun ship and at the beginning of the action she had been
immediately astern of Alava's 112-gun *Santa Ana*. As will be
related later, it was between these two ships that Collingwood's
division had broken the line. In going to the *Santa Ana*'s assistance the *Fougueux* had been raked by the 100-gun *Royal Sovereign*
and two 74's, *Belleisle* and *Mars*. With topsail and lower yards shot
away she had drifted to the north-west in thick smoke. This cleared
in a gentle breeze just in time for Harvey to see her. The *Téméraire*'s powerful starboard broadside had not yet been fired, and

Harvey paused, as a spider waiting for the fly to walk into its web, until the *Fougueux* was within one hundred yards.

On all three decks the second captains had cocked the locks and the gun captains were crouching beyond the recoil of the guns, peering over the sights and out into the smoke and daylight beyond the ports. Slowly, like a huge animal lost and blundering about in a yellow fog, the *Fougueux* came into their sights. The lieutenants waited until the *Téméraire*'s starboard side began a downward roll. "Fire!"

An almost solid wall of round-shot and grape smashed into the *Fougueux* at a range when even grape-shot would go through more than six inches of fir and four inches of oak. The effect on the French ship was devastating: the main and mizenmasts started to totter; Captain Baudouin collapsed, dying, on the quarter-deck; carriages of many guns were smashed to matchwood; grape-shot and splinters cut down scores of seamen at the guns and soldiers waiting at the bulwarks with muskets. Commander Bazin, the second-in-command, who had been wounded several times earlier, took over command; but the *Fougueux* was out of control, and while the *Téméraire*'s gunners reloaded, the stricken ship glided on towards them through the smoke of the first broadside.

Bazin realized that it would be a matter of seconds before the ships collided, and anticipating the British would try to storm his ship, he ordered all the surviving sailors and soldiers detailed off as boarders to stand by with their muskets, pikes, cutlasses and tomahawks. Again the *Téméraire*'s broadside flung solid shot and grape screaming into the French ship, now almost completely hidden in the swirling, throat-catching smoke. Then, with a rending crash, the *Fougueux* ran into the *Téméraire,* and the impact snapped the wobbling main and mizenmasts and they collapsed over the side. Some of the *Téméraire*'s Marines and seamen tried to board, but they were beaten back. Captain Harvey then had the carronades, loaded with musket balls, fired across the *Fougueux*'s decks. (The *Fougueux*'s earlier moves, against Collingwood's division, are described in the next chapter.)

Bazin, with the captain dead, sent for the third-in-command to help him fight off the boarders and at the same time restore some order on the *Fougueux*'s shattered gun decks. The word soon came back that he too had been killed. Dismayed, Bazin sent for the fourth-in-command—but he was dying. The next in seniority, Lt. Peltier, was lying with a musket ball in the leg. Finally Bazin's messenger found one surviving lieutenant, who told him that almost all the lower-deck guns had been silenced and nearly every man who had been serving them was dead. Midshipman Dudrésit, the only surviving officer on the 18-pounder gun deck, reported every gun out of action and only fifteen of his men left alive. By this time British seamen and Marines, shouting and yelling, were swarming over the bulwarks, lashing out with newly sharpened cutlasses, stabbing with the short-handled boarding pikes, and using their muskets as clubs.

"Seeing the impossibility of repelling boarding, or of defending the ship against the number of the enemies who were getting aboard," wrote Bazin, "I gave orders to cease firing and dragged myself, in spite of my wounds, as far as the Captain's cabin to get and throw into the sea the [leaden] box containing the signals and instructions for the ship, and, reappearing on the quarter-deck, I was taken and conveyed on board the English ship; the enemy hauled down the colours and gradually the slaughter ceased entirely."

By this time the *Victory* had managed to boom herself off from the *Redoutable* and was moving off to the northward. Harvey sent his first lieutenant, Kennedy, to the *Fougueux* and another lieutenant to the *Redoutable,* with orders that both ships were "to be securely lashed to the *Téméraire.*" Then, Captain Harvey wrote in a letter to his wife, "behold, I was informed some of the enemy's ships were coming up astern of us."

TWENTY-THREE

DUFF IS KILLED

Naval tactics, or the art of war at sea, is limited by
the possibilities of navigation; and is therefore much less
capable of that variety of stratagem which belongs to the
hostility of armies.   —Steel's *Naval Tactics*, 1797

NELSON had ordered Collingwood with his fifteen ships to attack
the last twelve ships in the enemy's line, but Collingwood was
free to make his own dispositions and carry out the order as he
thought best. We have already seen that very early on he had
ordered his ships to form the larboard line of bearing (attacking
diagonally, whereas Nelson attacked in column), forming them up
diagonally with the *Royal Sovereign* leading to the north. But the
line of bearing was never properly formed, because Collingwood
would not reduce sail in the *Royal Sovereign* to allow the others
to get into position on his quarter: instead he contented himself
with signalling his ships to "Make more sail." The effect was to put
the *Royal Sovereign* well ahead, with seven more ships strung out
astern and the rest of the division well behind them.

Although Collingwood later reported that he broke through the
enemy line "about the twelfth from the rear," in fact, as we shall
see, he broke through between the fifteenth ship, the *Fougueux*,
and the sixteenth, Vice-Admiral Alava's flagship *Santa Ana* (see
Diagram 5 on page 282). The result was that the first eight of
Collingwood's division attacked sixteen ships of the Combined
Fleet: it was nearly an hour after the *Royal Sovereign* opened fire
that the first of the other seven managed to get into action.

The weariness wrought by years of responsibility vanished from
Collingwood as the *Royal Sovereign,* studding-sails set, bore down
on the enemy; gone, for the time being, was his longing for his
wife Sarah and the memory of his home and garden. The thought

of battle transformed this country-loving Northumbrian into a cold fighting machine, as brave as Nelson but considerably less exuberant. Because his personality was not as colourful, history was destined to pass him by with a nod.

The Plymouth-built *Royal Sovereign*, fresh from the dockyard and her copper bottom still free of weeds and barnacles, was belying her nickname of the "West Country Wagon" and slowly drawing farther ahead of the rest of the division. Rotheram, son of a doctor and like his Admiral a Northumbrian, counted off the enemy ships as they ranged across the *Royal Sovereign's* bow. Collingwood did the same and, probably not realizing that three more ships were to leeward of the line and masked by the others, numbered off twelve of them. This brought them to the *Fougueux*, which he could see was a 74-gun French ship. Just ahead of her was a Spanish three-decker, quite clearly a flagship. Collingwood pointed her out and told Rotheram to steer between the two ships. At the same time he told him to order the officers to make sure that all the men were lying down on the decks between the guns until they were to fire.

At the bows of the *Royal Sovereign* the figurehead gleamed in the sunshine. It was an appropriate one to adorn the first ship of the British Fleet to go into action in the great battle and was a full-length effigy of George III dressed as a Roman emperor, sword at his side and scarlet cloak on his shoulders. On one side of him was the emblem of Fame, on the other Fortune, and each was blowing a golden trumpet.

Sailing slowly but with easy grace across the swell-waves, the *Royal Sovereign*, the eyes of the fleet upon her, bore down on the *Santa Ana* and *Fougueux*. Slowly the minutes ticked by; the range dropped. From the *Royal Sovereign* sextants measured the angle between the *Santa Ana's* water-line and the truck of her masts, and reference to a table showed trigonometrically what the eye, because of the slow speed, hardly detected. Three degrees fourteen minutes—she was 1,300 yards away . . . three and a half degrees—1,200 yards . . . three degrees forty-nine minutes—1,100 yards. The mass of enemy ships ahead would be opening fire any second now. Four degrees ten minutes—that gave a range of 1,000 yards, and the time was 11.58 a.m.

"Open fire!" ordered Captain Baudouin aboard the *Fougueux*,

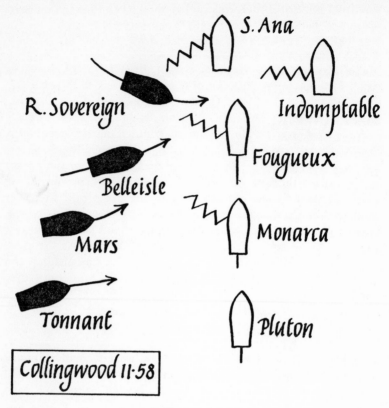

R. Sovereign

S. Ana

Indomptable

Belleisle

Fougueux

Mars

Monarca

Tonnant

Pluton

Collingwood 11·58

DIAGRAM 5: Approach of Collingwood's division: *Fougueux* opens fire at 11.58.

and from the *Royal Sovereign* they could see two lines of gun ports spout red flame and then breathe coils of yellow smoke. As the reverberating rumble of the first broadside reached them, more flashes rippled in a triple tier from the *Santa Ana* ahead of the *Fougueux,* and smoke wreathed the gun ports of the Spanish *Monarca* astern. They were followed by the *San Justo* and *San Leandro,* ahead of the *Santa Ana,* and the *Pluton* and *Algésiras* astern of the *Monarca.*

One of the *Royal Sovereign*'s seamen, writing to his father after the battle, said: "I told brother Tom I should like to see a greadly [*sic*] battle, and I have seen one, and we have peppered the Combined [Fleet] rarely; and for the matter of that they fought us pretty tightish for French and Spanish. . . . But to tell you the truth of it, when the game began, I wished myself at Warnborough [Hampshire] with my plough again; but when they had given us one duster, and I found myself snug and tight, I . . . set to in good earnest, and thought no more about being killed than if I were at Murrell Green Fair, and I was presently as black as a collier."

Unlike Nelson's column, where most of the vessels went through the gap torn in the line by the *Victory,* the ships of Collingwood's division, advancing on a broad front, were steering for individual French and Spanish ships. For a minute or two the enemy's shot hissed into the sea round the *Royal Sovereign* or whined through the rigging; then an occasional crash showed they were hitting the hull, either with direct hits or ricochets from random shots bouncing off the water. Collingwood, partly in order to hide the ship in smoke, told Rotheram to order some of the forward guns to be fired. Within a few moments, after midshipmen had run to pass the word down the hatches, the muzzles of the guns, poking out of the ports like pointing fingers, erupted their quotas of flame and smoke and recoiled in again, as if ashamed of firing without having a proper target. The minutes dragged by. With the enemy's shot falling round them like hail on a pond, each minute seemed a lifetime; but magnificent in her stateliness, apparently unperturbed, the *Royal Sovereign* bore down for the gap between the stern of the *Santa Ana* and the bows of the *Fougueux.*

She was only a few hundred yards away when Captain Baudouin of the *Fougueux* made a desperate attempt to close the gap: he ordered the main-topgallant sail to be hoisted and sheeted home and the main-topsail braced around and sheeted in so that it would fill. Gradually the *Fougueux* gathered way, and at the same time the Spanish *Santa Ana*'s mizen-topsail was backed to slow her down. The sharp-eyed Rotheram pointed this out to Collingwood; but the Admiral knew it was too late to try to break through elsewhere.

"Steer for the Frenchman and carry away his bowsprit!" ordered Collingwood. Rotheram quickly passed new helm orders to the Master, and slowly the *Royal Sovereign*'s massive bowsprit began to swing slightly to starboard as Rotheram, allowing for the headway the *Fougueux* was making, selected a spot for the two ships to meet. Baudouin, realizing at the last moment that the British ship intended to smash her way through, quickly ordered the *Fougueux*'s main-topsail to be backed. Almost immediately his ship slowed up, leaving the *Royal Sovereign* just enough room to get past.

As she forged through the gap, the British ship's larboard guns fired a whole broadside into the unprotected stern of the *Santa Ana*. The effect was even more dreadful than in the *Bucentaure* and *Santissima Trinidad*. As successive guns bore and fired their triple-shotted quota, much of the solid planking and rich carvings on the transom was smashed in as if by huge invisible fists, and the shot and splinters spun on down the decks, cutting down men and overturning fourteen guns. Rotheram ordered the helm to be put over and as the men worked swiftly in the choking smoke to reload the larboard guns, the *Royal Sovereign* swung round to larboard to come alongside the Spanish ship. But as she turned, Baudouin fired the *Fougueux*'s full broadside into her starboard quarter, and the 80-gun *Indomptable,* from only five hundred yards away on the British flagship's starboard beam, fired another. (See Diagram 6 opposite.)

In the meantime the *Santa Ana*'s captain had guessed that the *Royal Sovereign* would swing round and come alongside to leeward, and had brought all the larboard guns' crews over to reinforce those on the starboard side. When the British ship came alongside, their yardarms touching as the two great vessels rolled in the swell, the Spanish gunners fired. According to Collingwood's biographer the *Royal Sovereign* heeled considerably under the

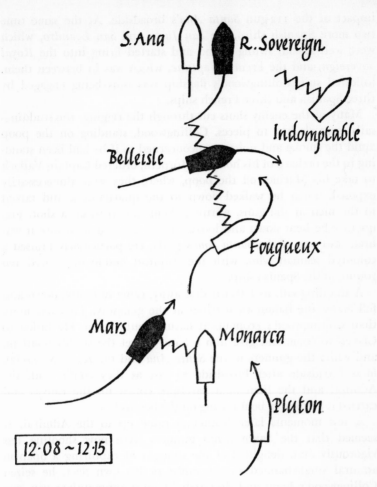

S. Ana

R. Sovereign

Indomptable

Belleisle

Fougueux

Mars

Monarca

Pluton

12·08 ~ 12·15

DIAGRAM 6: At 12.08 *Royal Sovereign* rakes *Santa Ana* and then luffs alongside. *Indomptable* opens fire on *R. Sovereign.* 12.11 *Belleisle* rakes *Santa Ana* and opens fire on *Fougueux.* 12.15 *Mars* engages *Monarca.* *Pluton* passes *Monarca* to leeward.

impact of the 112-gun *Santa Ana*'s broadside. At the same time two more Spanish ships, the *San Justo* and *San Leandro*, which were well ahead, swung round and started firing into the *Royal Sovereign*, and the French *Neptune*, which was in between them, followed suit. Collingwood's flagship was thus being engaged by three Spanish and three French ships.

Many of the enemy shots cut through the rigging; the studding-sails were slashed to pieces. Collingwood, standing on the poop amid the smoke and noise as unconcerned as if he had been standing in the orchard of his home at Morpeth, ordered Captain Vallack to take his Marines off the poop, where they were unnecessarily exposed. Then he walked down to the quarter-deck and talked to the men at the guns, warning them not to waste a shot. Frequently he bent down and looked along a gun-sight before it was fired into one of the *Santa Ana*'s ports. He particularly praised a coloured seaman who, with the Admiral beside him, fired ten rounds at the Spanish ship.

A studding-sail, its halyard shot away, came tumbling down and fell across the hammock nettings at the gangway. This was more than Collingwood's economical nature could stand. He called to Clavell to come and give him a hand to get the studding-sail in, and while the gunners in the *Santa Ana* and the *Royal Sovereign* fired broadside after broadside as fast as they could load, the Admiral and the lieutenant carefully rolled up the canvas and carried it across to a boat resting on the booms.[1]

A few moments later Rotheram came up to the Admiral. It seemed that the *Santa Ana*'s gunners were now shooting less vigorously and, delighted at the thought of capturing a Spanish admiral single-handed in the midst of his own fleet, he seized Collingwood's hand and declared: "I must congratulate you, sir: she is slackening her fire and must soon strike." But they were to be disappointed: even though the larboard gunners did their best, the Spanish ship kept pounding away. Collingwood escaped death by what was almost a miracle and was wounded, although he refused to have the fact officially reported. It was five months later

---

[1] Nearly nine years earlier, in the middle of the battle of Cape St. Vincent, where he had commanded the *Excellent*, Collingwood had looked up and then called out to the bosun, "Bless me, Mr. Peffers, how came we to forget to bend our old topsail? They will quite ruin that new one! It will never be worth a farthing again."

that he wrote to his wife, "Did I not tell you how my leg was hurt? It was by a splinter—a pretty severe blow. I had a good many thumps, one way or the other; one in the back, which I think was the wind of a great shot, for I never saw anything that did it."

The *Royal Sovereign*'s Master, Mr. William Chalmers, was killed at Collingwood's side, and in the same letter the Admiral described this. "A great shot almost divided his body: he laid his head upon my shoulder, and told me he was slain. I supported him till two men carried him off. He could say nothing to me, but to bless me; but as they carried him down, he wished he could but live to read the account of the action in a newspaper. He lay in the cockpit, among the wounded, until the *Santa Ana* struck; and, joining in the cheer which they gave her, expired with it on his lips."

By now the other ships in Collingwood's division were coming into action. The *Belleisle,* which had been on the *Royal Sovereign*'s starboard quarter, had suffered worse from the enemy broadsides as she approached the line. Captain Hargood, short and stocky, a man of few words, had previously sent for his officers and said: "Gentlemen, I have only this to say: that I shall pass under the stem of that ship." He pointed to Vice-Admiral Alava's flagship, whose great figurehead, an effigy of the mother of the Virgin, garbed in red, could now be clearly seen in the sunlight.

"Put in two round-shot and then a grape," he said, "and give her *that.* Now go to your quarters and mind not to fire until each gun will bear with effect." With this laconic instruction, reported Lt. Nicolas, of the Royal Marines, "the gallant little man posted himself on the slide of the foremost carronade on the starboard side of the quarter-deck."

By this time several ships were firing at the *Royal Sovereign* over on the larboard bow and others, says Nicolas, were beginning to shoot at the *Belleisle,* "and gave us an intimation of what we should in a few minutes undergo. An awful silence prevailed in the ship, only interrupted by the commanding voice of Captain Hargood. 'Steady! Starboard a little! Steady so!' echoed by the Master directing the quartermaster at the wheel.

"A shriek soon followed—a cry of agony was produced by the next shot—the loss of a head of a poor recruit was the effect of the succeeding—and, as we advanced, destruction rapidly increased."

Hargood suddenly fell from where he was standing on the

carronade slide, hit in the chest by a flat side of a splinter. He escaped with severe bruising, and refused to be taken below. Within a few minutes he was back on the slide, directing operations. He had given orders that as many people as possible were to lie down, to avoid being wounded. The shot were by now streaming in over the bow, tearing at the heavy timbers, the sails and the rigging, sending up sparks as they crashed into metal, and scooping up scores of splinters as they burrowed into wood.

"Those only who have been in a similar situation to the one I am attempting to describe," declared Lt. Nicolas, "can have a correct idea of such a scene. My eyes were horror-struck at the bloody corpses around me, and my ears rang with the shrieks of the wounded and the moans of the dying.

"At this moment, seeing that almost everyone was lying down, I was half disposed to follow the example, and several times stooped for the purpose, but—and I remember the impression well—a certain monitor seemed to whisper 'stand up and do not shrink from your duty.'

"Turning round, my much esteemed and gallant senior [Lt. John Owen] fixed my attention; the serenity of his countenance and the composure with which he paced the deck, drove more than half my terror away; and joining him, I became somewhat infused with his spirit, which cheered me on to act the part it became me!"

Nicolas goes on: "It was just twelve o'clock[2] when we reached their line. Our energies became roused and the mind diverted from its appalling condition, by the order 'Stand to your guns!'

By this time the French and Spanish broadsides were beginning to tell against the British 74. "Although until that moment we had not fired a shot, our sails and rigging bore evident proofs of the manner in which we had been treated: our mizen-topmast was shot away and the ensign had been thrice re-hoisted; numbers lay dead upon the decks, and eleven wounded were already in the surgeon's care. The firing was now tremendous, and at intervals the dispersion of the smoke gave us a sight of the colour of our adversaries."

There was no need to send men aloft to cut the halyards and bring the studding-sails in with a rush at the last moment, for

2 In fact it was 12.11 p.m.

the enemy's swirling chain shot had torn them down, and before the *Belleisle* could bring her first broadsides to bear, more than fifty of her men had been killed or wounded. Soon she had the *Santa Ana* in the sights of her guns, and the whole larboard broadside crashed out; almost immediately the starboard broadside was fired into the *Fougueux,* and the smoke drifted on ahead of the *Belleisle,* almost hiding the *Indomptable* ahead and the *San Justo* beyond the *Santa Ana.*

Nicolas describes the next few moments: "At this critical period, while steering for the stern of the *Indomptable* (our masts and yards and sails hanging in utmost confusion over our heads), which continued a galling raking fire upon us, the *Fougueux* being on our starboard quarter and the Spanish *San Justo* on our larboard bow, the Master earnestly addressed the Captain, 'Shall we go through, sir?'

" 'Go through, by——' was his energetic reply. 'There's your ship, sir; place me alongside her!' "

The Master brought the *Belleisle* round to starboard (see Diagram 6) to go round the stern of the *Indomptable* and come up on her lee side, but suddenly out of the great banks of smoke, sails hanging from masts like old clothes on a scarecrow, the *Fougueux* loomed up very close on the starboard quarter, and in a few moments her larboard bow crashed against the *Belleisle*'s starboard gangway.

While the after guns on the *Belleisle*'s starboard side fired into the *Fougueux* at the range of a few feet, the crews of those farther forward hastily got their handpikes under the carriages to heave them round to get them to bear. As the two ships drifted together, almost covered in smoke, the conditions on the gun decks were appalling. One man wrote: "At every moment the smoke accumulated more and more thickly, stagnating on board between decks at times so densely as to blur over the nearest objects and often blot out the men at the guns from those close at hand on each side. The guns had to be trained, as it were, mechanically by means of orders passed down from above, and on objects that the men fighting the guns hardly ever got a glimpse of. In these circumstances you frequently heard the order on the main and lower deck to level the gun 'two points abaft the beam,' 'point blank,' and so on.

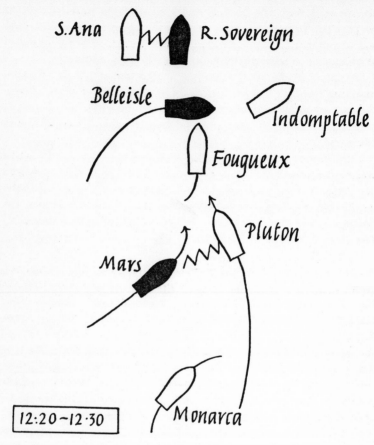

DIAGRAM 7: At 12.20 *Mars* and *Pluton* in close action. 12.30 *Fougueux*
collides with *Belleisle*. *Monarca* bears away.

"In fact, the men were as much in the dark as to the external objects as if they had been blindfolded, and the only comfort to be derived from this serious inconvenience was that every man was so isolated from his neighbour that he was not put in mind of his danger by seeing his messmates go down all round.

"All that he knew was that he heard the crash of the shot smashing through the rending timbers, and then followed at once the hoarse bellowings of the captains of the guns, as men were missed at their posts, calling out to the survivors: 'Close up there! Close up.' "

The *Indomptable,* saved by the *Fougueux,* turned to starboard and fired a broadside into the *Belleisle.* Then, as if she considered her part in the battle fulfilled, she drifted away to leeward into the smoke, like a poacher vanishing in the mist. Locked together, the *Fougueux* and *Belleisle* slowly fell away to leeward, hammering away at each other.

By now Captain Duff's 74-gun *Mars* was in action. The *Fougueux,* going ahead to engage the *Royal Sovereign* and then the *Belleisle,* had left a gap which the Spanish *Monarca* was slow to close. Captain Duff planned to pass through there, but Captain Cosmao Kerjulien in the 74-gun *Pluton* quickly set all possible sail to pass the *Monarca* and head off the *Mars.* Captain Duff came down to fire a broadside into the *Monarca,* who turned away, but within a few minutes the *Pluton* had ranged ahead into the gap, nearly across the bows of the *Mars,* a position from which she would be able to pour in a raking broadside. (See Diagram 7 opposite.) To avoid this, Captain Duff luffed up the *Mars* to windward on to a course parallel with the *Pluton,* who kept up a heavy fire. But now the *Mars* was fast approaching the *Santa Ana,* who was still locked in a violent struggle with the *Royal Sovereign,* and Duff had to luff up and then heave to in order to avoid her. With the *Mars* stopped, the *Pluton* was in an ideal position on the starboard quarter of the British ship. Desperately the British gunners tried to get their guns to train round far enough aft to bear, but Cosmao realized that he had only to luff and to pour a raking broadside into the stern of the *Mars.* (See Diagram 8 on page 292.)

A young Banffshire midshipman, Robinson, wrote: "Captain Duff walked about with steady fortitude, and said: 'My God,

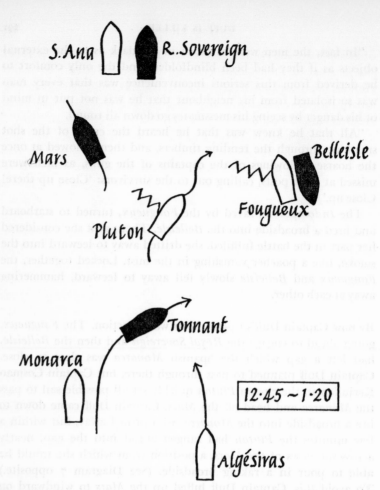

S.Ana R.Sovereign

Mars Belleisle

Fouqueux

Pluton

Tonnant

Monarca

12.45 ~ 1.20

Algésiras

DIAGRAM 8: At 12.45 *Mars* luffs to avoid *Santa Ana.* 1.00 *Pluton* rakes *Mars. Tonnant* bears down to rake *Pluton.* 1.10 *Fouqueux* drifts clear of *Belleisle,* rakes *Mars* and falls away to leeward, where eventually meets *Téméraire. Algésiras* runs aboard *Tonnant.*

what shall we do? Here is a Spanish three-decker raking us ahead [*Santa Ana*], a French one [*Pluton*] under our stern!' In a few minutes our poop was totally cleared, the quarter-deck and foc's'le nearly the same, and only the Boatswain and myself and three men left alive."

The British ship *Tonnant* was now entering the fray and bore down to rake the *Pluton*, who luffed to try to rake her first. But at this moment the *Fougueux*, in action with the *Belleisle*, shot away her antagonist's mizenmast and drifted clear, getting into a perfect position to rake the stricken *Mars*.

Captain Norman, commanding the Marines on board the *Mars*, spotted the French ship through the swirling smoke and ran to the quarter-deck to warn Captain Duff; but the *Mars* was hemmed in, and this, combined with the fact that the wind had fallen away, prevented the ship from manoeuvring. Norman pointed out the *Fougueux*. "Do you think our guns will bear on her?" asked Duff.

"I think not," replied Norman, "but I cannot see for smoke."

"Then we must point our guns on the ships on which they will bear," said Duff. "I shall go and look, but the men below may see better, as there is less smoke there."

He went to the end of the quarter-deck to look over the side, followed by his aide, Midshipman Arbuthnot. By leaning over he could just see the *Fougueux* on the starboard quarter through the smoke, and he told Arbuthnot to go below and order the guns to be pointed farther aft. The boy was just turning away towards the hatch when the *Fougueux* fired a full broadside into the British ship. One shot decapitated Duff and went on to kill two seamen who were standing just behind him. Duff's body fell on the gangway. Word was sent to Norwich below that his father had perished. When the men heard that their captain had been killed, wrote Midshipman Robinson, "they held his body up and gave three cheers to show they were not discouraged by it, and then returned to their guns."

Lt. William Hennah was now in command. The ship's main-topmast and the spanker-boom were shot away; the foremast was tottering, riddled with shot and about to crash over the side, and the other two masts were in little better condition; several guns had been smashed and the stern quarter and rudder were badly damaged. Already killed, in addition to Norwich's father, were

Lachlan Duff's son Alexander, who died in his younger brother's arms, two midshipmen, seventeen seamen and eight Marines. Thomas Norman, the Captain of Marines, was dying, and five midshipmen, forty-four seamen and sixteen Marines were wounded.

Almost helpless, the stricken ship paid off, presenting her damaged stern to the *Pluton*. Cosmao, in the process of luffing round to port to rake the *Tonnant,* promptly flung the helm over the other way, paid off and raked the *Mars* with another broadside and then turned away, drifting to leeward after the *Fougueux* until she found the *Belleisle* lying helpless. Cosmao then hove-to the *Pluton* on the British ship's port quarter and opened fire.

The *Tonnant* (which, we have already seen, had fired at the *Pluton* in an attempt to help the *Mars*) had earlier come down to break the line through the gap between the stern of the Spanish 74-gun *Monarca* and the bows of the French *Algésiras*, which was flying the flag of Rear-Admiral Magon. Two of the *Tonnant's* bandsmen, who had been busy playing "Britons, Strike Home!," were wounded, along with nine other men during the approach. Captain Tyler took his ship between the *Monarca* and *Algésiras* —"so close," according to Lt. Hoffman, "that a biscuit might have been thrown on either of them." (See Diagram 8 on page 292.) He adds: "Our guns were all double-shotted. The order was given to fire; being so close, every shot was poured into their hulls, and down came the Frenchman's [*Algésiras's*] mizenmast, and after our second broadside the Spaniard's [*Monarca's*] fore and cross-jack yards."

Her third broadside at the *Monarca* thundered out as the *Tonnant* came on to a course parallel with the Spanish ship. "We gave her such a murdering broadside," wrote one officer, "that she did not return a gun for some minutes." But even when some of her guns did get into action the *Monarca* was too badly damaged to put up a fight, and gradually she dropped astern, hauling down her colours. The *Tonnant* went ahead, still firing at the *Algésiras* to starboard. Then the *Monarca,* apparently finding herself safe for a while, rehoisted her colours.

Seeing the *Pluton* ahead on the starboard bow sending broadside after broadside into the helpless *Mars,* Tyler brought the *Tonnant* round to starboard and fired his larboard broadside into Cosmao's ship. But this was the chance for which Magon, in the *Algésiras,* was waiting: quickly he had the main and mizen-topsails braced round and sheeted home so that the ship would forge ahead and cross under the *Tonnant*'s stern, giving him a chance to cripple her with a raking broadside. Tyler immediately brought the *Tonnant* round to starboard and before Magon could do anything the *Algésiras*'s bow had crashed into the *Tonnant* amidships on the starboard side, her long bowsprit hooking into the British ship's main rigging, holding her in position. None of the French guns could be brought to bear, but almost every one of the *Tonnant*'s starboard guns was able to rake the *Algésiras*. Her carronades, loaded with musket balls, and her quarter-deck guns fired and, reported Commander Laurent Le Tourneur, commanding the *Algésiras*, "totally stripped us of our rigging."

Magon at once gave orders for the *Tonnant* to be boarded. Lt. Verdreau gathered a boarding party while sharpshooters in the *Algésiras*'s top kept up a heavy fire on the *Tonnant*'s upper works with their muskets. Led by Verdreau, the boarders ran to the bows, intending to scramble on to the bowsprit and clamber on board the British ship, but at that moment the British carronades and quarter-deck guns blasted them with grape-shot and musket balls and most of them, including Verdreau, were killed.

One of the Frenchmen, however, escaped and managed to get aboard the *Tonnant*. He had no sooner set foot on her quarter-deck than a British sailor lunged at him with a half-pike, which went through his right leg. Another was just about to cut him down with a cutlass when Lt. Hoffman shouted to him to put up his sword and take the Frenchman down to the cockpit to have his wound dressed.

The battle between the two ships went on for more than an hour. Passing British ships sent their broadsides into the *Algésiras*, which gradually swung round until she was alongside the *Tonnant*, instead of being held by the bowsprit. Hoffman wrote that the sides of the two ships were grinding against each other so much as they pitched and rolled in the swell "that we were obliged to fire our lower-deck guns without running them out."

Blazing wads from the *Tonnant*'s guns eventually started a fire in the French ship's boatswain's store, killing three men. "At length," Hoffman wrote, "both ships caught fire before the chess-trees, and our firemen, with all the coolness and courage so inherent in British seamen, got the [fire] engine and played it on both ships, and finally extinguished the flames, although two of them were severely wounded in doing so."

Firing with great coolness, the British gunners gradually got the upper hand. Commander Le Tourneur reported that on board the *Algésiras,* Magon, "feeling our position to be critical, went about everywhere encouraging us by his presence and displaying the most heroic coolness and courage." While he was doing this he was hit in the arm by a musket ball, and later a splinter hit him in the thigh; but the Breton carried on cheering up his men. The *Algésiras's* foremast crashed over the side and the *Tonnant's* fire continued clearing the enemy's upper decks.

Le Tourneur was wounded in the shoulder; his second-in-command, Morel, was soon carried down to the cockpit after him. The navigating officer, Lt. Leblond-Plassan, was hit in the chest with a bullet. Then Magon, who had refused the pleading of his officers that he should go below to have his wounds dressed because he was bleeding badly, collapsed on to the deck, killed by a bullet in the chest.

"Our 18-pounder battery was at this time deserted and utterly silenced," says Le Tourneur. "We collected all our men in the 36-pounder battery, which continued to be served by them with the utmost activity."

These guns were doing a considerable amount of damage in the *Tonnant.* Captain Tyler had been carried below wounded and Lt. John Bedford had taken over command. Down in the cockpit the surgeon, Forbes Chevers, was busy amputating torn limbs by the dim and flickering light of tallow candles held by two assistants, whom he had told, "If you look straight into the wound, and see all that I do, I shall see perfectly." (When later he washed his face he found that the candles had completely burnt his eyebrows.)

Chevers was being helped by the purser, Mr. George Booth, and "a very powerful and resolute woman," the wife of a petty officer, who had somehow contrived to be on board. She and Booth, who was a small but agile man, "carried the sailors who had been operated upon to their temporary berths, taking them up in their arms as if they had been children, in a manner which Chevers, himself a tall and very strong young man, always spoke of with expressions of wonder."

But not all the wounded had gone down to the cockpit. White, one of the captains of the carronades on the poop, had his right toe nearly severed. He took his knife and cut it off, and when Hoffman told him to go below to the cockpit he replied, "No, sir, I am not the fellow to go below for such a scratch as that. I wish to give the beggars a few more hard pills before I have done with them." He then untied the handkerchief round his head, used it to bind up his foot, and went back to his carronade.

Another seaman, Fitzgerald, climbed over the side of the *Tonnant* and scrambled up the rigging of the *Algésiras* to where a Tricolour was lashed. After cutting it away he tied it round his waist and began to climb down again, but a French sharpshooter saw him and opened fire. Fitzgerald was hit and fell, plunging between the two ships.

When Captain Tyler sent for Hoffman, the young lieutenant went down to the cockpit where he saw a Marine he knew standing in a queue, an arm shattered by grape-shot.

"What's the matter, Conolly?"

"Not much," replied the Marine. "I am only winged above my elbow, and I'm waiting my turn to be lopped."

At this time there were fourteen men waiting to have an arm or leg amputated. (Of the sixteen men who were eventually to undergo amputations, only two survived.)

Up on deck again, says Hoffman, they had the satisfaction of seeing the *Algésiras*'s remaining mast "go by the board, ripping the partners up in their fall, as they had been shot through below the deck, and carrying with them all their sharpshooters to look sharper in the next world, for as all our boats were shot through we could not save one of them in this."

The French ship was now at the end of her resistance. "The final broadsides from the enemy so crippled us that they forced us to cease fire," wrote Commander Le Tourneur. Immediately Lt. Bedford ordered the second lieutenant, Charles Bennett, to take the boarding party and capture her. Waving cutlasses, pikes and tomahawks, sixty of the *Tonnant*'s crew, with Bennett leading them, scrambled on board the *Algésiras*. "They cheered and in a short time carried her," according to Hoffman. Seventy-seven Frenchmen had been killed and 142 wounded. The boarding party found Magon's body lying at the bottom of the poop ladder.

But the battle, for the *Tonnant,* was not yet over. Commodore Churruca's *San Juan Nepomuceno* had, as will be told later, already been in action with the *Defiance* and the *Dreadnought.* Now badly damaged, she appeared to the south. The *Algésiras* drifted away, and the *Tonnant* was able to use her whole starboard broadside to engage the Spanish vessel. "We returned her salute with interest, and her foremast went about four feet above her deck. We cheered and gave her another broadside, and down came her colours."

The fourth lieutenant, Benjamin Clement, hailed her amid the smoke and noise to make sure she had struck, and when a Spaniard shouted back that they had indeed surrendered, Clement ran aft to tell Lt. Bedford. He was then ordered to go aboard the *San Juan Nepomuceno* and take possession of her. "We had no boat but was shot, but he told me I must try," says Clement.

With Maclay, a quartermaster, and Macnamara, a coloured seaman, he climbed down into a damaged jolly-boat and they started to row the few score yards to the Spanish ship. They had not covered a quarter of the way when a random shot skimming over the waves smashed in the transom, swamping the boat. Maclay and Macnamara immediately struck out to swim back to the ship, but when they saw that Clement could not swim they turned back and supported him, one on each side. Slowly the trio made their way to the *Tonnant,* bobbing up and down on the swell, until they reached the ship's side, where they found the jolly-boat falls—the tackles used to raise and lower the boat—still hanging down in the water.

Clement managed to get his leg over one of the falls, and "as the ship lifted with the sea," he wrote, "so was I, and as she descended I was ducked; I found myself weak and I thought I was not long for this world."

Macnamara managed to scramble on board and found a rope, which he flung over the side. He jumped back into the water and secured it under Clement's arms. The bedraggled lieutenant was then hauled in through a stern port. "In a short time I felt better and the anxiety of the time roused me, and I soon returned to my quarters," he reported.

TWENTY-FOUR

THE SHARPSHOOTER

Our God and sailor we adore
In time of danger, not before,
The danger past, both are alike requited,
God is forgotten and the sailor slighted.
—Old saying quoted by Nelson

THE FIFTH ship in Collingwood's division, Captain John Cooke's 74-gun *Bellerophon*, had come down on to the Combined Fleet's line where there were four 74's—the French *Aigle* and *Swiftsure*, and the Spanish *Montañes* and *Bahama*, which were well up to windward of the others. The *Swiftsure*, although now flying the Tricolour, was a former sister ship of the *Bellerophon* and was laid down in the same building programme during the American war, later being captured by the French.[1]

Cooke was steering the *Bellerophon*, in the rapidly falling wind, to pass under the stern of the *Bahama* and ahead of the *Aigle*. The latter, although a 74-gun ship like herself, was more powerful, having 40-pounders to the British 32-pounders. About a hundred and fifty of the *Aigle*'s crew of 750 were soldiers; her tops were packed with sharpshooters. Dozens of other men were standing by with grenades, ready to lob them on to the *Bellerophon*'s decks. The *Bellerophon*, her black-and-yellow sides gleaming, was ready for battle: her guns were double-shotted, the two carronades on the fo'c'sle were each loaded with 32 pounds of musket balls, and the six smaller ones on the poop held 18 pounds.

On the quarter-deck Captain Cooke watched and waited with Cumby, Wemyss and Overton. Nearby was Cooke's thirteen-year-old aide, Midshipman George Pearson, the son of a West Country

---

1 The *Bellerophon* was built at Frindsbury, on the Medway, to Sir Thomas Slade's design, dated 1759. She cost £30,232 14s. 3d. and was launched on October 6, 1786.

parson. On the poop the Marines stood with muskets loaded, while the signal lieutenant chatted to Midshipman Franklin. Alexander Whyte, the surgeon, was waiting in the cockpit with his surgical instruments; Russel Mant, the bosun, was on the fo'c'sle watching the ships ahead. Altogether nearly six hundred men in the ship waited for their part in the battle to begin.

The *Royal Sovereign* had just broken through the line and the *Belleisle* was about to follow her when, at 12.10 p.m., one of the *Bellerophon*'s midshipmen tripped over a trigger-line. The lock was cocked and the gun went off. The enemy ships ahead apparently thought that this must be some pre-arranged signal, according to one of the *Bellerophon*'s officers, and the *Aigle, Bahama, Montañes* and *Swiftsure* opened fire on her together. As the enemy shots started whining through the rigging and crashing into the hull, Captain Cooke ordered some of the forward guns to be fired, so that the *Bellerophon* would be partly hidden in her own smoke, which would drift down ahead of her on to the French and Spanish ships.

There was almost a calm now; the *Bellerophon* was down to under two knots—a little faster than a horse dragged a plough across the flat soil of Cooke's native Essex. Slowly she bore down on the enemy line until, at 12.25, seventeen minutes after the *Royal Sovereign* broke through to the northward, she had the *Bahama* coming into the sights of her larboard guns and *Montañes* into those to starboard.

The tension in the belly of every man on the gun decks, forced to endure the broadsides of four enemy ships without being able to fire back, eased as the lieutenants raised their speaking-trumpets. The guns were trained as far forward[2] as possible; and crouched well back, his eyes squinting over the sight, each captain took a firm grip on the trigger-line.

"Fire!"

One after another the larboard guns plunged in a welter of noise and smoke, the crash of the explosions merging into the rumble of the trucks recoiling across the decks.

A few moments later the *Montañes* loomed up in the sights of the starboard guns. There was a brief pause as the gunners waited for

2 The words "fore" and "aft" were not used, when training the guns, however: the orders were "left" or "right."

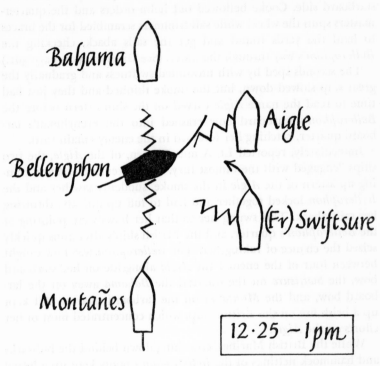

DIAGRAM 9: *Bellerophon* under fire from *Algésiras, Bahama, Aigle* and *Montañes*; breaks line, raking *Bahama* and *Montañes*. 12.30 *Bellerophon* sees *Aigle* through smoke and *Aigle* tries to avoid collision. French *Swiftsure* luffs to avoid *Aigle* and gets raked by *Bellerophon*, who then goes aboard *Aigle*.

the ship's roll, and then, with shattering suddenness, the broadside smashed into the Spanish ship. While the guns on both sides were being reloaded, Captain Cooke ordered Overton to bring the *Bellerophon* round to larboard to range up alongside the *Bahama*, but as the ship was swinging they saw in the dirty yellow smoke off to leeward the topgallants of another ship, very close on the starboard side. Cooke bellowed out helm orders and the quarter-masters spun the wheel while sail-trimmers scrambled for the braces to haul the yards round and get the sails aback, checking the *Bellerophon*'s way through the water. (See Diagram 9 on page 301.)

The seconds sped by with unwonted swiftness and gradually the great ship slowed down, but the smoke thinned and they just had time to read the name *Aigle* carved on the ship's stern before the *Bellerophon*'s starboard bow crashed into the Frenchman's lar-board quarter, catching her foreyard in the enemy's main yard.

Immediately, reported Lt. Asmus Classen, of the *Aigle*, the two ships "engaged with the utmost fury." The French *Swiftsure*, com-ing up astern of the *Aigle* in the smoke, suddenly saw her and the *Bellerophon* locked together and had to luff up quickly, throwing her sails aback. This swung her so that her bows were pointing at the *Bellerophon*'s quarter, and the British ship's after guns quickly seized the chance of raking her. The *Bellerophon* was now caught between four of the enemy: the *Aigle* alongside on her starboard bow, the *Swiftsure* on the quarter, the *Bahama* away on the lar-board bow, and the *Montañes* on the larboard quarter. All kept up a brisk fire on the British ship, which concentrated most of her efforts on the *Aigle*.

While the British Marines, crouching down behind the bulwarks and hammock nettings of the *Bellerophon*'s poop, kept up a heavy fire with their muskets at the men on the *Aigle*'s quarter-decks, the gunners at the carronades sent a rain of musket balls and shot smashing across her decks, cutting down men in swathes. The *Aigle*'s commanding officer, Captain Gourrège, collapsed, dying from five wounds, and was carried down to the cockpit, leaving Commander Tempié in charge.

Aboard the *Bellerophon* Captain Cooke, realizing that the battle with the *Aigle* would be a bitter one, ordered Cumby to go round the main and lower decks and order the officers to keep the star-board guns firing at all costs, using the men from the larboard side as reinforcements or replacements if necessary, and at the same time elevating the guns so that the shot would smash upward through the enemy's decks, causing the maximum amount of damage.

Cumby went down to the main deck where, amid the thick smoke, he found the lieutenants and gave them their instructions. He then plunged down to the din and darkness of the lower deck, where the massive 32-pounders were crashing out and recoiling like great berserk animals trying to break free from restraining ropes. Threading his way through scampering powder monkeys, avoiding trigger-lines, coughing as the acrid smoke entered his lungs, he gave his orders and scrambled up the ladder to the main deck.

As he walked aft, senses reeling from the din and lungs gulping fresh air, he saw a couple of men carrying Overton, the Master. He had one leg hanging down, shattered by a shot, and as blood trailed dripping to the deck and mingled with the sand, his life ebbed away. Before Cumby reached the quarter-deck ladder a quartermaster ran up to him. "The Captain's been wounded, sir!" he shouted. "I believe he's dead!"

Cumby found the quarter-deck and poop a bloodstained shambles. Of the fifty-eight men who had been on the *Bellerophon's* quarter-deck, fifty-four had been cut down by shot, splinters, grenades or musket balls. Captain Cooke had been firing his pistols at Frenchmen on the *Aigle's* quarter-deck and was just reloading them—standing at the same spot where Captain Paisley, commanding the ship at the "glorious first of June," had his leg shot off—when two musket balls hit him in the chest. He collapsed and a quartermaster ran to his side, asking if he should take him below.

"No," gasped Cooke, "let me lie quietly one minute."

But before the minute passed he had died. His aide, young Midshipman Pearson, had run across the deck to him but was hit in the thigh with a splinter and fell a few yards away. A burly seaman picked up the boy to carry him down to the cockpit, and at the quarter-deck ladder they met Cumby coming up to take command. Seeing the white-faced lad Cumby paused a moment and above the din said: "Pearson, my boy, I am sorry you have been hit, but never mind—you and I'll talk over this day's work fifty years hence, depend upon it."

On the lower decks the French and British guns' crews were

fighting each other through the ports. A midshipman at one group of guns reported that they were battering each other with rammers, slashing out with cutlasses and firing muskets. The French were also hurling grenades through the ports. One of these, wrote another midshipman, burst and killed or wounded more than twenty-five men, "many of whom were dreadfully scorched. One of the sufferers, in his agony, instead of going down to the surgeon, ran aft and threw himself out of one of the stern-ports."

The French sailors and soldiers mustered several times on the poop and quarter-deck to attempt to board, and their officers could be heard shouting *"A l'abordage!"* Several Frenchmen, armed with cutlasses, clambered on to the *Bellerophon*'s spritsail yard and began to work their way along to the bowsprit. A seaman named MacFarlane saw them and ran to the starboard side of the fo'c'sle where the spritsail brace, supporting the end of the yard, was made up on the cleat. He quickly threw the rope off the cleat and the yard canted sharply, toppling the Frenchmen into the sea.

Midshipman Franklin wrote later to his brother-in-law that with both ships locked together by the yards the space between their sides was not wide enough to prevent the French sailors and soldiers from leaping across, grabbing a handhold wherever they could. "In the attempt their hands received some severe blows from whatever the English could lay their hands on. In this way hundreds of Frenchmen fell between the ships and were drowned."

The heavy fire from the *Aigle* was slashing the British ship's rigging, and among the ropes cut were those to which the colours were lashed. When they came down for the third time the veteran Yeoman of Signals, Christopher Beatty, one of the few men left unwounded on the poop, growled, "Well, well, that's too bad. . . . The fellows will say we have struck!" He searched around for the largest ensign he could find, flung it over his shoulder and clambered up the tattered mizen rigging.

Every British seaman who had tried to climb aloft to repair rigging up to that time had been shot down by the French sharpshooters; and as soon as Beatty began his hand-over-hand scramble a hail of musket balls whistled round him. He stopped several feet above the deck and, taking the flag from his shoulders, began to spread it on the shrouds. Almost at once the sharpshooters stopped firing, as if they understood his motives and admired his courage.

The ensign lashed, he climbed down to the deck again, unharmed.

Cumby, apparently unworried by the new-found responsibility of command, was standing on the gangway when a French grenade thumped down nearby, its fuse sizzling. He quickly stooped down, picked it up and threw it over the side. Describing the effect of another grenade which had been flung in at a lower-deck port, Cumby wrote: "Its explosion had blown off the scuttle of the Gunner's store-room, setting fire to the store-room and forcing open the door into the magazine passage. Most providentially this door was so placed with respect to that [door] opening from the passage into the magazine that the same blast which blew open the store-room door shut the door of the magazine, otherwise we must all in both ships inevitably have been blown up together.

"The Gunner [John Stevenson], who was in the store-room at the time, went quietly to Lt Saunders on the lower deck, and acquainting him the store-room was on fire, requested a few hands with water to extinguish it; these being instantly granted, he returned with them and put the fire out without its having been known to any persons on board except those employed in its extinction."

The other enemy ships were closing in round the *Bellerophon* by now: the *Bahama* was only a few score yards away to windward, and although her gunners were firing slowly, they were doing considerable damage. Above the deep thunder of the guns and the crackling of the muskets came the sound of wood splintering aloft, and the *Bellerophon*'s main-topmast tumbled down, dragging a tangled mass of rigging with it. The topsail fell on the starboard side, hanging like a curtain over the guns as they pounded the *Aigle*. In a few moments the flash from the muzzles set the canvas ablaze, and the flames threatened to set both ships on fire. Cumby soon had the sail-trimmers cutting it free with axes, and the boarders joined in with their cutlasses. The burning sail dropped into the sea. By now, with sails and rigging slashed, main- and mizen-topmasts shot away, several feet of deck smashed and the hull riddled with shot-holes, the *Bellerophon* was in a precarious position. Cumby went round the guns' crews "to stimulate their exertions," telling them that they had nothing else to trust to as the ship aloft "has become an unmanageable wreck."

However, the *Aigle*'s fire, like that of the *Bellerophon*, was beginning to ease up appreciably. Each ship's guns were taking a heavy toll: at least half the *Aigle's* crew had been killed or wounded, while by now more than twenty in the *Bellerophon* had been killed and a hundred wounded. The French sharpshooters were still busy. Midshipman Franklin had seen one, complete with cocked hat, shoot several men from his perch in the *Aigle's* foretop. Franklin was talking to a great friend of his, Midshipman John Simmonds, when the Frenchman fired again and Simmonds fell dead. A few minutes later Franklin was helping a Marine sergeant to carry a coloured seaman down to the surgeon when the sharp-shooter fired once more, hitting the wounded man in the heart and killing him.

"He'll have you next!" Franklin exclaimed.

"Indeed he will not!" declared the sergeant, who swore he would get a musket, find a sheltered spot, and not stop firing until he had finished off the sharpshooter.

A little later, as Franklin walked back to the quarter-deck, he saw the Frenchman lift his musket to his shoulder and take aim. But Franklin, says his biographer, "with an elasticity very common in his family, bounded behind a mast," the musket ball hitting the deck just behind him. By this time the Marine sergeant had the sharpshooter in his sights and fired. Franklin, stepping warily from behind the mast, saw the Frenchman, "whose features he vowed he would never forget so long as he lived, fall over head foremost into the sea."

Seeing the Marine sergeant later, Franklin asked how many times he had fired. "I killed him," was the reply, "at the seventh shot."

By now the *Aigle* had had enough. Her rate of fire had slackened considerably, and a few minutes later from the *Bellerophon's* quarter-deck they could see the French seamen hoisting a jib and sheeting it home. Slowly the *Aigle* dragged herself clear and sagged away to leeward. The *Bellerophon's* gunners fired one more raking broadside. "Her quarter was entirely beaten in," wrote an officer. "I have no doubt she would have struck had we been able to follow and engage her for a quarter of an hour longer."

However, even though the *Bellerophon* had rid herself of the attentions of the *Aigle,* she was still in grave danger: at 1.50 p.m. Churruca's *San Juan Nepomuceno*—before her encounter with the

Tonnant—came out of the smoke, manoeuvring into position to fire a broadside into the *Bellerophon*'s stern, a broadside which might well have put her out of action altogether. But a huge British three-decker, the 98-gun *Dreadnought*, loomed up alongside her, and in a few seconds the pulsing darts of flame and spurts of smoke rippling along the triple tier of gun ports heralded a devastating broadside. (This action will be described later in the narrative.)

The *Bellerophon* at this time, wrote Cumby, "was totally unmanageable, the main- and mizen-topmasts hanging over the side, the jib-boom, spanker-boom and gaff shot away, and not a brace or bowline serviceable. We observed that the *Aigle* was engaged by the *Defiance* and soon after two o'clock she struck," he added.

As the smoke cleared away he could see several enemy ships had struck, including the Spanish *Monarca,* which was lying nearby, a shattered hulk with 101 men lying dead and another 154 wounded. Cumby sent a boarding party to take possession of her. "We were now without any opponent within reach of our guns, and our fire consequently ceasing, I had a message from the surgeon stating that the cockpit was so crowded with wounded that it was quite impossible for him to attempt some operations that were highly requisite, and begging I would allow him to bring some subjects up into the Captain's cabin for amputations if the fire was not likely to be renewed for a quarter of an hour. I gave the requested permission with an understanding that he must be prepared to go down again if any of the enemy's van who had not been engaged should approach us."

Cumby then describes how he met the Marine captain, Wemyss, who had been wounded several times but had previously refused to go to the surgeon. Wemyss came up the quarter-deck ladder and Cumby, seeing the darker stains of blood almost covering the scarlet jacket, said: "Wemyss, my good fellow, I'm sorry you've been wounded, but I trust you will do well."

Wemyss replied cheerfully, " 'Tis but a mere scratch, and I shall have to apologize to you bye and bye for having left the deck on so trifling an occasion." He was in fact on his way to the Captain's cabin where Whyte, the surgeon, was waiting to amputate his right arm. The *Bellerophon* had lost twenty-seven men killed while 123 had been wounded.

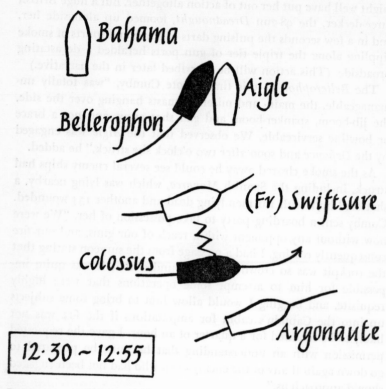

DIAGRAM 10: *Colossus* passes astern of French *Swiftsure* and down starboard side. 12.40 meets *Argonaute* to leeward and falls aboard her.

In four days' time Captain James Morris, of the *Colossus*, was due to celebrate the third anniversary of his marriage to Margaretha Cocks, daughter of a Charing Cross banker.[3] But for the moment all thoughts of his wife and home were driven from Morris's mind as he steered his ship, the sixth in Collingwood's division, for the enemy's line. Many of the French and Spanish ships were completely hidden in the smoke which was rolling to leeward in majestic clouds, here opening to reveal a toppling mast, there showing, for a moment, a shattered stem or some floating wreckage rising and falling on the swell.

The *Colossus* got into close action at about 12.30 p.m., five minutes after her next-ahead, the *Bellerophon*, and seventeen minutes after the *Royal Sovereign*. The first ship she met was the French *Swiftsure*, which was falling away after avoiding a collision with the *Bellerophon* and *Aigle*. (See Diagram 10 on opposite page.) Captain Villemadrin was able to bear up in time to avoid the *Swiftsure*'s being raked by the *Colossus*, but Morris managed to fire his larboard broadside into her before the *Colossus* sailed into a great cloud of smoke which prevented his distinguishing one ship from another. The British 74 had run only a few score yards to break through the line when suddenly out of the whirling smoke the French *Argonaute* appeared on the starboard side, almost alongside and on a slightly converging course. There was nothing that Morris or Captain Epron of the *Argonaute* could do: in a few seconds the two ships crashed together. There was a rending and splintering of wood as gun-port lids were wrenched off; some guns were flung from their carriages as their muzzles caught in projections; up aloft the yardarms, with their complicated webs of rigging, locked together.

Swiftly the British seamen, many of them flung off their feet by the impact, scrambled back to their guns and opened fire on the *Argonaute*. Working like machines in the smoke and din, they loaded and fired double-shotted broadsides, while on the poop the Marines kept up a fusillade with their muskets. Within ten minutes, according to the British accounts ("at the end of half an hour's bloody fighting," according to Captain Epron), the *Argo-*

3 By a coincidence Margaretha's sister Maria was, in four years' time, to marry William Hargood, now commanding the *Belleisle*, the second in Collingwood's line.

naute's guns were almost silent and the swell, which had been lifting the two ships and crashing them together again, finally drew them apart, and the French ship drifted clear.

Almost the last shot fired by the *Argonaute* hit Captain Morris above the knee, wounding him badly, but he refused to be taken down to the cockpit. Instead he lashed a tourniquet round his thigh to stop the bleeding and stayed on the poop.

By this time Commodore Galiano, of the Spanish *Bahama*, who had previously hauled clear of the onslaught of the *Bellerophon*, had found his former assailant fully occupied with the *Aigle* and decided to rejoin the fight—a decision which was to cost him his life. The *Bahama* opened fire from the *Colossus*'s larboard beam, but a few minutes later the French *Swiftsure* joined in from the quarter, forging ahead between the two ships to mask the *Bahama*'s fire and get the full force of the *Colossus*'s broadside. The British gunners fired so rapidly and with such accuracy that she soon dropped astern, leaving the *Bahama* once again in the line of fire. The effect on the Spanish ship was devastating.

Commodore Galiano had earlier told his officers, "Gentlemen, you all know our flag is nailed to the mast," and turning to Captain Butron, commanding the troops on board, he said, "I charge you to defend it. No Galiano ever surrenders, and no Butron should either."

The rapid broadsides from the *Colossus* soon slashed away a lot of the *Bahama*'s rigging; other shot crashed through her hull, several hitting below the water-line as she rolled. One shot flung out a splinter which hit Galiano on the foot, badly bruising him; a few minutes later another gashed his scalp, but he refused to go below to the surgeon. "Alcala Galiano gave his orders and directed his guns as if the ship had been firing salutes at a review," says one Spanish account.

It was not long before the constant training which the British gunners had received began to make itself felt: they were firing faster than the Spaniards, and more accurately. The *Bahama*'s mainmast fell.

Galiano was standing on the quarter-deck when a shot passing close spun the telescope out of his hand and made him stagger. His coxswain picked up the telescope and hurried to Galiano's side to see if he was all right, and Galiano gave a reassuring smile.

At that moment a cannon ball hit the coxswain, cutting him in two and covering Galiano in blood; a second later another shot from the same broadside hit Galiano in the head, and he fell dead beside the remains of his coxswain. Although a flag was flung over his body so that the men should not know their fearless captain had perished, the news spread rapidly through the whole crew, and the heart went out of them. The surviving officers held a rapidly summoned council of war. Some seventy-five officers and men had been killed and sixty-six wounded—141 casualties out of a crew of 690 sailors and soldiers. The council decided the time had come to take down the nailed-up flag. To emphasize the urgency, the mizenmast crashed down about their ears. Within a few minutes the *Bahama* "gave signs, by showing an English jack, that she had surrendered."

However, there was no time to send a prize-crew across from the *Colossus:* the French *Swiftsure* had dropped astern and Captain Villemadrin thought he saw a chance of turning suddenly under the stern of the *Colossus* to pour in a raking broadside. But Captain Morris, although faint from loss of blood, was too experienced and too alert to be caught. He gave the order to wear ship: the helm was put up and as sail-trimmers hauled in braces and sheets the *Colossus* swung even faster than the *Swiftsure.* A few of the French ship's larboard guns fired and then, with a succession of deafening crashes, the *Colossus* fired her broadside. The French ship's mizenmast slowly toppled over the side as if weary of staying upright, followed by the main-topmast.

Then Codrington's *Orion* came in astern of the *Swiftsure,* half hidden in the smoke, and luffed up to fire a broadside into her stern. Reloading, she fired a second and then a third broadside. Their effect was disastrous: according to Captain Villemadrin "they brought down my mainmast, carried away part of the taffrail, the wheel, and dismounted most of the guns on the main deck and killed many of the people.

"In this painful situation the senior surgeon sent a midshipman from the lower deck to inform me that he was unable to make room for any more wounded, that the spaces cleared in the hold and the orlop deck were thronged. I then sent all the men that I had available—both from the main deck and from the upper works —to the lower deck to continue fire."

The *Swiftsure*'s foremast then followed the other two over the side. "Having no longer any hope of being supported—seeing the Fleet at a great distance and having at hand only the *Achille*, who caught fire an instant later," wrote Villemadrin, "and [having] five feet of water in the hold—I gave orders to cease fire and I hauled down my colours."

The *Colossus* hauled up to windward to take possession, and her mizenmast, cut away by several enemy shot, began to creak ominously and sway. Morris, quitting the poop for the first time in the action, hobbled down the ladder to the quarter-deck just in time to avoid being crushed as the mast toppled over the side.

"Sent Lt Huish to bring the two captains on board, who returned with the captain of the French ship *Swiftsure*, and second [-in-command] of the Spaniard, her first being slain," Captain Morris noted tersely in his journal.

The seventh ship in Collingwood's division to get into action was Captain Richard King's 74-gun *Achille*, not to be confused with the French ship of the same name. King, the son of an admiral, brought his ship down to pass through the enemy's line astern of the *Montañes* and ahead of the *San Ildefonso*. He chose the former for his victim, steered boldly under her stern and fired a broadside into her quarter as he passed.

The British ship's broadside was perfectly controlled: the *Montañes*'s senior surviving officer, Lt. Alejo de Rubalcava, wrote that the *Achille* "poured a terrible fire into our larboard quarter, which caused great havoc among the crew, to the hull and to the rigging." (See Diagram 11 opposite.)

Captain Salzedo, commanding the Spanish 74, at first set the topgallants and main-topmast staysail to get more way on the ship so that he could luff up and bring his larboard broadside to bear on the British *Achille* before she reached him, but King was too quick and the *Achille*, after passing under the Spaniard's stern, came up alongside. Wreathed in thick smoke, the two ships lay close to each other, firing broadsides as boxers might exchange punches. Within half an hour Captain Salzedo was killed and his second-in-command carried wounded to the cockpit. Lt. Perez, the only officer left alive on the quarter-deck, sent for the next senior officer, Rubalcava. And when he came to the quarter-deck he found

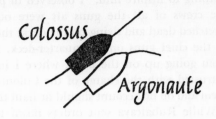
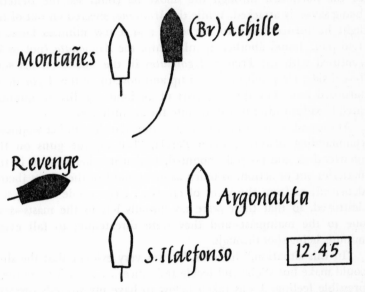

DIAGRAM 11: British *Achille* breaks line, rakes *Montañes* and ranges alongside to engage for forty minutes. *Colossus* passes on as *Argonaute* bears away.

nothing to inspire him. "I observed in passing the main deck that the crews of all the guns aft were out of action, many being stretched dead and dying on the deck; the same thing was apparent in the chief guns on the quarter-deck, but it did not detain me from going up on the poop, where I instructed the midshipman entrusted with the charge of the Colours that he should stand by them and on no account should he haul them down."

While Rubalcava sent orders down to the gun decks that all available men were to be collected to handle the guns left undamaged, Captain King realized the *Montañes* was beaten and up to the north-east through the smoke he could see the *Belleisle* being savagely attacked. While the *Montañes* sheered off out of the fight he turned away to starboard and a few minutes later, at 1.30 p.m., found another Spanish ship, the *Argonauta* (not to be confused with the French *Argonaute*) in the smoke on his starboard side. He promptly luffed up and hove-to on the *Argonauta*'s larboard bow. For the best part of an hour the British gunners fired broadside after broadside into the Spanish ship.

At the end of that time the *Argonauta,* according to her wounded commanding officer, Captain Pareja, "had all the guns on the quarter-deck and poop dismounted, a great number of guns in the batteries out of action, as much as on account of the pieces [being damaged] as from the want of crews . . . the whole rigging was destroyed, so that there were no shrouds left to the masts—save one to the mainmast—and they were threatening to fall every minute, being shot through.

"In this situation," he adds, "it was very evident that the ship could make but slight and feeble resistance. . . . With these inexpressible feelings I was taken below to have my wounds dressed, expecting every minute to find myself brought to the grievous point of having to surrender."[4] But for the moment the *Argonauta* had won a brief reprieve: the French *Achille* (which, as will be related later, had been in action with the *Revenge*) arrived on the British *Achille*'s larboard side and opened fire.

---

[4] The *Argonauta* was to surrender half an hour later, with 100 men killed and 203 wounded out of a total crew of 780. Lt. Owen, of the *Belleisle*, taking possession of her, wrote: "On getting up the *Argonauta*'s side, I found no living person on her deck; but on making my way, over numerous dead and a confusion of wreck, across the quarter-deck, I was met by the second captain at the cabin door, who gave me his sword."

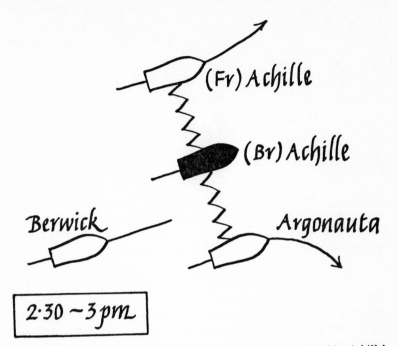

2·30 ~ 3pm

DIAGRAM 12: At 2.30 French *Achille* comes down on British *Achille*'s larboard side and engages. 3.00 *Berwick* comes between British *Achille* and *Argonauta* and engages.

A short while afterwards the French *Berwick* sailed up on the British *Achille*'s starboard side, between her and the stricken *Argonauta*. For a few minutes the British ship was sandwiched between two of the enemy while the *Argonauta* drifted away to leeward, masts tottering, more like a floating coffin than a ship of war. (See Diagram 12 on page 315.)

The French *Achille* then went ahead, leaving the British *Achille* and the *Berwick* to fight it out. Although King and his men had already silenced two ship—the *Montañes* and the *Argonauta*—they still had plenty of fight left in them, and within half an hour they forced the *Berwick* to strike. When one of the British *Achille*'s officers went on board to take possession he "counted upon her decks and in her cockpit and tiers fifty-one dead bodies, including that of her gallant captain, M. Camas"; and the wounded in the *Berwick*, according to the report of her few surviving officers, amounted to nearly 200: her loss in officers was very severe, "the quarter-deck having thrice been cleared."

At 12.35 p.m. (at about the same time as the *Victory* and twenty-seven minutes after the *Royal Sovereign*) Captain Robert Moorsom brought the 74-gun *Revenge* into action. She was a new ship, built at Chatham and launched only a few months earlier.

"While we were running down to them, of course," wrote one of the sailors, "we were favoured with several shots, and some of our men were wounded. Many of the men thought it hard the firing should be all on one side, and became impatient to return the compliment; but our Captain had given orders not to fire until we had got in close with them, so that all our shots would tell.

"Indeed, these were his words: 'We shall want all our shot when we get close in; never mind their firing. When I fire a carronade from the quarter-deck, that will be the signal for you to begin, and I know you will do your duty as Englishmen!'"

The *Revenge* came up to the line obliquely, running almost parallel to the *San Ildefonso* and the French *Achille* (before the latter went north to engage the British *Achille*). Captain Moorsom ordered the *Revenge*'s gunners to open fire on both ships. His men were among the best-trained in the Fleet, Moorsom being one of the Navy's cleverest gunnery experts. One or more shot from

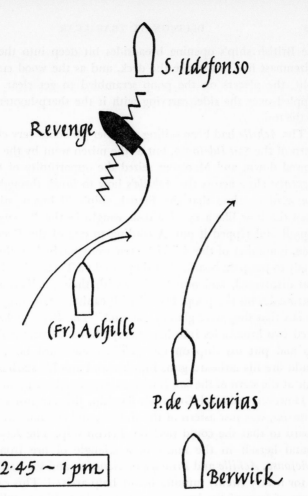

S. Ildefonso

Revenge

(Fr) Achille

P. de Asturias

12·45 ~ 1pm

Berwick

DIAGRAM 13: *Revenge* passes down side of French *Achille,* which loses a mast and falls back; *Revenge* crosses her bow, luffs up and engages her and *San Ildefonso*. *Principe de Asturias* bears away and rakes *Revenge*.

the British ship's opening broadsides bit deep into the *Achille*'s mizenmast five feet above the deck, and as the wood cracked and split, the officers on the poop scrambled to get clear. Slowly it toppled over the side, carrying with it the sharpshooters perched in the top.

The *Achille* had been sailing with her jib-boom very close to the stern of the *San Ildefonso*, but as the mizen went by the board she slowed down, and Moorsom seized the opportunity of taking the *Revenge* close across the *Achille*'s bow to break through the line. He went so close that the French ship's jib-boom, sticking out from the bow like a massive tusk, caught in the *Revenge*'s mizen-topsail and ripped it out. According to one of the *Revenge*'s seamen, a number of the *Achille*'s crew were perched on the bowsprit ready to jump on board, "but they caught a Tartar; for their design was discovered, and our Marines with their small-arms, and the carronades on the poop, loaded with canister shot, swept them off so fast that they were glad to sheer off." The *Revenge* had by then fired two broadsides into her enemy's bows. Moorsom then luffed up and put his ship on the *Achille*'s starboard bow, where he could fire his larboard guns into her and aim his starboard broadside at the stern of the *San Ildefonso*. (See Diagram 13 on page 317.)

However, Admiral Gravina's flagship, the 112-gun *Principe de Asturias*, was just astern of the *Achille*, and she bore away to starboard so that she could rake the British ship. The *Revenge* then found herself in the midst of a triangle of fire from the *San Ildefonso*, *Achille* and *Principe de Asturias*, and she had to endure it for nearly twenty minutes before help arrived. This came in the form of four of the last group of ships in Collingwood's division, led by Captain Durham in the *Defiance*. This gallant Scot—he was born at Largs, in Ayrshire—tried to pass ahead of the *Berwick* (this was before she went on to engage the British *Achille*) and under the stern of the *Principe de Asturias;* but the *Berwick* went ahead to close the gap and ran aboard of the *Defiance,* which tore off the French ship's bowsprit.

Gravina's flagship had, while this was going on, turned away to leeward to pass astern of the *Revenge* and rake her. Durham extricated the *Defiance* from the *Berwick*'s clutches and went off in pursuit of the Spanish flagship. The *Berwick,* apparently un-

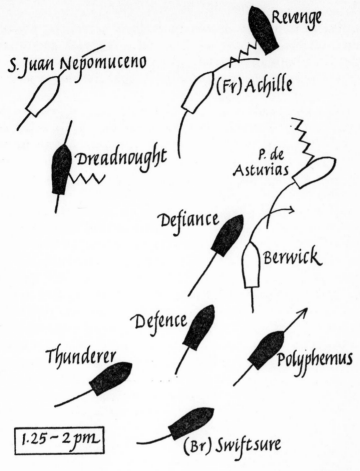

DIAGRAM 14: *Defiance* tries to pass under stern of *Principe de Asturias;*
Berwick closes gap but runs aboard *Defiance* and loses bowsprit. French
Achille tries to bear away under *Revenge's* stern but gets raked and,
1.25, loses mainmast. *Dreadnought* approaches *S. J. Nepomuceno,* opens
fire on *Principe de Asturias.*

willing to be left alone (for the *Defiance* was followed by the *Thunderer*, and the *Polyphemus* and British *Swiftsure* were coming up astern), followed the *Principe de Asturias*'s example and turned away to leeward. She was, as we have already seen, to fall into the clutches of the British *Achille*, which forced her to surrender.

Meanwhile Captain Moorsom and his *Revenge* had continued to battle with the French *Achille*. Finally the French ship wore and came round to starboard in an attempt to pass under the *Revenge*'s stern; but Moorsom's gunners raked her and the main-topmast came tumbling down, leaving her with only a foremast standing.

While the French *Achille* drifted away to leeward, Moorsom took the *Revenge* into action against the *Aigle*[5] which, as already described, had been involved with the *Bellerophon* and *Belleisle*, and raked her. Moorsom's ship had by now suffered badly: her bowsprit, all three lower masts and main-topmast were heavily damaged, nine shot had cut through the copper sheathing of the hull below the water-line and started leaks, and two midshipmen, eighteen seamen and eight Marines had been killed. Captain Moorsom, the Master and a lieutenant, the captain of Marines, thirty-eight seamen and nine Marines had been wounded.

Durham had to break off his chase of the *Principe de Asturias* because of damage to the rigging of the *Defiance*, and shortly afterwards met the *Aigle*, fresh from her encounter with the *Revenge* and, according to Durham's biographer, apparently having been severely handled. "She was, however, quite ready for action," he adds, "and defended herself most gallantly for some time; at length her fire began to slacken, and Captain Durham, thinking she had surrendered, called up his boarders to take possession." But every one of the *Defiance*'s boats was riddled with shot. There was little or no breeze to get the British ship alongside the *Aigle*, and this situation inspired young Midshipman Jack Spratt, described by Durham's biographer as a "high-spirited Irishman" and "one of the handsomest men in the service."

Spratt volunteered to swim over to the French ship, and Durham agreed. Sticking an axe in his belt, he "took his cutlass between

5 See Notes, pp. 373-74.

his teeth, called upon the boarders to follow, leapt overboard and swam to the *Aigle,* followed by a few men." On reaching the French ship he swam round her stern and scrambled up, by means of the rudder chains, to a gun port. Once on board he quickly discovered that she had not surrendered but—probably having surprise as an ally—he managed to fight through the decks to get up to the poop.

Here, according to one of his shipmates, three French soldiers with bayonets fixed to their muskets charged him. Grabbing a signal halyard, he swung himself up on to an arms chest, "and before they could repeat the operation, disabled two of them." Seizing the third soldier, he tried to fling him down the ladder on to the quarter-deck, but the Frenchman grabbed Spratt as he fell. The Frenchman landed on his head, breaking his neck, and Spratt sprawled unhurt on top of him. By this time some other men from the *Defiance* had managed to get aboard and were beginning to fight their way through the ship. Their yells, the clash of cutlasses, the popping of the muskets—sounding like toys against the heavy detonation of the guns of the ships around—echoed across the decks.

Spratt had just saved the life of a French officer who had surrendered when he saw another French soldier, bayonet fixed to his musket, making a lunge. Spratt parried with his cutlass and the Frenchman immediately aimed his musket at the midshipman's chest and squeezed the trigger. Spratt again struck out with his cutlass and managed to knock the musket barrel down as it fired, but the ball hit his right leg just below the knee, breaking both bones. Managing to avoid falling over, Spratt then hopped between two quarter-deck guns to get his back against the bulwarks and thus prevent anyone's cutting him down from behind. The French soldier made repeated jabs with his bayonet, and he was joined by two more men. All three attacked Spratt, but fortunately some of the boarding party arrived and saved him. These men had managed to get lines across to the *Defiance* from the *Aigle,* so that Captain Durham could warp the ships together. One of the first people that he saw through the smoke on the French ship's bulwarks was Spratt, who had dragged himself to the side and, holding his bleeding limb over the rail, called out, "Captain, poor old Jack

Spratt is done up at last!" He was brought on board and taken below to the surgeon, William Burnett.[6]

Another British seaman ran aft and hauled down the Tricolour, bent a British flag on to a halyard and ran it up. But the *Aigle* was not yet finished. The boarding party from the *Defiance,* fighting like demons, managed to drive the French seamen and soldiers out of the fo'c'sle and the poop; but the sharpshooters in the tops kept firing down, and many more Frenchmen were crouched behind the guns on the lower deck, firing muskets at the boarding party as they tried to scramble down the ladders. Others were busy throwing grenades through the *Defiance*'s gun ports, killing several men. Captain Durham, rather than lose any more of his men, called the boarding party back on board the *Defiance.* As soon as they had scrambled over, he ordered the lines holding the *Aigle* to be cut. When the two ships had drifted a few yards apart he ordered the guns to open fire. Shot after shot crashed with great precision into the *Aigle.* Lt. Asmus Classen, now left in command, was able to get back on his quarter-deck now that the British boarders had quit, but there was little he could do.

"We held out for some time," he reported, "but the enemy's flaming sulphur-saturated wads having set the gun room on fire close to the cable-tier . . . the ship being stripped of her rigging, most of the guns dismounted, the Captain and Commander killed, nearly all the naval officers wounded, and two-thirds of the crew disabled, the ship moreover—by what misfortune I know not— being isolated from the rest of the Fleet, we decided to haul down our colours in order to extinguish the flames and to preserve for the Emperor the scanty number of the gallant defenders who remained." Classen had not exaggerated: seven officers had been killed and ten wounded, and more than 250 of the crew were dead or wounded. "The slaughter on board of her was horrid," wrote one of the *Defiance*'s crew, Colin Campbell. "The decks were covered with dead and wounded. They never heave their dead

---

[6] A few days later Burnett went to Durham, asking for a written order to amputate Spratt's leg, saying it could not be saved and the Irishman was refusing to have the operation. Durham went below to remonstrate with him. Spratt thereupon held out the other leg and exclaimed, "Never! If I lose my leg, where shall I find a match for this?" Too crippled to serve at sea again, he was promoted to lieutenant and put in charge of the telegraph station at Dawlish.

overboard in time of action as we do." The *Defiance* had lost seventeen killed, while fifty-three more were wounded. (The disparity in casualties is partly accounted for by the fact that the *Aigle* had been engaged by several other British ships before the *Defiance* arrived.)

The report of the *Defiance*'s carpenter showed that "stopping the shot holes" in the British ship took one hundredweight and ninety pounds of sheet lead, twenty-one pounds of nails and forty-six pounds of tallow, while "replacing the bulkheads, cabbins [*sic*] and berths" in different parts of the ship "took eighty-six pounds of nails, three pounds of brads and a dozen pairs of hinges."

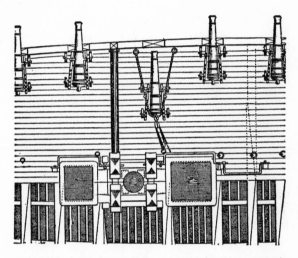

A section of the lower deck of a 74, showing a gun in the run-in position and the rest run out (tackles and breeching not shown). Between the second and third gun is the pump dale—a long wooden tube taking the water over the ship's side from the pumps, which can be seen behind the guns.

TWENTY-FIVE

JEANETTE'S RESCUE

How many ages hence
Shall this our lofty scene be acted o'er
In states unborn, and accents yet unknown?
—Shakespeare (*Julius Caesar*)

WITH THE LAST SHIPS of Collingwood's division coming into action, Nelson's main purpose had been achieved, although the battle was far from over. The van of the Combined Fleet under Dumanoir had been prevented for more than two hours from taking any effective part in the battle; Villeneuve had been captured, and those battleships round him in the centre which had not surrendered had been driven off to leeward out of the way. The rear ships under Gravina had been savagely handled and the rest of the British ships as they came into action were completing the task.

The 98-gun *Dreadnought,* which had been Collingwood's flagship until the *Royal Sovereign* arrived from England, had come into the battle late because she was a slow ship, but Captain Conn quickly brought her alongside Churruca's *San Juan Nepomuceno,* which was bearing down upon the crippled *Bellerophon,* intending to rake her. (See Diagram 14 on page 319.) The British threedecker's attack was overwhelming: in ten minutes the *San Juan Nepomuceno,* bravely fought, had surrendered. Churruca, according to one Spanish account, had "directed the battle with gloomy calmness. Knowing that only care and skill could supply the place of strength, he economized our fire, trusting entirely to careful aim, and the consequence was that each ball did terrible havoc on the foe. He saw to everything, settled everything, and the shot flew round him and over his head without his ever once even changing colour. . . .

"It was not the will of God, however, that he should escape alive from that storm of fire. Seeing that no one could hit one of the enemy's ships which was battering us with impunity, he went down himself to judge the line of fire and succeeded in dismasting her.

"He was returning to the quarter-deck when a cannon ball hit his right leg with such violence as almost to take it off, tearing it across the thigh in the most frightful manner. He fell to the ground, but the next moment he made an effort to raise himself, supporting himself on one arm.

"His face was as white as death, but he said, in a voice that was scarcely weaker than his ordinary tones: 'It is nothing—go on firing.'

"He did all he could to conceal the terrible sufferings of his cruelly mangled frame. Nothing would induce him, it would seem, to quit the quarter-deck. At last he yielded to our entreaties and then he seemed to understand that he must give up the command. He called for Moyna, his second-in-command, but was told he was dead. Then he called for the officer in command on the main deck. That officer, though himself seriously wounded, at once came to the quarter-deck and took command.

"It was just before he went below that Churruca, in the midst of his agonies, gave the order that the flag should be nailed to the mast. The ship, he said, must never surrender so long as he breathed.

"The delay, alas, could be but short. He was going fast. He never lost consciousness till the very end, nor did he complain of his sufferings. His sole anxiety was that the crew should not know how dangerous his wound was; that no one should be daunted or fail in his duty. He specially desired that the men should be thanked for their heroic courage.

"Then he spoke a few words to Ruiz de Apodoca, and after sending a farewell message to his poor young wife, whom he had married only a few days before he sailed, he fixed his thoughts on God, Whose name was ever on his lips. So with the calm resignation of a good man and the fortitude of a hero, Churruca passed away.

"After he was gone, it was too quickly known, and the men lost heart. . . . Their courage was really worn out. It was but too plain that they must surrender. . . . A sudden paralysis seemed to seize on the crews; their grief at losing their beloved leader apparently overpowered the disgrace of surrender.

"Quite half of the *San Juan's* crew were *hors de combat,* dead or wounded.[1] Most of the guns were disabled. All the masts except the mainmast had gone by the board. The rudder was useless. And yet, in this deplorable plight even, they made an attempt to follow the *Principe de Asturias,* which had given the signal to withdraw; but the *San Juan Nepomuceno* had received her death blow. She could neither sail nor steer."

When the Spanish ship surrendered Captain Conn brought the *Dreadnought* round and joined in the pursuit of the *Principe de Asturias.* The remaining enemy ships in the rear were soon crushed. At 3.15 p.m. the *Defence* attacked the *San Ildefonso* from to leeward, and in fifteen minutes the Spanish ship surrendered; at the same time the *Berwick* struck to the British *Achille.* Thus Gravina's flagship, the *Principe de Asturias,* was the only ship in his squadron which had not surrendered or quit the battle by running to leeward. But she was heavily engaged by several ships, and finally the last three-decker in Collingwood's division, the 98-gun *Prince,* under Captain Grindall, managed to catch up.

"She discharged all her guns at grape-shot range into our stern," wrote Escaño. "[Admiral Gravina] was wounded in the left leg; he was obliged to go below but while it was being temporarily dressed he gave orders that he should be conveyed back and placed sitting at his post on deck.

"Weakened by loss of blood he fell fainting; but quickly coming to himself and not perceiving the national colours, he ordered them to be hoisted without delay and he resumed command.

"In this critical position we sighted the [French] *Neptune* and the *San Justo* that were coming up to our aid, which was observed by the enemy, who obliged them to sheer off."

The French *Achille* was lying with her mizenmast and main-topmast down, wheel wrecked and her captain dead, when the three-decker *Prince* arrived close alongside at about 4 p.m. and fired a broadside into her. The shot bit into the French ship's mainmast and a moment or two later it crashed aft, along the centre-line of the ship, smashing boats and leaving her with only

1 Actually 103 were killed and 151 wounded out of a crew of 693.

the foremast standing. Lt. Cauchard, now in command of the *Achille,* was horrified to see flames coming from the foretop. They spread quickly along the dry wood, canvas and ropes. Several officers and midshipmen, with the carpenters and the few men left at the 18-pounder guns and some of those from the 36-pounders, ran forward with axes to chop away the tangle of rigging and then cut the mast over the side before the flames set fire to the whole ship. But even as they started hacking away, the *Prince* was ready with another broadside. This had no sooner been fired than the noise of splintering wood warned the Frenchmen men that the foremast was going to collapse, and a few moments later it toppled aft, the whole of the blazing foretop crashing down on to the boats stowed amidships, wrecking the fire engine. The *Prince* immediately sheered off, fearing the *Achille* would explode at any minute, but at the same time Captain Grindall ordered boats to be lowered and manned and sent off to rescue the French crew.

The *Achille*'s boats caught fire and burning debris started falling down the hatches. With the fire engine wrecked, the French crew had no chance of fighting the blaze, which rapidly spread; deck beams and planking smouldered and caught alight, rope burned like fuses, and canvas from the sails dissolved in flames. Lt. Cauchard ordered the bilge-cocks to be opened to flood the ship. "All hands then came up on deck," reported Lieutenants Lachasse and Clamart, "and losing all hope of extinguishing the fire, we no longer attended to anything except saving the ship's company, by throwing overboard all the debris that might offer them the means of escaping from almost certain death and awaiting the aid that the neighbouring ships might send them." With flames crackling up from the whole midship section of the ship, the crew started to leap over the side and swim towards the *Prince*'s boats and to the *Pickle* and *Entreprenante,* which were coming up to their rescue.

But trapped below decks in the *Achille* was a young Frenchwoman, wife of one of the main-topmen. During the battle she had been stationed in the passage to the forward magazine, passing up cartridges for the guns. When the firing had stopped, she later told Captain Moorsom of the *Revenge,* she had climbed up to the lower deck, anxious to get up to the main deck and find her husband. To her dismay all the ladders had been taken away or smashed by shot, and she could hear from the shouting that the ship was on fire.

Soon she could hear the crackling of the flames, and pieces of blazing wood fell down the hatches to start new fires on the deck on which she stood. She ran backward and forward along the shattered lower deck, scrambling over wrecked guns and dead and dying men, but could find no way of getting to the upper deck. . . . Some heavy crashes then startled her, and she saw that the main-deck planking above her was burning and some of the guns were falling through on to the lower deck. Terrified, she ran aft to the gun room and climbed through one of the ports whence, with the help of the rudder chains, she managed to scramble out on to the curved after edge of the rudder itself.

There, trembling with fear, she prayed that the ship would blow up and end her misery. Instead, the flames began to melt the lead lining of the rudder trunk and the molten metal dripped down on to her neck and shoulders. Her only chance now was the sea, and stripping off her clothes, she jumped in and swam to a piece of wreckage to which several Frenchmen were clinging. One of them, however, bit and kicked her until she had to let go. She then swam to another small piece of wreckage and a few minutes later another survivor from *Achille* swam past and seeing her, came over with a plank which he put under her arms, as if she were holding on to a rail. She was eventually rescued by one of the *Pickle*'s boats and taken on board the schooner with a hundred and twenty more survivors. Lt. Lapenotiere's crew—out-numbered four to one by the French—gave her a pair of trousers and a jacket, and a handkerchief to tie round her head. Then they treated the burns round her neck and shoulders.

Jeanette—for this was the only name by which the British knew her—was eventually transferred with other prisoners from the *Pickle* to the *Revenge,* where one of the officers noticed a youth "exhibiting a face begrimed with smoke and dirt, without shoes, stockings or shirt, and looking the picture of misery and despair." Curious, he asked some of the prisoners about this unhappy person and discovered Jeanette. "It was sufficient to know this, and I lost no time in introducing her to my messmates as a female requiring their compassionate attention."

"We were not wanting in civility to the lady," wrote Captain

Moorsom. "I ordered her two purser's shirts to make a petticoat." A lieutenant gave her his cabin (after the action was over the bulkheads were replaced) and needles and thread, while another came along with some material taken from a Spanish prize. The chaplain helped with a pair of shoes and someone else presented her with a pair of white stockings. Only one thing made Jeanette unhappy: her husband was missing. But four days later she found him on board, unhurt.

There was, according to Lt. Halloran of the *Britannia*, another woman rescued from the *Achille*. "This poor creature," he wrote, "was brought on board with scarcely any covering and our senior [Marine] subaltern, Lt Jackson, gave her a large cotton dressing-gown for clothing." He also noted that two Turks, father and son, were brought aboard from one of the ships. The father had both legs amputated, and both men died the same night.

At four o'clock the British ships to the south received a signal from Collingwood—"Come to the wind on the larboard tack." They had to leave off their pursuit of Gravina because Dumanoir had, at long last, arrived on the scene.

We left Collingwood's flagship engaging the *Santa Ana*, flagship of Admiral Alava, who had just been wounded. The Spanish ship's side, Collingwood wrote later, was "almost entirely beaten in" by the *Royal Sovereign's* gunfire. She had just surrendered when a boat from the *Victory* arrived alongside the British ship and Lt. Alexander Hills climbed on board, asking to be taken to Admiral Collingwood. The Admiral, his leg swollen and bleeding under its bandage, was told that Nelson had been wounded. "I asked the officer if his wound was dangerous," Collingwood later wrote to the Duke of Clarence. "He hesitated; then said he hoped it was not; but I saw the fate of my friend in his eye; for his look told what his tongue could not utter."

For the moment the *Royal Sovereign* was helpless. The crippled *Santa Ana* had a few minutes earlier drifted to leeward and then broached to, and the violent motion had brought her tottering masts tumbling over the side. Collingwood's ship was in little better shape, because at about 2.30 p.m. her mainmast, which had been swaying dangerously with only a few remaining shrouds to hold it, finally crashed down, and a few moments later the mizenmast followed. Blackwood's *Euryalus* was signalled to take her in tow. With his ship finally under way again, albeit at the end of the *Euryalus*'s tow-rope, Collingwood hailed Blackwood and told him to go aboard the *Santa Ana* and "Bring me the Admiral."

Blackwood lowered a boat and had himself rowed across to find Alava too badly wounded to be moved. He therefore brought Captain Gardoqui back with him. Hercules Robinson later wrote that when he met Alava five years later the Spanish admiral told him that one broadside from the *Royal Sovereign* had killed three hundred and fifty men, and "though he fought on afterwards for a couple of hours, like an old hidalgo, like 'a man of honour and a cavalier,' the first broadside did his business, and there was an end of him. . . ." Despite Alava's compliment to the efficiency of the *Royal Sovereign*'s broadside, according to Spanish official sources five officers and ninety men were killed, and ten officers and 127 wounded in the battle out of a total crew of 1,188.

When Captain Gardoqui got on board the *Royal Sovereign* he asked a sailor the name of the ship. On being told, he patted one of the guns, and said in broken English, "I think she should be called the 'Royal Devil.' "

Ship rig.

TWENTY-SIX

"NOBLE MADNESS"

Set honour in one eye and death i' the other,
And I will look on both indifferently.
—Shakespeare (*Julius Caesar*)

WE HAVE SEEN that just before the *Bucentaure*'s main- and mizen-masts toppled over the side, Villeneuve had signalled to Dumanoir that the van division—sailing north-westward away from the battle —was to wear together and come down to the rescue of the rest of the sorely tried Combined Fleet. "The over-light breeze checked the speed with which I desired to bear down to his assistance," Dumanoir later said in a report which was aimed at justifying his tardiness. He had ten ships with him—the original seven of his division, plus the *Intrépide*, which had not been able to get into her proper position before the battle, and the *Héros* and the *San Augustin*, which had been leading Villeneuve's division. (See Chart 2, page 228, and Diagram 1 on page 251.) The only way for Dumanoir's *Formidable* to wear was to lower a boat and use it to tow the ship's bow round. The *Scipion* tried to tack and failed, then could not wear because the *Intrépide* was too close, and finally put a boat over the side and was hauled round. The *Intrépide* managed to wear but collided with the *Mont-Blanc*, who smashed her own flying jib-boom and split the *Intrépide*'s foresail.

Then, wrote Captain Infernet, of the *Intrépide*, while the rest of the ships wore round or tacked, he "crowded on canvas and set my course for the ships foul of each other and dismasted, and particularly for the flagship [*Bucentaure*] which was amongst the number. I observed with sorrow," he added, "that I was followed only by the Spanish *Neptuno*, four French ships keeping to the wind on the larboard tack standing south and south-south-west, which caused them to pass a gun-shot to windward of the enemy

331

fleet, under full sail." The four ships were Dumanoir's *Formidable,* followed by the *Duguay-Trouin, Scipion* and *Mont-Blanc,* followed later by the Spanish *Neptuno.* They were sailing down for a point about half a mile to windward of the *Bucentaure,* towards the British *Spartiate* and *Minotaur,* which were just coming into the battle. Dumanoir wrote: "The Admiral [Villeneuve] was by then totally dismasted; I had still a hope that I might take him in tow and endeavour to get him out of [the line of] fire."

When Captain Hardy, from the bloodstained and shot-torn decks of the *Victory,* saw Dumanoir's ten ships turn back as though they intended at long last to join in the battle, he hoisted the signal for the British ships to come to the wind on the larboard tack, thus sailing clear of the scattered group of shattered enemy ships and getting into a position to beat off the new threat and at the same time guard the prizes which were to leeward.

However, only seven British captains saw the signal—Bayntun (*Leviathan*), Pellew (*Conqueror*), Bullen (*Britannia*), Digby (*Africa*), Fremantle (*Neptune*), Pilfold (*Ajax*) and Berry (*Agamemnon*). They formed themselves up in that order in a rough line of battle and headed northward.

Dumanoir's squadron had by now split itself into three distinct groups—Dumanoir's four, followed by the *Neptuno,* keeping up to windward and sailing back parallel with what had been the Combined Fleet's line; the *Intrépide* and *San Augustin,* heading bravely down towards the battle; and the *Héros, Rayo*—commanded by the Irishman MacDonell—and the *San Francisco de Asis,* which were to leeward and unashamedly about to steer away for Cadiz. In other words, out of the ten fresh and undamaged French and Spanish ships, only two were attempting to go to Villeneuve's rescue.

Dumanoir, at the head of the five ships to windward, was heavily engaged by the newly-formed British line as he passed them going in the opposite direction, heading down towards the *Spartiate* and *Minotaur.* However, neither Captain Sir Francis Laforey nor Captain Mansfield, both doing their best to get into the battle in the extremely light wind, seemed very concerned at the idea of tackling the five enemy ships now sailing down in line on their larboard side. (See Diagram 15 opposite.)

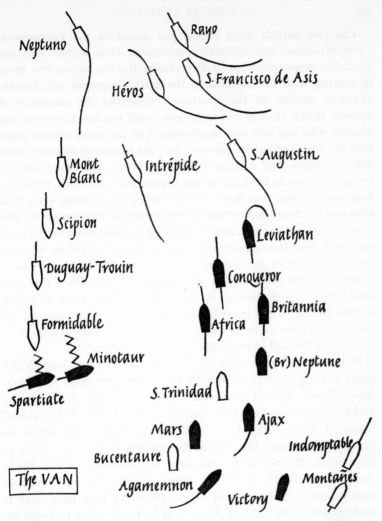

The VAN

DIAGRAM 15: British ships form line of battle. Dumanoir in *Formidable* sails down and is engaged by *Spartiate* and *Minotaur*. *Intrépide* and *San Augustin* make their brave attacks. *Rayo, S. F. de Asis* and *Héros* quit.

The two British ships passed just ahead of the *Formidable*. "The *Minotaur* and *Spartiate* commenced close action with the headmost ships, receiving and returning the fire of the five ships in passing with our topsails to the mast," reported Mr. Francis Whitney, Master of the *Spartiate*. "Observed the sternmost, a Spanish ship's, rigging and sails very much cut up. Lay-to on her quarter with our fore and main-topsails to the mast, all our after-sails set, firing obliquely through her, she returning at times from her stern-chase and quarter guns. . . . Wore, not being able to bring our guns to bear, to engage her on the other tack, the other four ships having left her." (See Diagram 16 on page 336.) The ship was the Spanish *Neptuno,* and Captain Valdés wrote: "At this time the mizenmast fell, and in its fall I was wounded in the head and neck and lost consciousness and was carried below, where I never thought to go notwithstanding that I had already been wounded three times during the action. . . . Finally, a few minutes before sunset, having thirty dead and forty-seven wounded, totally dismasted and overwhelmed by the superior number of the enemy who surrounded my ship—which was the only one in those waters—we decided to strike to such superior forces."

Dumanoir's descent with his five ships on the two lone British ships was a curious parallel with Nelson's approach to the enemy line. Whereas Nelson succeeded, Dumanoir lost the *Neptuno* and had to report that "the two vessels that I had intended to cut off managed to pass ahead of me at pistol shot and damaged me greatly." Even with the odds at five to two, he failed to make an impression. He was now well clear to windward of the battle. Anxious to acquit himself—on paper at least—he reported later that he ordered the captain of the *Formidable* to bear away to come down on to the rear ships, "but he came to me to point out that absolutely all rigging and the greater part of the shrouds were carried away, and that he could not change course without the certainty of losing his masts."

The Admiral bemoaned his fate: reasonably enough he felt the lack of the other five ships which had failed to follow him. "If I had had with me ten ships, however desperate our position, I should have been able to bear down on the scene of the action and fight the enemy to a finish—three of them were dismasted—

and perhaps it would have been reserved for me to have made the day glorious for the Allied Fleet." But he appeared to have forgotten that the opportunity had existed from the moment the action began at noon right up to 2 p.m., the time when he wore round; two hours when his intervention might well have had a considerable effect.

But the four ships now left to him—well, "to bear down on the enemy at this moment would have been a desperate stroke which would have only served to increase the number of our losses and augment the advantages to the enemy to whom, on account of the depletion of my division, I could not have done much damage." Then, in apparent contradiction, he added: "It was therefore my duty in this painful situation to endeavour to effect the repairs of my Division in the hope of more favourable chances on the morrow."

On the morrow, of course, the British ships would have carried out repairs, and also taken possession of the enemy ships which had surrendered. However, the quartet sailed on to the south, apparently satisfied. The *Formidable*, despite the damaged masts which kept her out of action, survived the great gales. Dumanoir was to meet Sir Richard Strachan on November 4 (and have his four ships captured), and eventually face two courts-martial and a court of inquiry.[1]

Meanwhile the *Intrépide*, with Captain Louis Infernet on the quarter-deck, was steering for the enemy to fight one of the most gallant actions of the whole battle. "We could hardly make out in the midst of the smoke and confusion of the battle," wrote the Marquis Gicquel des Touches, a young lieutenant on board, "the situation of our flagship [*Bucentaure*], surrounded as she was by the enemy and having near her only the *Redoutable*, a small 74, crushed by the overpowering mass of the *Victory*. . . .

"It was into the thick of this fray that our Captain Infernet led us. He wanted, he said, to rescue Admiral Villeneuve and take him

1 At the first, on his conduct at Trafalgar, he was cleared; at a court of inquiry on his actions on November 4 he was blamed for certain moves and was said to have "shown too much indecision in all his manoeuvres," and in a subsequent court-martial he was cleared.

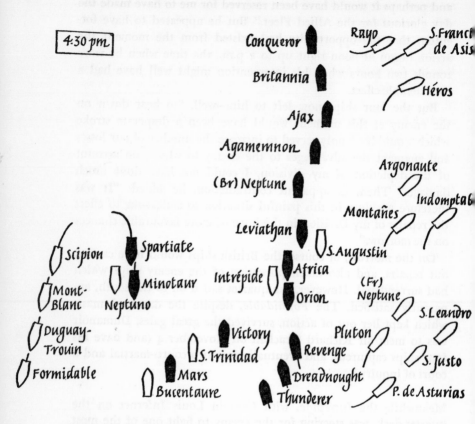

DIAGRAM 16: The probable situation at the end of battle showing the northernmost ships. Dumanoir in the *Formidable* quits to the southwest.

on board, and then to rally round ourselves the ships that were still in a fit state to fight. It was a reckless and forlorn hope, a mad enterprise; and he himself could not doubt it. It was the pretext Infernet gave for continuing to fight. He would not have it said that the *Intrépide* had quitted the battle while she still could fight a gun or hoist a sail. It was a noble madness, but though we knew it, we all supported him with joyful alacrity—and would that others had imitated his example!"

While Infernet steered the *Intrépide* down towards the new line of British ships, the *San Augustin* went down with him farther to leeward. (See Diagram 15.) The *Leviathan*, leading the line, was the first to engage the *San Augustin*, bearing down on the Spanish ship and turning out of the line to run alongside. After firing several broadsides, she attempted to board.

"It was inevitable to surrender to such superior numbers," wrote Captain Felipe Cajigal, commanding the *San Augustin*, "and having boarded twice I had not sufficient men to repel a third boarding, the few who remained being on the gun decks, continuing to fire into the other ships which were closing round me at pistol range."

Infernet saw the *Leviathan* engaged with the *San Augustin* and seized the opportunity to pass near the British ship and pour a raking broadside into her bow. The *Conqueror*, the nearest other British ship, was badly damaged aloft—most of her running rigging had been shot away—but opened fire on the *Intrépide* "at too great a distance to do any material execution," according to Lt. Senhouse, one of her officers. The little 64-gun *Africa* was the next nearest ship, and Digby quickly wore her round the *Intrépide*'s stern, luffed up on the starboard tack and opened fire. The *Britannia*, *Ajax*, *Agamemnon* and *Neptune* fired into the *Intrépide* as they passed on their way northward in pursuit of the *Rayo*, *San Francisco de Asis* and *Héros*, but for forty minutes the *Africa* kept firing her broadsides into the *Intrépide* until finally Codrington brought the *Orion* up and raked the French ship.

The young Marquis in the *Intrépide*, whose post was on the fo'c'sle in charge of the headsails, boarders and sharpshooters, was having a busy time amid the thick smoke and the crash of the guns. "What took much of my attention," he wrote, "was to prevent the masts and yards from coming down, and I was able to keep the foremast standing for a considerable time, by means of which we were able to manoeuvre the ship to some extent.

"While the fighting was very hot the British *Orion* crossed our bows in order to pour in a raking fire. I got my men ready to board and pointing out to a midshipman her position and what I wanted to do, I sent him to the Captain with a request to have the ship laid on board the *Orion*.

"I saw to the rest, and seeing the ardour of my men, I already imagined myself master of the British 74 and taking her into Cadiz with her colours under ours. With keen anxiety I waited; but there was no change in the *Intrépide*'s course.

"Then I dashed off to the quarter-deck myself. On the way I found my midshipman lying flat on the deck, terrified at the sight of the *Britannia*,[2] which ship had come abreast of us within pistol shot and was thundering into us from her lofty batteries. I treated my emissary as he deserved—I gave him a hearty kick—and then I hurried aft to explain my project personally to the Captain. It was then, though, too late. The *Orion* swept forward across our bows, letting fly a murderous broadside—and no second chance presented itself.

"At the moment I reached the poop the brave Infernet was brandishing a small curved sabre which struck off one of the pieces of wooden ornamental work by the rail. The sword blade went close to my face, and I said laughingly, 'Do you want to cut my head off, Captain?'

" 'No, certainly not you, my friend,' was the reply, 'but that's what I mean to do to the first man who speaks to me of surrender.'

"Nearby was a gallant colonel of infantry, who had distinguished himself at Marengo. He was terribly perturbed at the broadside from the *Britannia*. In vain he tried to dodge and shelter behind the stalwart form of the Captain, who at length saw what he was doing.

" 'Ah, Colonel,' called out the Captain, 'do you think I am sheathed in metal then?'

"In spite of the gravity of the moment we could not keep from laughing.

[2] The Marquis actually wrote "*Téméraire*," but she was still alongside Lucas's crippled *Redoutable*, and the *Britannia* was the only three-decker near in this position.

"But by now, indeed, the decks had been almost swept clear, our guns were disabled, and the batteries heaped up with dead and dying. It was impossible to keep up a resistance which meant the doom of what remained of our brave ship's company, and ourselves, without the means of striking back and inflicting harm on the enemy."

The heavily built Infernet, a Provençal by birth, rough in manner and uneducated, who started off in the French Navy as a cabin boy, wrote a report which gives some idea of the odds he was fighting by now.

"At four o'clock[3] I was dismantled to such a degree that all my rigging was cut to pieces and several guns on deck and in the batteries dismounted. At 4.45 I ordered the few hands remaining on deck to go below to the batteries in order to engage to starboard and larboard; at this minute the mizen yard where my colours were flying was carried away by a shot; I immediately ordered a flag to be flown from the mizen shrouds to starboard and larboard and continued the fight.

"At five o'clock the wheel, the tiller-sweep, the tiller ropes and the tiller were shattered to a thousand pieces; I at once had the spare tiller rigged and steered with it, always fighting desperately. At 5.15 the mizenmast fell; four or five minutes later the mainmast did the same; I still fought—and I am able to say so to the honour of those whom I commanded—undauntedly; I was then surrounded by seven enemy ships, which were all firing into me and I was making all possible resistance; I was firing with the stern-chasers, musketry from the upper works and from the foretops.

"At 5.53 p.m. the foremast fell; I was then left without masts or sails; seeing myself surrounded by enemies and not being able to escape, having, moreover, no French ships in sight to come to my assistance, the enemy keeping up a terrible fire into me, having about half my crew killed. . . . I was obliged to yield to the seven enemy ships that were engaging me."

Although the reports of the *Orion* and *Africa* do not bear out Infernet's report that there were seven ships engaging him simultaneously, Senhouse of the *Conqueror* wrote that the French captain surrendered "after one of the most gallant defences I ever

---

3 Infernet's times are an hour ahead of those recorded by the British ships.

witnessed. The Frenchman's name was Infernet, a member of the
Legion of Honour, and it deserves to be recorded in the memory
of those who admire true courage."

It was about 4 p.m. when the *Dreadnought, Revenge* and *Thunderer* came up to windward to ward off Dumanoir's apparently
impending attack and left Gravina's flagship the *Principe de Asturias* to roll and lurch her way towards Cadiz, with the French
Neptune, Pluton and *San Justo* in company. (See Diagram 16.)

At 4.30 p.m. Gravina ordered the remaining French and Spanish
ships to rally, and steered towards Cadiz. At 5 p.m. the frigate
Themis took his ship in tow and on their way they were joined
by the *Argonaute, Montañes, Indomptable, Rayo, San Francisco
de Asis* and *Héros*. Dumanoir was already well clear with his four
ships. But the drama off Cape Trafalgar was not yet over.

TWENTY-SEVEN

THE BARGAIN

He that outlives this day and comes safe home,
Will stand a tip-toe when this day is nam'd. . . .
                                        —Shakespeare *(Henry V)*

WHILE brave men and poltroons, silent heroes and noisy brag-
garts of many nations were fighting for their lives round the
Victory, Horatio Nelson lay on a purser's mattress with his back
against the ship's side, feeling death within him yet keeping a
tenuous but painful grasp on life. Burke had his arm round the
emaciated and pain-racked shoulders; Scott knelt beside his chief,
fanning him, massaging his chest or offering a drink. The steward,
Henry Chevalier, and Gaetano Spedilo, the Admiral's valet,
crouched nearby, waiting and anxious to have a task which would
ease their feeling of utter helplessness.

Beatty and his assistants hurried to and fro among the men
lying and sitting about waiting to have their wounds tended.
With bare arms and clothing bloodstained, crouching as they
walked because of the lack of headroom, they presented a macabre
sight in the fitful glow from the lanterns.

Looking pathetically small and helpless, his face white and his
breathing shallow, Nelson waited for Hardy to appear: more than
an hour had passed since the Admiral had been carried below
from the quarter-deck. For the whole of that time he had been
without real news of what was happening in this, his last and his
greatest battle.

Young Midshipman Westphal, lying next to Nelson with his
bleeding head resting on the Admiral's rolled-up coat, waited
patiently; on the other side the wounded Pasco tried to comfort
Nelson. Finally the huge bulk of Hardy scrambled down the

ladder almost opposite where Nelson was lying and, crouching low to avoid banging his head on the beams, he went over to the Admiral and shook hands affectionately.

"Well, Hardy, how goes the battle? How goes the day with us?"

"Very well, my Lord. We have got twelve or fourteen of the enemy's ships in our possession; but five of their van have tacked," said Hardy, referring to Dumanoir's squadron, "and show an intention of bearing down upon the *Victory*. I have therefore called two or three of our fresh ships round us, and have no doubt of giving them a drubbing."

"I hope," said Nelson, "none of *our* ships have struck, Hardy."

"No, my Lord, there is no fear of that."

Then Nelson, his voice dropping, said, "I am a dead man, Hardy, I am going fast; it will be all over with me soon. Come nearer to me. . . ."

Sensing that whatever the Admiral was about to say to Hardy would be private, Burke eased his arm from round Nelson's shoulder and made to move away, but he was motioned to stay.

". . . Pray let my dear Lady Hamilton have my hair, and all other things belonging to me," whispered Nelson.

Hardy, distressed at this turn in the conversation, said that he hoped that Beatty could yet hold out some prospect of life.

"Oh no," replied Nelson with what vehemence he could muster. "It is impossible. My back is shot through. Beatty will tell you so."

There was little more for Hardy to say, and at this moment his presence was wanted on the quarter-deck. He again shook hands with his wounded friend and with a sad heart climbed back up the ladder.

Beatty, who had been attending Midshipman Rivers's shattered leg, came back, but Nelson told him to go back and do what he could for the rest of the wounded, "for you can do nothing for me." The surgeon, to whom we are indebted for his description of these last hours, assured him the assistant surgeons were doing everything possible for the men, but Nelson insisted, and Beatty went off to attend to two wounded Marine lieutenants, James Peake and Lewis Reeves. He had not been gone long before Dr. Scott called him back.

"Ah, Mr. Beatty," said Nelson, "I have sent for you to say what

I forgot to tell you before, that all power of motion and feeling below my breast are gone; and *you* very well *know* I can live but a short time." Beatty knew that Nelson had a picture in his mind of James Bush, the seaman who had broken his back in the *Victory* the previous July, and in whose thirteen-day struggle for life, as mentioned earlier, Nelson had taken such a keen interest. The surgeon, confused at the Admiral's pronouncing his own death sentence, muttered, "My Lord, you told me so before," and knelt down to examine him again. But Nelson knew it was a useless gesture. "Ah, Beatty! I am too certain of it: Scott and Burke have tried it already. *You know* I am gone."[1]

By now Beatty realized that it was pointless to argue with his Admiral and unnecessary to comfort him. "My Lord, unhappily for our country, nothing can be done for you." As if saying aloud what his thoughts had tried to conceal broke his professional reserve, tears came to his eyes and he turned quickly and walked a few paces so that he could not be seen. Nelson said quite simply, and to no one in particular, as if he had come to terms with death, "I know it. I feel something rising in my breast"—he put his hand to his left side—"which tells me I am gone."

By now Dumanoir's ships were passing to windward, and the *Victory*'s larboard guns opened fire, their thundering reverberations once again rolling through the ship, followed by the heavy grinding of their trucks as they were run out and fired again.

"Oh *Victory, Victory,* how you distract my poor brain," groaned Nelson, and then, as an afterthought: "How dear life is to all men." Burke and Scott gave him sips of lemonade from time to time, and fanned him, but his brow was cold and he was breathing in short, uneven and painful gasps. Beatty came back and asked if the pain was still very bad. "It continues so severe," was the reply, "that I wish I was dead. Yet," he said, his voice dropping, as a confiding child might reveal a secret wish, "one would like to live a little longer, too."

He was quiet for a few minutes, as if he had gone into a world of his own where there was no pain but only happy memories, but then he came back from wherever he had been and said, "What

---

1 The italics are Beatty's. He often refers to himself as "the surgeon."

would become of poor Lady Hamilton, if she knew my situation!" Once again Beatty left, unable to do anything to ease the pain tormenting the Admiral's body, to attend to Midshipman Robert Smith who, like his Admiral nearby, was dying. From him he went to Lt. Bligh and then he came over to Midshipman Westphal, lying next to Nelson and still resting his head on the coat.[2]

Nearly an hour had gone by since Hardy's last visit. During that time Dumanoir had passed and Lt. Hills had been sent to tell Collingwood that Nelson had been wounded. The Dorset captain now had a few minutes to spare for another visit to the cockpit, which Beatty describes:

"Lord Nelson and Captain Hardy shook hands again, and while the Captain retained his Lordship's hand, he congratulated him, even in the arms of death, on his brilliant victory, which, he said, was complete; though he did not know how many of the enemy were captured, as it was impossible to perceive every ship distinctly. He was certain, however, of fourteen or fifteen having surrendered."

"That is well, but I bargained for twenty," said Nelson; then, gripping Hardy's hand tighter, he exclaimed with sudden emphasis, "*Anchor,* Hardy, anchor!"

He had seen the long white streamers of high cloud which had, from early morning, spread like the feathers of a peacock's tail from the westward and, coupled with the heavy swell, he knew this warned that a storm was coming up from the direction of the setting sun, and with the shoals of Cape Trafalgar and the rock-girt coast close under their lee, the British Fleet and the prizes were in great danger. Hardy evidently considered that the time had come for Collingwood to take over command, but it was a difficult suggestion to make to a dying man, and particularly to someone of Nelson's temperament. So he said, with as much tact as he could muster, "I suppose, my Lord, Admiral Collingwood will now take upon himself the direction of affairs." The effect on Nelson was

2 "When the battle was over," Westphal wrote later, "and they came to remove the coat, several of the bullions of the epaulettes were found to be so firmly glued into my hair, by the coagulated blood from my wound, that the bullions, four or five of them, were cut off, and left in my hair, one of which I have still in my possession."

startling: he reacted violently, trying to struggle up from the mattress. "Not while I live, I hope, Hardy!

"No," he added, " do *you* anchor, Hardy."

"Shall we make the signal, sir?"

"Yes—for if I live, I'll anchor."

Beatty says that Nelson meant by this order that if he survived until all enemy resistance had ceased, Hardy was then to anchor the ships, "if it should be found practicable." He adds that "the energetic manner in which he uttered these his last orders to Captain Hardy, accompanied by his efforts to raise himself, evinced his determination never to resign the command while he retained the exercise of his transcendent faculties, and that he expected Captain Hardy still to carry into effect the suggestions of his exalted mind, his sense of his duty overcoming the pains of death."

But, as if this last effort had taken him a few steps nearer to the end, he said to Hardy: "I feel that in a few moments I shall be no more. . . ."

A minute or two later he said in a low voice: "Don't throw me overboard, Hardy."

"Oh no, certainly not."

"Then," whispered Nelson, who had often discussed it with Hardy, "you know what to do: and take care of my dear Lady Hamilton, Hardy; take care of poor Lady Hamilton. . . . Kiss me, Hardy."

With every beat of his heart the little man's life was ebbing away fast, and Hardy knelt and kissed his cheek. Nelson looked up at Hardy's strained face and whispered, "Now I am satisfied. Thank God I have done my duty."

Hardy stood up, looking down at his dying friend, who was now lying back with his eyes closed, his breath so shallow that the narrow chest under the coarse, unbleached calico of the sheet barely moved. Hardy suddenly knelt again and kissed the forehead which was cold to his lips.

"Who is that?" Nelson whispered.

"It is Hardy. . . ."

"God bless you, Hardy!"

The Captain stood up and walked the few feet to the ladder,

between the mainmast and the hanging magazine, and clambered up to the quarter-deck.[3]

Nelson now told Chevalier to turn him to his right side, apparently hoping that this would ease the pain, and added, "I wish I had not left the deck, for I shall soon be gone." He was breathing with great difficulty as he drowned in his own blood, and he said in a faint voice to the chaplain, Scott, "Doctor, I have not been a *great* sinner. . . . *Remember* that I leave Lady Hamilton and my daughter Horatia as a legacy to my country: and never forget Horatia."

Now the pain seemed suddenly to increase to almost more than he could bear, and with it came a terrible thirst. He had difficulty in speaking, and when words came they tumbled over each other in their urgency. "Fan, fan!" he said. And to Scott, who had previously been massaging his breast with his hand and giving him some relief from the pain, "Rub, rub!" Then, says Beatty, "he every now and then, with evident increase of pain, made a great effort with his vocal powers, and pronounced distinctly these last words: 'Thank God I have done my duty'; and this great sentiment he continued to repeat as long as he was able to give it utterance.

"His Lordship became speechless in about fifteen minutes after Captain Hardy left him. Dr Scott and Mr Burke, who had all along sustained the bed under his shoulders (which raised him to a semi-recumbent posture, the only one that was supportable to him), forbore to disturb him by speaking to him; and when he had remained speechless about five minutes, his Lordship's steward went to the surgeon, who had been a short time occupied with the wounded in another part of the cockpit, and stated his apprehension that his Lordship was dying.

"The surgeon immediately repaired to him, and found him on the verge of dissolution. He knelt down by his side and took up his hand, which was cold, and the pulse gone from the wrist. On

---

[3] Beatty says that Nelson frequently told Hardy that if he was killed at sea he wished his body to be brought back to England, and that "if his country should think proper to inter him at the public expense," he wished to be buried in St. Paul's Cathedral. He preferred the Cathedral to Westminster Abbey because he remembered a tradition that the Abbey was built where a morass once existed, and he feared the Abbey would eventually disappear. If there was no public burial he wished to be buried beside his father at Burnham Thorpe, in Norfolk.

the surgeon's feeling his forehead, which was likewise cold, his Lordship opened his eyes, looked up, and shut them again.

"The surgeon again left him, and returned to the wounded who required his assistance; but was not absent five minutes before the steward announced that he believed his Lordship had expired. The surgeon returned, and found that the report was but too well founded: his Lordship had breathed his last, at thirty minutes past four o'clock; at which period Dr Scott was in the act of rubbing his Lordship's breast, and Mr Burke supporting the bed under his shoulders."

The *Victory*'s log recorded: "Partial firing continued until 4.30, when a victory having been reported to the Right Honourable Lord Viscount Nelson, he then died of his wound."

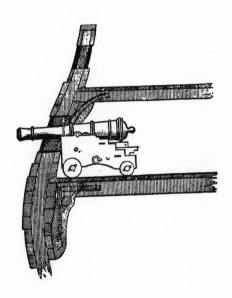

TWENTY-EIGHT

THE GREAT GALE

EVERY SHIP SET ABOUT clearing up the wreckage, tending the wounded and disposing of the dead. Lt. Paul Nicolas of the *Belleisle* gives perhaps the best description of the hours immediately following the end of the battle. There were two periods in the life of a sailor which were impressive above all others, he said. One was going to general quarters, when each man hoped to see his friends again; and the other was when the battle was over "and our kindlier feelings resumed their sway."

He wrote: "Eager inquiries were expressed, and earnest congratulations exchanged, at this joyful moment. The officers came to make their report to the Captain, and the fatal results cast a gloom over the scene of our triumph. I have alluded to the impression of our first lieutenant that he should not survive the contest [see page 230].

"This gallant officer was severely wounded in the thigh, and underwent an amputation: but his prediction was realized, for he expired before the action had ceased. The junior lieutenant was likewise mortally wounded on the quarter-deck. These gallant fellows were lying beside each other in the gun room preparatory to their being committed to the deep; and here many met to take a last look at their departed friends, whose remains soon followed the promiscuous multitude, without distinction of either rank or nation, to their wide ocean grave.

"In the act of launching a poor sailor over the poop he was discovered to breathe; he was, of course, saved. . . .

"The upper deck presented a confused and dreadful appearance: masts, yards, sails, ropes and fragments of wreck were scattered in every direction; nothing could be more horrible than the scene of blood and mangled remains with which every part was covered, and which, from the quantity of splinters, resembled a shipwright's yard strewed with gore.

"From our extensive loss—thirty-four killed and ninety-six wounded—our cockpit exhibited a scene of suffering which rarely occurs. I visited this abode of suffering with the natural impulse which led many others thither—namely, to ascertain the fate of a friend or companion. So many bodies in such a confined space and under such distressing circumstances would affect the most obdurate heart. My nerves were but little accustomed to such trials but even the dangers of battle did not seem more terrific than the spectacle before me.

"On a long table lay several anxiously looking for their turn to receive the surgeon's care, yet dreading the fate he might pronounce. One subject was undergoing amputation, and every part was heaped with sufferers: their piercing shrieks and expiring groans were echoed through this vault of misery; and even at this distant period the heart-sickening picture is alive in my memory. What a contrast to the hilarity and enthusiastic mirth which reigned in this spot the preceding evening.

"At all other times the cockpit is the region of conviviality and good humour, for here it is that the happy midshipmen reside, at whose board neither discord nor care interrupt the social intercourse. But a few short hours on these benches, which were now covered with mutilated remains, sat these scions of their country's glory, who hailed the coming hour of conflict with cheerful confidence. . . .

"About five o'clock the officers assembled in the Captain's cabin to take some refreshment. The parching effect of the smoke made this a welcome summons, although some of us had been fortunate in relieving our thirst by plundering the Captain's grapes which hung round his cabin; still, four hours' exertion of body with the energies incessantly employed, occasioned a lassitude, both corporeally and mentally, from which the victorious termination so near at hand could not arouse us; moreover there sat a melancholy on the brows of some who mourned a messmate who had shared their perils and their vicissitudes for many years. Then the merits of the departed heroes were repeated with a sigh, but their errors sunk with them into the deep. . . .

"A boat with a lieutenant from the cutter *Entreprenante* shortly after came on board, on his return from the *Victory,* to announce the death of the immortal Nelson. The melancholy tidings spread through the ship in an instant and the paralyzing effect was wonderful.

"Our Captain [Hargood] had served under the illustrious chief for years, and had partaken in the anxious pursuit of the enemy across the Atlantic, with the same officers and crew. 'Lord Nelson is no more!' was repeated with such despondency and heartfelt sorrow that everyone seemed to mourn a parent. All exertion was suspended: the veteran sailor indulged in silent grief; and some eyes evinced that tenderness of heart is often concealed under the roughest exterior."

The French *Achille* blew up at 5.30 p.m. and signalled the end of the battle. Midshipman Hercules Robinson wrote later of how boats from the *Euryalus* were engaged "getting hold of a dozen of her men who were hoisted into the air out of the exploding ship, cursing their fate, *sacré*-ing, tearing their hair, and wiping the gunpowder and the salt water from their faces; and how, in the evening these same fellows, having got their supper and grog and dry clothes, dancing for the amusement of our men under the half-deck."

Captain Durham left the *Defiance* to visit Admiral Collingwood in his cabin after he had transferred from the *Royal Sovereign* to the *Euryalus*. Going out on deck afterwards he saw a French officer leaning on the capstan. He discovered that it was in fact Admiral Villeneuve, and began talking to him.

"Sir," said Villeneuve, "were you in Sir Robert Calder's action?"

Durham replied that he was, and had commanded the ship which had first discovered Villeneuve's fleet, and that he had remained watching them for four or five hours until Calder arrived. Villeneuve sighed and said: "I wish Sir Robert and I had fought it out that day. He would not be in his present position, or I in mine."

When the sun went down that evening, its dying rays making a mauve patina on the high clouds, it left behind it a scene of grandeur and of desolation. The Combined Fleet of France and

Spain which, a few brief hours earlier, had been drawn up in fine array, was now so badly mauled as to be powerless. Seventeen French and Spanish ships had been captured and the eighteenth had blown up—just two short of the twenty for which Nelson had "bargained." Dumanoir, with four ships, was sailing off to eventual destruction, and Gravina with the remaining eleven was heading for the safety of Cadiz. Not one of the British Fleet of twenty-seven ships which had gone into action against the thirty-three of the enemy had been sunk, or forced to strike.

But the great swell which had rolled across the scene of battle and the fronds of high cloud which had finally merged into an ominous grey sheet, were no idle portents: by next day there was a gale blowing, and the day after that, October 23, great seas were sweeping in from the west, rolling along before the screaming winds. It was into this that Captain Cosmao, of the *Pluton,* led twelve French and Spanish ships (*Pluton, Indomptable, Neptune, Rayo* and *San Francisco de Asis,* with five frigates and two brigs) out of Cadiz to try to recapture some of the prizes which were now drifting at the mercy of the weather.

The remaining British ships in the area rallied, but the weather was too bad for battle. Cosmao managed to get the *Santa Ana* and French *Neptune* in tow and take them back to Cadiz, but the sally cost him three of his five battleships. The *Indomptable* was wrecked off Rota in the gale and most of her crew, along with about five hundred survivors from the *Bucentaure,* were drowned; the *San Francisco de Asis* went ashore in Cadiz Bay and MacDonell's *Rayo,* forced to anchor off San Lucar, rolled her masts over the side in the heavy seas. She was captured by the British next day, but later went ashore. Of the seventeen prizes left to Collingwood, six went ashore and were wrecked, two were retaken by Cosmao, five were scuttled or burnt because Collingwood thought he could not save them in the gale, and four were taken into Gibraltar. With Dumanoir's four ships captured by Sir Richard Strachan on November 4, the final result was that of the thirty-three French and Spanish ships in the battle of October 21, fifteen were destroyed by sinking or going ashore, eight were taken in as prizes, and ten managed to get into Cadiz, although many of these were very badly damaged and only three were fit for service.

Of the seven French and Spanish admirals who had watched

Nelson's coming into action against them, one was now dead and five were wounded. Two of the ten commodores had been killed and four wounded. Approximately 3,370 French officers and men had been killed or drowned and 1,160 wounded; and the Spanish casualties were 1,038 killed or drowned and 1,385 wounded—an approximate total (since French and Spanish reports were not complete) of 4,408 dead and 2,545 wounded. Against this total the British casualties were remarkably small—449 officers and men killed and 1,214 wounded. One admiral and two captains had been killed; one admiral (who failed to report the fact) and four captains wounded.

The *Pickle* was, as described at the beginning of this narrative, sent home with the news of the great battle. In the *Victory* Nelson's body had been put in a large cask—called a leaguer— which had been filled with brandy. The crew of the *Victory* were at first worried because of the rumours that reached them about the *Euryalus*'s returning home. As Marine James Bagley later wrote home to his sister, "They have behaved very well to us, for they wanted to take Lord Nelson from us, but we told Captain as we brought him out we would bring him home; so it was so. . . ."

But the ship was far from being safe. On the night of the battle Captain Hardy had set the crew to work getting runners and tackles fitted to secure the fore and mainmasts—the mizen had gone by the board. He managed to wear the ship round and, as the Master's log noted, "stood to the southward under the remnants of the foresail and main-topsail." At daylight next day, October 22, the men were still busy knotting and splicing, with the carpenter and his mates repairing the foremast. The old mainsail had been shot to pieces, so an old foresail was brought up and set in its place. Next day, the 23rd, as they tried to get the wreck of the mizenmast clear, the cloud and fresh breezes turned into a strong gale, with heavy seas threatening to roll what remained of the masts out of the ship. For the rest of that day and night the *Victory* wallowed; but just before dawn the weather eased up, and after breakfast Hardy mustered the crew to check the casualty list. At 11 a.m. Captain Redmill brought the *Polyphemus* close enough to pass a hawser from the middle-deck bow port of the *Victory* to the wardroom windows of the *Polyphemus*.

The high land of Rota, at the north end of Cadiz Bay, could be seen some fifteen to eighteen miles away to the eastward, and in fresh winds the two ships made their way towards Gibraltar. However, the strong gale returned next day, October 25; by the evening violent winds had carried away the *Victory*'s main yard and split the mainsail and main-topsail. By the time the wreckage was cleared away they suddenly saw the *Polyphemus* forge ahead —the towing hawser had parted. "We shipped three heavy seas which filled the deck," wrote Midshipman Rivers. "Turned all hands to the pumps. Hoisted the launch lug-sail to a rough spar attached to the cap of the ensign staff [which kept] the ship to and kept her from foundering."

The former flagship, left drifting almost helpless in the gale, had to be pumped the whole night, and dawn on October 26 brought little encouragement. Across the great grey and swirling waves to the north-east they could see the *Royal Sovereign* flying a distress signal, and the *Africa* near her with all her masts gone. Hardy, disregarding the *Victory*'s danger, sent the *Polyphemus* to the aid of the *Royal Sovereign*.

Later in the afternoon, when the wind had dropped slightly, Thomas Fremantle brought the *Neptune* down to take the *Victory* in tow. On the evening of October 28, Captain Hardy's journal noted: "At 7, anchored in Rosia Bay, Gibraltar."

On November 3, having been partially refitted, the *Victory* sailed for England to take Nelson's body home. On December 4 she anchored at St. Helen's, in the Solent, where, on September 14, Nelson had boarded her to sail for his last battle.

Six days passed before orders arrived to take the ship round to the Thames, and on December 22, after she had weathered the North Foreland and was heading up the Estuary, the *Victory* was met by Commissioner Grey's yacht *Chatham*. The Board of Admiralty had sent her to receive Nelson's body and take it to Greenwich. The body was taken from the cask in front of "all the officers in the ship, and several of his Lordship's friends," according to Beatty, and after being dressed in a shirt, stockings and uniform, was placed in the coffin which Captain Hallowell had had made from the *L'Orient*'s mast. This was placed inside a leaden coffin which was sealed and put in a wooden shell.

Commissioner Grey's yacht was brought alongside and the coffin lowered on board. As the yard-tackle lifted it from the deck of the *Victory*, Nelson's flag at the fore was struck for the last time and hoisted, at half-mast, aboard the *Chatham*. On January 9, 1806, Nelson was buried under the great dome of St Paul's Cathedral, and among those who saw the funeral procession were Vice-Admiral Villeneuve and Captain Magendie, who had been given permission to come up from Bishop's Waltham, in Hampshire, where they were living on parole.

The French prisoners—210 officers and 4,589 men—were brought to England. Those landed at Chatham were taken on board four prison hulks (shortly to be reinforced by two Trafalgar prizes, the *Bahama*[1] and the *Swiftsure*, the latter ironically enough renamed *Irresistible*). Those brought to Plymouth were taken to Millbay Prison or one of the eight hulks in the Hamoaze (some of them were eventually transferred to Dartmoor Jail after it was completed). The rest were landed at Portsmouth and put in prisons or hulks. Most officers were kept on parole at Crediton, Devon, and Wincanton, Somerset. Later, when Villeneuve was given a choice of any town more than thirty miles north or west of London, he chose Reading and was accompanied there by Magendie, Lucas and Infernet. Magendie was soon sent to France to arrange a proper system of exchange for the prisoners, while the other three were allowed to visit English families. Lucas became quite a popular figure in London society.

But in April, 1806, having been a prisoner for just over five months, Villeneuve was freed in exchange for four British post captains, and sent back to France. Crossing the Channel in a small boat, he landed at Morlaix, in Brittany. Settling himself in at an hotel, he wrote to Admiral Decrès, reporting his arrival. What were the Minister's instructions? He said he would go on to Rennes, to where the Minister's orders should be sent. Villeneuve then went by coach to Rennes and took a room at the Hotel de la Patrie to await the letter from Decrès. He discovered that Lucas and Infernet, who had already been exchanged and were in Paris, had been promoted to rear-admirals.

1 Desbrière says the *Bahama* was sunk, but she was in fact taken to Gibraltar and then to England.

But no letter came from Decrès; there was no summons from the Emperor bidding him to St. Cloud. And all the time, as the days passed, Villeneuve became more agitated. Finally, on the morning of April 22, he was found lying dead in his bed. An ordinary table knife had been driven up to its hilt in his chest, and there were five other stab wounds. The authenticity of a letter alleged to have been left by Villeneuve, addressed to his wife and saying that his life was a disgrace and death a duty, and asking her forgiveness for his suicide, has never been proved. Whether Villeneuve committed suicide or, as rumour had it, he was murdered on Napoleon's orders, will never be known for certain.

EPILOGUE

TRAFALGAR WAS ONE of the most decisive naval battles ever fought by the Royal Navy, and its effects are still felt in Britain today. Yet the day before Nelson defeated Napoleon at sea, the Emperor had won an apparently crushing victory on land. As we have already seen (pages 151-52) he had attacked General Mack's seventy thousand Austrians at Ulm with two hundred thousand of his highly trained, enthusiastic men, and forced him to surrender on October 20. When this news reached England nine days later—seven days before Lapenotiere arrived in a fog-bound London with Collingwood's Trafalgar despatch—the nation despaired: Pitt's masterly plan to bring the power of Russia and Austria to bear against Napoleon had failed even before it was properly launched.

"You have no idea of the consternation here," Lady Bessborough had written to Lord Granville Leveson-Gower. "I am so terrified, so shocked with the news, I scarcely know what to wish." And we have already seen that when the news of Trafalgar eventually arrived in London, the nation mourned the death of Nelson rather than celebrated the victory: they were far too close to the event to see exactly what it achieved.

As far as the war (which was to last another ten years) was concerned, there seemed at the time no hope for Britain. Pitt died less than three months after Nelson. Lord Sheffield spoke for many of the nation when he wrote: "Unless something extraordinary happens, I shall consider the game as lost."

Yet the tide *had* turned. After Trafalgar, Napoleon had no fleet to use in the Mediterranean, which was controlled by the Royal Navy. Sicily was in British hands and Napoleon's door to

Egypt was shut. With its slamming went his dreams of an Eastern empire.

Trafalgar finally cut Napoleon off from the sea. Forced into a purely continental strategy, he started off on the steps which led him inexorably to defeat on the snow-covered plains of Russia and, eventually, to the decks of the *Bellerophon* and exile. Thus, with the Fleet of France destroyed as a challenger—although Napoleon later partly rebuilt his shattered force—Britain was given more than a hundred years in which to build up and expand an Empire, a century in which the Royal Navy guaranteed that the sea lanes were kept open—not only for Britain but for every other law-abiding nation.

The effect of Trafalgar was still very evident in the Royal Navy's strength at the beginning of the First World War and, despite many sacrifices to political expediency, at the beginning of the Second World War. But the cost of defeating Hitler proved too much for Britain, and the demands of the welfare state and more political expediency have combined to lose for the nation many of the material benefits bestowed on it by Nelson's great victory.

Something which in the long run may prove more valuable than the material benefits still remains, and this book may serve to bring it once again into sharper focus: Nelson and Trafalgar established a tradition of bold tactics, a standard of personal bravery, of devotion, and a lesson in dedication to duty which has become a part of the British character. It made Britain stand firm at times of apparent defeat. Yet the victory was in one sense a mixed blessing: Nelson's methods at Trafalgar were so effective that they led to a stagnation in the study and practice of naval tactics which lasted for many decades. It also helped to foster that dangerous legend that Britain "muddles through": Nelson's victory in the midst of a war which Britain was singularly ill-equipped to fight has been taken as a justification for lack of political foresight and realism.

The muddlers and their apologists, however, have tended to lose sight of the fact that although Britain was ill-prepared for war in 1805, Nelson, the greatest admiral the world has ever seen, was at the height of his power: natural genius had blended with experience to make him, given reasonable odds, invincible. In a period when naval battles sometimes tended to be indecisive in the long run, it is worth noting that the Nile, Copenhagen and Trafalgar were three of the most decisive naval actions ever fought.

The battle of Trafalgar was not fought exactly in the way that Nelson had laid down in his Memorandum, but as we have seen, subsequent criticism has lost sight of the fact that it was a memorandum and not a rigid set of instructions: it was intended as an *aide-mémoire* after Nelson's discussion with his captains on board the *Victory*. At the last moment Nelson departed from a rigid movement to seize the advantage that speed would give him to smash an enemy making for its home port. He forced battle on an enemy which had a bolt-hole to leeward; he forced them to fight the battle the way he wanted. Villeneuve, as we have seen, guessed the method that Nelson would use, yet such was the brilliance of its conception that Villeneuve could not devise a method of defeating it.

"The risk he took of having the heads of his two columns isolated by a loss of wind or crushed prematurely by the concentration to which he exposed them naked, almost passed the limits of sober leading," says Corbett. "Its justification was its success and the known defects of his opponents. Yet it may be permitted to doubt whether if he had realized how much higher was the spirit of his enemy than he expected, he would have dared so greatly."

The main criticism has been that Nelson with his end-on approach laid his ships open to the risk of being dismasted by the massed broadsides of the enemy before they could break the line and bring their own guns to bear. Yet not one British ship was dismasted before it got into close action with the enemy. Nelson knew from long experience that the enemy gunnery tended to be wild—and it was; he knew the enemy officers and men were for the most part unskilled—and we have seen, from their own accounts, that he was right. Making allowances for the French, Spanish and British ships which came into action too late to affect the issue, twenty-three British ships fought twenty-eight French and Spanish ships and beat them. Yet several French and Spanish ships fought with remarkable bravery—the *Bucentaure, Redoutable, Intrépide and Santissima Trinidad,* to name a few. Although it may seem a harsh judgement, the fact is that when the French and Spanish ships found themselves trapped in the midst of the British ships they fought with skill and fury, but not enough of them found themselves in this situation to prevent victory's going to the British. It is quite clear, though, from contemporary accounts already quoted and particularly the council of war held in Cadiz, that many of the French and Spanish captains felt they were defeated even before they cleared the Cadiz roads.

However, Trafalgar was not a victory won cheaply by the British: many long months and years of ceaseless vigilance and blockade had gone into it. Then, as in 1940, Britain fought alone against the most powerful force in the world, holding the ring until other nations could be rallied round. And looking back over the whole campaign, one realizes more fully why Lt. Lapenotiere, bursting into the Board Room of the Admiralty in the dead of night, was not being melodramatic when his first words were: "Sir, we have gained a great victory, but we have lost Lord Nelson."

It was a woman, Lady Londonderry, stepmother of Lord Castlereagh, the Secretary for War, who wrote perhaps the wisest words about the death of Nelson shortly after his funeral: "Never was there indeed an event so mournfully and so triumphantly important to England as the Battle of Trafalgar. The sentiment of the lamenting the individual more than rejoicing in the victory, shows the humanity and affection of the people of England; but their good sense and reflection will dwell only on the conquest, because no death, at a future moment, could have been more glorious."

Then she added, with a mixture of logic and instinct, a few lines which crystallized all that the victory meant for the far distant future. "The public would never have sent him on another expedition; his health was not equal to another effort, and so might have yielded to the natural but less imposing effect of more worldly honours: whereas he now begins his immortal career, having left nothing to achieve on earth, and bequeathing to the English fleet a legacy which they alone are able to improve.

"Had I been his wife, or his mother, I would rather have wept him dead than seen him languish on a less splendid day. In such a death there is no sting, and in such a grave everlasting victory."

HMS *VICTORY*

Built to the design of Sir Thomas Slade, her keel was laid down at the Old Single Dock, Chatham, on July 23, 1759, and she was launched on May 7, 1765.

PARTICULARS

Length on gun deck	186′ 0″
Length of keel	151′ 5⁄8″
Moulded breadth	50′ 6″
Extreme breadth	51′ 10″
Depth in hold	21′ 6″
Displacement (approx.)	3,500 tons
Burthen	2,162 tons

ARMAMENT—1805

Lower deck	30—32 pounders and 2—12 pounders
Middle deck	28—24 pounders
Upper deck	30—12 pounders
Quarter-deck	12—12 pounders
Forecastle	2—68 pounders (carronades)

KEY TO DRAWING

1. Poop
2. Hammock nettings
3. Mizenmast
4. Quarter-deck
5. Steering wheels
6. Here Nelson fell
7. Pikes
8. Mainmast
9. Gangway
10. Foc's'le
11. Carronades
12. Foremast
13. Captain Hardy's cabin
14. Upper deck
15. Nelson's day cabin
16. Nelson's dining cabin
17. Nelson's sleeping cabin with cot
18. Shot garlands
19. Middle deck
20. Wardroom
21. Tiller head
22. Entry port
23. Capstan head
24. Galley and stove
25. Lower deck
26. Tiller
27. Chain & elm-tree pumps
28. Mooring bitts
29. Manger
30. Orlop
31. Sick bay
32. Aft hanging magazine
33. Lamp room
34. Midshipmen's berth —here Nelson died
35. Forward hanging magazine
36. Powder store
37. Powder room
38. Aft hold
39. Shot locker
40. Well
41. Main hold
42. Cable store
43. Main magazine
44. Filling room

APPENDIX I

COMBINED FLEET: Casualties and Damage

SHIP	KILLED	WOUNDED	FATE
Bucentaure (F) ..	197	85	Ran ashore, dismasted.
S. Trinidad (Sp) ..	216	116	Dismasted, captured and sunk.
Redoutable (F) ..	490	81	Dismasted, captured and sunk.
Monarca (Sp) ..	101	154	Captured, ran ashore, dismasted.
Argonauta (Sp) ..	100	203	Captured and sunk.
Neptuno (Sp) ..	38	35	Captured, ran ashore, dismasted.
Rayo (Sp) ..	4	14	Went ashore, burnt.*
S. Francisco de Asis (Sp) ..	5	12	Went ashore.*
San Augustin (Sp)	184	201	Captured and burnt.
Intrépide (F) ..	242	not known	Captured and burnt.
Indomptable ..	Two thirds	not known	Went ashore.*
Fougueux (F) ..	546 killed and wounded		Captured, ran ashore, dismasted.
Aigle (F)	Two thirds killed and wounded		Captured, ran ashore, dismasted.
Achille (F) ..	480 killed and wounded		Blew up.
Berwick (F) ..	Nearly all drowned		Captured, ran ashore, dismasted.
Swiftsure (F) ..	68	123	Captured, taken to Gibraltar.
Bahama (Sp) ..	75	66	Captured, taken to Gibraltar.
San Ildefonso (Sp) ..	36	129	Captured, dismasted, taken to Gibraltar.
S. J. Nepomuceno (Sp)	103	151	Captured, taken to Gibraltar.
Formidable (F) ..	22	45	Captured November 4.
Scipion (F) ..	17	22	Captured November 4.
Duguay-Trouin (F) ..	12	24	Captured November 4.
Mont-Blanc (F) ..	20	20	Captured November 4.
Santa Ana (Sp) ..	104	137	Recaptured, reached Cadiz, dismasted.
P. de Asturias (Sp) ..	54	109	Lost main and mizen in gale, reached Cadiz.
Pluton (F) ..	60	132	Again reached Cadiz, sinking.*
Héros (F)	12	24	Reached Cadiz, rigging and rudder damaged.
Neptune (F) ..	15	39	Again reached Cadiz, undamaged.*
Algésiras (F) ..	77	142	Recaptured, dismasted, reached Cadiz.
Argonaute (F) ..	55	132	Masts damaged, rudder lost, reached Cadiz.
San Leandro (Sp) ..	8	22	Masts, hulls damaged. Reached Cadiz.
San Justo (Sp) ..	—	7	Masts, hulls damaged. Reached Cadiz.
Montañes (Sp) ..	20	29	Lost foremast, reached Cadiz.

* After sailing on October 23 with Captain Cosmao.

APPENDIX II

BRITISH FLEET: Order of Battle and Sailing, and Casualties

Van Squadron—Starboard Division

Ship	Guns	Killed	Wounded	
Téméraire ..	98	47	76	Captain Eliab Harvey
Victory ..	100	57	102*	V-Ad. Lord Nelson; Captain T. M. Hardy
Neptune ..	98	10	34	Captain Thomas Fremantle
Conqueror ..	74	3	9	Captain Israel Pellew
Agamemnon ..	64	2	7	Captain Sir Edward Berry
Leviathan ..	74	4	22	Captain Henry Bayntun
Ajax	74	2	2	Lt. John Pilfold
Orion	74	1	21	Captain Edward Codrington
Minotaur ..	74	3	20	Captain C. J. M. Mansfield
Africa ..	64	18	37	Captain Henry Digby
Spartiate ..	74	3	17	Captain Sir Francis Laforey, Bt.

Rear Squadron—Port Division

Ship	Guns	Killed	Wounded	
Prince ..	98	—	—	Captain Richard Grindall
Mars	74	29	69	Captain George Duff
R. Sovereign ..	100	47	94	V-Ad. C. Collingwood; Captain E. Rotheram
Tonnant ..	80	26	50	Captain Charles Tyler
Belleisle ..	74	33	93	Captain William Hargood
Bellerophon ..	74	27	123	Captain J. Cooke
Colossus ..	74	40	160	Captain James N. Morris
Achille ..	74	13	59	Captain Richard King
Polyphemus ..	64	2	4	Captain Robert Redmill
Revenge ..	74	28	51	Captain Robert Moorsom
Britannia ..	100	10	40	R-Ad. the Earl of Northesk; Captain C. Bullen
Swiftsure ..	74	9	8	Captain William Rutherford
Defence ..	74	7	29	Captain George Hope
Thunder ..	98	4	12	Lt. John Stockham
Defiance ..	74	17	53	Captain Philip Durham
Dreadnought ..	98	7	26	Captain John Conn

* Twenty-seven more men reported wounded after the official return of 75 was made up, according to the *Victory*'s surgeon, Beatty.

			Frigates	
Euryalus ..	—	—	—	Captain the Hon. Henry Blackwood
Naiad ..	—	—	—	Captain Thomas Dundas
Phoebe ..	—	—	—	Captain the Hon. Thomas Bladen Capel
Sirius	—	—	—	Captain William Prowse
			Schooner	
Pickle	—	—	—	Lt. John Lapenotiere
			Cutter	
Entreprenante ..	—	—	—	Lt. Robert Young

Note: The ships did not eventually go into action in this order. The original order of battle and sailing included several other ships which did not arrive in time for the battle.

APPENDIX III

NELSON'S MEMORANDUM

NOTE: Subsequent insertions are shown within square brackets and deletions are given in italics.

Victory off Cadiz, 9 Octr. 1805

Mem^n.

Thinking it almost impossible to bring a Fleet of forty Sail of the Line into a Line of Battle in variable winds thick weather and other circumstances which must occur, without such a loss of time that the opportunity would probably be lost of bringing the Enemy to Battle in such a manner as to make the business decisive.

I have [therefore] made up my mind to keep the fleet in that position of sailing (with the exception of the first and Second in Command) that the order of Sailing is to be the Order of Battle, placing the fleet in two Lines of Sixteen Ships each with an advanced Squadron of Eight of the fasting [*sic*] sailing Two decked ships [which] will always make if wanted a Line of Twenty four Sail, on which ever Line the Commander in Chief may direct.

The Second in Command will *in fact Command* [his line] *and* after my intentions are made known to him *will* have the entire direction of His Line to make the attack upon the Enemy and to follow up the Blow until they are Capturd or destroy'd.

If the Enemy's fleet should be seen to Windward [in Line of Battle] *but* [and] *in that position that* the Two Lines and the Advanced Squadron can fetch them (I *shall suppose them forty Six Sail* [in] *of the Line of Battle)* they will probably be so extended that their Van could not succour their Rear.

I should therefore probably make *your* the 2nd in Commds signal to Lead through about their Twelfth Ship from their Rear (or wherever *you* [He] could fetch if not able to get so far advanced)   My Line would lead through about their Centre and the Advanced Squadron to cut two or three or four Ships Ahead of their Centre, so as to ensure getting at their Commander In Chief on whom every Effort must be made to Capture.

The whole impression of the British [fleet] must be, to overpower from two or three Ships ahead of their Commander In Chief, supposed to be in the centre, to the Rear of their fleet. [I will suppose] twenty Sail of the [Enemys] Line to be untouched, it must be some time before they could perform a Manoeuvre to bring their force compact to attack any part of the British fleet engaged, or to succour their own ships which indeed would be impossible, without mixing with the ships engaged.[1] Something must be left to chance, nothing is sure in a sea fight beyond all others, shot will carry away the masts and yards of friends as well as foes, but I look with confidence to a victory before the van of the Enemy could succour their *friends* [Rear] and then that the British Fleet would most of them be ready to receive their Twenty Sail of the Line or to pursue them should they endeavour to make off.

If the Van of the Enemy tacks the Captured Ships must run to Leeward of the British fleet, if the Enemy wears the British must place themselves between the Enemy and the captured & disabled British Ships and should the Enemy close I have no fear as to the result.

The Second in Command will in all possible things direct the Movements of his Line by keeping them as compact as the nature of the circumstances will admit *and* Captains are to look to their particular Line as their rallying point. But in case signals can neither be seen or perfectly understood no Captain can do very wrong if he places his Ship alongside that of an Enemy.

Of the intended attack from to Windward, the Enemy in Line of Battle ready to receive an attack:

B

E

The Division of the British fleet will be brought nearly within Gun Shot of the Enemy's Centre. The signal will most probably [then] be made for the Lee Line to bear up together to set all their sails even steering sails[2] in order to get as quickly as possible to the Enemys Line and to Cut through beginning from the 12 ship from the Enemies rear. Some ships may not get through their exact place, but they will always be at hand to assist their friends and if any are thrown round the Rear of the Enemy they will effectually compleat the business of Twelve Sail of the Enemy. Should the Enemy wear together or bear up and sail Large still the Twelve Ships composing in the first position the Enemys rear are to be [the] Object of attack of the Lee Line unless otherwise directed from the

---

[1] The   Enemy's Fleet is supposed to consist of 46 Sail of the Line—British Fleet of 40—if either is less only a proportionate number of Enemy's ships are to be cut off; B to be 1/4 superior to E cut off.

[2] *Vide* instructions for Signal Yellow with Blue fly, page 17, eighth Flag Signal Book, with reference to Appendix. [This and the above note were both written by Nelson in the margin.]

Commander In Chief which is scarcely to be expected as the entire management of the Lee Line after the intentions of the Commander In Chief is [are] signified is intended to be left to the Judgement of the Admiral Commanding that Line.

The Remainder of the Enemys fleet 34 Sail are to be left to the Management of the Commander In Chief who will endeavour to take care that the Movements of the Second in Command are as little interrupted as is possible.

NOTES AND BIBLIOGRAPHY

CHAPTER ONE (pages 17–33)

The *Pickle* and *Euryalus:* log of the *Pickle* (Public Records Office, Admiralty 53/3669, part II) kept by George Almy, Second Master and pilot; log of *Euryalus,* given in *Logs of the Great Sea Fights,* edited by Rear-Admiral T. Sturges Jackson, vol. 2 (Navy Records Society, 1900); Muster Book of the *Pickle* (PRO, Ady 36/1650). According to this the *Pickle* did not have a Master at this time. The assistant—and apparently sole—surgeon is given as L. G. Britton, although R. H. Mackenzie's *The Trafalgar Roll,* apparently erroneously, gives him as Simon Gage.

Details of the *Pickle* and the *Entreprenante,* the two smallest ships at Trafalgar, from Progress Books and List of Ships, Admiralty:

	Pickle	*Entreprenante*
Displacement (tons) ..	127	123
Length (on gun deck)..	73 ft.	67 ft.
Beam	20 ft.	21 ft.
Complement	40	40
Armament ..	..eight 12-pounder carronades	ten 12-pounder carronades

The *Pickle* was built at Plymouth and originally named the *Sting.* Bought by the Royal Navy in 1800, she was renamed the *Pickle*—the first ever to bear that name—in 1802. She had been under the command of Lapenotiere since December, 1804. The *Entreprenante* was captured from the French in 1798.

Collingwood's despatches: see *Letters and Dispatches of Lord Nelson,* edited by Sir H. Nicolas, vol. 7 (London, 1846); *London Gazette,* November 6, 1805.

Blackwood: see "A Memoir of Sir Henry Blackwood," in *Blackwood's Edinburgh Magazine,* No. CCX, vol. 34, July 1833; and Nicolas, vol. 7. The two versions of the letter vary slightly.

Lapenotiere: The family originally called itself La Penotiere. John was the son of an RN lieutenant and came from Ilfracombe, joining the Navy in 1780 at the age of ten. See also *The Enemy at Trafalgar,* by Edward Fraser (London, 1906).

The *Victory's* crew: Muster Book of the *Victory* (PRO, Ady 36/15900).

The *Nautilus:* She has variously been described as a cutter and a lugger, but the Progress Books and List of Ships, Admiralty, make it quite clear she was a 443-ton, ship-rigged sloop. She was built at Milford Haven and launched in April, 1804. For her movements, see log of the *Nautilus* (PRO, Ady 51/15441). Captain Sykes sailed for England on his own initiative. Some accounts say that he and Lapenotiere arrived at the Admiralty at the same time, but the logs of both ships and the direct written evidence of Marsden, Secretary to the Board, show this to have been impossible.

CHAPTER TWO (pages 34–46)

Lady Bessborough: see *Lord Granville Leveson-Gower, Private Correspondence 1781-1821,* edited by Castalia, Countess Granville, vol. 2.

Activities in the Admiralty: Tasks set out by Lord Barham, May, 1805 (PRO, Ady 3/256); *A Brief Memoir of the Life and Writings of the Late William Marsden, D.C.L., F.R.S.* (printed in 1838 for private circulation); *Correspondence of Vice-Admiral Lord Collingwood,* by G. L. Newnham Collingwood, vol. 2 (London, 1838); *Naval Chronicle,* vol. 17; *An Autobiographical Memoir of Sir John Barrow* (London, 1847); *Diaries and Correspondence of the 1st Earl of Malmesbury,* vol. 4; Fraser, *Enemy.* The letters from Colonel Taylor, including the one naming the battle, are in the possession of Mr. Christopher Marsden; Lord Arden's letter is given in *Marsden. Memoirs of the Life of Sir Edward Codrington,* by his daughter, Lady Bouchier, vol. 1; *The Wynne Diaries,* edited by Anne Fremantle, vol. 3 (London, 1940); Barham's letter to Lady Nelson, British Museum, Add. Mss. 28, 333.

CHAPTER THREE (pages 47–54)

The invasion: see *Projets et Tentatives de Débarquement aux Iles Britanniques,* by Colonel Edouard Desbrière (Paris, 1907); *Napoleon and the Invasion of England,* by H. F. B. Wheeler and A. M. Broadley, vol. 2 (London, 1908); *Years of Victory,* by Sir Arthur Bryant (London and New York, 1945); *Consulate and Empire,* by Adolphe Thiers, vol. 3 (English edition 1893, translated by Forbes Campbell and Stebbing); *Memoirs of Mme. Rémusat,* vol. 1.

CHAPTER FOUR (pages 55–61)

The invasion: see *Wynne Diaries;* Wheeler and Broadley; *The Three Dorset Captains at Trafalgar,* by Broadley and Bartelot (London, 1906); Bryant; *A Pop-gun Fired by George Cruikshank in Defence of the British*

Volunteers of 1803; English Caricature and Satire on Napoleon, by John Ashton; "A Sermon preached in a Country Village previous to the Enrollment of Volunteers," by the Rev. Cornelius Miles, "Rector and Captain"; *George Crabbe and His Times, 1754–1832,* by René Huchon, translated by Frederick Clarke (1907); *Narrative of Some Passages in the Great War with France from 1799 to 1810,* by Lt.-General Sir Henry Bunbury.

CHAPTER FIVE (pages 62–71)

The French Navy: see *The Influence of Sea Power on the French Revolution and Empire,* and *The Influence of Sea Power Upon History,* by Admiral A. T. Mahan; "The French Navy in 1805," by John Leyland, in *United Services Institute Magazine,* November 1905; Wheeler and Broadley; Fraser, *Enemy.*

The Royal Navy: see *Naval History of Great Britain,* by Captain E. P. Brenton, vol. 1; *The Naval History of Great Britain,* by William James (1902 edition); *Sea Life in Nelson's Time,* by John Masefield (London, 1905); *Naval Chronicle,* vols. 6 and 10; *Collingwood; Buckler's Hard and Its Ships,* by the 2nd Lord Montagu of Beaulieu (printed privately, 1909); *History of a Ship,* Anonymous.

Nelson letters: see Nicolas.

CHAPTER SIX (pages 72–84)

The Royal Navy: The wording of Loyagalo's attestation, oath, certificate and receipt was given in *Globe and Laurel,* May 1929; rates of pay in *Naval Regulations and Instructions;* the account of life afloat is taken from a large number of official and private sources and also from Masefield, the novels of Marryat, Chamier and Glascock, *Nautical Economy,* by "Jack Nasty-Face," court-martial reports, ships' logs, and officers' journals.

CHAPTER SEVEN (pages 85–90)

Napoleon's moves: see *Napoleon 1,* by Professor A. Fournier, vol. 1 (second edition, 1904–6, London, 1911); *The Campaign of Trafalgar,* by J. S. Corbett (London, 1910); *Mémoires de Miot de Melito,* vol. 2, quoted by Fournier, and Corbett; *The Trafalgar Campaign,* by Col. E. Desbrière (Paris, 1907). In the present narrative the excellent translation by Miss Constance Eastwick is used (London, 1933).

CHAPTER EIGHT (pages 91–101)

Villeneuve: see Desbrière, *Trafalgar;* Corbett; *The Life of Nelson,* by Admiral A. T. Mahan (London, 1897). Corbett says Villeneuve sailed on the 17th, but Desbrière, Mahan and Nelson himself give the 18th—"The

French Fleet sailed from Toulon on Friday last, the 18th," Nelson wrote to Sir John Acton on January 22.

Nelson: see Nicolas; *Nelson and His Captains*, by W. H. Fitchett (1902); Corbett; Mahan, *Nelson; Wynne Diaries; The Life of Nelson*, by Robert Southey (London, 1813); *The Life and Services of Horatio, Viscount Nelson*, by the Rev. J. Clarke and J. M'Arthur (London, 1809).

Napoleon: see Fournier; *Relations Secrètes des Agents de Louis XVIII*, by Remacle, quoted by Fournier; *Dispatches and Letters Relating to the Blockade of Brest*, by John Leyland, vol. 2 (Navy Records Society, 1902); Corbett; Desbrière, *Projets* and *Trafalgar*.

CHAPTER NINE (pages 102–112)

Napoleon and Villeneuve: see Desbrière, *Trafalgar;* Leyland, *Blockade;* Corbett.

Fleet movements and Admiralty orders: British Museum, Nelson Papers 34930, folio 74; PRO, Admiralty Secret Orders, 1636; Desbrière, *Trafalgar* and *Projets;* Corbett; Nicolas; Mahan; Leyland, *Blockade; Naval Chronicle*.

CHAPTER TEN (pages 113–117)

Fleet movements: see Desbrière, *Trafalgar;* Leyland, *Blockade;* Corbett; Mahan, *Nelson;* Nicolas; James.

CHAPTER ELEVEN (pages 118–127)

Nelson and Merton: see Nicolas; Fitchett; Clarke and M'Arthur, vol. 3; *Life and Correspondence of H. Addington, Viscount Sidmouth*, by G. Pellew; *Leveson-Gower; Naval Chronicle*. Keats's account of his conversation with Nelson is given in Nicolas, vol. 7.

CHAPTER TWELVE (pages 128–143)

Orders: see PRO, Ady 2/150 (for Berry, and the *Agamemnon, Thunderer, Ajax, Euryalus, Defiance, Superb, Royal Sovereign* and *Victory,* PRO, Admiralty In-Letters (Secret Orders), 1363, September 3; British Museum, Add. Mss. 34931.

Signals: see *Signal Book for the Ships of War, 1799*, with corrections; *Nelson's Signals: the Evolution of the Signal Flags*, Admiralty, NID, Historical, 1908; *Trafalgar Signals*, by Cdr. Hilary P. Mead (London, 1936); Corbett; *Barrow.*

According to Corbett, Barrow's memory is at fault in referring to an improved and enlarged version because the third and final part was issued in 1803.

Nelson in London: see *The Croker Papers*, vol. 2 (the Duke of Wellington gave an account of his meeting with Nelson to John Croker, Secretary to the Board of Admiralty, 1809–30, when in retirement at Walmer twenty-nine years later); Nicolas; Southey; Clarke and M'Arthur; *Life and Letters of Sir Gilbert Elliot, 1st Earl of Minto* (London, 1874); *Leveson-Gower; Nelson,* by Carola Oman (London and New York, 1947).

CHAPTER THIRTEEN (pages 144–149)

Napoleon and Villeneuve: see Desbrière, *Trafalgar* and *Projets;* Thiers; Corbett; Fournier.

Writing of Napoleon's decision to attack Austria, Professor Fournier says: "Until recent times wide credence was given to General Daru's statement that the idea of a continental war only occurred to Napoleon after receiving Villeneuve's dispatches, and that he then dictated the plan of campaign on a sudden flash of inspiration. But this is only part of the Napoleonic mythology. The struggle had long been foreseen and the time and mode of procedure decided upon after mature deliberation" (vol. 1, p. 365).

CHAPTER FOURTEEN (pages 150–156)

Napoleon and the Combined Fleet: see Desbrière, *Trafalgar;* Clarke and M'Arthur; Corbett.

CHAPTER FIFTEEN (pages 157–173)

Nelson: see Nicolas; *Codrington; Collingwood; Naval Chronicle;* Leyland, *Blockade;* James.

Nelson's captains: For details of their length of service with Nelson, the author has made use of material supplied by Rear-Admiral A. H. Taylor, to whom he is indebted. The details were also given in Rear-Admiral Taylor's article "The Battle of Trafalgar," in the journal of the Society for Nautical Research, vol. 36, no. 4, October 1950. See also *Codrington; Wynne Diaries; Naval Chronicle; The Book of the Duffs,* by A. and H. Taylor, vol. 2 (Edinburgh, 1914); *The Naval History of the Patey Family,* by C. Harvey (published privately); *Jane Austen's Sailor Brothers,* by J. H. and E. C. Hubback (London, 1906); *Memoirs of the Life and Services of Admiral Sir Philip C. H. C. Durham,* by Captain A. Murray (London, 1846).

For additional information the author is also indebted to the Misses Duff, of Bolton Gardens, South Kensington (descendants of Captain George Duff), who gave him permission to use documents in their possession, and to the Earl of Northesk, who owns many hitherto unpublished documents concerning his forebear, and also Nelson and Trafalgar.

CHAPTER SIXTEEN (pages 174–186)

Villeneuve and his officers: see Desbrière, *Trafalgar; Collingwood;* Fraser, *Enemy* (which gives a lot of detail unobtainable from any other source); *Sea Drift,* by Vice-Admiral Hercules Robinson.

Fraser says only thirteen officers—seven French and six Spanish—attended the council of war, but he is in error: fourteen signed the Minute (Desbrière, vol. 2, p. 107)—seven French and seven Spanish. Fraser includes Churruca, who did not sign the Minute, and omits Hore and MacDonell, who did. This is borne out by Villeneuve's letter to Decrès of October 8 which enclosed the signed Minute.

Corbett has apparently misunderstood Escaño's report of the council's meeting (Desbrière, vol. 2, pp. 107–10) and says it was Prigny who made the speech quoted on p. 178. He also refers to Galiano as a brigadier commanding some of the Spanish troops, whereas he was a commodore commanding the *Bahama.*

British ship movements: see Desbrière, *Trafalgar;* Corbett; the letter from the midshipman of the *L'Aimable* is used by permission of the Earl of Radnor; Robinson; Broadley and Bartelot; Cumby in a letter printed in the *Nineteenth Century Review,* November 1899.

CHAPTER SEVENTEEN (pages 187–204)

French and Spanish movements: see Desbrière, *Trafalgar,* and *Projets;* Fraser, *Enemy.* The reports of the French and Spanish ships differ considerably over the times that signals were made from October 18 until after the battle. There are discrepancies of up to five hours in the logs.

British movements: see *Logs;* Nicolas; Corbett; Robinson; *Codrington; Report of a Committee Appointed by the Admiralty to Examine and Consider the Evidence Relating to the Tactics used by Nelson at the Battle of Trafalgar* (hereinafter referred to as *Report*), published 1913 (HM Stationery Office); *English Illustrated,* October 1905, in which extracts from Lt. Halloran's journal are given in an article written by his granddaughter. The letter of the Earl of Northesk, previously unpublished, is in the possession of the present Earl.

CHAPTER EIGHTEEN (pages 205–223)

British Fleet: see Robinson; *Five Naval Journals* (Navy Records Society); *Collingwood;* Captain Duff's letter is in the possession of the Misses Duff; "Blackwood" (the wording varies slightly from that given in

Nicolas, vol. 7); *The Sailors Whom Nelson Led,* by Edward Fraser (London, 1913); Muster List of the *Victory; Personal Narrative of Events from 1799 to 1815,* by Vice-Admiral William S. Lovell (Badcock assumed the surname Lovell in 1840); Halloran; *Codrington;* "Minutes of the Action of Trafalgar," by W. Thorpe, one of the officers of the *Minotaur,* hitherto unpublished, in National Maritime Museum, Ms. 9735; *Naval Chronicle; Memoirs of the Life and Services of Admiral Sir William Hargood,* by Joseph Allen; *Bijou* magazine, 1839; *Britain's Sea Soldiers,* by Col. C. Field (1924).

"The Fleet to bear up and sail large" (see page 210). It is over these two signals that a great deal of controversy has arisen. They naturally had a considerable bearing on the point which was at issue: did the two columns go about "in succession"—each ship turning when it reached the point that its next-ahead turned—to attack in line ahead; or did Nelson want them to manoeuvre "together," so that he could attack in line abreast? Even to outline the controversy would take two long chapters. The present author's views on how the attack was carried out are made clear in successive chapters. The complexity of the subject can be gauged by the fact that the Admiralty in 1912 appointed a special committee to report on it.

British signals: There is considerable variation in the time that individual ships report signals being made and received. Since most of them originated from the *Victory,* her times are used (see *Report*) in preference to the *Euryalus* and other ships (see *Logs*).

CHAPTER NINETEEN (pages 224–234)

British Fleet: As for previous chapter, and *A Sailor of King George, the Journal of Captain Frederick Hoffman, RN, 1793–1814,* edited by A. Beckford Bevan and H. B. Wolryche-Whitmore (London, 1901); Cumby; Report of the *Defiance*'s carpenter, hitherto unpublished, National Maritime Museum; Midshipman Aikenhead's letter in *Naval Chronicle; The Life of Sir John Franklin, RN,* by H. D. Traill (London, 1896).

CHAPER TWENTY (pages 235–247)

French and Spanish movements: see Desbrière, *Trafalgar; Trafalgar,* by Perez Galdos, quoted in Fraser, *Enemy.*

British movements: Nicolas; *Narrative of the Death of Lord Nelson,* by Dr. Beatty; *Journals;* Midshipman Rivers's account is from his "Notes on Trafalgar and Naval Affairs," National Maritime Museum, Wellcome Mss. 30; the account of Pasco is in Nicolas; Fraser; Lt. Nicolas in *Bijou,* 1929; Blackwood's account in Nicolas.

CHAPTER TWENTY-ONE (pages 248–264)

The battle: see James; Desbrière, *Trafalgar;* Beatty; Fraser, *Sailors* and *Enemy;* Clarke and M'Arthur; *The Trafalgar Roll,* by Col. R. H. Mackenzie.

CHAPTER TWENTY-TWO (pages 265–279)

French and Spanish movements: as for Chapter Twenty.

British movements: see *Wynne Diaries;* Lovell; James; *Logs;* letter of Lt. (later Sir) Humphrey Senhouse, printed in *Macmillan's Magazine,* April 1900; Halloran; Fraser, *Sailors;* Robinson; *Regulations and Instructions.*

Certain accounts say that Prigny was taken prisoner, but Prigny's own report (Desbrière, *Trafalgar,* vol. 2, pp. 148–56, dated Cadiz, October 25, 1805) makes it clear that this was not the case.

The exact times at which individual British, French and Spanish ships engaged each other, according to their own reports, are almost impossible to determine accurately. Certain times are taken from Desbrière, James and individual logs; but this narrative relies principally on a detailed time-table worked out by Rear-Admiral Taylor, who kindly placed it at the author's disposal.

CHAPTER TWENTY-THREE (pages 280–298)

British movements: see *Report;* Corbett; James; Taylor; *Logs;* Fraser, *Sailors* (which also gives the letter from the Warnborough sailor, who signs himself "Sam"); *Collingwood;* Hargood (which gives Lt. Nicolas's account as an appendix); *Duff; Naval Chronicle;* Hoffman; *Notes and Queries* (Sixth Series, vol. 4); *Sir Charles Tyler, G.C.B., Admiral of the White,* by Col. Wyndham-Quin (1912); Lt. Clement, British Museum Add. Mss. 24,813.

French and Spanish movements: Desbrière, *Trafalgar;* Fraser, *Enemy; Logs; Report.*

CHAPTER TWENTY-FOUR (pages 299–323)

Movements of both fleets: see Desbrière, *Trafalgar;* Cumby; Franklin; *Logs; Hargood; Bellerophon, the Bravest of the Brave,* by Edward Fraser (1909); Durham; Fraser, *Enemy* and *Sailors;* James; Corbett; Mahan, *Nelson.*

There has been a certain amount of confusion over the *Revenge* and the French *Achille* (see page 320). James refers to her as the *Aigle—* which was busy engaging the *Bellerophon* at that moment. Moorsom does not mention his opponent's name, although other sources make it clear it is the *Achille*. Desbrière says, erroneously (vol. 1, p. 274), that the *Revenge* later passed astern of the *Principe de Asturias*, but Moorsom says she passed ahead.

CHAPTER TWENTY-FIVE (pages 324–330)

Movements of both fleets: As for Chapter Twenty-four, and logs of the *Pickle* and *Entreprenante*, PRO.

Santa Ana: The Spanish newspaper *Tribuno*, according to Fraser, *Enemy*, reported in April, 1882, that Gaspar Vasquez, who had been one of the *Santa Ana*'s crew in the battle, had just died aged 105. The last surviving seaman of the *Victory* in the battle, James Chapman, died in Dundee in 1876, aged ninety-two, while the last surviving officer of the *Victory*, Admiral Sir George Westphal, died a few months earlier. The last two survivors of the battle, both officers, were Admiral Sir George Sartorious (a midshipman in the *Tonnant*), who died in 1885, aged ninety-four; and Lt.-Col. James Fynmore, RM (of the *Africa*), who died in 1887.

Achille (French): see Desbrière, *Trafalgar*; Moorsom in letter to son; one of the *Revenge*'s lieutenants, quoted in Fraser, *Enemy*; "Jack Nasty-Face," who gives a slightly different version; Robinson; Durham.

CHAPTER TWENTY-SIX (pages 331–340)

French and Spanish movements: see Desbrière, *Trafalgar*; Fraser, *Enemy*; *Revue des Deux Mondes*, July, 1905.

British movements: see Senhouse; *Codrington*; *Logs*.

CHAPTER TWENTY-SEVEN (pages 341–347)

Death of Nelson: see Beatty; Nicolas (which also gives a note from Westphal).

CHAPTER TWENTY-EIGHT (pages 348–355)

Desbrière, *Trafalgar*; *Prisoners of War in Britain, 1756–1815*, by Francis Abell (London, 1914); Fraser, *Enemy*; James; Brenton; *Letters of the English Seamen*, by E. Hallam Moorhouse (London, 1910); Rivers.

INDEX